WELCOME TO MY WORLD

Flinx instinctively threw up his free hand to protect his face as he fumbled at his recalcitrant holster with the other. Something shattered the air just above him with an explosive pop.

Then he was enveloped by a mass of transparent wings and pulsing organs. The flesh he kicked at frantically as he sought to keep those glass-toothed jaws away from his neck felt like sheets of water-filled plastic.

It struck him that the creature was hardly moving. When he crawled out from beneath the quiescent mass, he saw why.

Its head was gone. Pink blood pumped from severed arteries in rapidly decreasing streams.

Pip! Flinx climbed shakily to a crouch. Pip, where...?

The flying snake lay off to his right, on her back. She didn t move...

By Alan Dean Foster
Published by Ballantine Books:

THE BLACK HOLE
CACHALOT
DARK STAR
THE METROGNOME and Other Stories
MIDWORLD
NOR CRYSTAL TEARS
SENTENCED TO PRISM
SPLINTER OF THE MIND'S EYE
STAR TREK® LOGS ONE–TEN
VOYAGE TO THE CITY OF THE DEAD
. . . WHO NEEDS ENEMIES?
WITH FRIENDS LIKE THESE . . .

The Icerigger Trilogy:
    ICERIGGER
    MISSION TO MOULOKIN
    THE DELUGE DRIVERS

The Adventures of Flinx of the Commonwealth:
    FOR LOVE OF MOTHER-NOT
    THE TAR-AIYM KRANG
    ORPHAN STAR
    THE END OF THE MATTER
    BLOODHYPE
    FLINX IN FLUX
    MID-FLINX

The Damned:
    Book One: A CALL TO ARMS
    Book Two: THE FALSE MIRROR
    Book Three: THE SPOILS OF WAR

MID-FLINX

Alan Dean Foster

A Del Rey® Book
BALLANTINE BOOKS • NEW YORK

A Del Rey® Book
Published by Ballantine Books
Copyright © 1995 by Thranx, Inc.

htpp://www.randomhouse.com

Library of Congress Catalog Card Number: 96-96371

ISBN 0-345-40644-3

Manufactured in the United States of America

First Hardcover Edition: November 1995
First Mass Market Edition: October 1996

10 9 8 7 6 5 4 3 2 1

Chapter One

If everyone's going to chase me, Flinx thought, I should've been born with eyes in the back of my head. Of course, in a sense, he had been.

He couldn't *see* behind himself. Not in the commonly accepted meaning of the term. Not visually. But he could "sense" behind him. Most sentient creatures generated patterns on the emotional level that Flinx could, from time to time, detect, descry, or perceive. Depending on the wildly variable sensitivity of his special talent, he could feel anger, fear, love, sorrow, pain, happiness, or simple contentment in others the way ordinary folk could feel heat or cold, slipperiness or stickiness, that which was sharp and that which was soft.

The emotional states of other beings prodded him with little jabs, twitches, icy notions in his brain. Sometimes they arrived on the doorstep of his mind as a gentle knock or comforting greeting, more often as a violent hammering he was unable, despite his most ardent efforts, to ignore.

For years he believed that any refining of his talent would be an improvement. He was no longer so sure. Increased sensitivity only exposed him to more and more personal distress and private upsets. He had discovered that the emotional spectrum was a roiling, violent,

1

crowded, generally unpleasant place. When he was especially receptive, it washed over him in remorseless waves, battering and pounding at his own psyche, leaving scant room for feelings of his own. None of this was apparent to others. Years of practice enabled him to keep the turmoil inside his head locked up, hidden away, artfully concealed.

Much to his distress, as he matured it became harder instead of easier to maintain the masquerade.

Used to be that he could distance himself from the emotional projections of others by putting distance between himself and the rest of humanxkind. Now that he'd grown more sensitive still, that kind of peace came to him only in the depths of interstellar space itself.

His situation wasn't entirely hopeless. With advancing maturity had come the ability to shut out the majority of background low-level emotional emanations. Spousal ire directed silently at mates, the petty squabbles of children, silent internalized hatreds, secret loves: he'd managed to reduce them all to a kind of perceptual static in the back of his mind. He couldn't completely relax in the company of others, but neither was his mind in constant turmoil. Where and when possible, he favored town over city, hamlet over town, country over hamlet, and wilderness over all.

Still, as his erratic control of his fickle talent improved, his worries only expanded, and he found himself plagued by new fears and uncertainties.

As he watched Pip slither silently across the oval glassine tabletop, hunting for fallen crumbs of salt and sugar, Flinx found himself wondering not for the first time where it would all stop. As he grew older and taller he continued to grow more sensitive. Would he someday be privy to the emotional state of insects? Perhaps a couple of distraught bacteria would eventually be all that was necessary to incite one of his recurring headaches.

He knew that would never happen. Not because it wasn't theoretically possible—he was such a genetic anomaly that where his nervous system was concerned, *anything* was theoretically possible—but because long before he could ever attain that degree of sensitivity he would certainly go mad. If the pain of his headaches didn't overwhelm him, an excess of knowledge would.

He sat alone in the southwest corner of the restaurant, but for all it distanced him from the emotional outpourings of his fellow patrons, he might as well have been sitting square in their midst. His isolation arose not from personal choice but because the other diners preferred it that way. They shunned him, and not the other way around.

It had nothing to do with his appearance. Tall, slim but well-proportioned, with his red hair and green eyes he was a pleasant-looking, even attractive young man. Much to his personal relief, he'd also lost nearly all the freckling that had plagued him since his youth.

The most likely explanation for his isolation was that the other diners had clustered at the opposite end of the dining room in hopes of avoiding the attentions of the small, pleat-winged, brightly colored flying snake which was presently foraging across her master's table in search of spice and sustenance. While the combined specific xenozoological knowledge of the other patrons peaked not far above zero, several dutifully recalled that contrasting bright colors in many primitive creatures constituted a warning sign to potential predators. Rather than chance confirmation of this theory, all preferred to order their midday meal as far from the minidrag as possible.

Pip's pointed tongue flicked across the tabletop to evaluate a fragment of turbinado sugar. Delighted by the discovery, she pounced on the energy-rich morsel with a languid thrust of her upper body.

Credit was due the restaurant's host. When Flinx had appeared at the entrance with the flying snake coiled decorously about his left arm and shoulder, the older man had stiffened instinctively while listening to Flinx's explanation that the minidrag was a longtime pet fully under control who would threaten no one. Accepting the tall young guest at his word, the unflinching host had led him to a small, isolated table which partook fully of the establishment's excellent view.

Samstead was a peaceful world. Its three large continents were veined by many rivers which drained into oceans congenial of coast and clime. Its weather was consistent if not entirely benign, its settlers hardworking and generally content. They raised up light industries and cut down dense forests, planted thousands of fields and drew forth from the seas a copious harvest of savory alien protein. In dehydrated, freeze-dried, and otherwise commercially profitable compacted forms, this bounty found its way packed, labeled, and shipped to less fruitful systems.

It was a world of wide-open spaces buttoned together by innumerable small towns and modest, rurally attuned metropolises. While air transport was widely available, citizens preferred where possible to travel by means of the many rivers and connecting canals. Working together, humans and thranx had over the years woven a relatively pleasant fabric of life out of the natural threads supplied by their planet, which lay on the fringes of the Commonwealth. It was a pleasant place to call home.

Perhaps the most remarkable thing about Samstead was that there was nothing remarkable about it. It had been a long time since Flinx had come across so docile an outpost of civilization. Since his arrival he'd given serious thought to extending his visit beyond his original intent, perhaps even settling down—if such a thing were possible for him.

It was a world where a new colonist might be able to lose himself in villatic contentment. A world where even he might no longer need to continually employ those figurative eyes in the back of his head. Flinx wasn't paranoid, but bitter experience had taught him caution. This was the inevitable consequence of an adolescence that had been, well, something other than normal.

For the moment, he was content to travel, to observe, to soak up the gentle, genial, country feel of this place. If its appeal held, he would linger. If not he would, as always, move on.

Departure would be effected by means of his remarkable ship, the *Teacher*, presently drifting in parking orbit over Samstead's equator in the company of several hundred other KK-drive craft. As far as Samstead Authority was concerned, it was bonded to a Mothian company, which was in fact a fiction for private ownership: a not uncommon practice.

As he slipped a forkful of some wonderful grilled fresh fish into his mouth, he drank in the view beyond the sweeping glass wall that fronted the backside of the restaurant. The establishment clung to the edge of a thirty-meter-high bank of the Tumberleon River, one of Samstead's hundred principal watercourses. Translucent graphite ribs reinforced the wall, becoming soaring arches overhead. These supported a ceiling of photosensitive panels which darkened automatically whenever Samstead's sun emerged from behind the clouds.

At this point, three-quarters of its way to the Kil Sea, the river was some three kilometers wide. All manner of contemporary rivercraft plied the languorous yet muscular stream: sailboats whose ultralight fabrics responded automatically to shifts in wind speed and direction, hovercraft built up out of ultralight composites, MAG barges which utilized the minute differences in electric charge between air and water to lumber along several centimeters above the surface of the water, big power-boats, tiny superfast pleasure craft, and land-based skimmers.

There was even a small group of children splashing about in some nearby shallows, looking for all the world like an undisciplined pod of playful amphibians. They seemed to be having a good time without the aid or intervention of any advanced technology whatsoever. Though timeless, it was a tableau less frequently encountered on the more urbanized worlds like Terra or Centauri.

Flinx found himself envying that unrestrained innocence. The pace of life on Samstead was much slower. It was a world on which one could live and work and still take time.

Flinx had managed to live, but so far his work had consisted of trying to stay alive and unnoticed. As for time, there never seemed to be enough of that intangible yet most precious of commodities.

Raising the upper third of her body off the table, Pip fully unfurled her pleated pink and blue wings and stretched. Across the room a family of four, stolid farmers clad in dress-gray coveralls and green paisley shirts, did their best to ignore the display. All except the youngest, a perfect little blond girl of seven who excitedly called attention to the unparalleled flash of color.

Her mother leaned over and spoke sharply, quickly quashing the girl's initial delight at the sight, while her father growled something under his breath and remained hunched over his meal. They were trying their best to ignore him, Flinx knew. He cast his perception their way. Instantly Pip froze, the better to serve as an empathetic lens for her master's talent.

He sensed fear lightly tinged with revulsion. There was also curiosity, which emanated principally from the children. This was directed more toward Pip than himself, which was to be expected. It would be remarkable if there was another Alaspinian minidrag anywhere on Samstead. This system was a long way from Alaspin, and Pip was usually an exotic no matter where they were.

Flinx was thankful he was no taller, no handsomer, no more distinctive in appearance than he was. The singular alignment of neurons within his cerebrum was distinction enough. The last thing he wanted was anything that would call additional attention to himself. He lived in constant terror of sprouting a third eye, or horns, or a bulging forehead. Knowing what had been done to him before birth, none of those developments would surprise him.

Sometimes it was hard to wake up and look in a mirror for fear of what he might see there. Others might wish for more height, or great beauty, or exaggerated muscularity. Flinx prayed frequently for the daily forgiveness of normalcy.

Pip attacked a pretzel while her master drank deep from a tall curved glass fashioned of self-chilling purple metal. An import, most likely. Though nearly done with his meal, he was reluctant to abandon the view. His fish had probably been netted in the river below that very morning. While it could not project, food possessed an emotional resonance all its own.

How wonderful were those times when he could simply sit and *be*.

Pip rose to land gently on his shoulder. This time it was the boy who gestured and exclaimed, only to be hastily slapped down by his father. Flinx sensed the older man's unease, but continued to ignore the family. That was what they wanted, anyway.

Fear of a different kind abruptly rippled through the dining room. Flinx tensed and Pip lifted her head from his shoulder, responding to his heightened emotional state.

That was odd. Calmly he scrutinized his fellow diners, seeing nothing to inspire such a sudden upsurge of apprehension. The ground was stable, the sky clear, the view outside unchanged. Raising his glass, he searched for the source of the disturbance.

Three men had arrived. They paused just inside the entrance. Two were much bigger than average. All three were exceptionally well dressed and would have stood out in any crowd on Samstead, though they would have been far less likely to attract attention on sophisticated Terra or Hivehom.

It was clear that the one in the middle was in charge. He wasn't more than four or five years older than Flinx; shorter, ordinary of build and sharp of countenance. His dark maroon whispershirt concealed a sinewy muscularity.

Over the top of his glass Flinx studied the narrow, pale face. The uncleft jaw protruded distinctively. It was matched above by an aquiline nose and unusually deep-set black eyes. The forehead was high, the black hair combed straight back in the most popular local fashion.

Eyeing him, Flinx decided that this was a man for whom any expression would be an effort. His two overbearing associates were much more animated.

Flagrantly indifferent to the reaction his arrival had engendered, the young man scanned and dismissed the room with a flick of his eyes before moving off to his left. The self-important heavies continued to flank him.

To Flinx, the lessening of emotional tension in the dining area as the new arrivals turned away was palpable. A measurable quantity of joie de vivre having been sucked out of them, the patrons gratefully returned to their conversation and meals as the recently arrived trio disappeared through a service doorway.

Flinx returned to the last of his meal, but unlike everyone else, continued to monitor the disturbance that centered around the recently arrived trio. It had simply shifted from the dining room proper to the kitchen in back.

After a while the three reemerged, followed by a very attractive young woman dressed in chef's whites. Save for her red hair, her features reflected an Oriental heritage. Her prosaic attire could not completely conceal her figure.

Flinx couldn't hear a word they were saying. He didn't have to; not while he could effortlessly monitor the ebb and flow of their respective emotional states. The greatest intensity emanated from the slim young man and the chef, the two heavies projecting nothing more vivid than mild amusement leavened with boredom.

One leaned back against the wall and crossed his lower left leg over his right, while his counterpart took in the view and occasionally cast an intimidating glare at any diners bold and foolish enough to glance in the direction of the altercation.

As the conversation reached audible levels, the degree of emotional distress intensified correspondingly. The woman was shouting now. She sounded defiant, but alone in the room only Flinx could sense her underlying terror. A mother shook a child too young and innocent to remain indifferent. Near the back, two couples rose and left quickly without finishing their meals.

The chef turned back toward the kitchen, only to have the heavy who'd been leaning against the wall step sideways to block her retreat. Flinx saw him grin. His employer grabbed the woman by her left arm, none too gently, and spun her around. The surge of fear that rushed through her started a throbbing at the back of Flinx's head.

That was typical of his unpredictable, erratic talent. A whole room full of uneasy people hadn't caused him so much as a twinge, but one woman's distress sparked the inevitable headache.

It was evident that the young man wasn't going to let her return to the kitchen until he'd achieved whatever sort of satisfaction he'd come for. Even without the two heavies, it was an unequal confrontation.

Flinx had passed by or otherwise ignored a thousand such encounters. Calmly he worked on the last of his meal. For all he cared or could do about it, the confrontation taking place behind him could escalate to actual violence. Either way, it was none of his business. Nothing that happened in this city, along this river, or on this rustic world of Samstead, was any of his business. Circumstances beyond his control, indeed, beyond his birth, had estranged him from the rest of humankind. It was a separation that for his safety and peace of mind he was forced to acknowledge. All he wanted was to finish his food, pay, and leave quietly.

That didn't mean he wasn't upset by the situation. Having been looked down on for much of his life, he hated to see anyone bullied. But interfering would draw attention to him, something he was at constant pains to avoid.

An older man emerged from the kitchen, painfully intent on resolving the confrontation. If anything, Flinx decided, the level of tension and unease he was generating exceeded that of the young woman. The heavy who'd been enjoying the view promptly put a palm on the senior's chest and shoved him back toward the kitchen doorway. The woman tried to intercede but the man holding her arm refused to relinquish his grip.

The heavy finished pushing the oldster back into the kitchen and turned, blocking the doorway with his bulk. Flinx wondered at the old man's interest. Was he merely an associate, or perhaps a relative? An uncle, or even her father? Again, it was none of his business.

Noting her master's steadfast emotional keel, a relaxed Pip fluttered back down to the table and resumed picking among the crumbs there. Flinx watched her fondly. Digging through the remnants of his lunch, he slipped half a nut onto his spoon and flipped it into the air. With a lightning thrust of neck and flash of wings, Pip darted up and snatched it before it could hit the table, swallowing the morsel whole.

"Just a minute."

The voice came from behind him, completely under control yet hinting it was always on the verge of violent exclamation. It suggested tension without edginess. Unintentionally, Flinx had attracted the attention of the principal protagonist in the unpleasant domestic drama being played out near the entrance to the kitchen.

"Are you going to let me go now?" The woman's voice was insistent and frightened all at once. Her emotional temperature was fully reflective of her false bravado. Flinx had to admire her for it.

"Yes, Geneen." It was the tight, soft voice of the man who'd been holding, and hurting, her arm. "Go back to your cooking. For now. We'll continue this later."

"But Jack-Jax . . ." the heavy blocking the doorway protested.

"I said let her go, Peeler." Paradoxically, the quieter he became, the more intimidating the speaker managed to sound. "Don't try to leave, Geneen."

Flinx didn't have to turn to know that the three had started toward his table. He sighed resignedly. At the first sign of trouble he should have risen quietly from his chair, paid his bill, and departed. Now it was too late.

Only the one called Jack-Jax evinced any real emotion. The two heavies were emotional blanks, waiting to be imprinted by the whims of their master. As they drew near, Peeler projected a modicum of disappointment, no doubt displeased at the interruption of what had been for him an amusing diversion. Flinx disliked him immediately.

Reflexive as automatons, the two big men took up positions on either side of the table. Peeler stopped behind Flinx while his counterpart eyed the recumbent minidrag curiously. Neither showed any fear. They were paid not to.

The one called Jack-Jax, whose presence had so thoroughly and effortlessly intimidated the entire dining establishment, sauntered around the table until he was blocking the view. His piercing jet-black eyes bordered on the remarkable. The emotions Flinx sensed behind them were uncontrolled, unformed, and immature. Outwardly he was the soul of calm, but internally the man seethed and boiled like a sealed pot on a high flame. Only Flinx knew how close to the proverbial edge his visitor was treading.

Unable to ignore that intense stare, he raised his own gaze to meet it. "Yes?" he ventured politely.

The response was as cordial as it was superficial. "That's a very, very interesting pet you have there."

"Thanks. So I've been told."

"I'm Jack-Jax Landsdowne Coerlis." A little emotional pop accompanied each name.

It was an innocuous enough salutation. "Lynx," Flinx replied pleasantly. "Philip Lynx." He didn't offer a hand. Neither did Coerlis.

Lips didn't so much smile as tighten. "You don't know who I am, do you?"

"Sure I do. You're Jack-Jax Landsdowne Coerlis. You just told me so."

"That's not what I mean." Impatience bubbled beneath the other's impassive visage. "It doesn't really matter."

Knowing he should leave it alone and, as was too often the case, unable to do so, Flinx nodded tersely in the direction of the kitchen. "Girlfriend?"

"After a fashion." The lips thinned like flatworms. "I have a lot of girlfriends. It's a matter of timing."

"You didn't seem to be getting along too well."

"A minor disagreement easily resolved. I'm good at resolving things."

"Lucky you. I wish I could say the same."

This semicomplimentary rejoinder caused Coerlis to mellow slightly. His attention shifted back to the snake shape relaxing on the table.

"Absolutely gorgeous. Really magnificent. It's an Alaspinian miniature dragon, isn't it? Warm-blooded, toxic reptiloid?"

Flinx displayed surprise, deliberately flattering the other. "You're very knowledgeable. It's not a well-known species and we're a long ways from Alaspin."

"Exotics are a hobby of mine, especially the resplendent ones. I have a private zoo." Flinx looked appropriately impressed and was rewarded with something akin to a genuine smile of satisfaction. "I collect all kinds of beautiful things. Animals, sculptures, kinetics." Coerlis jerked a thumb in the direction of the kitchen. "Women."

"It must be nice to be able to indulge in such a diversity of interests." Despite the cordial banter, Flinx was very much aware that Jack-Jax Coerlis was an emotional bomb waiting to go off. For one thing, beneath the underlying tension and anger a vast sorrow lingered, turgid and repressed, which bordered on despair.

Curious patrons kept sneaking looks in their direction, frantic to ignore the confrontation but unable to wholly rein in their curiosity.

"How much?" Coerlis said abruptly.

"How much what?"

"How much did she cost you?" He indicated the flying snake.

"Nothing." Reaching out, Flinx gently rubbed Pip on the back of her head. The minidrag couldn't purr. Beyond an occasional expressive hiss, she made hardly any noise at all. Instead her eyes closed contentedly and a small but powerful warmth emanated from within her pleasure center.

"I found her. Or rather, she found me."

"Then that should make my offer all the more inviting. What do you say to fifty credits?" When no response was forthcoming, Coerlis added, as if the actual amount was a matter of supreme indifference to him, "How about a hundred? Two hundred?" He was smiling, but internally the first stirrings of irritation were beginning to surface.

Flinx withdrew his finger. "She's not for sale. At any price."

Coerlis's emotions were as easy to read as if he'd presented them to Flinx in the form of a printed hardcopy. "Three hundred."

A flicker of interest showed in Peeler's eyes.

Flinx offered up his most ingratiating yet apologetic smile. "I told you: she's not for sale. See, she's been with me since I was a child. I couldn't part with her. Besides, no one knows how long Alaspinian minidrags live. She could up and die on you next year, or next month. A poor investment."

"Let me be the judge of that." Coerlis was unrelenting.

Flinx tried another tack. "You're aware that Alaspinian minidrags spit a highly lethal poison?" This time both heavies reacted. Flinx sensed a jolt of real unease in the one standing behind his chair. To his credit, the man held his ground.

Coerlis didn't flinch. "So I've heard. She doesn't look very threatening. If she's sufficiently domesticated to allow you to pet her like that, I think I could handle her. She'll be in a safe cage, anyway." He reached toward the table.

The flying snake instantly coiled and flared her wings, parting her jaws and hissing sharply. Coerlis froze, still smiling, while his companions reached for their jacket pockets.

"I wouldn't do that." Flinx spoke softly but firmly. "Alaspinian minidrags are telepathic on the empathic level. She's sensitive to my feelings. If I'm happy, she's happy. If I'm angry, she's angry. If I feel threatened— If I feel threatened, she reacts accordingly."

Impressed, Coerlis slowly withdrew his hand. Pip shuttered her wings but remained alert, watching the stranger. "Not only beautiful, but useful. Whereas I have to rely for that degree of protection on these two clumsy, ugly lumps of mindless protein." Neither of the heavies reacted. "She can ride your arm beneath a jacket, or sleep inside a travel bag. I'm sure she's capable of delivering a really nasty surprise."

Flinx said nothing, willing to let Coerlis draw his own conclusions. He was growing tired of the game, and the confrontation was attracting entirely too much attention. By now it was reasonable to assume that someone in the kitchen, the old man if not the pretty chef, had taken the step of notifying the authorities. Flinx didn't want to be around when they arrived. He glanced toward the service doorway.

Though he wasn't telepathic on any level, Jack-Jax Coerlis had a feral understanding of human nature. "If you're waiting for someone to call the police to come and mediate, I wouldn't. You see, in Tuleon Province I pretty much go where I want and do as I please." Keeping a thoughtful eye on Pip, he leaned forward slightly.

"Any decisions reached between you and I will be achieved without the intervention of any outside parties." With a finger, he nudged the purple glass. "Anything else you'd like to know?"

"Yes. Who have you lost recently?"

The question took Coerlis completely by surprise. He straightened, gaze narrowing. "What are you talking about?"

"You've lost someone close to you, someone very important. You're still mourning them. The result is anxiety, fear, sorrow, and a mindless desire to strike out at those less powerful than yourself. It's a way of reasserting control: not over others, but over yourself."

Coerlis's uncharacteristically unsettled tone reflected his sudden inner turmoil. "Who are you? *What* are you?"

"A perceptive visitor."

"You some kind of traveling therapist?"

"No." Flinx had very slowly edged his chair away from the table.

Attempting to reassert himself, Coerlis's tight grin twisted into an unpleasant smirk. "You've been poking around, asking questions. I'll bet my cousins hired you. Not that it matters. They can dig all they want. They're still getting nothing." He plunged on without waiting for his assumptions to be confirmed or denied. "So you know about my father. What of it? He's been dead two years last month."

"You still mourn him. His memory plagues you. He dominated you all your life and you suffer from consequent feelings of inferiority you're unable to shake."

Flinx's evaluation of his antagonist's emotional state of mind was part reading, part guesswork. Coerlis's hesitation suggested that he had deduced correctly. Now the question was, how far could he push this paranoid without nudging him over the edge of rationality? It wouldn't do to embarrass him in front of his flunkies, much less the other diners. A glance showed the young chef and her elder protector watching from the safety of the kitchen portal.

"I've run the House of Coerlis as well or better than the old man did ever since the accident! I don't know what you've heard or who you've been snooping around with, but I've done a damn good job. The interim administrators all agree."

Paranoid, neurotic, and pathologically defensive, Flinx decided. Traits that did not necessarily conflict with ability or intelligence. Coerlis had been forced to assume control of a large trading House hastily and at a young age. No wonder he bristled at any hint of defiance, any suggestion of a challenge to his authority. He was secure within his position, but not within himself. The shade of a domineering sire loomed over everything he did. It went a long ways toward explaining his anger and frustration, without in any way lessening the danger he posed to those around him.

"I haven't been doing any snooping," Flinx protested mildly.

"Of course you have!" Dark eyes glittered as Coerlis convinced himself he'd regained the conversational high ground. "Not that it has anything to do with the business at hand."

Flinx shrugged mentally. It had been worth a try. Though he doubted its appeal to someone like Coerlis, there was one more thing to be tried.

"At least you knew your father."

This admission appeared to please Coerlis rather than spark any sympathy. "You didn't? That's tough."

It was also, Flinx concluded resignedly, probably the last chance to end the confrontation peaceably.

"Didn't know my mother, either. I was raised an orphan."

Coerlis's expression remained flat. "You don't say. It's been my experience that the cosmos doesn't give a shit. Better get used to it.

"All that matters now is our business together. Dead parents don't enter into it. Four hundred. That's my last offer."

Flinx stiffened, knowing that Pip wouldn't have to look to him for directions. She knew what he was feeling the instant he did himself.

"Try to understand. You're not making the connection. I never knew my mother or father. An old lady raised me. She was my whole family. Her—and this flying snake. I had a sister once, too. She's dead also."

Coerlis's smirk widened ever so slightly. "With a run of bad luck like that you can probably use the money."

Flinx met the dark gaze evenly. "One more time: she's not for sale."

Coerlis inhaled an exaggerated breath as he ran the fingers of his left hand through his curly black hair. "Well, I guess that's that. If she's not for sale, she's not for sale." He smiled reassuringly.

Flinx was unconvinced. Alone among those in the dining room, only he could sense the near-homicidal fury that was mounting within the other man. Compared to the emotions boiling inside Coerlis, the mixture of anticipation and eagerness Flinx sensed in the two heavies was negligible.

He felt rather than saw the sudden movement of the big man standing behind his chair as a rush of adrenaline sparked an emotional surge in the man's brain. At the same time, Peeler's hand slid deep inside his open jacket and Coerlis reached for his own concealed weapon. Raising his legs, Flinx put his feet on the edge of the table and shoved, sending himself and his chair smashing backward into the figure behind him. Jarred off balance, the big man stumbled backward.

Patrons screamed and parents shielded children. The more alert among them dove for cover beneath their tables. One elderly couple, eschewing temporary salvation, staggered as best they could toward the exit.

The big man behind the chair recovered quickly and threw both arms around his quarry as the younger man rose. Flinx offered no resistance. Removing the needler from his jacket, Peeler aimed it with practiced ease. At the same time, Coerlis threw his open jacket over the table, pinning Pip beneath. Grinning broadly, he carefully gathered the material together, bundling his prize tightly within.

Chapter Two

"Got 'er!" Breathing hard, Coerlis gazed triumphantly at Flinx. "Wouldn't want to leave you thinking I was some kind of thief."

"We both know what you are." Flinx spoke quietly, unresisting in the heavy's grasp.

For an instant Coerlis's expression flickered, like a video image subject to momentary blackouts. Then the smile returned. "If you'll give me an account number I'll see that payment is forwarded. Four hundred. I'd be grateful, if I were you. At the moment, it strikes me that your bargaining power is severely reduced."

"I told you. She's not for sale."

Holding the bundled jacket securely, Coerlis made a show of pondering this last remark. "Maybe you're right, boy. Maybe I haven't been paying attention. I guess in spite of everything, I can't buy her after all. What that says to me is that you'd prefer to make her a gift. Oh, don't worry. She'll be well looked after. I take good care of my zoo. Even have two vets on permanent staff."

"Mr. Coerlis, sir?" Peeler's eyes were dilating.

"Not now, Peeler," growled Coerlis impatiently. "Can't you see I'm in the midst of delicate negotiations?"

"But sir—" The big man started to explain himself. He didn't have time.

Smoke was rising from the middle of Coerlis's heavy jacket. He barely had time to gawk at the widening hole in the center before he screamed and flung the bundle aside, shaking his right arm violently. A few wisps of smoke curled upward from the back of his hand. Flesh curled away from the source like the peel off a potato.

Stumbling backward, Coerlis banged into another table, sending silverware and plates clattering to the floor. With his left hand he grabbed the standing pitcher of ice water in the center and dumped the contents over his smoking hand. Unbeknownst to him, this action saved his life by flushing away the corrosive before it could get into his bloodstream.

Emerging from the steaming hole in the jacket, wings fully unfurled and buzzing like the grandfather of all hummingbirds, a pink, blue, and green blur erupted toward the ceiling. Flinx took advantage of the diversion to break free of the stunned heavy's grasp. Meanwhile Peeler was trying to divide his attention between the angry, buzzing reptilian shape hovering overhead and the moaning, unsteady form of his master.

Coerlis shakily wrapped a linen napkin around his injured hand, making a crude bandage. His pain almost overrode his rage. "Shoot him, you idiot!" With his good hand he pointed at Flinx. "Shoot them both!"

Peeler's reactions were excellent, but no match for a predator of Pip's quickness. As the muzzle of the needler shifted in her master's direction, she dove straight at its wielder. Knowing what was coming, Flinx did his best to project an air of compassion. He was only partially successful.

Waving wildly at the darting, weaving flier, the big man tried to bring his pistol to bear. Pip's mouth opened, jaw muscles contracted, and from a groove in her upper jaw a needle-thin spurt of poison shot forth. Because of Flinx's emotional intervention it struck Peeler on the back of his gun hand instead of square in the eyes.

Letting out a surprisingly high-pitched shriek, the gunman dropped his weapon and clutched at the wrist of his injured hand. The caustic toxin ate into his flesh.

"Need to wash it off quick," was Flinx's calm advice. He glanced back at the heavy who'd been restraining him. "Better help your buddy. If the poison gets into his bloodstream, it'll kill him." He turned back to Peeler. "He's not paying attention."

"Get him, you imbecile!" Tears were streaming from Coerlis's eyes, and his injured arm was trembling uncontrollably.

"I . . ." The big man came to a decision. Ignoring his master, he snatched up two pitchers of water from a pair of nearby tables and hurried to assist his associate. As their quarry backpedaled, the two men combined efforts to douse the steaming wound.

Flinx extended an arm. Pip immediately darted down to curl her body around her master's bicep. Her head remained up and alert, her wings still spread.

Ignoring his apoplectic employer, the big man looked anxiously back at Flinx. "What now?"

"Keep flushing the site. As soon as possible, apply an antibiotic sealant. And see that he gets five cc's of a general neurotoxin antivenin once a day for a week. Just to be safe. Bluorthorn and Tan-Kolenesed both work."

The big man nodded nervously. He was afraid now. Angry, but afraid.

"Never mind that now!" An enraged Coerlis flung an empty platter against the nearby wall. It bounced and clanged noisily to the floor. "Get *him*." He whirled to face Flinx.

"But Mr. Coerlis, sir—"

The disgusted merchant waved indifferently at the injured Peeler. "He's not dying! The thing doesn't have any fangs. It can't bite, it can only spit." The uninjured heavy hesitated, uncertain what to do next.

"That's true." Flinx turned and headed toward the exit.

He sensed the three of them moving to pursue. He could simply have taken cover and unleashed Pip with a flick of his wrist. Without any emotional restraint on his part she would surely kill all three of them.

But Coerlis was a citizen of some substance, and his sudden, violent death would draw attention of a kind Flinx had worked hard to avoid. On the other hand, so to speak, a little seared skin should pass unnoticed.

Once clear of the restaurant, he glanced quickly in all directions before choosing the right-hand path. The paved service road narrowed rapidly. Olenda was not only the capital, it was the oldest city on Samstead. Roads tended to follow the casual meanderings of the Tumberleon and its tributaries rather than some imposed, arbitrary grid pattern. Side streets as often as not led to narrow closes, quaint cul-de-sacs, or dead-ended atop high stream banks. He ought to be able to lose himself without too much of an effort.

Zoned and fully fueled, the *Teacher*'s shuttle awaited his arrival at the city's eastern shuttleport. But while he was anxious to escape Coerlis's unbalanced attentions, he wasn't about to let the smug maniac run him off a planet he'd grown rather fond of. Tuleon was a big place. There was room enough for both of them. Besides, the young merchant and his bodyguard needed immediate medical attention. Coerlis might be irrational, but he wasn't stupid.

Their emotional auras persisted behind him as he jogged along. That fit Coerlis's mental pattern, but Flinx was still confident he could lose them. Pip slithered up his arm to assume her favorite perch on his shoulder.

Where could he go? Not the local police depot. Coerlis was likely to have influence there. Tuleon was urbanized but hardly urbane, and Flinx had learned early on that large amounts of credit had a way of fogging Truth's vision. You might not be able to break laws by hammering on them with money, but subtle circumvention was another matter entirely.

It felt as if they were gaining on him. Flinx knew that Coerlis's ireful persistence could result in the man's death, something he would still prefer to avoid. He was familiar with the type. Coerlis wouldn't rest now until the perceived insult had been avenged. It had passed beyond being a simple question of whether or not he would obtain ownership of a flying snake.

Obsession, Flinx knew, was often one of the first steps on the road to madness. He knew because there was always more truth in emotions than in words.

Still running easily, he turned up a gently sloping side street. Maybe they'd continue straight, believing he was headed for the waterfront and a faster means of escape. It would be a logical assumption. The occasional passing pedestrian glanced in his direction, drawn to him more by his height and haste than the almost invisible minidrag coiled securely about his shoulder. Samstead was not a fast-paced world. It was unusual to see anyone running in the center of the capital.

He passed entrances to office towers and residential complexes, knowing he'd have to present appropriate identification to gain entry to the smallest of them.

Tuleon might be a relatively easygoing metropolis, but crime was not unknown within its boundaries.

The meretricious facade of a hotel beckoned. Too obvious, he decided, and ran on. He needed someplace less conspicuous. In ancient times a bank would have afforded some safety, but such things no longer existed. Money and credit were largely abstract components of computer storage space, to be manipulated electronically. That was a refuge he could not enter.

Then he saw the building, a stark triangle whose bladed crest topped out at a modest six stories. The familiar emblem, hourglass-on-globe on a field of green, was emblazoned over the always unlocked entrance. Gratefully lengthening his stride, he ascended the curving ramp and entered.

Once inside, he slowed to a respectful walk. The sanctuary was empty save for a couple of elderly supplicants. One was on her knees before the altar, praying before a brilliant depth depiction of swirling nebulae and galaxies. The reality injection was two stories tall and rendered in exquisite, awe-inspiring detail. In conjunction with the subdued, concealed illumination, it imparted to the vaulted sanctuary an air of eternal peace and reassurance. Natural light fell from tinted windows high overhead.

He'd visited the sanctuaries of the United Church before, though never to attend formal services. No doubt there were several dozen similar sites scattered throughout the city. He was tempted to settle into one of the comfortable seats. At this point even the several thranx body lounges looked inviting. But he decided to move on. The sanctuary itself was too open.

Without warning, the persistent fury he identified with Coerlis vanished. That was his damned talent, flickering in and out like a short in his brain. He eyed the entrance uneasily, unable to tell now if Coerlis and his minions were still pursuing or if they'd taken a different turning. The warning wail of emotion in his mind had winked out, and strain as he might, he knew there was no way he could simply turn it back on.

He glanced down at Pip. Have to keep an eye on her now, he knew. Unlike his own erratic abilities, hers were the result of natural evolution. She was on permanent alert. The trouble was, she was not intelligent enough to sort out hostility directed specifically at him. Detection usually went hand in hand with physical proximity, by which time it was often too late to run. But unless his talent reasserted itself, she was all he had to warn him of Coerlis's possible presence.

He looked to his left. If tradition held, there would be a row of library reading rooms there. He could lock himself inside, but while providing privacy and some security, that would also eliminate all avenues of flight. This wouldn't do, he told himself. He was too exposed in the open sanctuary.

Choosing a hallway off to the right and adopting the attitude of one who knew what he was doing, he abandoned the worship center. Small glowing letters hovered before successive doors, rising or descending as he approached until they were exactly at eye level. Some identified individuals, others specific departments.

Avoiding the lift, he took some fire stairs two at a time until he reached the third floor. There he turned down another hall. It was quiet and very few workers were about, as befitted the contemplative nature of the structure's owner.

He'd passed several open doors without incident when a voice from within one office slowed him.

"You look anxious, my son. And tired." Flinx hesitated. "May I be of any assistance?"

Flinx glanced back the way he'd come. The corridor was still deserted. Suspecting the outcome, he strained internally. Nothing. The emotional nova that had been Coerlis might as well never have existed. For the moment, his empathic palette remained precariously blank.

The man standing just inside the portal was much shorter than Flinx, and older. Disdaining a depilatory, he revealed a skull bare save for an elfish fringe of white curls. These continued around his face to form a pair of thick muttonchop whiskers. His self-pressing aquamarine uniform was spotless.

A glance at Pip showed her eyes shut. Flinx considered. He'd been running for quite a while and needed to stop and rest. This seemed as likely a place as any. The jovial, stocky padre was regarding him with friendly curiosity, and regardless of what he decided, some sort of response was clearly in order.

"I'm running from a confrontation. I try to avoid fights when I can."

The kindly visage beamed back at him. "Fighting is a good thing to avoid. Won't you come and sit a moment? You look like you could use a rest."

"Thank you. I think I will."

The padre's office was awash in the usual ecclesiastical paraphernalia. There were the twin monitors on his desk, assorted homey holos and flatscale representations on the walls, a box of spherical drive files on the floor in one corner, and a back wall vid of boreal forest dominated by an energetic, flowing stream that smelled of humus and damp morning. It was designed to relax and reassure, and Flinx allowed himself to fall under its cleverly constructed spell. Even more satisfying was the comfortable, old-fashioned chair to which the padre directed him.

He glanced back at the gaping doorway.

"Privacy?" inquired the padre. When Flinx nodded gratefully, his host murmured into a vorec designed to resemble a tulip. Immediately a real door, much more reassuring than the usual flimsy privacy curtain, closed off the office from the hall.

In return for this largesse of surcease, Flinx knew he was expected to talk, or at least to make casual conversation. No more than that. A proper padre would put no pressure on him to pray or do anything else. One of the attractions of the United Church was that it was a very low-key organization. It offered help and asked nothing in return except that supplicants act rationally. Not necessarily sensibly, but rationally.

"I am Father Bateleur, my son." He nodded in the direction of Flinx's occupied shoulder. "An interesting pet. Is it dangerous?"

"Watchful."

"Those who wander beyond the sanctuary usually have a reason for doing so." The older man smiled expectantly.

"There were some men chasing me." He caressed the back of Pip's triangular head, and one pleated wing unfurled partway, quivering with pleasure. "One of them wanted to buy her."

"Her?" Bateleur smiled. "How do you sex such a dangerous animal?"

"In my case, by dumb luck. She had babies. Anyway, I told this man I wouldn't sell. I couldn't. She's been with me most of my adult life."

"No offense, my son, but you don't look old enough to me to have had much of an adult life yet."

"I've had to grow up fast. I've lived sooner than most people."

"Not faster?" The padre pursed his lips. "Interesting way of putting it." He folded his hands on his lap. "These men who wanted to buy your pet: they were very insistent."

"The disagreement escalated beyond discussion of price. A couple of them got hurt. Pip would have killed them if I hadn't restrained her."

"I see." The padre glanced involuntarily at the coiled minidrag. Flinx sensed no fear in the man, which could have been a consequence of a steely constitution, or the fact that his talent was still inoperative. When Pip didn't return the stare—always a good sign—Flinx allowed himself to relax.

"Restraint is a sign of confident intelligence. How many of them were there?"

"Three."

"Three," murmured the older man, as though the number held some unique significance for him. "It's good that you came here."

"He's apparently well-known in the community," Flinx went on. "Wealthy, not a lot older than me. Jack-Jax Coerlis?"

Bateleur nodded without hesitation. "The House of Coerlis is one of the oldest mercantile enterprises on Samstead. The father passed away not too long ago; a noteworthy death. I myself have had no personal contact with the family. They live outside the city, beyond the boundaries of my parish. There are stories about the heir which do nothing to flatter the reputation of the clan. He's rumored to be something of a hothead."

"Try homicidal maniac." Flinx smiled pleasantly.

"So you had a run-in with young Coerlis. You did well not to kill him. While he may be personally unpopular, the family has powerful friends in Tuleon and elsewhere."

As if on cue, the door slid open. His arm still wrapped in the bloodstained tablecloth, Jack-Jax Coerlis stood in the portal, panting heavily. A round red spot showed on his neck where he'd received an antivenin injection. A small electronics pak dangled from his other hand: the device he had doubtlessly utilized to pick the door seal.

Bateleur's tone and expression were appropriately disapproving. "You are violating the sanctity of the office, my son."

Swiveling in the chair, Flinx saw the two heavies bulking large behind Coerlis. Peeler's arm was similarly bandaged. Both men were straining to see into the room. Though he concentrated hard, for all his effort Flinx drew a trio of emotional blanks. There was no predicting when his sensitivity would return, but he didn't really need it at the moment. Anyone could tell what all three men were feeling from their expressions.

Though confirmation was hardly necessary, Pip provided it. Suddenly she was awake and alert, both wings half spread, ready to rise from his shoulder. With a hand, Flinx held her back. There were no guns in evidence. Only a complete fool would try to enter a church with weapons drawn.

"Didn't expect us to follow you this far, did you?" Coerlis was grinning unpleasantly. "We just waited to see where you'd turn in. Called ahead for a courier to airdeliver the antivenin you so thoughtfully recommended. Peeler and I are feeling better already.

"We've been checking rooms. Fortunately, it's still too early for services and the place isn't busy. City parish, you know. Most people work."

Father Bateleur slid open a drawer on his right. "I must ask you to leave or I will have to call for assistance."

Coerlis eyed him contemptuously. "Call anyone you want, padre. We'll be gone before they can get here."

Bateleur spoke into a concealed pickup. "Father Delaney, Father Goshen, could you come here, please? We are experiencing an incident." He turned back to the intruders. "Really, my son, this sort of thing is not good for one's hozho. Not to mention your blood pressure."

"Your concern touches me, padre." Coerlis turned back to Flinx, gesturing at the minidrag. "Remember: she's real fast, but this room is pretty cramped." Stepping inside, he made space for the two heavies. Both men drew compact needlers. "They're set to stun, and I don't think she's faster than a needle beam."

"You'd be surprised," Flinx replied calmly. "You won't touch her, and she'll end up killing all three of you."

"You underestimate Peeler and Britches. Before, they had no idea what to expect. Now they do, and they'll react accordingly. Of course, there's always the possibility that I'll have to kill you to keep you out of the way. Are you willing to take that chance?"

"Life is the taking of calculated chances," declared a voice from the hall. "The universe throws dice with predictable regularity."

"Please put your weapons on the floor," requested a second voice. "Carefully."

The two padres had come up silently behind the intruders. One was even bigger than Peeler, and both gripped projectile weapons, one of which was aimed directly at the back of Coerlis's head.

"Why, padre." Coerlis spoke to Bateleur without turning. "This hardly seems in keeping with the tenor of a sanctuary."

The older man's smile was wan. "This isn't a sanctuary; it's an office. Do as Father Goshen says."

The two heavies complied. Bateleur looked satisfied. "Now then, my sons, you may leave the building wiser and, I pray, somewhat chastened in spirit." He steepled his fingers in front of him.

"Otherwise," rumbled Father Goshen softly, "we will be most regretfully compelled to preside over the releasing of your immortal souls."

"What?" Peeler sounded as unhappy as he looked.

"I'll blow your head off."

The other man needed no further clarification.

For the barest instant Coerlis hesitated, and Flinx feared he was going to try something truly stupid. Then he smiled and gave a little shrug. "Sure, why not?" Eyes cold and flat as a shark's glanced Flinx's way. "I'll be seeing you."

Bateleur nodded. "Father Goshen, Father Delaney, would you show our visitors the way back to the street? Unless they wish to remain in the sanctuary and pray. Properly supervised, of course." Peeler grunted derisively.

"With pleasure." Using his gun, Father Delaney prodded the nearest intruder in the back of his neck. "Move it!"

As soon as the uninvited visitors and their escort had departed, Father Bateleur rose and shut the door, this time latching it manually from the inside. Back in his chair, he smiled once more at Flinx.

"It would seem you have made an enemy, young man."

"He wouldn't be the first." Flinx immediately regretted the comment, then discovered he didn't really care. He was tired, so very tired. Tired of secrets and of searching, of inexplicable mysteries that seemed to lie teasingly forever beyond his ken. It would be wonderful to have someone to confide in besides the aged Mother Mastiff. So much of what he wanted to say and share was beyond the comprehension of her caring yet simple self.

There were Bran Tse-Mallory and the Eint Truzenzuzex, but he hadn't seen the philosopher-soldiers in years and didn't even know if they were still alive. It was hard to envision either of them dead. Both man and thranx were a force of a nature.

"Is there anything else I can do for you, my son?" Bateleur seemed earnest enough. "If not, there is a concealed and secure rear exit to the church which you may make use of whenever you feel the time is right. Will you be staying much longer in our city?"

"I don't think so," Flinx told him. "Not under the circumstances."

Bateleur nodded approvingly. "A regrettable but probably wise decision."

"In fact," his visitor added, "it looks like I'm going to have to leave Samstead itself now."

"I see. Do you need help in booking passage?"

"No, thank you. I've already made arrangements." Flinx wasn't about to divulge to anyone, not even the sympathetic Father Bateleur, that at the ripe old age of twenty he was the master of his own KK-drive vessel.

Rising to leave, he found himself hesitating. "Padre, what can you tell me about the nature of evil?"

Chapter Three

Bateleur's heavy white eyebrows rose. "In what sense is the question posed, my son?"

Flinx settled back into his chair. "Well, for example, what does the Church say about it? I've never been what you'd call a disciple."

"As you may know, that doesn't matter. People come and go within the Church as their spiritual needs require. As to evil, that is what occurs when sapient creatures who understand the difference between good and bad intentionally do the latter. It's not nearly as complex a matter as philosophers once made it out to be."

"But what about evil in a physical sense, padre?"

"A physical sense . . ." Bateleur pondered uncertainly. "Are you asking if there is a way to quantify evil?"

"Yes, that's it exactly!" Flinx responded eagerly.

Bateleur punctuated his response with delicate gestures. "That's something theologians have debated since sapients first huddled in caves and developed organized religions. I'm still not entirely sure I understand your question."

Once released, the words spilled from his visitor. "I mean, can evil be real in the physical sense? Can it have physical properties, like light or energy? I'm no physicist, but I know that everything is composed of particles and waves. There are strong forces and weak forces, colors and flavors, directions and sensations." He leaned forward so intently that Bateleur was momentarily taken aback.

"Could some combination of forces or particles constitute that which we have always referred to as 'evil'?"

"Interesting notion. I suspect I'm even less the physicist than you, my young friend. But speaking theologically, these days we tend to regard evil as an embodiment of immorality, not an actual presence."

"What if it's not?" Flinx pressed his host. "What if it's a combination of forces, or particles? What if there's such a thing as an evil wave-form? Wouldn't it explain a lot, about how people are influenced and why seemingly rational beings commit inexplicable acts?"

"Be nice if that were the case," Bateleur admitted. "Then someone could build an 'evil-meter' or some such similar device. It would be a great help in my line of work. But I'm afraid I simply don't have the specialized knowledge necessary to respond intelligently to your question. I suppose anything that hasn't been overtly disproved is theoretically possible. Tell me, my son: what led you to this intriguing line of speculation?"

"I've seen it," Flinx informed him tersely. "Or sensed it, anyway."

There. Whatever happened now, he'd shared what he'd experienced with another person. Even if the padre decided he was insane, it felt good to have it out.

No question that it led Bateleur to speculate on the stability of his visitor. That was part of his job. "I see."

"It's out there," Flinx went on. "That way." Raising his right hand, he pointed. As a melodramatic gesture, it was decidedly understated.

"You don't say. People commonly tend to think of evil as lying in this direction." Smiling, Bateleur tapped the floor with a foot.

"What I'm referencing has nothing to do with archaic, traditional concepts of Hell. I'm talking about an actual physical presence that's pure distilled evil. Do you have access to star charts?"

"This is the United Church. Of course we have charts." Turning, Bateleur made the request of the nearest monitor, then pivoted the screen so Flinx could see it as well.

"How's this?" the padre asked when the screen came to life.

"No." Flinx contained his impatience. "That's just the immediate stellar vicinity around Samstead. You need to pull back by several orders of magnification."

Bateleur nodded agreeably and directed the monitor to comply. After a moment he glanced expectantly at his visitor.

"No, no. Farther out. Much farther."

"That's the whole galaxy we're looking at now, with the Magellanic Clouds off to the lower left," Bateleur informed him. "You said that you saw, or sensed, this presence yourself?"

"That's right." Having come this far, Flinx saw no point in holding back any longer. Let the padre think him mad if he wished. Regardless, they would play the scenario out to the end.

Bateleur surprised him by chuckling softly. "For such a young man, you've been around quite a bit."

Flinx looked up out of bright green eyes. "Padre, you don't know the half of it."

Bateleur directed the monitor to remove the view by several orders of magnitude yet again.

"That's better." Flinx studied the image. "Can you rotate the field about forty degrees to the east? I know you can't change the perspective."

"Not working with distances like this." He complied, until Flinx felt he was looking at a section of sky he recognized.

"There! That's the place."

"The evil place?"

"No, no." Flinx shook his head restlessly. "The location isn't evil. It's what's occupying the location. What's out there."

Bateleur considered the monitor. "I'm sorry, my son, but it doesn't look any more evil to me than any other section of the cosmos."

"I've seen it!" Flinx was insistent. "I—I've been there. Not physically, of course. Mentally. I'm still not sure how it was accomplished, but I know it wasn't a dream. It was completely real, even to the jolt I felt just before achieving full perception."

"That's certainly very interesting. I hope you won't mind, my son, when I say that I think you have a very vivid imagination."

"Yes." His guest sighed, having expected that reaction sooner or later. "I suppose I do. But will you at least admit that my basic idea has some merit?"

"Let's just say that I'm open to anything I can't disprove," Bateleur replied kindly. "You must understand that until now I never had occasion to consider evil as a function of unidentified subatomic forces."

"I know. It was a shock to me as well." Rising, Flinx extended a hand. Bateleur took it firmly. "You said something about a back door?"

"Yes." The padre came around from behind the desk and started to put a reassuring arm around his guest's shoulders. A hiss from Pip caused him to reconsider. "You strike me as an unusually independent and resourceful young man, but even though we'll see you safely out of here, don't forget about or underestimate Jack-Jax Coerlis."

Flinx nodded appreciatively. "I won't, I promise." Out in the hall he loomed over the stocky churchman.

"Your accent immediately marked you as offworld," Bateleur commented. "You have no drawl at all. Where do you call home?"

A fair question. "Moth. It's capital city of Drallar."

"I've heard of it. A freewheeling sort of place, I believe. Not as receptive to the Church as some others."

"I like the freedom it affords its citizens," Flinx replied.

"I will pray that you maintain it, my son." They turned down another corridor. "What ship will you be departing on?"

"I don't recall, padre." Flinx lied readily, with the skill of many years practice. "The information's in my baggage."

"And your destination? No, forget that I asked." The older man waved diffidently. "It's none of my business."

"That's all right. I don't mind telling you that I'm heading home." They passed more offices and, as they descended a ramp, a noisy children's crèche.

That much wasn't of a lie, he mused. He *was* going home. Not today, perhaps, or tomorrow, or even next month. Not, in all likelihood, for some time. But eventually.

"I wish you a safe journey, young man. I hope you will have no more trouble."

"I can deal with it. I'm used to dealing with it. I've had to grow up very fast, padre."

There was something so ineffably sad in the young man's voice that Father Bateleur was moved to ask him to remain, to talk more, to come to his home and sup with his family. Despite the young man's outward confidence and evident brilliance, it was clear to Bateleur that his guest was seriously in need of comforting and reassurance. Something within him was crying out for help, and try as he might, Bateleur had no idea what it might be.

He didn't have the chance to offer further. They were already at the back door and his visitor was bidding him good-bye. As expected, the rear serviceway was quite deserted.

"Follow this for several blocks. You'll come to a door which opens into the lower level of a major financial complex downtown. It's always crowded there and you should be able to lose yourself easily. I'd keep your pet under cover to avoid attracting attention, but I suppose you're used to doing that." Flinx nodded.

"If you change your mind and see your way to staying awhile longer," Bateleur added, "my wife and I have room in our home. It sits on an island upstream and—"

"Thanks," Flinx replied warmly, "but I need to be on my way. I'm more comfortable when I'm moving around."

Bateleur found himself watching the tall youth until the shadows enveloped his lanky form. Then he shut the door and started back to his office, barely acknowledging the greetings and comments of colleagues and coworkers along the way. As he walked, an unaccustomed contentment flowed through him, the mental equivalent of sunning oneself beneath a heat lamp. Once, he looked around sharply, but there was no one there.

Taking a left turn, he found himself in the sanctuary. There he knelt and began to pray. Not only for the continued safety of his recent visitor, as he'd promised he would do, but for guidance.

When he was done he returned to his office and activated the nearest monitor. It automatically saved to memory everything that transpired within range of its pickup. There was the young man's arrival, the ensuing confrontation with the hostile Coerlis and his minions, and his visitor's subsequent eccentric dissertation. Bateleur had to smile as he saw for a second time the young man insisting he had visited a place impossibly far away.

What was intriguing was that instead of speaking in generalities, his visitor had chosen and chart-sequence-searched a specific point in the sky. The honestly deluded were not usually so precise.

As an amusing curiosity, Bateleur referred it to local Church headquarters, which in turn dutifully catalogued and filed it via space-minus tight beam to Church science headquarters in Denpasar, on Terra. There it shuttled around in the company of a hundred thousand similar low-key reports, passing the notice of a number of researchers who understandably ignored it.

Except for a certain Father Sandra. She picked it out of a large study file, did some cross-checking on the accompanying visuals, and decided to share the result with Father Jamieson, with whom she'd had an ongoing relationship for nearly a year.

"Shiky, I've got something here I'd like your opinion on."

Shikar Banadundra turned to smile up at her as she handed him the hardcopy. He took a moment to flip through the folder, frowned, scanned it a second time more carefully.

"You sure about this, Misell?"

"Of course not, but a lot of it checks out. The resolution on some of the old visuals is pretty bad. The computer says there's a good chance it's a match. I had to do some scrambling around."

"Voiceprint?"

"Only the new interview with this Father Bateleur on Samstead. Unfortunately, there isn't anything similar in the earlier references."

"Pity. Can you get enough enhancement to do a retinal match?"

She shook her head sorrowfully.

Banadundra eyed the hardcopy afresh. "That's not very encouraging."

"I think the interview itself is encouraging. He's supposed to be dead."

"He may be. Computer opinion or not, this is pretty inconclusive." He concentrated on the last page of the report. "I don't see anything remarkable here. This individual had a run-in with a small-time local merchant. So what?"

She pulled a page from the folder. "What do you think about this business of physically measurable evil existing in a specific cosmic location?"

Banadundra shrugged. "Mildly interesting from a theological point of view. I don't see that it has anything to do with our division."

"I ran a follow-up. For hundreds of years it was generally supposed there was nothing in that location. That it was a big, fat, empty space, a vast section of sky devoid of nebulae, stars, or interstellar hydrogen. Just a lot of dark matter."

"So?"

"Most theories of universal creation call for a relatively even distribution of matter throughout the cosmos.

This place is an anomaly. A big one. No quadrant of space that big is supposed to be that empty."

"Again: so?"

"According to the updated file of Papers, Astronomy, being prepared for general distribution, a couple of months ago a team based on Hivehom found a source of strong radiation deep within the region. They can't see it, of course. It's hidden by all the dark matter. But they're convinced it's there. From what I was able to make of it, there may be some unique electromagnetic properties involved."

Banadundra smiled. "Like evil?"

"I have no idea. What intrigues me is how this young man," and she tapped the hardcopy, "knows about it."

"We don't know that he does."

"He claims to know about *something* out there. You read the printout. He says he's been there. Just not physically."

"Right." Banadundra's smiled widened. "His 'soul,' or whatever, went there. Or maybe he died and went there and came back."

"Thranx researchers don't release experimental data until they're sure of their results. No one is conversant yet with the conclusions of this particular research group. They haven't appeared in the general scientific literature, and this preliminary report has only just been passed along to the Church's Science Department. How did this person Father Bateleur talked with, whoever he is, find out about it?"

Banadundra was growing impatient. He had other work to attend to. "I don't know, Misell, but if he actually does know anything, I find it easier to believe that he had contact with this thranx group than that he traveled a couple of million light-years by some kind of wacky astral projection, or whatever. A search of the tabloid media would probably yield a thousand similar stories."

"Such fictions rarely include discussions of the nature of subatomic matter."

"All right, a couple of dozen stories, then. The numbers mean nothing, just as the interview signifies nothing."

"Shikar, did you ever hear of the Meliorare Society?"

He blinked. "The renegade eugenicists who were wiped out a few years ago? Sure. Everybody in the department remembers that one. What of it?"

Father Sandra tapped the hardcopy. "You remember some trouble involving a radical antidevelopment group on a colony world called Longtunnel?"

Banadundra nodded slowly. "I think so. It was properly taken care of, wasn't it? I don't follow colonial politics."

"If the computer correlations are correct, this young man was present there as well. He became involved with the group. Also with a gengineer working for a company called Coldstripe. Her name," Sandra checked the printout again, "was Clarity Held. At the conclusion of the confrontation she filed a report of her own with the appropriate regulatory authorities. It includes mention of a young man whose description closely matches that of Father Bateleur's interviewee."

"You're losing me, Misell."

"When the last known adherents of the Meliorare Society were destroyed, it was on a world called Moth."

"Never been there," he told her. "Heard it's an interesting, wide-open sort of place."

"I sweated correlation. Not easy when you've got the whole Commonwealth to cover. There are records of a young man named Philip Lynx. Credit tallies through a trading concern called the House of Malaika, a few other ancillary notations. Not much."

"I take it you've drawn some conclusions?"

She leaned forward earnestly. "Look, Shiky. We've got a young man who's on Moth and in the general vicinity when the last of the Meliorares are put down. A niece of one of the last Meliorare practitioners, a woman named Vandervort, is on Longtunnel working with Coldstripe and has contact with what may be this same young man. She died in the confrontation, by the way. Now this person shows up on Samstead. I haven't checked travel records—I'm not a detective—but for such a young man, he seems to have uncommon resources. Far more than his credit records on Moth would suggest."

"Are you suggesting this is someone who's trying to carry on the work of the Society?"

"No. He's much too young. But if there's any kind of connection at all, I think it's worth following up. What I've got right now is a fascinating young man with a blurry past, a tenuous but distinctive link to the Society, and an inexplicable tie to an unreleased astronomical discovery."

Banadundra made a face. "If you can pull all that together into something sensible I'll nominate you for the Obud Prize myself."

She reached out and caressed his cheek. "I don't want any nominations for any prizes. You're my prize, Shikar. What I want is your help accessing the history of the Meliorares."

Concern crossed his dark face. "There's a Moral Imperative seal on those records. There are still mindwiped participants walking around. Access is above both our classifications."

"We can at least try. If nothing else, we can pass what I've found out on up the ladder."

"What's our justification?" he wanted to know. "That there still might be adherents to the Society's philosophy running around loose? Or that we're researching the nature of evil? Or is it strictly an astronomical problem? What you've formulated here would be a conundrum for the Devil himself."

"That is a concept which may be involved as well."

He looked for a smile, frowned when he didn't see one. "Better back up a step or two there, woman. You'll be sent down for instability."

"I assure you, Shiky, I'm talking straight physics. Philosophy's only tangential to what I've been looking into. But," she added, "it may be an *important* tangent. I need you to back me in this."

"Subatomic properties?" he asked hesitantly.

She raised a hand, palm facing him, and replied solemnly. "Subatomic properties. Give me no forces and I'll draw you no lies."

He took a deep breath. "All right, Misell. Just be careful what you say to people." After a moment's thought he added, "Maybe this kid's trying to start a new religion. Happens all the time."

"I wouldn't think so. Not after reviewing the copy of Father Bateleur's interview with him. He doesn't strike me as the messianic type at all. Much more inwardly focused. As far as religion goes, I don't think he's trying to explicate any of the traditional ones, either. I think *he's* convinced he's on to something. Whether it actually is anything more than a coincidental personal hallucination is one of the things I'd badly like to find out.

"I think there are enough interesting coincidences here to intrigue the department. Both this Philip Lynx and what he told Father Bateleur are worth taking a closer look at. At the very least someone of higher rank than a metropolitan padre ought to do an in-depth interview with our well-traveled young man."

"This is obviously important to you, Misell."

"Then you'll get to work on obtaining access to those records?" she asked eagerly.

He sighed. "I suppose. I'm not sure I'll get anywhere, love, but I'll try."

She bent, and he rose on tiptoes to kiss her.

Chapter Four

The ride in the commercial taxi out to Tuleon's northern shuttleport was uneventful. The sky was overcast, the air moist and warm, the scenery pleasant. While not having completely returned, Flinx's talent was flickering in and out, periods of emotional rush alternating with calm and quiet.

A short-circuit in my brain, he rhymed, *which I work on in vain.* Together with the condition that inspired it, the little ditty had stuck with him for years. He couldn't shake either of them.

Following his instructions, the taxi circled the port twice. He was grateful that it was fully automated and he didn't have to answer questions from a querulous driver. There was no sign that he was being followed, and while not conclusive, the additional circumnavigation added to his confidence.

Instead of stopping at one of the passenger debarkation lounges, the vehicle halted midway between those hectic terminals and the cargo depot. With his Ident fully in order, no one questioned his progress, though he did draw the usual curious glances. He was very young to be traveling by private craft. It was assumed he was the scion of one of the wealthy Houses. If challenged by some overzealous official, he could call on his friendship with the

House of Malaika, but such confrontations were infrequent. Since the beginning of civilization, bureaucrats were reluctant to impugn the wealthy, especially if the latter seemed to know what they were doing.

Climbing into an empty, four-person port bubble, he punched in the appropriate pad coordinates. The compact maglev transport accelerated down a tunnel, speeding beneath the green belt that separated the terminals from the pad itself. The actual launch area occupied an open plain several kilometers from the port proper.

Moderating its horizontal velocity, the bubble entered a vertical shaft and began to ascend. At the surface it deposited him on open tarmac. There, he was surrounded by shuttles of varying size, each snugged neatly within the artificial crater of a landing site.

Fat cargo craft were sucking modular transport containers from multiple shafts flanking their sides. With safety tube deployed, a passenger shuttle was unloading nearby, the dome of an arrival center having sprouted from the nearest receiving shaft. When the last passenger had disembarked, the center would automatically be deflated, rolled up, and secured in a protective bunker.

No such elaborate facilities were provided for Flinx, nor did he require any. He simply walked over to his waiting shuttle, communicated the requisite security code, and waited while a simple lift descended from the craft's underside.

"All systems functioning," the shuttle informed him once he was aboard. "Minor discrepancy in the port lift engine. Eighty percent efficiency."

Have to get that fixed someday, he told himself. "Fueling status?"

"Complete," replied the shuttle via its vorec interface.

Flinx settled into the pilot's chair, Pip resting comfortably on his shoulder. Spread out before him were the manual controls, whose proper function had and probably always would remain a mystery to him. Flight navigation and ship operation were matters better left to computers, a state of affairs with which he was quite content and had no desire to challenge.

"Back to the *Teacher*." He adjusted his harness. The shuttle's AI had no difficulty interpreting the routine nontechnical instruction.

"Please secure yourself, sir," the melodious artificial voice requested. "Is there any baggage to come aboard?"

"No." Flinx checked his harness. Except for occasional visits to more distant regions of Samstead, he'd been living out of the shuttle. It knew that, but had been programmed to offer the reminder.

Instruments set flush into the smooth contour before him came alive. He was familiar with the colors if not the functions. A low rumble began as first the starboard, then the port VTOL engines came to life.

"Port Authority has cleared for departure. Lift in ten seconds," announced the shuttle in its pleasant male baritone. Next week Flinx might change it to high thranx, or seductive female. The tone of his mechanical companions depended on his mood, and the *Teacher*'s voice library was extensive.

At the appointed time the stubby craft rose noisily into the air, its internal guidance system in constant contact with every other active shuttle and aircraft in the vicinity. Collisions were all but nonexistent.

At two thousand meters the rear engines took over and the VTOLs shut down. Gentle pressure pushed Flinx back in his seat as the scramjets shoved the ship high into Samstead's relatively unpolluted upper atmosphere.

"Ascend and circle," he ordered the shuttle.

"I am compelled to mention that climbing in such a fashion involves an unnecessary expenditure of fuel."

"Do it," he reiterated. The craft complied.

Now he could make out the great winding water snake that was the Tumberleon, its major tributaries, and the sprawl of the capital. The geometric patterns of farms and ranches quilted the surrounding terrain in green and brown patches.

As the ship continued to spiral upward, the vast blue reaches of the Chirapatri Sea came into view, darker in hue than the endless ocean of space toward which he was climbing. A metallic flash to the east marked the razor path of a shuttle descending toward Peridon, the capital's harbor city.

Turquoise to azure to cerulean to purple and lastly to black, the change in the sky shade delineated increasing altitude as sharply as any instrument. The pressure of his harness lessened along with the maternal pull of the planet, and he was soon resting in zero g. No shuttle was big enough to support a posigravity generator, nor was any needed.

Lights falling like golden teardrops marked the path of a pair of shuttles descending in tandem, probably cargo craft from the same parent vessel. As his own ship rotated, the *Teacher* hove into view; an elongated ovoid of modest proportions from which protruded a cylindrical shaft. The other end of the column terminated in a bulge to which was attached a huge parabolic dish shape: the Caplis generator and KK-drive field projector.

Though not a large vessel and in no way outwardly imposing, in one important respect it exceeded the capability of any other vessel in the Commonwealth. Its secret remained hidden beneath an unremarkable exterior.

The scramjets having long since been silenced, attitude jets took over and carefully maneuvered the shuttle into the docking bay that gaped in the side of the interstellar craft. Confident that the shuttle's instrumentation was communicating silently and efficiently with the much larger AI on board the *Teacher*, Flinx paid no attention to the maneuvers. He was luxuriating once more in the emotional vacuum of space. Here there were no throngs to crowd him, no silent screams of agonized individuals to spark another of his innumerable headaches. It was a place of peace in which his talent was neither a blessing or a curse, a place where he could look forward to an extended period of relaxation and mental ease.

It was *quiet*.

Once the shuttle had been secured in its braces, the exterior door slid shut and the bay was pressurized. As posigravity powered up, Flinx felt weight returning. He released himself from the flight harness and slid out of his seat. On his shoulder Pip stirred in her sleep.

It was good to be back in the familiar confines of the *Teacher*. Within the designated living areas, he'd added what homey touches he could: live plants to supplement the artificial ones, bright colors, a ragged bedspread from Mother Mastiff's pack-rat jumble of a domicile on Moth. There were enterprises and individuals specializing in vehicular decor who could have transformed the interior into a space-traversing palace, but Flinx was reluctant to allow strangers on board his vessel, for all that its singular secret was well-camouflaged and concealed. The result was that the ship exhibited a cool functionality which was wholly in keeping with his own personality.

The posigravity field was reassuring. Not quite one g, but sufficient to keep him attached to the floor. Beyond emptying his duffel and dumping dirty clothing into the sanitizer, there wasn't much else to do. He ate an indifferent meal before moving up to the control room.

Two small ports revealed the view aft, while the fore port displayed a halo of stars around the drive parabolic. Lazy blue light rose from Samstead's atmosphere, the sensuous arc of the planet glowing like porcelain on fire. It was time to bid that beauty farewell, as he'd been compelled to do with so many beautiful things throughout his life.

"Activate drive. Prepare for system departure."

"Very well, sir," replied the *Teacher*. A subtle vibration impregnated the deck underfoot. That was expected.

What followed was not.

"We are being hailed, sir."

Flinx pursed his lips. A customs vessel, or perhaps a nearby ship noting the activation of his drive and seeking clarification of intentions. Easy enough to find out.

He flopped into the pilot's seat. "Acknowledge."

The com screen off to his left cleared immediately. He tensed. The face displayed was all too familiar.

"I'm sure you thought I'd given up by now." The edgy yet disciplined voice was also familiar.

"No." Flinx's tone was resigned. "But I'd hoped you had. You said that you own a whole zoo. Why this unreasonable obsession with my pet?"

Coerlis shrugged imperceptibly. "I don't have an Alaspinian minidrag. And your ship is a lot closer than Alaspin. Why don't you just come on over in your shuttle? Or if you prefer, I'll send someone over to you. It won't take but a few minutes. Your internal systems will confirm that I'm very nearby." As Flinx moved to check, Coerlis added, "Where'd you steal that ship? It looks new."

"I didn't steal it. It's mine."

"Yours?" Coerlis didn't laugh. "You don't have to lie to me. I can find out the truth anytime I want."

"It was a gift," Flinx informed him quietly.

Coerlis's eyebrows rose. "Someone must think highly of you."

Flinx had to smile as he thought of the Ulru-Ujurrians and their fanciful permutations of physics, logic, reason, and matter. "To tell you the truth, I'm not sure if they do, but a gift from friends it was."

"Doesn't matter. It's not your ship I want. The House of Coerlis isn't hurting for transport. Take the craft I'm aboard right now, for example. Latest drive and navigation technology, or so I'm told. Very responsive, very efficient. I really ought to get off Samstead more often, but I've a lot of business to attend to. That's why it upsets me to have to spend so much time on something as minor as our mutual enterprise. It's wasteful. I hate waste.

"While you're checking on my location you might as well have your instrumentation confirm something else about my vessel. It's armed. She's no peaceforcer, but she's lethal enough to make me feel secure. Also confident."

"How did you follow me?"

"It wasn't hard." Coerlis sounded matter-of-fact rather than boastful. "If you're looking for an individual who's reasonably distinctive in appearance, and you saturate your search area with enough people, you can find anybody. As soon as you were spotted it was easy to set professionals in your wake. I have resources.

"Once your intent was clear, I boosted before you did. After that it was simply a matter of having ground control track your shuttle. I was prepared to delay and board a commercial craft, but this is better. Privacy facilitates commerce." He shrugged anew. "Such things aren't difficult to manage. All it takes is money."

Another screen showed Coerlis's vessel orbiting behind and slightly below Flinx, gaining on the *Teacher* with its drive silent. "How do I know you're really armed?"

"I've no reason to lie to you. I've a belt-mounted energy weapon and a couple of older-model but quite adequate projectile launchers. Not enough to threaten a small peaceforcer, but more than enough to reduce you to scrap."

"Do that, and you don't get your new pet."

From her favorite perch on a tree sculpture fashioned of metallic glass fibers Pip looked up curiously. Since her master was projecting no fear, she relaxed.

Tired, Flinx thought. So tired. And not a little fed up. How could he contemplate doing anything for humanxkind if humanxkind wouldn't leave him alone?

"All right. If it's that important to you . . . I can't believe you'd really use spatial weaponry in close orbit around an inhabited world."

"At this range? Why not? Ships have 'accidents' all the time. A small electrical interrupt, someone fiddling with the wrong control; easy enough to explain an incident away. Money mutes any complaint. But why should any of that be necessary? Do us both a favor: save me credit and yourself your life."

Flinx couldn't sense directly what the other man was feeling, but he had a reasonably good idea: the small sensation of triumph, the juvenile feeling of satisfaction, self-elevation at the expense of another. It was all so discouraging and predictable.

"I'll get my shuttle ready," he told the other man. "You're still going to pay, of course."

"Certainly." Coerlis smiled as widely as he could. "Why make trouble? If you have friends with resources enough to give you a ship like that, they might come looking for me if anything happened to you. I don't want the aggravation; just the flying snake."

"I'm secured for changeover. It'll take a couple of minutes to prepare for an exchange of shuttles."

"I'll wait." Coerlis was more than agreeable. "Meanwhile don't think about trying to boost. We're much too close for you to try a run. If you don't believe me, check with your computer."

Flinx had no idea how accurate or efficient Coerlis's weapons systems were. He doubted they were any more effective than his own, but he had no intention of surprising the merchant by selectively destroying a portion of his vessel, for example its drive components. Such activity would be detected by orbital monitors and the *Teacher* would be permanently identified and marked for attention by Commonwealth and Church authorities.

"I'll take any universal credit chit." Flinx made conversation while the *Teacher* made ready. "We can run it through a neutral ground-based system."

"Sure." Despite the obvious exertion, Coerlis was unable to be truly cheerful.

"Shuttle will depart in five minutes."

"Three." Coerlis smiled relentlessly.

"All right: three." Flinx terminated transmission and turned toward the omnidirectional voice recognition pickup. "*Teacher*, I want drive activation in three minutes."

"Difficult." Lights flickered on the layout before Flinx. Pip stirred slightly but remained on her perch, wings furled against her blue, pink, and green body.

"It may also be necessary to engage in evasive action," Flinx added. "We have been threatened by the KK-drive vessel nearest to us."

"The situation is understood, sir." Flinx's chair quivered beneath him.

Coerlis's voice grated over the wide-open com, restive and suspicious. "You're moving. What's going on?"

"Adjusting attitude. My shuttle's low on fuel and you're a fair ways off. Check your own readouts. I'm moving toward you, not away."

A pause, then, "So you are. Take it easy."

"Relax. I'm entirely on automatics. Do I look old enough to you to handle manual piloting?"

"All right, but no tricks."

"What tricks?" Flinx replied. "The closer I come, the simpler it is for your weapons systems to target me."

"Just don't forget that," Coerlis replied testily. He subsided a little when Flinx reestablished visual contact. "Not that I feel bad about this, but I see no reason for you to leave with just money. Would you like a puppy?"

"That's all right. I've been to Alaspin. I can get another minidrag."

Coerlis eyed him curiously. "Then why give me such a hard time over this one? Just because it's been with you for a while? It's only an alien analog."

"Sixty seconds," announced the *Teacher*, too softly for the pickup to transfer the information to Coerlis's craft.

"Emotional attachments can be hard to break."

"They can also be damaging if you let them get to you," Coerlis replied. "Look, no hard feelings. You're a pretty resourceful kid. Why don't you come work for me?"

"Because I haven't been a kid for quite some time, and because I don't think I'd like working for you. In fact, I doubt anyone does. But you'll never know that. Pumped credit buys a lot of fawning, and humankind's never suffered from a shortage of sycophants."

"Drive activation imminent," murmured the voice of the *Teacher*.

Someone offscreen shouted urgently and Coerlis turned in their direction. A moment later he was glaring icily back at Flinx. "I told you no tricks. I get what I want, and if I can't get what I want . . ." He turned away to shout an order.

At that instant the *Teacher* twitched and the view outside all three ports spun wildly. Communication with Coerlis was lost as Flinx's vessel accelerated sharply, to pass directly above and dangerously near to the other vessel. Though very mild, the initial gravity wave generated by the *Teacher*'s drive perturbed the orbit of Coerlis's craft enough to make precision weapons targeting impossible.

Flinx allowed himself a slight smile as he envisioned his frustrated nemesis screaming and yelling at his subordinates. Meanwhile the *Teacher* continued to accelerate exponentially.

"Any indication of hostile reaction?"

"One object-seeking weapon launched," replied the vorec promptly.

"Potential?"

"Far below SCCAM velocity, sir."

"I know that. If it was a SCCAM projectile we'd already be dead." The computer did not object to its inclusion in Flinx's evaluation.

"Improperly aimed, sir. It is not a threat." A brief pause, then, "The vessel which undertook the reaction has activated its own drive and is attempting to pursue."

"Are they closing on us?"

"No, sir. Maintaining projected interval and velocity."

"Good enough." As long as Coerlis remained out of weapons range there was no harm in both ships accelerating in tandem. Projectiles were no longer a concern. Everything depended now on the sophistication of Coerlis's single energy weapon. It could prove difficult to evade. KK-drive ships weren't designed for sharp, quick maneuvering.

A military craft would already be solidifying its targeting procedures. Coerlis's people should take somewhat longer. Meanwhile the *Teacher* headed outsystem, where the full power of its drive could be safely engaged.

"Heavy particle burst detected, sir," announced the *Teacher* gravely. "Capable of causing significant damage if we are hit. Shall I respond actively?"

"No. Evade and avoid. See that we're not impacted. How long before we reach changeover?"

"Crossing the orbit of the sixth and outermost planet, sir. Two minutes thirty seconds." There was a pause, almost an electronic hesitation, then, "Allow me to point out that it would be useful to select a course prior to insertion, sir."

"I don't give a damn." Watching Pip, Flinx was reminded of his childhood on Moth: free-roaming, without responsibility, dangerous but exciting, and largely devoid of headaches. He missed that freedom, missed the easy laughter and camaraderie of fellow street children. He'd grown up too fast and learned too damn much. It was somebody's fault, and he knew who they were.

But there was no use blaming them anymore, because they were all dead.

"We are being hailed, sir."

"Ignore all transmissions." He was sick of Jack-Jax Coerlis's pinched, pasty, psychotic face and hoped never to have to look upon it again.

How much longer would he have to put up with the cavalier madness of individual antagonists? How much longer would he have to restrain himself? He felt a headache coming on, a throbbing at the back of his skull. Even here, in the sanctuary of emptiness, he wasn't always immune.

"Forty seconds. Course, sir. Please."

"I told you; it doesn't matter. Anyplace—anywhere on our current vector. The next habitable world. I don't care. Just go."

"Very well, sir. Changeover is imminent."

A different sort of shudder ran through the ship. He fancied he could hear Coerlis's howl of outrage as the *Teacher* leaped off his screens. The starfield outside the ports dopplered and his stomach did an amiable flip-flop. In the time it would take Coerlis's vessel to achieve equal velocity, the *Teacher* would be long gone in the unnatural immensity of space-plus.

And that would be the end of that.

As for what lay ahead, it didn't matter. Flinx never gave much thought to tomorrows. He was by nature reactive rather than protagonistic. For the present he was content to let the cosmos bounce him where it would.

Chapter Five

Flinx didn't bother to count the days. He was content simply to be going. It wasn't necessary to ponder where he'd been or where he was heading. In space-plus, cocooned in the responsive and caring confines of the *Teacher*, he was free from the emotional roar and babble of thousands of sapient beings. Here there were no headaches, no need to wonder at the true motivation of supposed friends or old acquaintances. The *Teacher*'s AI existed to serve, and serve emotionlessly. There was only one problem.

He was not, at heart, a hermit.

He loved the feel of solid ground underfoot, the flash and static of new worlds, the company and conversation of intelligent life. The paradox had always existed within him: solitary of mind but gregarious of nature.

If only he could blind himself to their emotions, shut out their feelings, ignore their petty internalized tantrums and upsets, he would be as comfortable in a crowd as in the familiar chambers of the *Teacher*. But he could not. They raged and tore at him, demanding his notice, pricking his talent and worming their distraught selves into his mind. He almost smiled. Maybe that was the cause of his headaches.

Overcrowding.

He elevated himself with philosophy, diverted himself with music, expanded his perceptiveness with art, and made yet another stab at the physics of his private revelations, until one day the ship announced brightly, "Preparing for changeover, sir. Reinsertion into normal space imminent."

"Only entropy is imminent, *Teacher*. Didn't you know that?"

"You've been reading Sheckley again, sir. Insightful, but lacking in depth."

"Truths are no less real for being transitory."

"I cannot debate with you now, sir. There are adjustments to be made. Unless you wish us to be turned inside out upon changeover."

"Don't think I haven't thought about it."

"I remind you that I am programmed to recognize facetiousness, sir."

Flinx closed down the library, made certain the painting he'd been working on was properly stabilized, dismissed the entertainment block, added a few bars to his ongoing symphonic mass, and prepared to rejoin the real universe. Lazing on her perch, Pip followed him with piercing, slitted eyes.

"Where are we, anyway?" Flinx settled himself into the pilot's chair, from which he'd never done nor hoped ever to have to do any piloting.

"The world is not named, sir."

The last vestiges of *a capella* polyphonics faded from his mind. "What do you mean, it's not named?"

"You asked that we travel to the next habitable world on our original vector, sir. No other specifications were provided and no limitations set."

"We've been a long time in space-plus." He checked one of numerous readouts. "A very long time. What are you telling me?"

"It's an odd entry in the files, sir. There's virtually nothing in the way of description beyond the fact that it is Earthlike and habitable. It's more of a statistic than a realized place."

"You're telling me that it's habitable but uninhabited."

"Insofar as I am able to determine from the very limited information available to me, sir. It's little more than a listing. Unclassified."

Flinx frowned. "That's odd. Why not label it a class ten and leave it at that? If enough is known about it to list it as habitable, enough must be known for a formal classification to apply."

"I do not dispute your logic, sir. I am only reporting what information is in my files."

"Is it a new entry?"

"No, sir. It appears to be quite old."

"Curiouser and curiouser. Something someone wants kept secret?"

"Not so much secret as perhaps overlooked, sir. You know that I have access to files which are unavailable generally."

"If you say so." Flinx considered the refulgent orb they were decelerating toward. "I would've preferred Tehuantepec." That well-developed world, with its partially above- and partially belowground society, would have been a fine and active place in which to submerge himself.

Maybe this was better. Something completely new. Flinx had always liked surprises because his talent made genuine ones difficult.

"Any sign of communications, at any level of proficiency?"

"A moment, sir. I am scanning. No sir, nothing. Only the expected local and background stellar output."

Flinx studied those readouts whose function he could comprehend. The world expanding before him massed slightly less than Terra and orbited a little nearer its star. It hugged close a dense but breathable atmosphere. Additional details would become available subsequent to more intimate observation.

"Let's take a closer look."

"Very well, sir. How close? We are alone here."

The ship was being careful, as it was programmed to be. It wouldn't do to have some lone Commonwealth survey drone note the fact that a KK-drive ship could descend to within touchdown distance of a planetary surface without generating the usual cataclysmic side effects both to ship and surface. Alone among known vessels, only the *Teacher* could manage that trick, and Flinx guarded its secret zealously.

"I know we're alone, but let's hew to minimum Commonwealth orbital standards anyway. At least until we're doubly sure nobody's watching. Then we'll see."

"As you wish, sir."

They dropped to the specified altitude and commenced a steady circumnavigation of the planet, moving from west to east and occasionally shifting to a circumpolar orbit. It didn't much matter. Except for an occasional outbreak of blue ocean, the surface was practically uniform.

There was also a vague feeling of having been here before, stronger than déjà vu but far less than certitude. He had to grin. If the *Teacher* was correct, *no one* had ever been here before, except the robot drone that had long ago noted its coordinates.

"Visuals confirm preliminary observations," he murmured aloud. "It looks as well as tests habitable. Wonder why no one's come here?"

"I don't know, sir. There are many discrepancies in the old files. Record-keeping was much less efficient hundreds of years ago."

Flinx heard a deep hum and felt a weight on his shoulder. Pip had fluttered over to join him. It was unusual for her to be so active so soon after changeover, but he didn't have time to wonder about her behavior. He was too busy staring out the port as they slowly circled the cloud-swathed planet.

There was at least one sizable ocean. There might have been others but it was difficult to tell, since even the surface of the water was heavily masked in green. What pelagic growth there was, was thick and cloying.

The few eroded mountain ranges were completely smothered in greenery, as were the occasional isolated canyons and depressions. Except for disparate shades of that dominant hue, there were only varying densities of white cloud and the isolated patch of blue, struggling to be seen. The *Teacher* soared high above greens so pale as to be translucent, shading to green dark enough to verge on black. Within the tightly constricted palette there was immense variation.

Instruments searched for an open space in which to set down: the crumbling gray of a high mountain plateau, the baneful yellow of open desert, even the pallid glare of a glacier or ice cap. In vain. Save for the already noted patches of open ocean maintained by a few strong currents, this world was an unrelenting, unremitting green from its equator to its poles.

"I don't think there's much question about the presence of indigenous life," Flinx commented. "Not of the botanical variety, anyway. That's certainly noteworthy enough to be included in any records. But you say there's nothing."

"No sir. Only the coordinates and the simple basics already alluded to." After a period of silence in which man and machine silently contemplated the world below, the ship ventured, "Would you like me to construct a vector to Tehauntepec, sir?"

Flinx considered. There was no one to talk to here, no convivial strangers with whom to share conversation or debate. After so much time spent in the isolation of space-plus, he was in need of conversation. It was a function of his age as much as his personality. Much easier to observe in isolation when one has turned eighty or ninety and has a store of old conversations to draw upon.

The voice of the *Teacher* interrupted before he could make a decision. "Sir, instruments have detected a metallic anomaly within the surface."

"Within?" Flinx's eyebrows rose.

"Yes sir. The surface we are viewing is neither uniform nor solid."

"Where is this anomaly located?"

"Behind us now, given our velocity."

Could be an old meteorite lying within the vegetation, Flinx mused, or an outcropping of a concentrated ore deposit. Or . . . ?

"Find it again and position us overhead."

"Yes sir." The ship adjusted orbit to comply. Not much later, "We are directly above it now and holding, sir."

Flinx examined the surface via the view offered up by the *Teacher*'s scopes, eyeing the relevant monitors with interest. All that could be seen was the all-pervasive green, albeit at a higher magnification.

"I am unable to further resolve the anomaly," the ship informed him. "It is relatively small."

Still a meteorite or ore outcropping, Flinx decided. "There's nothing about it to suggest that anyone else is here?"

"No, sir. The communications spectrum for this entire system is completely blank."

He considered. "Then take us down."

The ship complied, descending slowly to an altitude that would have stunned any observer conversant with the physics of KK-drive technology. Only when they had fallen far enough for Flinx to make out individual tree-tops did he direct the *Teacher* to pause and hover.

"It's all like this?" he asked rhetorically.

The ship replied anyway. "All that I have been able to survey so far, sir. Of course, we have only made a dozen or so passes."

"What are our landing prospects in this vicinity?"

"The local vegetation rises to heights in excess of seven hundred meters, sir. There is some question as to the stability of the actual surface, even if it could be reached."

"So there's nothing?"

"I have noted the presence of a very few relatively growth-free mountain peaks which rise above the surrounding greenery. These exposed barrens may owe their existence to altitude, the absence of suitable soils, or a combination of factors. There are none next to the anomaly, but one is relatively close."

"Define 'relatively' in this instance."

"I believe that would be misleading, sir, given the energetic nature of the surface. Linear and chronological distance are not likely to correspond in any meaningful fashion."

"Is there room enough to land?"

"The space is inadequate and the topography unsuitable," the ship replied discouragingly. "There are one or two places where a properly piloted shuttle might safely achieve touchdown."

"Good enough. Take us back to a normal orbit."

"Yes sir." A tremor ran through the ship as it balanced on its unique drive and began to ascend. "Further observation reveals that the exposed area is composed of especially tough granites, very difficult for organics to break down. This could account for the absence of the otherwise omnipresent vegetation."

"What an amazing place." Flinx continued to gaze out the port as they returned to orbit. "I wonder what kind of animals, if any, live here? Surely in all this world-spanning forest there has to be a variety of mobile life forms."

"In the absence of high-resolution observations, it would be premature of me to speculate, sir."

Time to reprogram the *Teacher*'s voice, Flinx decided as he rose and headed for the shuttle bay.

"We'll go down and have a look around," he told his companion. Pip eyed him uncomprehendingly. "A world capable of supporting this kind of life deserves to be reported. Settlements would do well here."

"Your appraisal is similarly premature, sir. If you would like my opinion—"

"I always want your opinion, ship." Flinx turned down a corridor.

"The biotic density far exceeds that of any previously recorded rain forest. Even the thranx, who are partial to such conditions, might have difficulty establishing themselves here. The growth may not be manageable, and I remind you that we know nothing of the actual surface, which must be shrouded in perpetual darkness."

"I didn't say potential colonizers wouldn't have problems. They could start by clearing a wide section of forest."

He halted sharply and had to place one hand against a wall for support. An alarmed Pip raised both wings and immediately began hunting for an unseen enemy.

"Sir?" The voice of the ship was concerned.

"Whew!" Flinx put the hand to his head. "Just had something shoot through me like you wouldn't believe. Not like one of my usual headaches. I guess I'm going to have to adapt to a new round of pain." He straightened. "It'd be worse on Samstead. Or Terra." Cautiously he resumed walking.

On board the shuttle he addressed the vorec which was permanently linked to the *Teacher*'s neutral nexus. "You're sure there's a place to set down? I don't want to burn any vegetation if I don't have to."

"There should be adequate room, sir, though there is little margin for error."

"I'm not worried." He slipped into harness. "You don't make errors."

"No, sir."

The shuttle detached cleanly from its bay, pivoted in nothingness, and engaged a preprogrammed angle of descent, aiming for an infinitesimal spot of gray/brown that just barely protruded above the sea of green. As he dropped, Flinx marveled through the port at the virescent surface. Colossal emergents with overarching crowns a hundred meters across dominated the chlorotic topography, while smaller yet still gigantic growths fought for a share of life-giving sunlight. Utilization of every shaft of sunshine, every stray photon, was contested. On this world photosynthesis had gone wild, and chlorophyll was the addiction of choice.

As they descended, the roar of the shuttle's engines was a steady, reassuring thrumming in his ears. He reached back to his childhood, when, as a carefree ward of the tolerant Mother Mastiff, he'd spent days climbing the gnarled evergreens of Drallar's public parks. Other children might have mothers and fathers, but few had enjoyed his degree of freedom.

As he monitored the *Teacher*'s ongoing observations, he knew he wouldn't be doing much tree-climbing here. How did one scramble up a seven-hundred-meter-tall trunk? At what height did the incredible growths begin to put out branches?

Something vast and superbly colored swept past the foreport like a shower of stained glass and was gone. The shuttle rocked ever so slightly. Startled and excited, Flinx leaned forward and peered to his left. The flying creature, or whatever it had been, was gone, its chromatic brilliance a fading memory on his retinas. He considered ordering the shuttle to alter course to follow, then decided against it. Where one aerial apparition existed, there were sure to be others.

So there were at least aerial life forms here, he realized, and big ones at that. How had the details of such a world gone missing from the Commonwealth archives? It wasn't Under Edict, like Ulru-Ujurr. Just forgotten.

And he had it all to himself.

Vibration increased as the engines worked harder, braking against thick atmosphere. Through the port Flinx could make out a riot of color within the treetops, bright patches of vermilion and chartreuse within the greenery.

Flowers, perhaps, their shapes blurred by distance and movement.

He leaned back in harness, making certain it was secure. Touchdown was liable to be rough. Below lay no smooth-surfaced shuttleport, no forgiving tarmac, no land-based controller to offer last-minute advice. He had only the *Teacher*'s assurance that a landing was even possible.

Ahead he made out a few rugged splotches of gray rising above the forest, lonely islands in a sea of green. The shuttle's thrumming became a whine as it switched smoothly from scramjets to VTOLs. Forward motion slowed and it fell precipitously on a cushion of heated air. Flinx closed his eyes.

There was a jolt and his fingers tensed on the armrests. Motion ceased, the whine faded. A deafening silence settled over the shuttle. He was down.

A glance outside showed broken rock cresting against straining greenery less than half a dozen meters from the fore landing strut. There was more open space toward the stern. Coached by the *Teacher*, the shuttle had handled the landing perfectly.

Slipping out of harness, Flinx double-checked the *Teacher*'s original observations. The atmosphere was indeed breathable. Combined with the high oxygen content, the slightly less than T-normal gravity promised easy hiking.

Microbiological screening revealed the presence of several million airborne organisms. This was to be expected on such a fecund world. Detailed sampling suggested the absence of any likely to seriously affect his otherworld constitution. He'd use the airlock anyway, as a safety precaution. Better if possible to keep the shuttle's atmosphere inviolate. To conserve power he would utilize the foldout ramp instead of the shuttle's internal powerlift.

When Flinx cracked the outer door, the humidity hit him like a hot, wet towel. The humidity, and the rush of alien odors. These ranged from a sharp suggestion of fine perfume to something that stank worse than an overloaded waste treatment plant.

It required an effort to realize that he was looking out across the top of an immense forest and not at some poorly maintained garden. The actual ground lay hundreds of meters below, and he was standing on a mountaintop, not a rocky outcropping in the middle of a lawn. This knowledge was as energizing as it was disorienting.

Vegetation struck and clawed at the exposed granite, seeking to submerge even this last bastion of bare rock, as if driven into a chlorphyllic frenzy by the absence of any plant life upon the peak. Pip riding easy on his shoulder, Flinx started down the metal rampway. He left the lock ajar. There was no one here to disturb anything inside, and he wasn't going to wander very far.

At the bottom of the stairs Pip unfurled her wings and soared toward the sun, relieved to be free of the ship's confines. She needed the exercise, he knew. There was a limited amount of space for aerial maneuvering on board the *Teacher*.

"What do you think, Pip?" She dipped close, wings ablur. "Quite a place, isn't it? What say we go for a little walk?"

Reentering the shuttle, he made his way to the supply locker and packed a service belt with everything from survival rations to compacted water. Lastly, he snapped on a holster holding a fully charged needler. If the traditions of exploration held true, it was possible that not every life form they encountered would prove amiable. Certainly none would have any instinctive fear of a human.

Besides, he'd learned early on to always enter a strange environment, no matter how outwardly civilized or pacific, expecting trouble. The efficacy of this maxim was attested to by his continued existence.

The belt heavy against his waist, he sealed the inner door, once again opened the outer, and descended the deployed ramp, content in the knowledge that his only means of returning to the *Teacher* was secure. At such moments he was ever mindful of the famous story of the Commonwealth liner *Kurita*. She had been paralyzed in orbit above Terra, a thousand passengers and crew forced to wait impatiently while dozens of engineers and specialists had swarmed her instrumentation and equipment in search of the difficulty.

Only to find that a tiny spider had spun a web not much larger than itself at a critical electronic junction. Flinx had no intention of losing control of the shuttle to such an oversight.

Stopping at the base of the ramp, he once more scrutinized the boundless sea of green. There was a distinct yellow-green tint to the atmosphere that was compounded by the reflective quality of numerous low-lying clouds. Prodigious transpiration from the forest maintained the ambient humidity at near maximum levels. Already he had begun to perspire heroically. The high humidity didn't bother Pip. Much of Alaspin was also thick with rain forest, though on a much more modest scale.

Strolling toward the nearest patch of vegetation, he felt a muscular thrust from Pip and instinctively dropped, reaching as he did so for his handgun. The minidrag just did manage to interpose herself between his crumpling form and the vast shape plunging toward him out of the clouds.

The reason for its unseen approach was immediately apparent. Despite a wing span of some four meters, it was practically invisible against the limpid sky. Not only its membranous wings, but its bones were perfectly transparent. Only the muted colors of its internal organs and the pale pink blood that coursed through transparent arteries and veins were readily visible, along with the partially-digested remains of an earlier meal.

The swart skull boasted jaws set with backward-curving teeth that appeared fashioned of glass. Three eyes protruded from the wedge-shaped forehead. Evolved for optimum predation, one looked forward while the other two were set off to the sides of the head. This distinctive ocular architecture allowed for more than three hundred degrees of uninterrupted vision, while the fore eye functioning in tandem with either of the others gave the creature excellent depth perception as well.

A third, shrunken wing ran the length of the meter-long body and served as a maneuvering keel in place of the expected tail. Three short, clawed feet provided a solid landing platform.

A more difficult-to-spot aerial predator would be hard to imagine, Flinx decided even as he struggled to unlimber his weapon. Silhouetted against the sun, his attacker would be virtually invisible to prey flying or crawling below.

All this flashed through his mind in an instant, as Pip prepared to counterattack. Flinx instinctively threw up his free hand to protect his face as he fumbled at the recalcitrant holster with the other. Something shattered the air just above him with an explosive pop.

Then he was enveloped by a mass of transparent wings and pulsing organs. The flesh he kicked at frantically as he sought to keep those glass-toothed jaws away from his neck felt like sheets of water-filled plastic.

It struck him then that the creature was hardly moving. When he crawled out from beneath the quiescent mass he saw why.

Its head was gone. Pink blood pumped from severed arteries in rapidly decreasing streams.

"Pip!" He climbed shakily to a crouch. "Pip, where . . . ?"

She lay off to his right, on her back. For a horrible moment she didn't move. Then she twisted onto her belly scales, spread her wings, and fluttered briefly into the air before crashing back to the ground, obviously dazed. He stumbled toward her. His ears rang as if someone had been using his head for a clapper inside a gigantic bell.

Behind him the decapitated alien raptor flopped against the rocks, wings and body twitching spasmodically. Flinx's first thought was that an explosive projectile had obliterated the predator's skull. If that was the case, he would have expected a cry of greeting from whoever had fired the saving shot. Nothing of the sort was forthcoming.

Up close he saw that Pip was unhurt, only stunned. Not unlike himself, he knew. Then he saw her tense as she rose to land on his shoulder. He followed her reptilian gaze.

From the body of a huge emergent, just beneath its capacious, shadowy crown, a thick brown cable had emerged. It crept along the rocks, prodding and probing, a second following close behind. At first Flinx thought they were some kind of impossibly attenuated snakes. He soon learned otherwise.

The tip of the nearest cable made contact with the still quivering corpse of the raptor. With a speed that took Flinx's breath away, the two cables lashed out and contracted. One encircled the dead predator's body, the other a crumpled wing. Together they dragged the corpse toward the forest.

From his perch atop the exposed rock, Flinx watched as the cables drew their prize across the treetops. At first he thought they originated within the tree itself. Closer inspection revealed that they were retracting not into the trunk but into a large lump on its side that differed only slightly in color from its stolid host. He envisioned a limpet the size of a grizzly.

As he looked on, the tentacles lifted the body toward the pale brown lump. A toothless maw gaped in the side. Flinx found himself wondering if the tree drew any benefit from the lump's presence. Perhaps in the course of its natural predation it and others like it kept the emergent's crown free of winged grazers who might otherwise devastate its vulnerable, sun-loving leaves.

He wasn't about to investigate any closer. The tentacles coiled tight against the lump's side as the body of the transparent flier disappeared within the receptive cavity. As he looked on, a smaller flying creature approached. It had pink and red feathers, a long neck, and a beak like a roseate stiletto. Skimming gracefully over the top of the forest, it was intent on the branches below.

The instant it entered the shadow of the emergent's crown, one of the coiled tentacles snapped out. There was a concussive bang, an echo of the sound that had temporarily stunned him and Pip. The feathered flier's head vanished and the limber body crashed into the treetops below, tumbling once before coming to rest. Another tentacle reached for the fresh catch.

Fortunately for Flinx, the tentacled mass, which he promptly dubbed the whipbump, only seemed to attack airborne life forms. Its perception was directed permanently skyward.

"Remind me not to do any recreational gliding around here," he murmured to Pip. The flying snake glanced up at him querulously.

He'd been outside the shuttle for only a couple of minutes, and in that time had encountered not one, but two indigenous predators, neither of which resembled anything previously encountered or read about. The initially peaceful appearance of the warm, moist forest took on a sinister aspect. A breeze would have helped, but the air was as still and heavy as an old pot of stew.

He shaded his eyes against the yellow-green glare, acutely aware now that he was dangerously exposed on the bare mountaintop. It was obviously not a safe place to linger, and he'd do better to get under cover. In the distance he could see fuzzy shapes rising and diving above the green canopy. Surely not all of them were predators, but until he was more familiar with the local fauna, he'd do well not to take any chances.

A series of mournful, echoing cries reached him, and he tilted his head back. High overhead a flock of streamlined, cream-colored creatures soared past on prismatic wings. Each was perhaps half the size of his shuttle. Farther to the west a cluster of mewling grazers drifted above the treetops by means of three gas-filled sacks growing from their spines. Multiple legs dangled beneath some, tentacles twitched and coiled beneath others. There were many varieties of these drifters. To his untrained eye they looked like airborne jellyfish.

Not all were ample of dimension. As he stood observing, several hundred gas-bag floaters appeared from behind the stern of the shuttle. Each about the size of his closed fist, they drifted lazily past, their single supportive balloons flashing iridescent in the hazy sunlight.

Their tails resembled the aft wings and rudders of ancient aircraft. Six thin, flexible blades, three to a side, propelled the tiny bodies briskly through the damp atmosphere. Individuals were either azure with yellow stripes or white on purple. Flinx fancied, without any proof, that the color differences might indicate sex. He noted the presence of three tiny, simple black eyes and long coiled snouts like those of butterflies or moths. The six small legs each ended in a clasping hook.

Nectar feeders, he decided. Experimentally, he waved at the school as it floated past, nudging several of the floaters with his fingers. They paddled harder with their fragile wing blades as they struggled to avoid his attentions. Those thus disturbed emitted tiny burbling squeaks. As the melodic discord spread throughout the school, Flinx felt as if he was surrounded by a stately procession of musical soap bubbles.

Beautiful, he mused. Initial encounter to the contrary, not everything here was out to make a meal of him.

A glance skyward revealed several larger fliers dipping low, whether to examine him or the shuttle, he couldn't tell. Several looked large enough to try and make a meal of the latter.

"We'd better get under cover," he told the minidrag. As always, she offered companionship without comment. He headed for the nearest patch of verdure.

Choosing the thickest branch he could find, Flinx bent down and pushed his way into the brush. Several leaves gave off an aromatic scent as he eased them aside. The living pathway expanded rapidly and the undergrowth became less impenetrable. Before long he was able to walk upright while descending the gentle slope of the branch.

Wonders large and small flew, swung, fell, flitted, and swelled before his eyes. Despite the incredible density of the hylaea, dropoffs of ten meters and more were common on either side of his chosen path. By this time the branch he was walking along was more than a meter wide, however, and unless he took a careless misstep there was little danger of falling. From time to time he would have to step over a thick vine or epiphyte, or work his way around a subsidiary branch growing upward, but with care he was able to continue on his way in relative safety.

Something so enormous it blocked out the diffuse sunlight passed by close overhead. Rising slowly from his crouch as the shadow passed, he looked around until he found a suitable creeper. As Pip effortlessly paralleled his descent on her brilliant wings, he lowered himself twice, to a still larger branch, until he felt reasonably confident no aerial predator could reach him through the tangle of growth that now crisscrossed above his head.

A quick check indicated that the tiny positioner attached to his service belt was functioning properly, keeping him in constant touch and in return line with the shuttle, and through it, with the *Teacher* orbiting high overhead. Thus reassured, he moved on, following the gently curving route provided by the branch.

Bursts of color like small frozen explosions splotched the forest with a riot of hues as radiant flowers burst forth from bromeliads, epiphytes, and other growths which were in turn parasitic or symbiotic on the trees themselves. Many of these subsidiary growths were as big as normal trees and provided sites for still smaller plants. The largest trees must be immense, he knew, not only to reach such heights but to support such a weighty biomass of subsidiary growth.

Sound as well as color surrounded him, an irregularly modulated cacophony of screams and bellows, squeaks and pipings, honks and hisses, whistles and whines. A few sounded almost familiar to his alien ears, while others were like nothing previously encountered in all his travels. He was traveling within a green sea, many of whose inhabitants he could hear but not understand.

Coming to a slightly more open space, he clutched a sturdy vine the color of aged rum and leaned over the side of the branch. It was twenty meters down to the next solid wood, and in places more than that. Incredible to think that the actual surface lay hundreds and not merely dozens of meters below.

He found himself wondering; if he fell, would he bounce from branch to branch all the way to the ground, or would he fetch up before that in a tangle of branches or flowers? Something the size of his little finger darted in front of him, paused to hover a hand's length in front of his nose as it studied him. It sang like a shrunken calliope and its body was painted with alternating crimson and green stripes. Three bright blue compound eyes regarded him somberly. Finding in the tall, gangly alien nothing of interest, it pivoted in midair and sped away.

The air was so rich and thickly flavored with alien smells he felt he should be spooning it into his mouth like some frothy whipped dessert instead of simply inhaling it. The effect was as if a perfume factory and a fertilizer plant had been raised up and smashed together, resulting in what Flinx chose to think of as aromatic critical mass.

An all-pervasive warmth enveloped him, which he attributed to the perpetual and for the most part pleasurable assault on his senses. Not a single threatening mental throb disturbed his musing. No headaches to be had here.

Pip sometimes trailed behind, sometimes raced out in front to investigate a new flower or slow-moving creature. She appeared to be coping effortlessly with the deluge of new sensations.

He paused to examine a flower whose petals twisted to form perfect spirals. The top of each petal was bright silver-green, the underside green-gold. Each a meter or so in diameter, half a dozen such flowers grew upon every parent plant. They looked like decorations for a gigantic Christmas tree and smelled of sandalwood and cinnamon. Overwhelmed by their magnificence, he moved on.

Numerous small life forms skittered along the branch and its wooden tributaries, adroitly avoiding his approach by means of legs or wings. Most hewed to the three-eyed, six-legged standard which seemed to be the norm, though there were plenty of variations in the number of limbs and other organs.

A single bloom three meters across blocked his path. The hundred slender petals of the incredible blossom were dark green laced with tartrazine, while the center of the flower bulged with thick orange nodules whose purpose was not immediately apparent. Purple stamens thrust skyward, drusy with yellow pollen. Its elegant perfume was so heady it all but made him dizzy.

Reaching down, he broke off a piece of damp deadwood, intending to use it to nudge the petals aside so he could pass without having to walk on so much beauty. As he took a step forward he thought he saw the purple stamens twitch. There were more than a dozen of them, each as thick around as his thumb. He hesitated, having already escaped one encounter with vines that had turned out to be tentacles.

Tentatively, he extended his arm to the fullest and managed to reach the nearest stamen. Surprisingly tough, it was as if he were prodding a stick of rubber. The stamen bent and released a blast of still stronger perfume. Woozy with pleasure, Flinx turned away and sucked fresh air to clear both his lungs and his head.

Nothing made a grab for him. The amazing blossom was the reproductive portion of a plant and nothing more. Reaching down, he used the piece of wood to push the first petal aside.

It contracted viciously around the stick and snapped it neatly in half. Flinx jumped back and Pip let out a startled hiss.

As he watched, half a dozen wiry tendrils that glistened like corn silk crept out from beneath the base of the flower. Like pale worms, they examined the wooden fragments from top to bottom before curling around them and dragging them to the edge of the branch. The deadwood was dropped over the side and the tendrils withdrew out of sight, leaving the astonishing flower once more quiescent and wondrous.

Flinx backed slowly away from the botanical phantasm. Securing a grip on a suitable creeper, he leaned far out over the side of the branch and looked down. Half a dozen meters below, whiteness gleamed amidst the green. He wondered what the creatures who had encountered the flower before him had looked like.

Certainly their broken and scattered skeletons were interesting.

Finding the exquisite fragrance that issued from the blossom no longer quite so appealing, he sought a safe way around the innocent-looking petals. Closer inspection revealed that the silvery glint that emanated from their edges was decidedly metallic in nature. Somehow the plant extracted and concentrated metal along the rims of its alluring petals. Flinx knew of plants whose leaves could slice flesh, but none that incorporated actual razors into their blossoms. Here was a plant whose perfume masked the presence of swords.

A brace of stout vines and a twisting aerial root allowed him to descend to the next major branch. Despite the resultant gap, he took care not to pass directly beneath the great flower.

As a lesson, the brief encounter was simple and straightforward. On this world, equating beauty with harmlessness could prove fatal. He considered returning to the shuttle. Even a cursory exploration of the surrounding forest might better be left to an experienced and properly equipped survey team.

If only it wasn't so beautiful.

Something was moving sluggishly through the branches and lianas just ahead. It looked like a dun-colored, black-spotted stump suspended from a hanging creeper. The three eyes were half closed, giving the creature a decidedly somnolent appearance. The short tail was striped with gray, and a pink patch flashed above each of the three eyes. It had no legs and hung from the creeper by six long, triple-jointed arms. In this fashion it moved along hand over hand over hand.

As Flinx looked on, a dozen similar individuals of varying size materialized from the green depths, following the leader along the creeper like so many upside-down elephants. The smallest ones gamboled among the vines and branches, occasionally leaping by means of their sextupal arms from adult to vine and back again. Meanwhile the adults advanced with an unconscious solemnity so profound Flinx found himself grinning at the sight.

Suddenly the lead adult spotted him. All three eyes dilated and a concealed round mouth pumped out a series of shrill hoots. The troop immediately leaped in a series of floral crashes from their chosen creeper to another farther away.

It was a relief to encounter something more afraid of him than he was of it. Flinx watched as the troop of ambling armatures vanished into the glaucous depths, the leader lingering behind to favor him with a few last disparaging hoots. He found himself waving amiably.

A swarm of tiny creatures momentarily enveloped him in a cloud of powder-blue wings before moving on. Nearby, a cluster of leathery cylinders the color of dried blood weaved back and forth to a silent floral beat. Flinx saw a waterfall of silver-sided vines plunging into the abyss, flashing light from leaf to reflective leaf as they bounced precious sunshine to light-hungry growths down in the emerald depths.

"Look at that," he murmured to Pip. "Isn't adaptation wonderful? Wish it were as easy for me." The shuttle could wait, he decided. With a new wonder presenting itself at every step, he had no choice but to continue on. Beauty aside, the sheer profusion and diversity of life was overwhelming. He felt more alive than he'd ever been.

And there was something else. Something thus far undefinable. An all-pervasive feeling of peace and wellbeing that persisted and survived despite the aggressive attempts of various representatives of the local flora and fauna to consume him. It washed over and through him in an irresistible, soothing wave, almost as if the forest itself was projecting a homogeneous emotional calm.

Which was absurd, of course. Only sapient beings emitted emotions his aberrant talent could detect. Plants did nothing of the sort. What he was experiencing was nothing more than a deception promulgated by a subtle combination of fragrance, humidity, and increased oxygen levels. It was a physical rush masquerading as mental.

The astonishing alien zoo kept his attention occupied. A two-meter-long, rippling crawler the color of clotted cream was advancing down the branch toward him, scuttling along on hundreds of tiny legs. It looked innocuous enough. Half a dozen small black hairs or antennae protruded from each end. Several bulged at the tips, suggestive of eyestalks.

Flinx retreated a step. Sensing movement, the creature halted, then turned to its right. Increasing its pace, it came to the edge of the branch and without hesitating dropped off the side.

Leaning over, Flinx saw it land in a cluster of flowers with leaves the texture of split blue leather. To his surprise, the crawler promptly split into half a dozen independent sections, each with its own now visible face. These organic components engaged in some brief foraging before reforming their original lineup, the protuberant face of each section fitting seamlessly into the concave depression that formed the backside of its colleague immediately in front of it. Once more resembling a two-meter-long—and presumably more formidable—animal, the communal crawler continued on its leisurely way.

Shaking his head, Flinx resumed his pace. Before long he came to a section of branch devoid of animal or secondary plant life. The barren place caused him to halt. After several close brushes with death, he'd learned to suspect anything out of the ordinary. On this world, a place where nothing grew certainly qualified.

While he waited he watched the local fauna. Everything that came close was careful to bypass the seemingly innocuous section of branch. Their unanimous avoidance only heightened Flinx's suspicion.

The slight depression that ran the length of the open space was filled with fresh rainwater, surely an attraction to any passing animal. Then Pip, before he could call her back, zoomed over and lowered her head to take a drink. He held his breath.

Nothing happened. None the worse for the experience, she returned to resume her familiar perch upon his shoulder.

Either he continued forward or looked for a way around. No easy alternate routes presented themselves. Advancing cautiously, he examined the waterlogged section of wood without seeing anything that resembled an eye, a limb, a claw.

Then it occurred to him that anything that tried to grow in the depression would find itself subject to permanent if shallow inundation. Any hopeful epiphyte that took root in the hollow would find its roots rotting quickly. Striding forward into the liquid, he watched it slide over the tip of his boot. A swarm of tiny red ovals with outsized black eyespots scurried away from his foot. Apparently they lived in the water without coming to any harm.

He was halfway across the depression when he was forced to pause. His right foot was refusing to comply with the instructions from his brain. Irritated that he might have momentarily stepped in a deeper crack and caught himself, he looked back and down.

There was no crack. It was the water itself that had undergone a startlingly rapid transformation. He leaned forward. His leg refused to move. When he tried to turn to gain more leverage, he found that his left foot was also stuck fast. He was locked in place, unable to advance or retreat, his boots entrapped by a thick, transparent, tarlike substance. Furthermore, it wasn't inactive.

Very much to the contrary, it was slowly but inexorably crawling up the sides of his boots even as he watched.

Alarmed at the abrupt change in her master's emotional state, Pip rose to hover anxiously. From time to time she dove combatively toward the depression, perceiving it to be the source of Flinx's upset, but there was nothing she could do. This time there were no inimical eyes to focus upon, no head to strike at.

The branch beneath him quivered slightly and Flinx flailed wildly to keep his balance. If he fell over and got his front or back stuck in the thickening goo, he'd be unable to move at all. He tried not to think of what might happen if he fell facedown. He would suffocate rapidly and unpleasantly.

A section of branch directly in front of him suddenly rose. It was pointed, rough-edged, and designed to fit flush with the top of the hollow that had been excavated in the living wood. Reaching down, Flinx fought to release the rip-fastener that secured his front boot. If nothing else, he could try stepping out of his footwear and making a leap for safety, an alternative denied to this extraordinary predator's accustomed prey. If he could make it over the side of the branch he would be safe.

Depending on how far he fell and what he landed on, he reminded himself.

A semicircle of nine opalescent orbs bordered the apex of the creature's head, if such it could be called. Devoid of irises or pupils, the organs might be no more than primitive light-and-motion sensors. More than adequate for the creature's needs, he told himself. The gunk gripping his boots continued to flow energetically upward. When it reached his pants he'd have to consider abandoning them as well.

As he reached for his boot fastener, a deep bubbling noise emerged from the depths of his undefinable assailant. The surface heaved beneath him and he found himself, arms swinging madly, catapulted over the side of the branch. As he fell he realized that the predator must have some way of separating what was edible from what was not. Leaves, branches, and other debris must frequently fall from above, he realized. Like a spider cleaning its web, it was natural to expect that the glue-sucker would have a way of detecting and ridding itself of the inedible.

Plasticized travel boots, for example.

It was seven hundred meters or so to the actual ground. Surely he would fetch up against something before he reached that final, unyielding destination.

Even as he pondered the possibilities, he found himself entangled in a cluster of thin, unyielding green vines. His momentum snapped several before his fall was arrested. For several moments he hung twisting in their knotted grasp, his feet kicking at the air, before he realized they were pulling him *up*.

Tilting back his head, he found himself staring at the source of the vines: something like a giant lavender orchid squatting on a dense mound of reeds. Only the dark, ominous opening in the underside spoiled the otherwise elegant effect. Within the gaping maw, sharp-pointed cilia palpitated expectantly.

Another plant evolved to act like an animal, he thought. Another camouflaged carnivore. Wasn't there anything on this world that didn't grasp or bite? He struggled to reach his needler, but the tendrils' grip was unyielding. He continued to rise.

Darting upward, Pip released a stream of venom at the source of her master's distress. The corrosive liquid burned a section of the puffy, main mass but did nothing to halt Flinx's inexorable rise toward the waiting mouth. The area affected by the minidrag was too small and neuronically insensitive to trouble the expansive growth.

Another three, four meters and those questing, eager cilia would be able to reach his head. Propelled by tendril and cilia, he would enter the creature's stomach head first, no doubt to be consumed slowly and as necessary. First the head, next the shoulders, then the torso, much as he would munch satay on a stick.

Still, it was with quite a start, despite his situation, that he found himself gazing across open space at an obviously intelligent green face directly opposite his own.

Chapter Six

The owner was short and stocky. Though it was hanging upside down, it was clearly not a permanent dangler like the six-armed hooters he'd encountered earlier. About the size of a St. Bernard or small mastiff, it hung from a thick creeper by means of six short, powerful legs. Each foot ended in half a dozen long, curving, and very impressive claws.

Three eyes ran across the front of the blunt-snouted head. A pair of pointed ears faced toward him. An upward-curving tusk protruded from either side of the powerful lower jaw. As he stared, a snort came from the large nostrils. The creature was covered completely in short, thick, green fur.

Moving foot over foot along the creeper, it approached to within half a meter of his face, supremely indifferent to however the carnivorous quasiorchid overhead might choose to react. The large, limpid eyes examined him curiously. Then it spoke, in comprehensible if strangely accented symbospeech.

"Stupid person."

"Not a person," insisted a second voice, pitched slightly higher than the one challenging Flinx.

He managed to twist around just far enough to see another of the green talkers squatting on quadruple haunches on a nearby branch, surveying the scene with bucolic aplomb. The differences between the two were minor: a notched ear on the first speaker, a slightly longer tail on the second. As he gaped and Pip darted in tight nervous circles, the one on the branch swatted lazily at a brightly colored insectoid.

"Is." The upside-down scrutinizer regarded Flinx with comical seriousness.

"Is not." The sitter ignored Pip, who buzzed the blocky head several times. "Just look at it, Moomadeem." A heavy paw waved in Flinx's direction as he continued his inexorable ascent toward the waiting, cilia-lined digestive cavity. "See how tall it is. And it has reddish fur."

"Green eyes, though." Triple oculars squinted at Flinx's face. "That's right."

"Not a person," the other continued to insist.

"Has to be, Tuuvatem." Advancing, it came to within licking range. A thick, musty, but not entirely unpleasant odor assailed Flinx's nostrils. "Everything else right."

"Look at its feet," suggested Tuuvatem. "Too stubby. *Not a person.*"

"Maybe an old injury."

Flinx didn't have time to wonder what was wrong with his hair and his feet. The top of his head was less than a meter from the dark, slimy maw. Fringing cilia twitched expectantly.

"Save him and then decide." Moomadeem swung effortlessly from his vine.

"Save not. Not a person." Tuuvatem was inflexible.

All Flinx needed to hear was the word "save." "Look, I don't know what *you* are, or how you learned my language, but if you can understand me, all I can tell you is that by any standard you'd care to apply I am a 'person,' and if you can do anything to help me out of this, afterward I'll personify myself to your satisfaction the best I can."

"He talks." Moomadeem looked smug. The lower lip curled up over the upper. "Has to be a person."

"Does not!"

"Can't we argue about it later?" Flinx struggled violently in the creepers' grasp.

The one called Moomadeem shoved out its lower jaw, thrusting the sharp tusks into even greater prominence. "Speaks sense, too!"

Up on the branch, Tuuvatem groomed the front of her furry muzzle and executed a startlingly humanoid shrug. "Well—maybe *half* a person."

The one called Moomadeem emitted a snort of satisfaction. Retreating slightly, it drew back a powerful, clawed foot. Flinx flinched, but the blow wasn't intended for him. Instead, the sharp claws snicked through the air just above his head, cleanly severing a couple of the numerous creepers engaged in hoisting the plant's intended prey. Flinx felt himself drop a few centimeters and bounce to a stop.

"That's it! Keep going, don't stop now. I *am* a person! A—visiting person. A person from elsewhere."

"See?" Moomadeem looked back. "He is a person from a faraway tribe."

"Makes sense." Tuuvatem conceded the point grudgingly. "But *very* stupid."

Flinx knew they were intelligent because, to his great surprise, he found that both were generating emotions strong enough and developed enough for him to detect. Primitive and childlike they might be, but they were far in advance of anything else he'd encountered on this world.

But how had they come to learn the Commonwealth lingua franca?

Displaying an agility all the more astonishing for the indifference with which it was employed, the solemn skeptic jumped off the upper branch and latched effortlessly onto another vine on the side opposite Moomadeem. With both of them methodically ripping and tearing at the creepers, Flinx found himself jostled about like a preadolescent in a stim-can.

When a pair of tendrils reached for Tuuvatem, Flinx shouted a warning. Showing no reaction, the creature used the claws on its front feet to shred the futile counterstrike. Trailing glutinous sap, shards of shorn creeper spun in ever-increasing lengths down into the green depths.

Finally, the plant responded to the ongoing devastation of its underside by releasing its intended prey. Thus freed, Flinx would have offered his heartfelt thanks except for the fact that he was now plunging downward, grabbing futilely at inadequate lianas and branches as he fell. Pip followed, hissing helplessly.

From above, his lugubrious saviors followed his descent with interest. "Maybe less than half," declared Tuuvatem. "Can't climb worth a crap."

Flinx would have argued with them had he been close enough to overhear. He let out a yelp as he struck something unyielding yet comparatively soft. Dazed, he felt himself being turned upright and gently set on a solid surface. Pip immediately landed on his shoulder and began caressing his cheek with her tongue.

Shaking his head in an attempt to clear it, he turned to confront the creature who had caught him. It was identical in most respects to the two who had freed him from the grasp of the creepers while simultaneously debating his personhood. The most notable difference was in size. This one was many, many times larger than his original rescuers, massing as much as the Kodiak bears that still roamed protected islands in Terra's chill northern hemisphere.

He noted the same six legs and massive claws, the three eyes and twin tusks, and a slightly higher, more intelligent brow. While the two who had saved him from the carnivorous plant had done effective combat with the inimical growth, this was an altogether more formidable creature.

The three eyes regarded him thoughtfully, the head tilted slightly to its right. While the posture duplicated the quizzical aspect of a curious dog, it was clear this was a far more intelligent animal. For one thing, its perceived emotional state was much more complex.

It snorted, and the exhalation washed over Flinx; warm, moist, and pungent. Pip reacted with spread wings, but Flinx put out a hand to restrain her.

"Take it easy, girl. I think these are friends. Unless I've been saved to make a meal."

"You can cook?" rumbled the huge green shape.

A choice slice of the surreal, Flinx decided. "That's not what I meant. Are you a friend?"

"Have to be," grunted the creature. "You a person, I a person. All persons are friends."

Flinx wasn't about to argue the point. A crashing from above revealed the two much smaller animals descending toward him with casual abandon. For such burly creatures, their agility was astonishing. He found himself wondering if the smaller pair were the offspring of the adult who'd caught him. They certainly acted like a family group. But a family of what?

Answers were to be forthcoming from still another and even more unexpected source. "Moomadeem, Tuuvatem—behave yourselves! Be nice to the new person."

"See?" Flinx watched as Moomadeem, clinging to a thick maroon vine, took a playful swipe at its companion. "Told you was a person!"

"Three-quarters," argued back the other, conceding points only with the greatest reluctance.

A rustling behind him prompted Flinx to turn. When the first of the creatures had spoken to him, he'd believed himself immune to any greater shock. He was wrong.

The woman and two children didn't so much emerge from the vegetation as silently manifest themselves. They'd been standing just behind him for some time, blending in perfectly with their surroundings as they took the measure of the strange visitor. He'd been concentrating so hard on the emotions of his alien rescuers that he hadn't sensed the human feelings immediately behind.

Now he adjusted his perception and felt the jar in his mind of familiar yet very different emotions. There was curiosity, concern, and wariness all mixed up together. The emotions of the children were less intense, not as complicated by experience. All three likewise projected that same feeling of internal warmth he had been experiencing since he'd first stepped off the landing site and made his way down into the hylaea.

All three were clad in a minimum of clothing woven from some dark green fiber. Each wore a cloak fashioned of similar material as well as a backpack and belt made from something sturdier and darker. In addition, a green pipe or tube of some kind was strapped to the woman's back.

She approached him without fear, perhaps due to the presence of the massive animal next to Flinx. It was evident from her call to the two small ones that all six were traveling together. Her next words confirmed it.

"Thank you for catching him, Saalahan. He could have been seriously hurt."

The creature grunted softly. "Very strange person. Very strange and very clumsy."

The young woman looked up at Flinx. Though well-proportioned, she was quite short, and the children shorter still. "Why didn't you catch a vine after Moomadeem and Tuuvatem freed you?"

Flinx knew there was no reason for him to be embarrassed, but he felt himself flushing anyway. "It's not like I didn't try."

She considered this. "I am Teal." When she extended her hand, he reached out to shake it. Instead, her palm rubbed against his. He memorized the greeting and made no move to inflict the more traditional one on her.

The children crowded closer. "This is Dwell," she said, indicating the boy. Flinx guessed him to be about ten. "And Kiss." The girl was perhaps a year younger.

Certainly they came from the same stock. All three had long brown hair and green eyes, a deeper green than Flinx had ever seen. His own were pale by comparison. Their skin was a uniform light coffee color. Most remarkable of all were their feet. The toes were long and flexible, longer even than their fingers.

Except for that and their short stature, they were as human as anyone who walked the streets of Terra or Moth or any of the other humanx-colonized worlds. That they or their forbears had originated on one of those worlds he didn't doubt for a moment. Either that or he was witness to the most extraordinary instance of convergent evolution on record.

Besides, there was their use of familiar and easily understandable symbospeech, even if their accent was sharp enough to qualify as archaic.

"What are these?" He gestured back at the enormous green shape that had saved him from an uncomfortable landing. It blinked at him once before turning away.

The woman gawked at him. "You mean you don't know? Saalahan is a furcot, of course. My furcot."

"Let me guess. The others belong to your children."

"Belong?" Her brow furrowed. "Furcots don't belong to people any more than people belong to furcots. At least, not in the way you are meaning. Moomadeem is Dwell's furcot, and Kiss is Tuuvatem's person."

"Fur coat?" said Flinx.

"Furcot." She leaned to look past him. "Where is yours?"

"Mine? I don't have one."

Tuuvatem was sniffing his leg. "Who ever heard of a person without a furcot?"

Flinx didn't feel deprived. "I have Pip." He caressed the flying snake as it slithered forward on his shoulder, straining for a better look.

The two children tensed. Apparently his winged pet and companion bore a resemblance to something local and dangerous. Considering some of the life forms he'd encountered in the short time he'd been on this world, he could only sympathize with their caution.

"She's not a furcot," he told them, "but she is my friend. It's all right; she won't hurt you."

"She?" Teal rose on tiptoes to see better.

"Yes. Like you and Kiss and Saalahan."

"Like Kiss and I," she corrected him. "Saalahan is not female."

"Oh. He's the father of the other two, then."

"Saalahan is not male, either."

Flinx made no effort to hide his confusion. "I don't understand. Then what is—it?"

"I told you. Saalahan is a furcot." And that was all the explanation he could get out of her. The creature's sex organs, assuming it had any, were not readily in evidence, and Flinx wasn't about to venture any requests that might be construed as impolite. Not after he'd seen what those claws could do. It was a quandary that could be resolved later.

"You should know that," the woman told him. "Can't you emfol them?"

"Emfol? I don't know that word."

Teal's look was pitying. "You are a strange person indeed. Any person should be able to emfol their furcot along with everything else."

"I don't know what you mean." He didn't see any harm in revealing a little of himself to these abandoned, isolated people. "I can sense what Pip is feeling and she can do the same to me. Is that kind of what your relationship to your furcots is like?" He didn't say anything about being able to sense her emotions or those of her children.

"Emfoling is different." She shook her head slowly, registering bafflement. "How different you are."

Odd little lady Teal, he thought, you don't know the half of it.

"And ignorant." Tuuvatem stalked fearlessly up to Flinx. "Stepped right into a mistyr, he did. And that after almost sticking his arm in a spiralizer."

Flinx thought back to the breathtakingly beautiful flower with the razor-edged petals. "You were watching me then?"

"Been watching you long time," the furcot informed him. "Trying to decide what you were."

"I'm human. A person," he corrected himself. "Just like Teal and her children. They are your children?" Teal nodded and smiled.

He extended his open palm. Dwell ignored it, while his sister put a finger to her lips and gazed up at him in wonder.

"You're awful tall," the boy proclaimed.

"Am I?"

"Yes," put in Teal. "Very." Quite unexpectedly, her eyes grew wide and she retreated several steps, pulling the children with her. Flinx tensed immediately, until it finally struck him that *he* was the source of her sudden distress.

"What is it, what's the matter?"

"Skyperson. You are a skyperson, from beyond the Upper Hell!"

A low growl rose from the giant furcot behind him. It was echoed by Tuuvatem and Moomadeem. Responding to the growing emotional upheaval, Pip rose from Flinx's shoulder to interpose herself between the big carnivore and her master. Her wings buzzed furiously.

Instinctively he reached toward the needler holstered at his waist—and hesitated. The emotions he was sensing were fear and uncertainty, not anger.

"It's true that I'm not from this world," he confessed, "that I'm from up there." He stabbed a finger in the direction of the distant sky. "Why does that frighten you? I mean you no harm, and I owe you my life."

She relaxed somewhat, still watching him guardedly and keeping the children behind her. "There is a well-known tale oft told around the night fires. Of tall persons with different-colored hair and eyes and stunted feet who came among us long ago. But—you have the right eyes."

"Go on," he encouraged her.

"They came to hurt the forest, and none of them could emfol. Like you."

"I may be wrong about that," he replied. "I think I can do a little of this emfoling. We may just be using different words to describe the same thing. What happened to these skypeople who looked like me?" Evidently he had been preceded here, and if Teal's account was to be believed, some time ago.

"They died," she replied simply. "It was inevitable. They hurt the forest and the forest hurt back. They wanted the persons to help them, and of course the persons helped the forest instead."

"How did these skypeople get here? Do you know?"

"The story says they fell from the Upper Hell in big pieces of metal. They brought more metal with them." She pointed into the trees. "They fell in that part of the world."

Flinx checked a sensor on his service belt. He was not surprised to find that both it and Teal were pointing in the direction of the metallic anomaly the *Teacher* had detected from orbit. So the anomaly that had drawn him to this location was an old shuttlecraft—or something more.

"How long ago did this happen?"

"The story does not say exactly. Several generations, at least. It was when there was only one tribe of persons. Now there are six. The Tallflower, the Sinvin, the Calacall, the Firsthome, the Seconds, and the Redflitter. We are Tallflower."

Flinx searched for an analogy. "Since there are six tribes here, it shouldn't be difficult for you to grasp the idea of there being many tribes of skypeople. Actually, there are hundreds."

"Hundreds!" Kiss's eyes grew even wider.

"Yes." He smiled down at her. "And I come from a completely different tribe than the one that came here so long ago to cause trouble. In fact, I know less about them than you do." He didn't know that for a fact, but felt it was a reasonable enough assumption.

To his surprise, it was the big furcot who responded. He still wasn't used to having the animals participate in the conversation.

"I think he may speak truth." Saalahan snorted warningly at Pip, who darted past the massive skull. The furcot followed the warning by taking an irritated swipe at the minidrag, missing her completely.

"That's enough," Teal admonished the creature.

"Pip, get over here!" Making a reluctant landing on her master's shoulder, the minidrag fixed the furcot with a wary eye.

Saalahan turned and, in a diffident demonstration of effortless power, leaped easily across to the next large branch. Moomadeem and Tuuvatem elected to remain with the humans.

"The cubs don't go with their mother?" Flinx inquired.

"Moomadeem and Tuuvatem aren't Saalahan's cubs," Teal corrected him.

He knew he was overlooking something vital. "They're adopted, then?"

Dwell looked at his mother. "This man speaks strangely. And he sounds funny, too."

Teal tried to explain. "Furcots don't have children."

Flinx blinked. "Then where do they come from?"

She continued as if lecturing an infant on the most obvious thing in the world. "When a person is born, their furcot comes to them. Person and furcot are always tied—here." She put a hand over her heart. "What about your snake? Where did she come from?"

"She came—" He stopped, remembering. To this day he wasn't sure if he'd found the minidrag or she'd found him. But at least he knew she'd been born. He'd seen her give birth himself.

"Never mind," he told the woman. "You can explain it to me later."

Dwell eyed Pip curiously and she returned the boy's stare. "Does everyone in your tribe have one of those?"

"No. Among my tribe, Pip and I are unique."

"It is good to be unique," noted Teal approvingly. "You are fortunate—except that you have no furcot." Again she shook her head. "It is a terrible thing for a person to be without a furcot. I cannot imagine how one would live."

Flinx grinned as he nuzzled the back of Pip's head with a fingertip. "We manage."

"You say you are not of the tribe of skypersons that came before," Teal pressed him. "Yet if you can emfol, how is it that you stepped into the mistyr?"

"I'm new to this place," he replied. "I've only been here a little while."

"That's plain enough to see," observed Dwell sardonically as he picked at a nearby branch. He had exposed a cavity in which tiny bright red creatures dashed about on pink legs. They hopped around energetically, refusing to abandon their little celluloid caldera as the boy teased them with a twig.

"You see, Mother? He can't help us." His eyes darted about rapidly. "We've been too long out in the open."

"Dwell is right." Moomadeem glanced upward with all three eyes. "Still very close to Hell."

"You speak of the Upper Hell." Flinx followed the antics of the tiny red hoppers with interest. "Does that mean there's a Lower Hell?"

Teal sighed. "You are truly ignorant."

"Thank you," he replied cheerfully.

"There are seven levels to the world. Persons choose to live on the third. At the top is the Upper Hell, at the bottom the Lower. Very few persons have gone there and returned. More have visited the Upper, but it is nearly as dangerous. There are sky-devils and more."

"If it's so dangerous this near to open sky," he asked, "then what are you doing here?"

"Trying to find a bearing," she responded. "We are in bad trouble . . ."

"Flinx," he told her, "and Pip you already know."

"We were out gathering. This is the season of the sugararries. They need a lot of sunshine and so only grow close to the Upper Hell. It takes a brave family to go gathering." She touched the two small sacks fastened to her belt. One was half full.

"Those who bring back sugararries are accorded much honor by their tribe. After some have been given to the Home-tree, the rest are divided."

"So you do it for honor?" Flinx inquired.

"Everyone shares." Teal looked at him sideways. "Without sharing, a tribe could not survive. Everyone relies on every other person and furcot. That is the way of survival."

"I understand," he assured her. Cooperation would be vital in a place like this, where a harmless-looking blossom was as likely to assassinate as astonish you. It occurred to him that while he had yet to see a large, mobile, tree-bound predator— the furcots excepted—they must certainly exist. "How did you get lost?"

"Jerah was much better at finding the way than I," she explained quietly. "He chose our course."

"Your husband?" he asked. She nodded. He lifted his gaze, expecting at any moment to see a larger version of the boy Dwell emerging from the verdure. "Where is he now? Out trying to find the way back?"

"He's dead," she told him.

The emotions he sensed within her were as confused as they were powerful.

Chapter Seven

"Jerah was a good hunter," she went on. "Usually it was he and Ark and Brean who brought back the best food, the biggest game. It is the hunters who know the wide ways of the world, who can out-track and follow-back and find their way home.

"But one hunter can only carry so much. In certain things it is traditional for entire families to participate. Children are especially good at gathering sugararries. Their small fingers can fit more easily between the thorns.

"I always felt safe with Jerah. He believed he could find a place where the sugararries grew thicker and sweeter than anywhere else. We walked a long ways without finding any, but Jerah was sure, so we kept going."

"What happened?" Flinx's tone was subdued. Recognizing and responding to her master's feelings, Pip assumed a more solemn aspect than was usual for her.

Teal chose her words carefully, remembering. "We felt safe and had relaxed. The sugararry patch Jerah led us to was virgin and dripping with sweetness. After eating their fill, the furcots spread out to scout the area. While they were gone, Jerah decided to climb up a little ways to see how high the patch grew. I remember him calling down to us from a branch far above. The light was brilliant so high up. Sugararry vines need lots of light." Her tone was flat, matter-of-fact.

"That's when the diverdaunt struck. Jerah almost got away—he was a very quick man. Ordinarily, if a diverdaunt doesn't kill its prey on the first strike it gives up and flies away. But this one was very persistent. It kept striking, and Jerah fought back. We could hear it clearly. There was a lot of yelling and screaming.

"Jerah had no chance to use his snuffler." She indicated the tubular weapon strapped to her back. "Before the furcots could climb up in time to help, both he and the diverdaunt came crashing down through the green, locked in each other's grasp. By the time a tangle of creels caught them up and halted their plunge, the diverdaunt was dead. But Jerah couldn't free himself from its talons. It landed on top of him and he struck a branch.

"The fall broke his back. There was nothing that could be done."

"I'm sorry," Flinx whispered. "I don't know what to say." Reaching out to her, he sensed only regret. There was no surge of deeply felt emotion, no sense of overpowering loss. The children were nearly as stoic.

Clearly, self-control was an important component of survival on this world. Regrets had to be expressed economically and then put aside. Sorrowful moping was a sure prescription for joining the already deceased. You needed your wits about you at all times. Bawling and crying might attract curious predators.

"A second diverdaunt struck at Dwell and Kiss," Teal was saying. "There must have been a flock of them patrolling that part of the first level. Saalahan knocked it down and Moomadeem and Tuuvatem tore it apart. After that there were no more attacks.

"But Jerah was the one who knew the way back to the Home-tree. Saalahan has tried, but furcots are not explorers. They keep to their humans and follow their lead. We have been lost now for many days."

Flinx surveyed the all-encompassing sea of viridity, wherein every direction looked the same as any other. The diffuse sunlight offered no help in finding one's way. "I sympathize. There isn't anything that stands out as a landmark. Or treemark." He nodded toward Moomadeem. "What about scent? Couldn't your furcots find their way back by smell?"

"The forest is showered with smells," she replied. "And a scent-trail is only good for one day, until the night's rain."

"Lost," grunted the big furcot, peering across at them from the branch on which it sprawled. As Flinx looked on, Saalahan proceeded to clean all three paws on the left side, one after another.

"You spoke of 'the night's rain.' " Flinx turned his attention back to Teal. "If it rains a lot during the night you wouldn't be able to use the stars to guide you, either."

"A lot?" She gave him a funny look. "It rains *every* night."

"There must be exceptions. It can't rain every night."

She just smiled at him. "The rain starts at dusk and stops an hour or so before the dawn. Every night. In between the rain and the sun we see the stars and the moons, but not for very long and then only when someone is brave or foolish enough to ascend to the uppermost reaches of the first level."

"I see how you could have trouble finding your way around."

"We have tried," she told him. "We crossed back and forth many times looking for signs, but the forest grows back so quickly that scuffed bark and broken leaves are remade overnight. There are plants that sprout so fast you can see them growing."

"So your village, your 'Home-tree,' lies on the forest's third level?" He considered thoughtfully. That meant not only direction but altitude had to be taken into consideration. He could overfly the community numerous times in the *Teacher*'s shuttle without spotting its location buried deep within the hylaea. Nor would it reveal itself to instrumentation, fashioned as it doubtless was of native, natural materials.

What if they had scavenged metal from the original, downed ship? Of course, the forest might have completely reclaimed that by now, but there was one other possibility.

"Could you find your way home from the place the bad skypersons lived when they came among you?"

She started and her eyes widened slightly. "No one goes there! It is the site of past horrors; an evil, unnatural place. The forest there is still trying to heal itself."

"Yes, but at least you know where it is. If you *were* there, could you find your way back home?"

She glanced briefly at Saalahan, who responded with a sleepy-eyed sniff. "It is a long way, but—yes. That way is well known to all the people."

Pip chose that moment to loft from Flinx's shoulder. The minidrag darted across to Kiss and paused to hover before the little girl, the flying snake's pointed tongue flicking in and out in the direction of the child's face. Nearby, Tuuvatem stiffened but made no move to intervene. Wide-eyed with delight, Kiss stared back at the minidrag. Then she threw up her hands to mock-shield her eyes and turned away, giggling musically.

Flinx let the pleasure of her reaction wash over him like a splash of cool water even as he sensed the flying snake's more primitive but no less affable reaction.

"Gotcha!" Displaying uncommon quickness, Dwell leaped at the minidrag from behind with hands outstretched.

They clutched only empty air. Pip simply rose a meter vertically and paused there, brilliant wings humming loudly. Slitted eyes considered her would-be young captor. Letting out a growl, Dwell whirled instantly and jumped as high as he could. Pip zipped to one side.

Kiss quickly joined in the game, and the three were soon flashing through the air, Pip on wings of scarlet and azure, the children by means of vine and branch. The furcots watched indifferently, mildly disproving of the exorbitant waste of energy.

"Your little companion is very understanding of children," Teal observed.

Flinx stood close to her, observing. "I think Pip's enjoying it as much as they are. I don't play with her as much as I once did."

As he watched he felt slightly guilty knowing that, unlike his newfound friends, he could return home whenever he wished. His positioner would guide him infallibly back to the shuttle. All he had to do was avoid the rabid attentions of the local flora and fauna. That would mean abandoning this family to whatever fate might provide. Teal was putting on a brave face, but unbeknownst to her, Flinx had been reading her emotions all along. She was worried, and afraid.

It was clear that despite the best efforts of the furcots, she and her children weren't likely to see their home again without his help. Although he knew next to nothing about this world, he thought he had found a way to do this.

"I think I can help you, Teal."

As she spoke she caressed the thin, wispy petals of a black flower. It seemed to tremble in response. "How? You are more of a stranger here than we."

He touched the positioner. "This tells me where my shuttle—my transportation—is located. Up there," and he gestured skyward, "is my sky ship. It knows the location of the bad skyperson's place." Again he indicated the positioner. "With this I can keep track of both places at once, as well as my own location. I can follow its directions to the place built by the bad skypersons. If Saalahan is right, from there you can find your home."

She wanted to believe but remained skeptical. "You can tell all that from a little gray pod?" He nodded. "If you are wrong we could become more lost than we are now."

He grinned gently. "If you're already lost, what difference does it make if you become more lost?"

"Try explaining that to a human," Saalahan whispered to Moomadeem.

"We can always find this spot again," Flinx insisted. "Surely you don't think I'd go wandering off into this forest without being confident of finding my way back?"

"I don't know . . ." She was still unsure.

"You know how many days you've been away from your Home-tree." She nodded slowly. "Give me that many days to find a way back. If by that time we haven't found the place where the bad skypersons lived, we'll come back here." He kicked the solid wood underfoot.

"Don't do that!" Instantly alert, she reached out to put a hand on his chest. Her eyes were darting in all directions, and Flinx saw that the furcots had risen sharply from their near-sleep.

"What is it, what's the matter?" He tried to look every which way at once.

"Stupid skyperson." Moomadeem stretched and yawned. "Better learn fast."

Flinx jerked his head in the young furcot's direction. "What was that all about?"

Teal hastened to explain. "When you strike a branch like that, you send out vibrations. Those who live in the forest are very sensitive to such things. For example, you could draw the attention of a Chan-nock."

"I don't know what that is, but I see your point." Moomadeem was right. Once again he felt like a prize incompetent. It made him that much more determined to see this family safely home.

Meanwhile he would learn. He'd have to. He couldn't rely on Teal and her children and furcots to look after him every minute of the day.

"That way?" she asked him, pointing.

"Give me a minute. I want to be sure before we start out, and frankly, I need to sit down for a little while. I've been on my feet all day."

"Not when the *griple* had you," Tuuvatem reminded him.

He smiled embarrassedly as he found himself a smooth, bare place on which he might sit. Only when he was certain it was solid, toothless, and fangless, however, and unlikely to be concealing anything capable of tearing the bottom out of his pants, did he actually sit down. Crossing his legs, he began to work with the positioner. Pip landed gently on his right thigh and peered curiously at the softly glowing readout.

Teal came over to watch him work, but the children were more interested in play. They amused themselves while the three furcots slipped into a contented semi-slumber.

He felt her curiosity. She was a study in contrasts: outwardly assured and in complete control, inwardly rife with turmoil and uncertainty. That was natural enough, given her situation. She was putting on a brave face for the sake of her offspring.

To his relief, the *Teacher* responded promptly via the shuttle's relay. It would take only a moment for it to plot the best route. Unfortunately, it could only provide linear directions. In the course of following the prescribed path, they might have to detour up or down to accommodate local conditions.

While he waited, he felt himself surrounded by that inscrutable dark green warmth. It fuzzed his perception while simultaneously invigorating his spirit. He likened it to a nurturing, all-encompassing blanket that was not quite transparent. Something was at work here deserving of deeper study, something stronger than the exotic aromatics that permeated the cloying atmosphere and threatened to overwhelm his olfactory senses. Further study would have to wait, as would everything else, until he had helped these people find their way home.

The *Teacher* responded to his request by providing precise directions in the form of a blinking arrow on the positioner's screen. Set between a pair of notches, it pointed the way toward the metallic anomaly he had first noticed from orbit. All they had to do was walk, keeping the arrow positioned between the notches. Via the shuttle, the *Teacher* would track them while providing automatic updates.

The ship also calculated the distance to be traveled. It was respectable without being overawing; about what he had expected. After all, Teal and her late mate had managed to cover the same distance with two children in tow.

He rose and pointed. "We go that way."

Teal moved to stand close to him, staring in wonder at the positioner. "It could be, I suppose." She encompassed the section of forest ahead with a wave of her hand. "Somewhere out there."

"There's more." He looked down at her. "If we pass close by your Home-tree I will probably be able to tell. I can—He searched for a way to explain his talent. "—I can sort of 'emfol' people."

That made her frown. "Only plants can be emfoled."

"I said 'sort of,' " he reminded her.

"You *are* different. Is this a true thing you are telling me?"

He nodded. "I can often tell how people are feeling. Not what they're thinking, but how they're feeling."

Her gaze challenged him. "Then you know what I am feeling, right now?"

He closed his eyes. Not because it was necessary, but because he thought it might make his ability more comprehensible to her. "Nervousness. Uncertainty. Hope." He blinked.

She nodded slowly. "Emfoling people. What a peculiar notion. How many other skypeople can do this?"

"As far as I know, Teal, I'm the only one."

She nodded solemnly. "So you are the only one of your tribe."

"I hadn't thought of it that way."

"I hope it is not so. Because if it is, then you, Flinx, are more lost than we are." She turned and called out to her children, beckoning them to rejoin her.

Flinx pondered her response. To a greater or lesser degree he'd always been lonely. But he'd never considered himself lost. Perhaps on this world the two terms had come to mean one and the same thing.

"If you want to get going now, I'm game," he told her once the children had run and swung over to join them.

"Not *now*," Dwell told him, speaking as one would to a simpleton. Moomadeem added a snort of confirmation.

In the absence of his father, the boy's assertiveness was understandable. Flinx held his temper as he glanced skyward. "Why not? There should be another hour or so of daylight."

"Time enough to seek or make shelter," Teal reminded him. "Do not forget about the night-rain."

Kiss peered up at him. "Are you a rain person?"

"All right, I get the point." He considered leading them back to the shuttle, which would certainly be the driest as well as the safest place, but he wasn't sure how they would react to the idea. The children in particular were still wary of him. He needed to work on gaining their trust. Also, he was pretty sure he was more than an hour's trek from the landing site. Already he'd reached the conclusion that on this world one could move either with speed or stealth. The former exposed one to far more dangers than the latter.

The plethora of perils that roamed the hylaea made the contentment he was feeling seem more than a little paradoxical.

"What's wrong with camping right here?"

"See any shelter?" the boy challenged him.

"Your mother said something about making shelter."

"Easier to find it." Grabbing a vine, Dwell swung effortlessly across to a paralleling branch. Kiss went next, and then her mother. The furcots simply jumped across. Grateful that he was both tall and slim, Flinx followed clumsily. Pip circled above them all, penetrating the dense brush more easily than anyone as she investigated each new flower, each scurrying three-eyed, six-legged creature, each fluttering multiwinged arboreal.

Teal led the way, pausing occasionally to allow Flinx to check their location on the positioner. Just because they were seeking shelter didn't mean they couldn't make a little progress in the right direction.

A looming gap in the branches forced them to descend to another sublevel. Having learned his lesson, Flinx ignored the thick, sturdy creeper that dangled promisingly before him and followed Teal's lead in shinnying down a section of a secondary trunk, carefully placing his feet in convenient scalloped gouges formed by the rust-colored bark. While he dug his fingers into the woody surface and descended with utmost care, the children laughingly climbed circles around him, making a game of it as they mocked his caution. Their strong fingers and prehensile toes made easy work of the descent. He smiled back at them, knowing that if he lost his grip he'd look considerably more foolish lying broken and twisted on a branch below.

He slipped only once, hurriedly digging his fingers into the obliging wood to halt his fall. A protruding shard of bark scraped his cheek, and Teal hastened to assure him that the secondary tree they were utilizing was in no way toxic. He resumed his descent, envying the furcots their powerful feet and claws as they leaped effortlessly from bough to trunk and back again.

Walking along a branch wide enough to allow six people to march abreast atop it, they came eventually to the emergent's trunk. Even at this height, more than five hundred meters above the ground, its diameter was impressive.

From his position out in front, Dwell called back to them. He'd found a split in the side of the tree, a place where lightning had struck and burned. In this perpetual humidity natural blazes of any kind must be quite rare, Flinx mused. The resulting charred cavity had been further enlarged by some now-departed inhabitant.

Following a well-rehearsed routine, the children tucked themselves all the way in the back. Teal followed, leading Flinx by the hand, and indicated that he should sit down beside her. Next came the two young furcots. Saalahan entered last, the great green bulk forming a living barrier between the hollow's opportunistic denizens and the hylaea outside.

As they swapped answers to many questions, Flinx shared his rations with them. Even Dwell was forced to concede that chocolate was almost, if not quite, as tasty as sugararries.

The foods they offered him in return assaulted his palate with a rich variety of alien flavors, outlandish and new. He tried them all save for something that looked like the dehydrated remains of a cilia-lined, three-centimeter-long pink grub. Not even the raspberry-flavored gel or sap Teal spread on the preserved carcass could induce him to take a bite. The children found his reluctance incomprehensible.

"We will have to hunt for food soon," Teal told him when they'd finished. "As you know, we have been away longer than we ever expected to be and our supplies are very low. Saalahan and the others will help."

Flinx tapped the needler holstered at his belt. "So can I, if it's meat you're after."

She leaned forward to squint at the weapon. "It's very small. Do you really think it will be useful?"

He smiled reassuringly. "Just give me a chance."

As she was leaning forward he noted how her green cloak covered much of her body. No doubt it served to camouflage the wearer as well as protect her from the elements. The weave was tight and smooth.

Invisible in the dense, mist-impregnated air, the orb of the sun did not drop from sight so much as melt away like a lemon candy left out in the heat too long.

As darkness encroached, so did the first rain. Its arrival heralded by scattered peals of distant thunder, it descended in sheets, forceful and unrelenting. Any travelers unfortunate enough to be caught out in the downpour would find themselves drenched to the skin in a very few minutes.

"This lasts all night?" he queried Teal once more, mightily impressed by the force of the deluge.

"Nearly always." Her leg bumped his thigh repeatedly. Physical contact here was accepted without apology.

By stretching, Flinx could just see past Saalahan's bulk. It forced Pip to shift her position on his shoulder, and she hissed her displeasure. In the rapidly failing light he watched the big, heavy drops drum relentlessly on the branch, slide off leaves and flowers, slick down bark and the irregular surface of creepers. Nearly all the leaves and petals had pointed tips, the better to efficiently drain off the nightly precipitation.

Dwell had chosen well. Within the fire-scarred hollow they stayed dry and comfortable. The slight drop in temperature induced by the rain and the onset of darkness was offset by the proximity of so many warm bodies.

Flinx scrunched as best he could up against the wooden wall behind him, listening to the rain. Teal was very close. Because of the children, he knew she was probably anywhere from five to ten years his senior, but because of her diminutive size the difference seemed much less.

She was gesturing at the positioner. "You're sure that will keep us from getting lost?"

"Absolutely."

Kiss crowded close. "Can you emfol it?"

He shook his head. "No. It's just a tool, like the clothes you wear or the sugararry sacks each of you is carrying. See? You can even use it in the dark." He slid his thumb along one side.

Soft light illuminated the transparent readout. Instantly, miniature growls issued from Moomadeem and Tuuvatem, while Saalahan rolled over to stare at him. They needn't have bothered. Teal quickly put her hands over the positioner, smothering the light. Her bright green eyes peered past the big furcot, out into the sodden night.

"No light!" she whispered urgently. "There are creatures that hunt the night."

"Even in this?" He indicated the rain.

She nodded solemnly. "Even in this. They seek out movement—and light."

He flicked off the positioner's internal illumination. "All right. Kiss, I'll show you more in the morning."

"A tool." The girl turned away, silent and contemplative.

"Is a furcot a tool?" he asked her, not wanting to leave her feeling deprived.

"No. A furcot is a person," she replied.

"Maybe you're a tool." That was Dwell's sharp, clipped tone.

In the darkness Flinx smiled. "No, I'm a person, too. Or maybe in a way, we're all tools at least some of the time."

"Not me," Dwell snapped.

Flinx patiently ignored the boy's hostility and suspicion. Not for the first time he wondered about himself. *Come to think of it, what am I, exactly? How much person and how much tool?*

"We should all try to get some sleep." Teal's announcement signaled the end of childish commentary.

The ensuing silence found him staring out into the murky downpour, wondering what inimical life forms might be prowling the branches and creepers in search of sleeping or unprotected prey. He marveled that anything could maneuver effectively through both darkness and deluge. The damp, musky odor of furcot marked a reassuring barrier against whatever might be crouching just outside their protective hollow. With the familiar weight of Pip snuggled tight against his shoulder and neck, he edged forward until he could lie flat. One foot contacted furcot and it snuffled in its almost-sleep.

Occasionally a cry or whistle would pierce the thrum of falling rain. Once, there came a succession of deep, reverberant booms that had to arise from a throat of generous dimensions. It escalated for a while, then drifted away, swallowed by the rhythm of the rain. At that moment it personified perfectly the world on which he found himself.

He nudged Teal, who responded sleepily to his question. "It's a thumber."

"Dangerous?"

He detected slight movement. "No. A lot of meat but not very good to eat. Too greasy. Easy to catch, though."

"As wary and cautious as everything here seems to be, I'm surprised there's any creature that's 'easy to catch.'"

"Bad taste combined with big size makes for a good defense. Go to sleep, Flinx." He felt her turning away from him.

Small breathy noises sounded behind him. The children were already fast asleep. He considered breaking into his rations for a last-minute snack, decided against it. The memory of the cilia-fringed grub they'd offered him, or whatever it was, remained vivid in his mind. Better to ration his rations for as long as possible.

He envied their ability to easily fall asleep in such cramped quarters. The wooden surface beneath him was as uncomfortable as it was unyielding. Trying not to toss and turn, so as to disturb the others as little as possible, he was startled when, an hour later, a bare warm arm flopped loosely across his chest. In her sleep Teal nestled tight against him. Pip stirred but did not wake.

Reaching down to gently move her arm, he realized that her nearness was more agreeable than displeasing. Resting his own arm across hers, he closed his eyes. Her body heat offset some of the discomfort of his hard bed, and while he tried to analyze and dissect what he was feeling, he fell into a deep and contented sleep.

Chapter Eight

There wasn't much room left on the exposed mountain-top, but the pilot of the shuttle that descended carefully next to the one from the *Teacher* knew her trade. She monitored every critical readout and screen continuously, tweaking the command program structure whenever necessary.

Larger than Flinx's craft, the sturdy lander still managed to set down on the bare granite without disturbing its predecessor. Rock pulverized and then vaporized beneath its exhaust. Gravel was blown aside, tearing into and battering the nearest plants. Moments later all went quiet as the new arrival's engines shut down.

For a while nothing happened, as the occupants of the second shuttle were intent on monitoring the status of the first. Then a portal appeared in the newly arrived craft's flank and a service ramp descended.

Three heavily armed humans appeared in the opening and promptly slid down the sharply raked ramp. From the bottom they ran toward the other shuttle, spreading out to cover its deployed walkway.

In their wake came a creature massive enough to shake the ramp with its weight. Its strapping, muscular body advanced on four legs. The front portion of the broad-chested torso flowed into a thick, long neck that terminated in a tapering, heavy-browed skull. The jaws were long and flattened, the two nostrils set on the very end. Four arms protruded not from the body but from the neck. A pair of small, round ears listened intently, each pivoting independently of the other. Set beneath the protective, bony ridge of the naked forehead, the two eyes were oval-shaped and alert with intelligence. Sweeping from side to side on the end of that powerful neck, they had tremendous range of vision.

The upper pair of hands gripped two identical weapons, while the lower set of fingers manipulated instrumentation. A truck-sized pack was strapped to the broad back, while the torso and legs were encased in a brown canvaslike bodysuit. Each stumpy foot was enclosed in a matte black boot. In hue the creature was a pale beige. Longitudinal white slashes striped the exposed neck, vanishing beneath the leading edge of the bodysuit.

The Mu'Atahl joined one of the humans whose weapon was zeroed in on the entrance to Flinx's shuttle. After a brief exchange of opinion, the quadruped spoke into the pickup attached to its head. Its voice was deep, its symbospeech thick but competent.

"No sihgn of lihfe, sihr. The approach is secured."

A moment later the ramp extending downward from the new arrival was withdrawn, its function replaced by a proper powerlift. It positioned itself automatically, the sensors on the bottom of the cab slowing to meet the rock.

A man and a woman exited, neither as heavily armed as their predecessors. They paused to inspect their surroundings before the woman turned to beckon back into the cab. Another man emerged to join them. Murmuring to his predecessors in passing, he advanced to the Mu'Atahl's side.

"It is as we essayed status from orbiht, sihr, and con-fihrmed durihng descent. This landing craft appears deserted."

"Thank you, Chaa." Jack-Jax Coerlis removed his hand from his belted sidearm and scoped the sea of vege-tation that lapped energetically at the edges of the ex-posed rock. "Hell of a place. You saw the survey readouts?"

"Yes, sihr. An ihmmense forest covers this contihnent and may ihn fact domihnate this entihre world."

Coerlis's fingers rapped absently on his belt buckle, drumming his anxieties to a nonexistent audience. "An inhabitable world that wasn't in the files. I wonder if he's been this way before or if he ended up here by accident?"

"I would think the latter, sihr." The Mu'Atahl never looked back at Coerlis, keeping his eyes focused at all times on the surrounding vegetation. "The profuse flora suggests a varihety of endemihc lihfe forms. It would be reasonable to assume that at least a small percentage are inihmihcal."

"Nervous?" Coerlis challenged the Mu'Atahl with a look.

"I am always concerned when your safety is ihn-volved, sihr."

"Good boy. That's what I like to hear."

Flanked by the man and woman who'd exited the lift cab ahead of him, and with the Mu'Atahl bringing up the rear, its arching head and neck forming a protective canopy, Coerlis walked over to where the ramp emerged from the other shuttle. One of the three who had first spread out to cover the craft joined him.

Coerlis eyed him expectantly. "Well, Damas?"

"I went up, sir. As you'd expect, the exterior lock is sealed. There's no response from inside."

A shout made them turn. Another of the men had descended the slight slope to the edge of the forest to inspect the fringing verdure.

"Over here!"

They gathered around him. One didn't have to be a professional tracker to see the clear depressions booted feet had left in the pocket of crumbled, decomposing rock. They inclined downward.

Coerlis nodded sagely to himself. "So he's gone for a walk. If he's using any kind of electronic positioner, and he'd be a fool not to, he'll be easy to locate." He glanced sideways. "Feng, get into his ship. Try not to damage it too much. I can always use another shuttle." The individual so identified turned and sprinted back toward their own craft to get the necessary tools.

"Aimee, once Feng opens it up you think you can disable his navigational matrix?"

"Shouldn't be any trouble, sir." She placed a hand on her equipment belt. "I can go that one better. I'll replace his navpak with one of our own. That way if he slips past us somehow and tries to make it back to orbit, his shuttle will only respond to our codes."

Coerlis rewarded her with a slight upward curling of his lips. "Excellent. After you've done that, extract his location from the shuttle's relay and set your own positioner to track. If he's moving around he'll want to stay in permanent contact with both the shuttle and his ship.

"Shouldn't take us long to catch up with him. He won't be expecting company." Coerlis's expression turned ugly. "I'm sure he's not used to my style of persistence. After all, only a madman would follow anyone all this way just to secure a small personal acquisition."

She kept a straight face. "Whatever you say, sir."

Coerlis put a paternal arm around her shoulders. "That's one of the things I like about you, Aimee. You have just enough of a sense of humor to make your presence tolerable. Nothing to excess. For that I hire others."

"I'm glad you're pleased, sir."

Peeler was grinning. "You must really hate this guy."

Coerlis replied calmly. "Hate has nothing to do with this. It's a matter of principle." He turned away to scrutinize the undulating ocean of green. "What do you think, Chaa? A day to catch up with him?"

"I don't know, sihr. It depends, of course, on how far he has gone. Myself, I am not a clihmber. I am not lookihng forward to trackihng hihm through this jungle."

"You worry too much. He won't be expecting us. We'll just drop in on him and then maybe we'll just drop him." He giggled, an unexpectedly terse, high sound.

"Peeler and Rundle have told me about your fihrst confrontation with the young man. Alaspihnian minidrags are lethal."

"There are seven of us, Chaa. We know what to expect. Shouldn't have any trouble surprising him, and as long as we can do that, I don't foresee any problems."

"Surprihse would be best."

"I don't want him harmed. At least, not right away. He didn't understand me before, and I want to make sure that this time he does. That's what led to all this trouble; a lack of understanding. I want to make sure he understands before I have him killed."

"You humans. You always have to know. Better sihmply to react."

"That's what I'm paying you for, Chaa. To react. Not to philosophize."

The flattened jaws stirred. "No sihr, Mihster Coerlis, sihr."

Feng had no trouble decoding the standard latch sequence and cycling the shuttle's lock. As soon as Aimee finished swapping out navpaks with the console, she fixed the absent owner's position and scheduled her own unit to copy. From now on it would both monitor and duplicate the information their quarry was receiving.

"Your assumption was correct, sir." She stood behind Coerlis as he continued his examination of the shuttle's interior. "He hasn't gone very far."

The magnate popped a storage locker, revealing only standard-issue equipment. "His own vessel will be more enlightening. He hasn't personalized this one at all. There's nothing on board suggestive of him."

"A shuttle's a tool, sir. Not much reason to personalize a tool."

"Spoken like an engineer."

She took no offense. "I'm curious to have a look at his ship. The visuals we made on arrival hint at some interesting modifications."

"You'll have plenty of time to poke, Aimee. I'm counting on you to bring it back to Samstead for me." She beamed at the confidence, anticipating the opportunity. "I'll have the codes changed, do a little simple external modification. No one will know and I doubt he'll be missed, no matter how well-off his supposed friends are."

"Why go through all this, sir?" She waved at the forest. "Why not just take his ship and leave him marooned here?"

He smiled delightedly. "Why Aimee! That's not thinking at all like an engineer. I like it!" He clapped her approvingly on the back. She responded to his enthusiasm with an uncertain smile.

Fearing the worst, she'd rebuffed his initial advances long ago. He'd simply shrugged and backed off, explaining that he valued her professional expertise far more than he did her body. Competent, slightly amoral professionals were hard to find, whereas mere physical satisfaction was cheap and plentiful. Despite this, there was often something in his expression, in his enigmatic smile, in his penetrating gaze, that left her feeling awkward and vaguely unclean.

But he paid very, very well.

"It's because of the flying snake, isn't it?"

"Only incidentally. It's also because of a number of other things, engineer. Personal pride, reputation, goals. Nothing for you to worry about. I pay others to worry. You concentrate on reading the positioner, and think about the fun you're going to have with his ship, and leave the rest to Chaa and Peeler and their kind.

"The idea of marooning him has merit, however. Of course, I would have to make certain he couldn't live out his life here in some bucolic, comfortable, Crusoelike existence. That denouement would hardly balance out the trouble and expense he's caused me. Cutting his Achilles tendons before we abandon him should equalize matters. What do you think?" She swallowed uncomfortably and his smile widened.

"See? I told you to leave it alone."

Damas, Peeler, and Rundle led the way, followed by Coerlis, Aimee, and Feng, with the Mu'Atahl bringing up the rear. Coerlis plunged eagerly into the verdure as he envisioned the look of shock and surprise that would appear on his quarry's face when his pursuers burst from the greenery to overpower him. They'd rehearsed the attack many times. Preparations had been made for dealing with the dangerous minidrag. Coerlis anticipated no trouble.

All of them wore chameleon suits that changed from gray to a mottled green as they advanced by means of vines and branches. All were armed, even his engineer. Attached to the front brim of the lightweight helmets they wore was a transparent quickflip shield that he'd been assured would prove impervious even to the minidrag's poison.

There was really no cause for concern. Peeler, Feng, and the others were trained for this sort of work. He doubted the same was true of their quarry. And in the event of any surprises, there was Chaa, whose strength and skills were exceptional. In addition to his other abilities, the Mu'Atahl effortlessly carried the majority of their supplies on his broad back.

He glanced over at the engineer's positioner. "How far?"

"In a straight line, not overmuch," she informed him. Obviously uneasy, she peered over the side of the branch along which they were marching, trying to penetrate the mysterious green depths. "But this won't tell us straight out if he's above or below because he's using a simple linear positioner. That's going to take more work." She chewed her lower lip. "I'm going to have to work out some way of measuring the intensity of the signal."

Coerlis was unperturbed. "Just get us close and we'll find him. What's the matter? Scared of heights?"

She smiled wanly. "Ever since I was a kid."

"I wouldn't worry. Look how dense this stuff is. Even if you fell, you wouldn't fall far." So saying, he gave her a sharp nudge, knocking her off balance. Arms flailing, she fought to steady herself. Her face was ashen. Coerlis chuckled contentedly and moved up to chat with Peeler.

"Look at these." Damas had paused to examine a cluster of tiny flying creatures. They hovered close together, their sextupal wings humming an alien syncopation. Each had three eyes arranged above a bright yellow, conical beak. He waved at them and they backed away, maintaining their spherical formation.

Abruptly, they scattered. Damas took a step in their direction. "Hey, c'mon back! Don't be afraid."

No one saw the shape that fell from the sky. It simply appeared, like a stone dropped from a great height. Plummeting through a gap in the canopy, it struck Damas in the middle of his back with a mauve, saberlike bill that was nearly two meters long. A sharpened ridge ran along its crest to terminate in a perfect point. This went right through his heart to emerge from his chest, killing him instantly. He jerked a few times and then was still. Powerful white wings beat at the air, striving to rise with the impaled prize. Tiny hooks fringing the bill kept the body from sliding off. A trio of wild red eyes focused singlemindedly on the task of raising the dead body.

Drops of blood flew as Damas's body shook on the end of the bill. Only his weight kept the arboreal killer from vanishing instantly with its prey. Despite the impressive span of its wings, it was having trouble with the heavy load.

Stunned by the suddenness and ferocity of the attack, Coerlis could only fumble clumsily with his holstered pistol. Though Feng and Peeler reacted more quickly, they were still a step behind Chaa.

Shells and energy beams ripped into the predator, which responded with a horrible screeching that assaulted their unprepared ears. A couple of bursts tore its two left wings to shreds. Beating furiously at the air and surrounding vegetation with the other pair, it toppled over on its side, the unfortunate Damas still impaled on the hooked bill.

Approaching wordlessly, the Mu'Atahl centered an explosive shell on the powerful skull, which exploded in a shower of blood and bone. The wings twitched a couple of times before folding like the sides of a collapsing tent. Blood, pieces of flesh, and shredded feathers flew everywhere, coating the survivors as well as the surrounding brush.

Damas lay crumpled, eyes open and staring. He'd never seen the creature that had hit him. Blood trickled from his mouth as well as his chest.

While his human companions gathered around him, mumbling to themselves and staring, Chaa backed beneath a shielding branch and kept his attention on the open patch of sky. After a moment he announced, "There are others up there. Perhaps different, perhaps simihlar. Some are larger. Much larger. I suggest we descend to a poihnt where we wihll be less exposed."

"Poor bastard never had a chance." Rundle's gaze turned nervously skyward.

"He's dead." Aimee stared at the body, pinioned in its alien embrace.

"Damn right he's dead. Voicing the obvious won't change it. Everybody do like Chaa says. Let's move down." Coerlis turned away from the impaled corpse.

"This way." The Mu'Atahl lowered himself to a branch that held even as it bent alarmingly under his weight. Once assured of its stability, he reached up with two of his four hands to assist Coerlis. The others made their way down on their own.

"Better," Coerlis declared as the patch of sky receded overhead. "We'll be perfectly safe as soon as the forest closes in around us."

Chapter Nine

Pip darting effortlessly along in front of him, Flinx picked his footing through the undergrowth of deranged epiphytes and syrupy bromeliads, clinging mosses, and psychotic fungi. One minute he was walking through a botanist's heaven, the next through an equivalent hell. It was all baffling, mind-numbing, and beautiful.

He was preceded by the big furcot, Saalahan, while the two cubs flanked the group as it advanced. They stayed out of sight on either side, making sure no predator had the chance to prepare an ambush. Flinx noted their distance from one another and worried.

"Will the young ones be all right out by themselves?" He ducked to pass under a branch that Teal cleared without having to stoop.

"The furcots? They'll be fine. If anything threatens they'll give warning, or deal with it themselves."

"But they're so much smaller than Saalahan." A sapphire leaf brushed his face and his nostrils were filled with the contrasting scents of honey and turpentine.

"Heard that!" called the always argumentative Moomadeem from off to the left. Flinx saw the dim green shape take a swipe at something. Faint thrashing sounds followed, but the young furcot had already moved on.

Pip dipped down to smell a purple and black flower with four thick, diametrically opposed leaves. She was almost too slow. The four leaves smacked together like a pair of clapping hands, just missing her head. With a contemptuous hiss she buzzed the plant repeatedly, each time just avoiding the grasping greenery. Its capture and destroy mode exhausted, it finally relaxed and allowed her to inhale the deep-seated fragrance.

There weren't many life forms on Alaspin faster than a minidrag. Fortunately, the same seemed to apply on this world as well. So far, Flinx reminded himself.

"I'm sorry about your mate," he murmured sympathetically. Though Teal kept her pace deliberately slow, the lanky Flinx had difficulty keeping up. Creepers and moss seemed to hang directly in his path, thorns intentionally clutched at his clothes, and smaller branches and aerial roots appeared magically beneath his feet and between his legs, trying to trip him. Tiny creatures wondrous of shape and bright of hue darted, crawled, slithered, or flew out of his path. Dwell charted the strange skyperson's progress with a mixture of amusement and contempt.

"Yes, it's too bad." Teal glanced back at him. Intermittent light tumbling through the irregular scrim of the forest flashed from the bright green cabochons of her eyes. "Jerah was a good man."

Flinx wrestled his way past a stubborn creeper. "Were you very much in love?"

"In love?" She blinked. "Not really. There are couples who have love. I know; I've seen it."

"Don't you wish it for yourself?" Looking down, he saw the barbed abdomen of a dull orange segmented crawler sticking out of his left boot. He moved to crush it underfoot and watched with interest as the segments promptly scattered for cover, leaving only the barbed stinger behind. Gently he scraped it out of the tough fabric with the heel of his other boot.

"Not especially." She considered. "This love seems nice, but dangerous. I would rather have by my side a strong, intelligent mate who knows how to survive than one who gawks stupidly at me and forgets where he is. A companion who is soon food for a bildergrass or a carnopter is no good at all. What matters love when your mate is meat?"

"I've never really looked at it that way." He was a bit taken aback by her cool, analytic response.

They walked on, pausing occasionally to check Flinx's positioner to ensure they were still on course. "What about you?" she asked him. "Have you ever been in love?"

"Several times. Always with a woman older than myself. The last time—the last time it was hard to leave. I had to force myself to do it."

She eyed him curiously. "Then why did you?"

"Because I'm not ready to mate." He could hardly tell her the truth. Not that she would understand anyway.

"You look ready enough to me."

He had the grace to blush. Life on this world was very direct, social niceties having been sacrificed on the altar of continued survival.

"The reason I'm not ready to mate isn't visible." He tapped the side of his head.

She frowned but didn't inquire further, though he could tell from her confused emotional state that she wasn't ready to let the matter drop.

"Mate or not, I think you would make a good survivor."

"Thanks. That's how I like to think of myself. But love?" He shook his head. "I don't know. I'd like to understand myself better, first."

"To understand oneself you must first better understand the world."

He looked at her sharply but there was no guile in her expression, no subtlety in her tone. Her emotional state was not that of one trying to hide some unknown secret. He continued to puzzle over her words even as she turned away from him to check the way ahead.

The branch they were currently traversing quivered under Saalahan's great weight, but it led in the direction they were headed. To allay his concerns, Teal assured him they would soon be able to switch to a thicker, sturdier pathway. No straight line led to their destination. Traveling a path through the hylaea was more akin to tacking a sailboat into the wind, only in their case an extra dimension was involved.

"Stormtreader." For his benefit she identified a massive tree off to their right. Leaves grew directly upon the trunk. What few branches there were appeared stunted and vestigial. All that he could see of the remarkable trunk was clad in an exceptional, silvery bark.

"Draws the thunderbolts," she explained. "A bad place to seek shelter in a storm."

"I'll remember." Had he known of the trees' role in utilizing lightning to fix nitrogen in the planet's soil, he would have been even more impressed.

Dwell and Kiss strayed freely from the main branch, cavorting among flowers and vines, instinctively avoiding those that were potentially dangerous while prodding and poking playfully at those that were not.

"You have a lot of confidence in your children."

"They are old enough to know the ways." Teal leaped to another branch and waited for Flinx to follow in his usual, tentative fashion. "If they are unfamiliar with something, they will ask about it. And a furcot is always at hand."

"Is that what furcots do? Watch over humans?"

"And each other as well, just as we look out for them. It is a partnership."

"Is there love between human and furcot?"

She reflected. "No. It's deeper than that, almost as if your furcot is a part of you and you are a part of it." A grunt sounded from up ahead and she turned sharply. "Saalahan wants us to come quickly." Without waiting to see if Flinx was following, she broke into a sprint.

Trying to pick his way yet still keep up, he followed as best he was able. Teal and her children seemed to know just where to put their feet, exactly when to shorten their stride or gather themselves for a jump. He was getting better, but he knew that even if he practiced for years he could do no better than match Kiss in agility.

Though he considered himself to be in good physical condition, he was still breathing hard when he finally caught up with them.

Lying in the crook of two large, pale blue branches was an adult furcot. It was clearly in an advanced state of degradation. Instead of a bright, healthy green, its fur had taken on a distinctly yellowish tinge. The chest bellowed in and out in long, painful contractions. Slumped on its side, it looked like a beached hippo. Already starting to fester, gaping wounds were visible between both sets of legs.

At their approach it tried to lift its eyes to greet them. Failing, the head sank back, exhausted.

Not knowing how he should react, Flinx studied his companions for clues. All were solemn and quiet, including the children. It was the first time he'd seen Dwell so subdued.

Saalahan nuzzled the fallen creature while Teal bent to stroke the blocky skull, rubbing gently between the ears. A muted grinding noise emerged from deep within the massive chest: a labored, falling sound. The three eyes remained half shut.

"Ciinravan," she informed Flinx, responding to his un-voiced question. "Jerah's furcot."

"I thought you said that when a person died, their furcot died with them."

"Soon enough," Saalahan growled softly. The ugly wounds confirmed the big furcot's words.

"Ciinravan tried to help Jerah but was too late." Teal continued to stroke the shivering brow. "This degeneration began soon after his death."

"Can't we make some kind of a stretcher?" Flinx studied the enormous mass. "With all three furcots pulling and the rest of us helping, maybe we could carry Ciinravan back to your home." He fumbled with his supply belt. "I have some medicines. I don't know how well they'll work, or even if any of them will work at all, but I'm willing to try."

"It doesn't matter. You can't do anything. Ciinravan will be dead by this afternoon."

"No matter what I do?"

She nodded slowly. "No matter what. Jerah is dead, so Ciinravan will die."

Flinx could see the life ebbing from the once powerful form. "Seems like an awful waste."

"It is the way of things." She was thoroughly resigned. "The forest gives life to us all, and to the forest each is destined to return. It is nothing to be sorrowful for. Ciinravan has no regrets."

"Tell me something. If Ciinravan had died instead of your husband, would Jerah have faded away like this?"

"Of course," she told him.

Something's going on here, he thought to himself. Something much deeper than friendship between human and beast. These relationships had more to do with true symbiosis than casual companionship.

But how had it all begun? Teal and her children were of traditional human stock. Their ancestors had come here from some other Commonwealth world. How had they become so tightly bound to this particular native species? Just how intelligent were the furcots, anyway? And what had prompted them to form such a close association with humans? The thousands of years of interaction that had gone into creating the relationship between human and dog, human and horse, didn't exist here. Everything had happened quickly.

Much too quickly, he thought, but he couldn't be sure. He was no behavioral biologist.

He studied the dying furcot. "I don't understand. Why couldn't Ciinravan attach himself to another person?"

"All persons already have furcots," Teal told him.

Flinx persisted. "I know that. Can't a person have two furcots?"

She blinked. "What a strange notion. Why would a person want to be with two furcots? And why would two furcots want to share a person?"

"I still don't get it. Where do the furcots *come* from?" Moomadeem was sniffing his leg, and he did his best to ignore the young animal. "Do you raise them? Is there a furcot herd living near your home that you select new young animals from whenever a child is born?"

She laughed at him. "When a person is born, their furcot comes to them. When a person dies, their furcot dies. This is the natural way of things."

The unnatural way of things, he thought.

Saalahan spoke before Flinx could ask another question. "It will not be long."

"Do not weep," Teal told her new friend. "Ciinravan is happy. Soon it will be with Jerah again."

The big furcot was in obvious pain. Flinx thought of the needler holstered at his hip. "Can't we make it any easier for him? Put an end to the misery?"

She frowned. "There is no misery in dying. It is part of the natural order. Death begets life. This is nothing to sorrow about."

"But if the animal is hurting—"

"Ciinravan shows more than he feels," Teal assured him. "It is not so bad as it appears."

"I was just thinking that—" Suddenly he paused and put a hand to the side of his head, turning sharply. His eyes scanned the impenetrable green walls. Alarmed, Pip took to the air, leaving her master's shoulder to search for the perceived danger.

"What is it?" Teal looked uncertain.

Rising on her hind legs, Tuuvatem sniffed the damp air before concluding with a soft snort. "There's nothing. The skyperson hears a flitter, and jumps." She dropped back to all sixes.

Teal glanced at him. "Flinx?"

"I thought—I thought I felt the presence of other persons." He looked down at her. "Would your people send out search parties to look for you?"

She shook her head. "They have more practical things to do with their time."

"Another family of sugararry gatherers?" Again she shook her head.

Moomadeem nudged him roughly with a shoulder. "Maybe you were sensing me?"

"No. These were human feelings."

"Not impossible," the furcot admitted, much to Flinx's surprise. He was convinced that the young creature was eager to dispute anything he said.

"I can't be sure of anything on this world," he muttered, as much to himself as to Teal. "I suppose the first thing is to get you all safely home."

"No," she replied. "First we must bury Ciinravan."

"Bury?" He eyed the rapidly failing animal. "It's a long ways to the ground."

"Why would anyone, person or furcot, want to be buried in the Lower Hell?" she asked him. "There are proper places. We can move the body. Saalahan will help. Even you can help."

"Of course," he told her, without comprehending. He let his gaze rove the hylaea, wondering where and how they intended to dig a hole large enough to accommodate the furcot's bulk.

Saalahan jumped easily to the next branch and vanished into the verdure. "Once a place has been found, we will move Ciinravan," she told Flinx. "Meanwhile we will attend the last moments. And we must also find shelter for the night."

Flinx glanced skyward. The torpid cloud cover was already beginning to darken.

Chapter Ten

"They're heading down again." Feng checked his own positioner. They each carried one, standard issue for travel on any world. He checked the readout with Chaa and then Peeler. Their numbers matched reassuringly. "You can tell by the variance in the signal. Nice job of tuning, Aimee." As she acknowledged the compliment with a nod, he brushed at a clinging vine covered with fuzz. Fine hairs came off in his hand, imparting a mild burning sensation. He rubbed the skin angrily against one leg of the chameleon suit.

"Why don't they keep to one height?"

"Maybe they don't like being exposed to the sky," Peeler suggested. "You could ask Damas about that."

"Real funny. Big joke." Feng examined the rash the hairs had inflicted on his hand. They carried gloves, but despite the suits' best efforts at cooling and dehumidifying, it was still oppressively hot. Wearing gloves was out of the question.

"Everybody hold up." Aimee had halted and was waving for attention. They crowded close to her.

The branch they had been following emerged from a trunk fifteen meters in diameter. There were no other branches within easy reach, and the trunk itself was as smooth as glass, offering nothing in the way of a toe- or handhold.

"Where did they go from here?" Rundle peered cautiously over the side. It was a ten-meter drop to the next suitable branch. Plenty of vines and creepers trailed from overhead down into the emerald depths, but no one was in a rush to test their strength.

"Over there." Feng was standing on the opposite side of the branch.

On the north side of the tree a cluster of thorns as long and thick as a man's arm protruded from the otherwise perfectly smooth bark, forming dense clusters directly on the trunk.

"Make a serviceable ladder, don't you think?" Feng beamed proudly at his discovery.

Aimee was less convinced. "I don't know . . ."

"You see a better way down? Look at those two." A pair of skinny six-limbed creatures were scampering up the far side of the trunk, utilizing the thorn clusters in much the same fashion as Feng had suggested. Each was about a meter tall. Their tiny heads were completely dominated by three oversized, pale brown eyes. Glancing anxiously in the direction of the party of humans, they fled as expeditiously as possible. Patches of electric-blue flashed from the backs of their otherwise dun-colored bodies.

Once safely overhead, they lingered on several thorns to peer down at the travelers, chattering and whistling emphatically. For such comparatively small creatures, they had exceedingly loud voices.

"Look at them," ordered Feng. "Do they look like they're worried about anything?"

Watching the obstreperous pair as they scampered restlessly from cluster to cluster, it was difficult to imagine that the thorns represented any danger. The sharp protrusions looked strong enough to support all of them, including the much heavier Chaa.

"You're right, it does look safe." Coerlis smiled at Feng. "You go first."

The other man's expression fell, but he nodded and reached tentatively for the nearest thorn. When it neither reacted nor broke off in his grasp, his companions relaxed.

"I don't understand how he can move so fast." Coerlis stood peering into the dense vegetation as he waited his turn at the thorn ladder. "He doesn't know anyone's chasing him so there's no reason for him to be traveling so rapidly. There are no set routes through this, no obvious paths left by animals, so he has to pick his way just like us. He hasn't been here before."

The engineer was stepping cautiously out onto one thorn while tightly gripping another. "How do you know, sir?"

"Because *no* one's ever been here before. Not according to general records, anyway."

"Records are not perfect." Chaa was scanning the forest, weapons at the ready as always. He would make the descent last, after everyone else was safely down on the next branch.

"Where the hell could he be going in all this?" Coerlis's brow furrowed as he sought rationale for the inexplicable.

"Maybe he's just out for a stroll. Maybe he likes to explore." Rundle was halfway down and feeling much more confident in their chosen route.

"Then he should be taking his time." Coerlis kicked absently at the woody surface underfoot. "It doesn't make any sense."

"We should be able to overtake him tomorrow." The Mu'Atahl exuded quiet confidence.

"We'd better. I don't like it here." Coerlis put a hand on the immense, glossy wall of the trunk. "Although there're definite commercial possibilities here. Exotic hardwoods, new biologicals, medicinal extracts: enough to justify sending out a full evaluation team. Later." His gaze narrowed as he sought to penetrate the all-concealing green. "Right now all I want is to add a certain specimen to my zoological collection."

Feng was almost down. The two big-eyed chatterers had scrambled down another part of the trunk and now waited just above the next branch as they continued to monitor the intruders' progress. "Look at them, whistling away. They're damn cute."

"They are." Carefully positioning her hands and feet, the engineer peered up at her employer. "Why don't you bring them back for your collection, sir?"

"Maybe on the way back," Coerlis replied diffidently.

"That's funny. They're not running away from us now." Rundle studied the pair as he followed in Feng's wake.

"That's because not everybody's face is as frightening as your ugly puss," the other man replied. He extended a friendly hand downward. "C'mere, guys. I won't hurt you."

The big-eyes responded with a flourish of incomprehensible chatter and promptly vanished into a hole in the trunk.

"So you don't scare 'em, huh?" Rundle grinned broadly.

"Where'd they go?" Peeler paused to let Rundle, who was just below, descend another step.

Feng leaned out. "They've got some kind of nest in the tree. There are some big thorns, but I could reach in and grab 'em easy if I had to. Their teeth are real small and flat." He moved sideways, positioning himself on one of the extra-long thorns. "Hey, guys, how're you doin' in there?" He reached in to stroke the thick brown fur of the animal nearest.

The entire immense mass of the tree shivered slightly.

Coerlis was jolted off his thorn, but Chaa, demonstrating inhuman speed and strength, reached down and grabbed the man by the collar of his chameleon suit, drawing him back to safe footing. Rundle and Peeler fell to the branch, Peeler landing hard and rolling, while Aimee clung desperately to one long thorn with both arms, her legs kicking at empty air.

A dull thump seemed to resonate through the entire forest. Panicked creatures flew or ran in all directions, flashes of color amidst the all-pervasive green. Above the whistling and howling and hooting, Peeler was shouting frantically.

"Feng! You all right?" From their location on the branch he moved as far as he could to his right to see what had happened to the other man. Rundle helped the shaken Aimee down the last couple of steps.

"I'm—I'm okay," came the shaken reply. "But I'm stuck."

"Stuck? What do you mean you're 'stuck'?" Coerlis reached the branch with Chaa close behind. With his long neck, the Mu'Atahl could see better than any of them.

"Some kind of a trap," the alien announced.

"Four big thorns," the engineer added. "They've folded right over him. Like this." She interlocked the fingers of both hands.

"They're not thorns. They are part of somethihng else that lihves on the tree." The Mu'Atahl pointed. "Look closely and you can see where it fihts perfectly ihnto a hollow in the trunk."

The thin, almost imperceptible line that delineated the creature's outline was nearly four meters in length and two wide. As they tried to make sense of what they were seeing, Feng was pushing and shoving at his prison. He managed to wedge his right leg between two of the thorns but could make the gap no wider.

"I'm sure it's real fascinating," he growled at his companions. "Now how about getting me out of here? Hey . . . ow!"

"What is it?" asked Peeler anxiously. "What's wrong?"

"One of those damn little monkey-things just bit the hell out of my right ankle. Little bastard, get away from me!"

"You—you all right?" Rundle stammered.

"Yeah. I smacked him good and he went to the back of his hole."

"We'll have to burn him out." Coerlis fingered his pistol speculatively. "We don't have anything else to cut with. Unless you think you can snap those thorns, Chaa."

The Mu'Atahl studied Feng's prison. "This wood supports my weight, but those are of a different composition. They are desihned to restrain ihntruders. I do not know if I wihll have success."

"Take it easy," Rundle shouted to his friend. "We'll get you out of there." He looked confidently back at his companions. "It's some kind of trap the big-eyes use to get food, but in this case the food's bigger than they are. Feng can fight them off until we get him out."

"C'mon, you guys, hurry it up." It was the prisoner, sounding anxious.

"What's the rush?" Peeler made a face at Aimee. "Accommodations not to your liking?"

"It's not that," the other man replied. "That place on my leg where the little shit bit me? I can't feel it. It's gone numb."

"Who the hell would want to feel your leg, Feng?" Aimee was doing her best to encourage him, but her expression was pale.

Peeler and Rundle carefully worked their way over to where Feng was imprisoned, each of them taking up a position on either side. When Peeler leaned close he saw that the pseudothorns had contracted even farther, shutting out the light and probably forcing Feng even farther inside.

"What's going on?" Coerlis demanded to know.

"Can't see him. The thorns are blocking the hole completely now."

"What do you mean, you can't see him? He's got to be in there. Feng, what the hell's going on?"

This time the other man didn't answer.

Chaa had worked his way across the side of the trunk. Now he settled himself just above the closed opening. "Both of you get out of the way." He cradled a heavy rifle in his lower hands while gripping supportive thorns with the other pair and all four legs. Peeler and Rundle scrambled hastily back down to the branch.

As soon as they were clear, the Mu'Atahl released a concentrated burst from the high-energy weapon. One of the thorns turned to brown powder laced with dark green. Sap bubbled from the neatly sheared stump. Two more bursts cleared the opening.

While Peeler went in, shining his service light ahead of him, the others waited silently. Hardly a moment passed before gagging, choking sounds came from inside the hole.

"Dammit," Aimee muttered tightly.

The buzz of a needler replaced the retching noises. Then Peeler stuck his head out where the others could see him.

"Feng's dead."

Coerlis's lips thinned. "What happened?"

"Those little monkey-things? I put a shot through each of 'em. Slimy little—"

"Get ahold of yourself!" Coerlis barked. "What—happened?"

"It wasn't the big-eyes. They're just some kind of mobile bait that bites back. There's a big pink sac in here, all covered with mucus. It dissolves whatever it touches. It dissolved part of my left boot before I pulled away from it. Feng was—inside. And one of those big-eyes had its head shoved halfway into Feng's chest. Now we know why they're so small in comparison to the rest of the body. The other one was ripping into his gut. God, it's sickening!"

"External stomach." The Mu'Atahl was calm as ever. "The creature extruded it to swallow Feng. It must utihlize highly acihdic gastrihc juices. The harmless-looking, bihg-eyed hexapods lure prey ihnto the hole, the thornlihke protuberances trap it, the hexapods bihte and ihnject some kihnd of paralyzihng toxihn, and then the external stomach takes over and begihns the process of dihgestion. There is much teamwork ihnvolved, and all parties clearly share in the fruihts of the capture."

Aimee put a hand over her mouth and turned away while Rundle cursed under his breath. "Fast," Coerlis observed coolly. "It works fast. I wonder if it's a plant or an animal?"

"I am not a xenologihst," the Mu'Atahl replied. Behind him the engineer had turned as green as some of the surrounding vegetation. "With its bait creatures dead and its imprihsonihng thorns burnt away, I wonder if it wihll regenerate ihtself or die?"

"I hope it dies! I hope it starves to death, slowly." Aimee was breathing hard. "What a lousy way to go. I *liked* Feng."

"A valued employee." Coerlis's tone suddenly changed as he peered curiously at her. "You two weren't . . . ?"

She turned a startled gaze toward him. "No, Jack-Jax, we weren't. He was a decent guy, that's all."

"Oh." The merchant seemed disappointed. "This will be a lesson to all of us. It should make everyone that much more anxious to catch up with our evasive friend."

"Yeah. Oh yeah." Grim-faced, she caressed her needler. "I want to find him. I want to find him and get the hell out of here."

"Then we need to move." Looking up from studying his positioner, Chaa pointed westward. "That way."

The others followed, ignoring a flock of delicate pastel flying creatures the size of overweight sparrows. The well-organized swarm swept past them and eagerly entered the still smoking cavity in the side of the tree. Each of them was a visual delight, an iridescent winged wonder that flashed ruby and lapis and topaz in the diffuse daylight.

They were almost too beautiful to be scavengers.

Aimee did her best to encourage Rundle, who shuffled along listlessly. Not because she was particularly fond of him, but because they all had to depend on one another, and it didn't help to have one of their number moping about aimlessly, not paying attention to his surroundings.

"Look, I liked Feng, too. He made a mistake, that's all." She eyed the surrounding verdure warily. "You don't go looking to pet anything here. You don't even *touch* anything unless you absolutely have to. It was his own fault."

"Got to get away from here." Rundle's voice had fallen so low she had to strain to understand the big man. "Got to get out." His eyes looked haunted. "Could've happened to any one of us, right about that." He nodded down at the branch they were traversing.

"This right here, somethin' in it could jump out and swallow us right up. Never notice it until it was too late." He looked around sharply. There was nothing there—and everything there.

Aimee put an arm through his and hugged gently. "Take it easy. Not everything here is carnivorous. It wouldn't make sense. This world is dangerous, but it's not irrational." Lifting one leg, she stomped hard on the underlying wood, twice. Four meters thick, it didn't even quiver.

"See? It's just a branch. Solid as any bridge, maybe more so. Plain, ordinary wood. Not everything here bites or snaps or stings. You just have to be careful." She lifted her gaze and smiled. "Look at those."

A tangle of slender blue-green vines tumbled from somewhere overhead. Thin and fragile, they formed elegant spirals of uncommon attractiveness. Dozens of tiny lavender flowers striped with gold lined the delicate strands, exuding a subtle yet rich fragrance. Even Coerlis was impressed.

"Striking appearance and aroma." He inhaled deeply before moving on. "Hopefully, it can be distilled."

"See?" The engineer gave her wavering companion a reassuring squeeze. "They're just flowers. Gorgeous flowers, at that. If you let this place get to you, you'll end up hiding under a leaf and just shivering. Paranoia's more dangerous than anything we're likely to encounter." She smiled comfortingly. "Just remember rule number one for this place: don't touch unless you're sure."

Pausing next to the glittering cascade of fragrance and color, she bent forward slightly to smell the most accessible cluster of blossoms. None were larger than a centimeter across. Each had the look of an individual, faceted gem. Petals flashed with absorbed silicon. When she brushed them with her hand, they sparkled like diamonds and the intense perfume went everywhere.

Nothing lethal responded. No creepers or tentacles reached for her, no hidden hands grasped at her throat. There was only the rush of dazzling beauty. Her smile widened.

Rundle's nerves steadied and his breathing slowed. The gold and crystal lavender blossoms put the most beautiful flowers he'd ever seen before to shame. The engineer was right: there was beauty here as well as death.

Taking out her service knife, Aimee excised a perfect natural bouquet and used a clip to fasten it in her hair. It caught the sunlight like a Marquise's tiara, as splendid as a crown of colored diamonds. She executed a small pirouette.

"What do you think, Charlie? Does it suit me?"

A reluctant smile crept over the big man's face. "Maybe you're right. Feng was stupid. It still stinks, but it was his own fault."

"That's right." She resumed her place alongside him. "Just don't touch anything."

He indicated the gleaming headdress. "You just did."

"I checked them out first. They're only flowers. Don't you see, Charlie? Everything here can't be dangerous." Her expression turned playful. "You still haven't told me what you think."

"It's very becoming." Coerlis shoved aside a handful of vines. They trembled slightly at his touch. "Keep up."

Rundle gripped the pistol he was holding a little tighter. "Be careful and try not to touch. Right. Got it." He managed a determined smile.

"That's better." She ducked beneath an overhanging limb. "We've made some mistakes, suffered some losses, but we'll be on this kid pretty quick and then we'll be out of here. Concentrate on that."

He nodded vigorously, feeling a little better about things. The image of Feng, his body engulfed by the pink membrane, the two adorable little furballs gnawing voraciously at his insides, began to fade from his thoughts.

But despite strenuous efforts, he could not make it disappear entirely.

Chapter Eleven

This time it didn't stop raining until less than an hour before sunrise. Though Flinx was eager to leave, he allowed Teal to restrain him.

"It's not good to move with the first light. Better to wait an hour or so."

"Why?" Curled up in a corner of the shelter, a sleepy Pip unfurled her glorious wings and stretched.

"Sunrise is the coolest part of the day." The perpetually saturated and perspiring Flinx accepted this as a relative term. "Those who hunt at night are seeking to make a final kill, while those who feed during the day are most active. Better to wait for the first frenzy of feeding to fade before moving."

Sampling the sodden air of morning, Flinx found himself agreeing. While he would have called it less saunalike rather than "cool," he had to admit it was easier to take than the atmospheric stew that was midafternoon. Something roared in the distance, its triumphant cry reverberating through the branches, and he willingly resumed his seat. Folding her wings, Pip slithered into his lap.

"It will not take long," Teal assured him. "Soon the hunters of the first light will lie down to eat. Then we will bury Ciinravan."

Flinx studied the surrounding forestscape, peering out from beneath the huge green-black leaf where they'd spent the night. Though a dozen or so such leaves grew from a single immense epiphyte, one was large enough to shelter them all. The plant could have sheltered an entire tribe.

Behind him, Dwell and Kiss were stirring. Given the opportunity, most children their age would sleep until awakened or till a much later hour. On this world, indulging in such a luxury would invite visitation by exploring, curious scavengers. They were soon wide-awake.

After a leisurely breakfast, Teal stepped out from beneath the leaf to study the verdure overhead. "We must go up."

Flinx rose to stand alongside. "Up? Isn't this the third level?"

"No. We are still on the second, and we must go up to the first."

"But you said that your people lived on the third, that they preferred the third, and that you fear the sky."

She lowered her gaze. "We will not go all the way to the openness of the Upper Hell. But it is good for a spirit to be near the sun. We will find one of They-Who-Keep and climb it." At Flinx's look of confusion she added, "There we will bury Ciinravan."

He frowned. "On the tree?"

"In the tree. In that way Ciinravan will be returned to the world."

Her guest turned thoughtful. "I hope we don't have to do much digging."

She laughed then. A nice laugh, he thought. Unpretentious and compassionate.

"You will see, Flinx."

With the help of the young furcots and the children, they managed to position the considerable dead weight of Ciinravan on Saalahan's broad back. Teal cut lianas, and with these secured the limp mass in place. Flinx's admiration for the furcots' abilities went up another notch as he watched Saalahan maneuver the great load upward. Powerful curving claws dug deep into the wood of branches and trunks as they began to ascend, searching for the right tree while doing their best not to stray any farther than necessary from the positioner's indicated course.

They were lucky, finding a They-Who-Keep that lay in their path. Seeking out an efficacious combination of vines, creepers, branches, and smaller trees, they started up. The hylaea began to thin perceptibly, and the already partially acclimated Flinx found himself watching the larger openings warily. Once, he had to follow the others in ascending a suitable creeper hand over hand. At such times it was best not to dwell on the fact that it was some six hundred meters to the actual ground, intervening vegetation notwithstanding.

The tree was the size of an office tower, a gargantuan spire of wood and greenery. When he remarked on this to Dwell, the boy responded with something less than awe.

"It's a good-sized They-Who-Keep, but I have seen larger. Besides, They-Who-Keep are not the biggest trees. That would be a Pillar."

Flinx looked to right and left, unable to see around the epiphyte-infested bole, and wondered what a Pillar tree might be like.

Teal called a halt and began to inspect each of several branches. Even this far from the base, they exceeded in diameter all but the largest trees on Moth or Terra. Their weight, Flinx decided, must be enough to depress the very earth beneath them.

"See the vines-of-own?" Teal pointed out a knot of flower-stricken creepers that clustered in a notch where the trunk split. Their scent was sharp but not unpleasant. "Don't brush against them. Their seed sacs are under great pressure and will burst on contact. The pollen expands inside the lungs and suffocates. It will kill anything that breathes it."

"These vines, they grow on your Home-tree as well?"

"Of course."

"You must have a hard time avoiding them."

She laughed again. "Not at all. Our Home-tree knows us."

"Knows you?"

"Yes. The vines respond to those who live with the tree. Their flowers recognize our spit. These flowers would not know us."

"Emfoling?" Flinx wondered aloud.

"No, chemistry," she corrected him.

Where the broad wooden avenue of a large branch paved with grasses, fungi, and small flowers emerged from the trunk, the wood had developed a massive crack. Often the cavity was the home of a creature Teal called a *volute*, but this one was dry and deserted.

After she cut away the binding creepers, the body of Ciinraven was carefully and reverently lowered into the crack. Humans and furcots then spread out to gather leaves, dried fruits, moss, and whatever other available and easily accessible vegetation they could find. This was alternately dumped, packed, piled, and pressed into the cavity, until Ciinravan was completely hidden from view and the upper edge of the opening was once again flush with the surface of the branch. In addition to hiding the body from view, the decomposing vegetation would speed Ciinravan along the proper path, while the neutralizing aroma of special mosses would discourage prowling scavengers.

Flinx did his best to help, until he was forced to dump his third load. His hands felt like he'd shoved them into an open fire. Shaking them wildly in an attempt to cool them off, he saw that tiny red pustules were breaking out all over his fingers and palms. Sensing her master's distress, Pip darted about anxiously. But this was no antagonist she could deal with.

Teal put her own armful down and hurried over. "What's the matter?"

He showed her his hands. "Stings," he told her.

"I'm sure it does. What did you pick?" He indicated the pile of soft, easily uprooted plants.

"Grivets." She was nodding to herself. "Its leaves are covered with fine hairs that release a strong chemical. Properly distilled, it makes a marvelous spice."

"I can understand that." He grimaced. "My hands feel like they've been shot with pepper."

"I don't know what that is. Come with me."

Eyes beginning to water, he followed her as she searched the surrounding vegetation. Eventually she paused next to a bromeliad whose tall green leaves were spotted with pink. Floating in the plant's internal pool were half a dozen thumbnail-sized pure milk-white spheres. As she reached in and pulled one out, he saw that each floating bulb was attached to its parent by a wire-thin stem.

"Hold out your hands, palms up."

Lips compressed against the pain, he complied.

When she squeezed the sphere, it released a large quantity of thin, clear fluid. "Don't drop any," she warned him as she flung the crushed pulp aside. "Rub your hands together. Rub it all over your fingers."

As he did so, the bulb's healing capabilities manifested themselves. Cool and soothing, the analeptic juice quickly took away the stinging. The pustules began to pale.

"O'opaa fruit," she informed him. "It's very good for any kind of skin irritation." Picking up her load, she carried it over to the crevice and began packing it in.

"I think from now on I'll just help you carry." He blew alternately on his spread fingers.

"You cannot emfol." She put a reassuring hand on his arm. "That is why you ignorantly picked the grivet."

"This emfoling's something I'm really going to have to work on," he replied earnestly. "Can it be taught?"

Her expression was one of honest surprise. "I don't know. I have no idea if it can be learned by one who was not born to it. We will have to ask Overt the Shaman."

He nodded, then turned suddenly and sharply to his right. Were those two bushes laughing at him? He put it down to an overactive imagination suffering from a surplus of stimuli.

When all was done, the little group assembled around the grave hundreds of meters in the sky. Led by Teal, the children recited several touching and straightforward verses, not all of which Flinx understood. When they finished, the three furcots put back their heads, tusks in the air, and began to howl. It was a strangely melodious, mewling sound, not unattractive but quite incomprehensible: what a trombone might sound like if it could be an amplified clarinet for a day.

When the furcots finished, everyone turned and started off through the forest as if nothing untoward had transpired. Following Flinx's positioner, Teal led the way westward and down.

"The imbalance has been addressed," she told him. "All will be well now." He chose not to comment, still woefully ignorant of her people's personal philosophy. He noted that despite her confidence and reassuring words, neither she nor the children had in any way reduced their constant vigilance.

"What happens when one of you dies?" he asked.

"Humans and furcots are treated alike." She looked back at him. "Balance. One of our elders knew of an ancient word handed down by his great ancestors. 'Hozho.' "

"Don't know it." Flinx spared a last look back at the rapidly receding burial site. At this distance it was quite indistinguishable from the rest of the branch. Speculating silently on the relationship between furcots and humans, humans and Home-trees, he realized that the nutrients in Ciinravan's body would be absorbed by the tree and not the ground, as would have been the case with a more traditional burial. Something Teal had said earlier flashed again in his mind: *Chemistry*.

Not for the first time, Flinx wished he had enjoyed the time and resources to indulge in advanced education. This was not a world where the ability to pick locks or unlatch sealed doors was of much use.

Teal slid lithely down a bundle of creepers, paralleled by Kiss and Dwell. The furcots jumped from branch to branch while Flinx did his best not to hinder the pace. Though he was agile and strong enough, and doing better, his size was still a disadvantage when it came to negotiating the intricate tangles of the hylaea.

A flock of fluorescent flitters flashed past, blurs of electric color amidst the green and brown. There was so much to see here, so much to absorb, and he was missing most of it because he had to be careful of where he put his feet. He resolved that once he had helped Teal and her family return to their home, he would make time simply to study and enjoy.

They found the most magnificent spot imaginable to spend his third night away from the shuttle. Expecting another hollow in a tree trunk or cluster of shed-sized leaves, he was completely unprepared for the excited Dwell's discovery. The boy came racing back to join them, the lumpish yet somehow lovable Moomadeem loping along at his side.

"Mother, Kiss—come and look, come and look!" Without waiting to see if they were following, he whirled and retraced his path, his green cloak flapping against his slim back.

"Must be something special to get Dwell that excited," Flinx commented.

"You mustn't be hard on him." Teal vaulted effortlessly over an intervening aerial root that Flinx had to climb. "You are his competitor."

Flinx frowned. "Competitor? For what?"

"Dominant human male in this family grouping."

"But I'm not—" he started to say, then stopped. In this place it was Dwell's perception that mattered, not his own.

The horizontal cavity had been caused by lightning. Located on the western side of the branch, it was a couple of meters high and three wide. The blackened gash penetrated deep into the wood, forming a cave in the curving brown flank. Flinx watched as the three furcots dug their claws into the wood and simply stepped over the edge, hanging out over emptiness as they walked into the hollow.

"It's safe!" Saalahan called out moments later. Leaning over cautiously, Flinx found he couldn't see the furcot.

Thus concealed, they would be able to spend a comparatively relaxed night.

"It's all right." Digging the claws of its four hind feet into the wood, the big furcot reached out and up for him. "Come down, Flinx person. I won't let you fall."

Flinx hesitated while Teal, Dwell, and even the diminutive Kiss scrambled over the side of the branch and swung with practiced skill into the waiting cavity. The dropoff below the branch itself was precipitous. It promised a safe night's sleep but did little for his nerves. Bracing himself, he turned his face to the branch and slowly eased himself over the edge. His fingers dug at the bark while his feet slipped and skidded on the wooden arc.

Then he felt powerful paws grasping his lower body, and he allowed Saalahan to pull him into the blackened opening. The adult furcot considered him with its three eyes.

"You have learned much in short time. Next, better learn how to climb." Flinx responded with a grateful if slightly embarrassed smile.

"I'm actually a pretty good climber, Saalahan. It's these surroundings I'm not used to." With a soft snort, the adult shambled off to inspect the underside of the branch, looking for concealed predators and leaving Flinx to take stock of his surroundings.

What made the site special was its location. The cave in the branch looked out across a valley in the forest, a vine-and-liana-swathed depression that dug all the way down to the fifth level. Thick moutire and coculioc vines dangled from branches above, shielding the cavity from attack by arboreal hunters. The panorama visible through the curtain of vines to anyone sitting on the edge of the opening was nothing less than spectacular, filled as the green valley was with a fecund riot of flowers and flying creatures. Gliding shapes great and small picked and grazed on the exposed vegetation as well as upon one another.

Dwell had stumbled upon something all but alien to his people: a safe view.

All the cavity needed, Flinx decided, were a pair of sliding glass doors and air-conditioning to justify an exorbitant rent. Given that, the branch would still be a hard sell as a vacation site. Too much of the local flora and fauna had already demonstrated a robust liking for the taste of unwary travelers.

For the first time he was able to get an idea of the true size of some of the trees. Though draped in clinging vines and parasitic smaller growths, the boles fringing the valley had trunks six and seven hundred meters tall. They were the largest living things he'd ever seen, and possibly the largest ever discovered. This world, he knew, was the proverbial heaven dreamed of by deserving botanists.

If the Home-trees and Pillars were so massive at this height, he wondered, what must they be like at their base?

After two days spent deep within the shadowed forest, the hazy unfiltered sunlight made him squint. He should have turned away, but the frenzy of uncontrolled growth held his mesmerized attention. Gradually his eyes readapted and he could make out individual, smaller features.

Nor was it a silent scene, alive as it was with buzzing, droning, humming, screeching, singing, whistling, cackling entities of every shape and size. Most adhered, as he had come to expect, to the pattern of physiologic trifurcation he had noted on arrival, though there were distinctive variants.

Occasionally an aerial predator would plunge into the green depths, only to emerge a moment later, often struggling to regain altitude, with some unfortunate canopy-dweller clasped in its talons or beak or teeth. Flinx particularly noted one flock of fliers that hovered on a dozen rapidly beating wings. They flashed up and down in succession like so many hooks on strings as each of the fascinating creatures sucked nectar from flowers through a meter-long tube of a tongue.

A bulbous, stubby-winged hunter shot into their midst, scattering the flock and its raucous chorus. Sharp spikes adorned the predator's entire body. Dropping like a dead weight into the flock, it emerged with two of the nectar-sippers impaled on its spikes. It was not necessary, Flinx saw, to boast of talons and teeth in order to be a successful hunter. There were innumerable other ways of killing.

Something vast dipped down into the hole in the canopy, shadowing the green wall where they lay. An immense, iridescent gas-filled sac trailing dozens of tentacles, it grazed the edge of the forest in search of prey. When it had concluded its circumnavigation of the valley and returned to the mist-laden sky, half a dozen small creatures could be seen struggling to free themselves from its lethal grasp.

"Buna floater." Teal leaned out slightly to make sure the dirigible-sized creature was truly departing. "It's not strong enough to carry off a human, but it can kill one."

Though imposing, the floater was not the most impressive flier they saw. That honor went to a gigantic blue-black glider with tercet tooth-lined jaws longer than Flinx was tall. Possessing the wingspan of a modest-sized aircraft, it resembled nothing so much as an enormous, airborne shark.

It was quite clear why Teal and her people had come to think of the sky above the canopy as the Upper Hell. Its revelations made him all the more curious to view the Lower.

But not right away.

The remote blob of diffuse light that was this world's sun melted into the indistinct yellow-green horizon, to be replaced by the steady drumming of warm rain. Nocturnal criers commenced calling to mates, communicating with offspring and warning one another of the possible presence of concealed killers who whispered their way through the hylaea, silent shadows of death.

Chirps and barks, whistles and screeches, moans and feral hiccoughings punctuated the onset of night. Following a procedure Flinx was now familiar with, he joined Teal and her children in the back of the burnt-out cavity while the furcots formed a protective barrier along the edge of the opening. Pale, tenebrous moonlight illuminated the valley in the forest and the falling rain. It was bright enough to hint of a full moon or two, whose outline Flinx knew was masked by clouds and mist.

Surrounded by warm bodies and the thick but not unpleasant musk of the furcots, he allowed himself to drift toward sleep, Pip curled snugly atop his chest. Once, something stout and many-legged marched past directly overhead, shaking the branch with its weight. With the rain dissipating their scent, they remained safe and secure in the cavity while the tread of the unseen giant soon vanished into the distance.

He glanced down at his hands. Not only had the irritation disappeared completely, the skin was as smooth and soft as it had ever been. The juice of the O'opaa fruit not only healed, it restored. What might it do for wrinkles? Not all the wonders of this place were large and fearsome.

Bearing Teal's warning in mind as he checked his positioner, he used his body to carefully shield its internal illuminator from outside view, and as soon as he'd noted the readout, quickly shut it off. They were on course.

Dwell was dreaming, a rush of indefinable sensation Flinx had no difficulty detecting. Dreams he was able, with an effort, to shut out. It was a skill he'd been forced to learn in order to get any sleep. Easier to do here than on Moth, or Samstead, where the nocturnal cacophony of millions of sleepers would have driven him mad had he not been able to master the shut-out technique.

It struck him forcefully that he had gone three days without a headache of any kind. Not a record, but close. This world was at once soothing and deadly. That was the last thought he had before passing over into a contented sleep of his own as the rain pounded on the stems and leaves and branches outside the refuge.

He dreamed of small biting things and the comforting emollient of cool liquids. Of vast shapes filled with teeth and others that only smiled. Of slipping, and of falling, to land unharmed in a hell he could not envision.

Permeating it all was an indefinable presence, alien yet somehow reassuring, full of questions he did not understand and answers to questions he did not know how to ask. It was, not surprisingly, green as well as formless. Bursting with life, it seemed too expansive to be contained only within a dream. All velvet ties and luxurious bindings, it encompassed without restricting, enveloped without imprisoning. It strove to draw him in even as it left him free. Seeking definitions in his sleep, he found only greater mysteries.

Amidst the assurance was an anxiety that correlated well with his own. Shining through it all, like a beacon, was the need first to survive and second to comprehend.

In particular there was a distant and voluminous mass, inconceivable in size and incomprehensible in its evil, that defied understanding. With a start, that part of Flinx's mind that was conscious in sleep recognized the pit at the center of his own encounter. The darkness was stirring, and scattered matter shifted imperceptibly on a cosmic scale. From seemingly stray neutrinos on up, the infinitesimal was alert.

Anxiety. Incomprehension. Flinx swam in a pool of shared glaucous concern, trying to keep his conscious unconsciousness from drowning in confusion, unable to offer succor or solution.

But there was a possible solution. Incredibly complex, difficult beyond imagining, the legacy of great thinkers long since departed, it hovered tantalizingly on the edge of his understanding. That was because he was not yet ready.

Not yet ready, but incontestably a part of it.

He twitched in his sleep. On his chest Pip, wide-awake, her triangular head centimeters from his own, stared at the face of her master with glazed reptilian eyes. She understood nothing of what he was feeling, nothing of the torrent of sensation and information that was flooding through him, but she remained as close as possible, concerned and protective.

It was the best she could do. She was not an interpreter, but a vector.

It was the middle of the night when he sat up sharply, wide-awake and staring. In the darkness he looked around, saw only the sleeping forms of his companions. Moomadeem snuffled and kicked out with a middle leg while Dwell swatted a nonexistent bug from his face. Teal was silent and motionless. Attentive as always, Pip licked at his face.

A presence had been in the hollow, and in him. The keen reality of certain dreams is often difficult to separate from wakeful thinking. Slowly he lay back down, resting his head on his hands as he pondered all that had washed through him, trying to fix it in his conscious memory. Much of it was already beginning to fade, indistinct and senseless. Despite his drowsy state, there was one characteristic of the experience he knew he would have no difficulty recalling.

It had been very, very important.

Chapter Twelve

"Peeler!"

Aimee screamed as she started to fall. The man next to her reached out but missed. It was Chaa who reacted in time. While his body remained securely atop the swaying liana they were traversing, he was able to twist his neck sideways and down and reach for her with three of his powerful arms. One caught her by her right forearm, another by the opposite shoulder of her suit. Slowly she felt herself rising in the Mu'Atahl's grasp.

Peeler leaned over and managed to get ahold of her other arm. Together they hauled her back up through the rain and onto the liana. She promptly lay back on the rufous walkway, hands on her stomach, and fought to catch her breath.

Lit by the reflected glow of its owner's flash, a face was staring down at her; expressionless, devoid of emotion. There was, however, some concern in the voice. Not necessarily for her personally, she knew. Coerlis was worried about losing any more of his party.

"What happened?"

She took a deep breath. "Slipped. Was trying to watch something in the trees and stopped paying attention." She sat up and put her arms around her knees as she drew them in toward her chest. "It's not easy moving at night.

You're trying to watch where you're going at the same time as you're trying to be careful where you put your feet. And everything's soaked."

Coerlis looked away. "If we don't try something different it's going to take forever to catch up to him."

"I know, I know," she snapped, reaching up with a hand. Peeler took it and helped her to her feet. His simple face was full of the kind of honest worry that was alien to Coerlis. She even felt closer to Chaa.

"Thanks, guys." She wiped bits of sodden plant matter and soil from her chameleon suit.

"You can pull me up when I slip." Chaa did not smile, but he had a pretty good understanding of the range of human expression. He showed his teeth.

She hesitated, then laughed. "Right, sure. With one hand. Just don't fall too far." The Mu'Atahl weighed in the neighborhood of half a ton.

Coerlis was peering through his night-vision monocular, searching the hylaea ahead. "I don't understand why we haven't caught up with him. There's no reason for him to think he's being pursued, therefore no reason for him to be moving so fast. You'd think he'd stop in one place for a while." He lowered the opticon. "And there's only one of him, and that minidrag. By rights he should be having a harder time of it in this morass than we are."

Shielding the tracker from the rain, Chaa checked the readout. "He continues to travel more or less in a straight line, as if he has a specihfic destihnation in mihnd."

Peeler tugged on the hood of his suit and waved at the sodden, smothering verdure. "How could anybody have a destination in this? It all looks the same."

"Maybe he's just trying to cover as much ground and see as much as possible." Aimee had risen to her feet again. She reached up, straightened her hood and touched her hair. A smile lightened her expression. "At least I didn't lose my flowers." In the crisscross of artificial light the spectacular specimen continued to twinkle like a bouquet of faceted gems.

"Let's get moving." Coerlis led the way off the liana and onto a convenient, more stable branch that led in the right direction.

"Lucky, that time," Peeler told her conversationally. Noting the look on her face, he frowned. "You sure you're okay?"

Her smile returned. "Just feel a little queasy all of a sudden." She fumbled for the medkit on her belt. "I'll go ahead and take something."

"Delayed reaction to your slip," Coerlis suggested without looking back.

"Or these stinking rations we've been living off for three days." Rundle was gnawing distastefully on a soaked protein block.

Eyes flashing, Coerlis turned on the big man. "Maybe you'd like to try some of the local fruit?"

"Uh-uh, no thanks, Mr. Coerlis, sir! It might bite back."

"I'm sure some of the local vegetation is not only palatable but tasty." As always, Chaa brought up the rear. "The problem is in decihding what is edihble and what is lethal."

"Yeah." Peeler chided his associate, nudging him in the ribs. "Go on, man." He aimed his light at a cluster of swollen, bright blue cylinders hanging temptingly from a nearby epiphyte. "Take a bite out of one of those."

Rundle glared back. "How about I shove a whole one down your throat and see if you blow up?"

"Quiet," Coerlis snapped. "Unless you want to see what kind of nocturnal carnivores your babbling can attract."

The two men went silent, abashed not because their boss had chewed them out but because they knew he was right.

"We wihll snare your quarry, sihr," Chaa assured Coerlis. "If necessary, you and Aimee can rihde on my back. That would enable us to increase our pace slihghtly."

"Not worth it." Coerlis wiped a mixture of perspiration and rainwater from his face. "I want you at full strength when we reach him. We're still going to have to deal with the flying snake."

"As you wish, sihr."

A grumbling Coerlis angrily shoved a clinging creeper out of his way. "At least he's stopping for the night." Feeling thoroughly miserable, he sneezed twice despite the temperature.

As if they weren't uncomfortable enough, the lingering moonlight faded and the downpour intensified, drenching them afresh.

Peeler mumbled something unrepeatable, and even the normally unperturbable Chaa had a few choice words to say in his own language. Their meaning and intent was obvious from his inflection even if a straightforward translation was impossible.

Coerlis's light found a shadow at the base of a large parasite. Looking exactly like another, smaller tree, it grew from the heart of the branch they were traversing, its roots penetrating deep into the heartwood of the emergent and nearly straddling their chosen course.

"Hold up!" He raised his hand. Huddling against the unrelenting deluge, the others halted gratefully.

Advancing on the secondary growth, Coerlis saw that the shadow that had caught his eye was a cavity that ran all the way through, a tunnel formed by fire or disease. Or maybe, he thought, the consequent growth was the result of two parasitic trees that had grown together and merged to form a single trunk. Whatever the cause, there was room enough within to shelter all of them from the rain. Even Chaa would be able to stand up and keep dry.

"Inside," he ordered curtly. They needed no urging.

"See." Shining his light downward, the Mu'Atahl scuffed the wood underfoot with one circular pad. "The interior is slihghtly higher because of root growth. Water runs around but not insihde." He tilted his head and neck back. "The ceihling rihses higher stihll. This wihll be very comfortable for the balance of the night."

Rundle leaned back against the interior wall and let out a relieved sigh. "As long as it's dry."

Peeler was inspecting their serendipitous refuge more closely. "Funny sort of place. Doesn't look damaged."

"Neither do you," quipped the big man. Peeler started to reply, then frowned. "Hey, where's Aimee?"

"Right here." Entering, she rustled the collar of her suit to remove the clinging drops. "Just got dizzy for a moment."

Coerlis eyed her unblinkingly. "How much medication did you take earlier?"

"Enough. Relax, Jack-Jax. I'm fine."

"You still nauseous?"

"A little. It comes and goes. I'm glad you decided to stop for the rest of the night."

The merchant looked resigned. "Doesn't do any good to close the gap if half of us don't make it." Sitting down with his back against the inner wall of the cavity, he fumbled for a food packet. Peeler settled himself nearby, while the exhausted Rundle stretched out on the delightfully dry floor. Chaa languorously twisted his neck around to rest his head on his shoulder.

"Hey!" Trying to clear her head, the engineer had tilted her neck back. "Something moved up there." She raised a hand and pointed.

Coerlis swung his light to the vertical. Sure enough, there were three, four—perhaps a dozen of the tiny creatures. Each small enough to fit in his palm, the fuzzy brown shapes clung to the apex of the conical cavity. Their flat, homey faces were covered with bands of shiny black keratin. The single horn that protruded from each forehead was flanked by a pair of bulbous eyes, with the third lying below and slightly forward of the horn. Each eye was capable of swiveling independently of the others. It was disorienting to see.

Protruding between two bands of hard keratin, the coiled muzzle or mouth was thin, gray, and strawlike. The creatures had no visible teeth, and clung to the ceiling of the shelter with six stubby legs. Each foot ended in an unintimidating but obviously efficient hook.

"Impressive secondary sexual display," commented Chaa, referring to the individual horns. "Or perhaps they are for defense."

"This must be their roost." An indifferent Coerlis eased back against the wood, trying to find the least uncomfortable spot. "I don't think they'll mind sharing."

When a nervous Peeler shined his light directly on them, the cluster of brown shapes drew back into a defensive knot, blinking painfully at the illumination. He cut the intensity of the beam by three-quarters.

"Mr. Coerlis is right." A grinning Rundle waved his own light at the mass, forcing them to huddle together even tighter. "They're afraid of us."

"They just want the same thing we do." Once the source of the shadowy movement had been revealed as harmless, Peeler had relaxed. "A nice, dry night's rest."

"Kittens with alien faces." Aimee was entranced. "Listen to them." Soft burbling sounds floated down from the ceiling, sounding like bubbles popping to the surface of a quiet pond. Whether it was an expression of mutual fear or some kind of group communication, the visitors had no way of knowing. Certainly it was anything but threatening.

Rundle was still standing and shining his reduced light on the cluster. "They're cute. C'mere, little pretty." Standing on tiptoes and reaching upward, he made scratching motions in the direction of the nearest.

It immediately swelled like a balloon to three times its previous size. On the taut skin pinkish flesh was visible through the individual hairs.

The Mu'Atahl looked back. "I don't think that's such a good idea, Rundle."

The big man looked over at him. "Aw, c'mon. What're you afraid of? It's not any bigger than—ow, *damn*!" He drew back his hand sharply. "Ow, ouch, look out!" Arms crossed over his head, he bent over and tried to present only the back of his chameleon suit to the ceiling.

Coerlis had rolled to his right, colliding with the engineer as she scrabbled backward on her hands and backside. Chaa had darted out the other side of the tunnel, while Peeler lay huddled against the far side of the cavity.

With an explosive *whoosh* half a dozen of the swollen creatures had sharply contracted. The compressed, expelled air had blasted each tiny horn free of its supporting face shield. Three protruded from the back of the startled Rundle's reaching hand. Another had stuck in his forearm, two more in his shoulder, piercing the thick weave of the chameleon suit. He wrenched one from his forearm, leaving a spot of red behind.

Above him the furry shapes were starting to move.

Ignoring them, a disgusted Rundle plucked the remaining pair from the back of his hand. "Last time I try to be nice to anything on this planet," he muttered. "Hey, how about giving me a hand with these?" His head tilted back, his expression malign. "I'm gonna fry every one of the little bastards. All I wanted was to pet one."

Aimee helped him remove the rest of the horn darts, carefully working them free of his flesh. "How do you feel? Besides angry, I mean."

"Little woozy. Not too—bad. *Whoo!*" He staggered, and it was all she could do to help him sit down. Peeler was too late to help.

Instead he rested a comforting hand on his associate's shoulder. "How you feeling, man?"

"Pretty potent stuff." Rundle blinked. "Spice it up a little and I think you could find a market for it." When he looked up at them, a stupid smile dominated his expression. "Tried a couple o' shots o' kentazene once. Just for kicks, of course. Felt kind of like this."

"There." Aimee removed the last of the horn darts. Favoring it with a look of distaste, she flung it out into the rain.

Employing a very subdued beam, Chaa was cautiously studying the inhabitants of the ceiling. "I wonder how long it takes them to grow new ones? It seems to be an effective defense. It's not necessary to kihll. Only to discourage. Any predator taking a couple of those in the face would most lihkely stagger off, stunned and destablized."

The engineer nodded ceilingward. "Look," she whispered.

It was clear now there were more than a dozen of the creatures. They had been so densely packed together that their true numbers had been effectively concealed. She counted twenty, thirty of them, making their laborious way down the sloping flanks of the cavity. Several simply rolled into balls, released their grip on the ceiling and dropped. They bounced a couple of times, unfolded themselves, and started crawling, their protruding, staring eyes fixed on Rundle's seated form.

Aimee rose, nervously using her light to scan the floor near her feet. "Come on, we've got to get out of here. Get up, Rundle."

"Why?" He smiled happily up at her. "It's the first night since we landed I haven't been soaked through."

Chaa was beckoning from out in the rain. "Outside, everyone. Now. We must get out of range." Coerlis was standing next to him. Eyeing his friend reluctantly, Peeler hesitated. There was an explosive pop and a dart horn struck his service belt. He nearly fell over his own legs in his haste to get clear.

Covering her head with her hands, Aimee started to retreat. Rundle grinned at her as he scuttled backward on his hands and feet, and propped himself up against the wall.

"What're you all afraid of? I can handle this."

One of the little creatures was approaching his right boot. Contemptuously, he drew back his leg and kicked out, sending it spinning all the way across the cavity. Fetching up against the far side, it righted itself, fluffed out its fur, and started back in Rundle's direction as if nothing had happened.

More of the fuzzballs were dropping from the ceiling and crawling down the walls. A wary Chaa inclined his neck for a better look.

"There must be another hollow high up inside the growth. There are many still emerging." Peeler's expression was grim. Coerlis peered inside enigmatically.

Aimee was pulling at Rundle's shirt. "Come on, you've got to get out of here!"

A powerful arm flung her aside. "No way! This is *our* tree!" Fumbling at his waist, he drew his needler and began waving it about.

Coerlis flinched. "Shit! Put that thing away, Chet! Aimee, get out of there!" The engineer hesitated, then stumbled out into the rain.

"Go ahead and soak if you want." Rundle returned his attention to the interior of the tree. "I'm stayin'." Taking careful aim, he fired once.

Following the familiar sizzle, something burbled loudly. The stink of burnt flesh filled the interior of the growth. Rundle's burst had caught one of the crawlers face-on, reducing it to a smoking shell.

Squinting, he fired again. Half its body gone, the crawler spun over and over, its long tongue uncoiling to flick futilely at its missing self.

Rundle grinned out at his wary, sodden onlookers. "Hell, this is fun!" Raising his aim, he neatly picked a crawler off the far wall. "You're all missin' out." Another fuzzball nearing his right foot was sent flying, its torso carbonized.

"Chet's right." Peeler started back. "A couple of minutes and we can have this place cleaned out."

"No!" Lunging forward, Chaa swept the man aside.

Peeler rolled over on the branch and climbed furiously to his feet. "Hey, what'd you do that for!"

"Look." The Mu'Atahl pointed to the wooden surface just outside the entrance.

It was lined with horn hypos. At least twenty of the creatures must have fired in Peeler's direction when he'd taken his step forward.

"Son of a bitch," the bodyguard muttered as he eyed the spines sticking out of the wood.

Chaa had retreated another couple of steps down the branch. "They are swarmihng ihnside now, eager to protect their home. Without armor, no one can get back ihn."

Aimee crouched down on the branch, struggling to see into the cavity through the darkness and steady downpour. "Chet, how're you doing in there?"

"You hurtin', man?" Peeler asked anxiously.

"Are you kidding?" They could hear the methodical sizzle of his needler above the downpour. "Maybe this juice freezes the local life, but it feels pretty swell to me. *Blammo*, got two with one shot that time! You just relax out there. I'll have this place sterilized in five minutes." Again the electronic surge of the needler flared above the drumming precipitation.

Water dripping from his long snout, Chaa glanced over at Coerlis. "We have no choihce. Anyone attempting to reenter rihsks an unknown number of punctures."

"So what?" They turned to Peeler, a shadow brooding in the rain. "They don't seem to be doing Chet any harm. He sounds higher than the ship. Hell, he sounds better than any of us has since we landed here." He stared into the dry, inviting cavity. "He's having such a damn good time in there I'm tempted to join him."

"It's a little early to draw any conclusions, Peeler. Hopeful or otherwise." Coerlis was eyeing the tunnel thoughtfully. "Rundle seems convinced he has the situation under control. All well and good, but I don't see any reason to expose any of the rest of us to potential danger at this time. We'll stay out here and monitor the situation within."

They stood or sat in the miserable rain, forced to listen to Rundle's delighted whoops from within. One time he announced, hardly able to control his laughter, that he'd nearly shot his own boot off while picking a crawler off his toe. The smell of burnt flesh from within the hollow was strong enough now to reach them even out on the sodden branch.

After a while the steady hiss of the needler faded. Aimee rose and, disregarding Coerlis's expression, cautiously approached the opening. The light from Rundle's beam showed clear and strong.

"Rundle? Chet, have you finished your party yet?"

"Careful," Chaa warned her.

"I don't see anything moving." She was very close to the entrance now. Bending, she scanned the interior, using her own beam to supplement Rundle's. "I don't see anything on the ceiling, or around the edge here."

"Maybe the fool's done it, made it safe. And had a good time doing it to boot." Coerlis moved to join her.

That's when she screamed. She continued to scream as the others crowded around her. Chaa uttered a private outrage in his guttural tongue while Peeler started mumbling under his breath. Only Coerlis said nothing. His curses and self-admonitions were composed silently.

At least the alien narcotic that had been injected into the big man's system seemed to have forestalled any discomfort. Rundle wore a broad smile of contentment. Much broader than usual because his head, like the rest of him, had collapsed into the remainder of his body. Only his skeleton retained any semblance of the human shape.

"Lihquification." The Mu'Atahl stared stonily into the tree. "The soft parts of his body, everythihng except the hard endoskeleton, have been turned to lihquihd. Some powerful enzyme ihn the narcotihc. Prey that ihsn't sufferihng struggles less."

"Like with a spider," Peeler whispered.

"Yes, like a spider." Coerlis was equally mesmerized by the gruesome sight. "You might as well stop screaming, Aimee. It won't do you or us any good, and Rundle can't hear you."

Her chest rising and falling violently, the engineer fought to calm herself.

The spongy, gooey mass that had recently been Rundle lay on the floor of the cavity like a blob of lumpy gelatin. Dozens, perhaps hundreds, of the brown-furred crawlers swarmed over it, thronging with turgid deliberation. Many had already embcdded their coiled snouts in the gluey mound and lay quiescent, sucking contentedly. Their bodies expanded perceptibly as they drank, siphoning up the nutrients that had recently combined differently to form a human being. Rundle's alien constitution was no inhibition. Protein, apparently, was protein.

"We may as well leave this place." Chaa shook raindrops from his snout. "There's nothihng more we can do here."

Coerlis agreed. "The stupid shit." A stirring in the night made him whirl. There was a shadow, a damp whisper in the leaves. He saw nothing more. His hands started to shake and he willed them steady, hoping that in the dark his moment of weakness hadn't been noticed by any of the others.

There were four of them now. Only four. Seeing his engineer continuing to stare blankly into the hollow, he grabbed her arm and spun her toward him, getting right up into her face.

"Forget it, *understand*? You want to watch until there's nothing left? Want to see if the bones dissolve, too? Think about it too much and it'll be just as bad for you as it was for Rundle."

She nodded jerkily. As his eyes challenged hers, he gave a gentle but unrelenting tug on her arm, turning her away from the secondary growth and back into the downpour. With Coerlis serving as guide, she allowed herself to be led away into the night. Peeler moved out in front, warier than ever, while Chaa placed himself between the rest of them and the tree. The light from Rundle's flickering beam gradually vanished behind them, swallowed up by the deluge and the night.

Chapter Thirteen

Flinx awoke with a start. Prodigious concepts slipped rapidly from the grasp of consciousness, sudden wakefulness serving to nudge a procession of alien thoughts just beyond comprehension. Dream worlds became subsumed in reality, swept away like shells on a wave-scoured beach.

It was still dark out and the night rain continued its fall unabated. Watching and listening, he felt as if he could cast himself into the curtain of water and swim off into the sky. It was the day's transpiration reversed, a kind of aerial communication between plant and atmosphere. Not privy to its subtler meanings, he was reduced to contemplating the poetry of it.

No thunder tonight, he realized, and not a breath of wind. He was aware of a warm and pleasantly rounded shape pressing up against him. Peering down in the dim light, he saw that Teal was awake and staring openly up at him. Her eyes were the hidden green of the forest, and when she smiled gently, her teeth flashed like the sun that had not yet risen. She had removed her cloak and simple, hand-woven garments and lay close, browned and open, her body adorned only by echoes of moonlight.

"Teal," he began, "I don't—"

She put a finger to his lips. She was older than him, but not by much, and her diminutive yet perfectly proportioned form made her appear younger. On this world he was the vulnerable one, not her.

Sensing the rising tide of conflicted emotions in her master, Pip stirred uneasily on his chest. Beginning with the jaws, a yawn passed through her, transformed into a muscular ripple that concluded with a last quiver of the tip of her tail. Half asleep, she slithered off his sternum and coiled peacefully against the very back of the cavity.

"I like your pet," Teal whispered. "Sometimes perception is better than intelligence."

Flinx found that he was trapped between her naked form and the slumberous green mountain that was Saalahan. Near their feet the children slept on, oblivious to the rest of the world. Moomadeem and Tuuvatem lay curled about one another like a pair of matching green salt and pepper shakers.

As near as Flinx could tell, his emotions and Teal's were the only ones active.

"You were dreaming," she whispered. "I know; I was watching you. What do you dream of, Flinx?"

"I can't remember," he replied honestly. "Different things. Big and small, bright and dark, green and black, cool and hot."

Nearly as supple as Pip, her arms flowed across his chest to meet behind his neck. "I like hot."

"Your mate—he just died," Flinx reminded her, keeping his voice down.

She sighed. "Jerah is gone. He has returned to the world. If I were gone and he were here and you were a suitable woman, he would not have waited this long."

"On my world it's customary to wait a little while."

"Then you must have time to waste on your world. Here life is threatened by too many things to lose it also to hesitation." She lowered her head, resting it on his stomach. "I have two children to care for, a much simpler task when two adults are present. My own parents help, but they are old and cannot stray from the Home-tree. I am fortunate they are both still living." She challenged his gaze with her own.

"Life here belongs to the quick, Flinx. Dwell and Kiss need a male parent. You have said that you are not mated."

"That's true."

"You are very ignorant of many basic things." This was uttered matter-of-factly, without any hint of insult. "But you learn quickly. And you are big, though not as strong as you might be. You are strong in other ways, and seem to me to be a good person."

"Teal . . ." He struggled to find the right words. "I'm not interested in mating with you. I'm not interested," he added swiftly, "in mating with *anyone*."

Lifting her head, she studied him curiously. "Why? Where you come from is there a rule or law against it? Have you rites of maturity still to complete?"

"No, it's nothing like that." He thought of the women he'd known; Lauren Walder and Atha Moon, Raileen Ts-Dennis and most recently and especially, the wonderful Clarity Held. There were even fond memories of one called Sylzenzuzex, who had not been human. "It's just that I'm not ready."

Propping her chin in one palm, she regarded him intently. "How old are you, Flinx? How many years?"

"Twenty. I think."

"Then you have been old enough for several years, and still have not mated."

He knew that her night vision was better than his, and wondered if she could see him blushing. "Like I said, in my society we tend to wait a little longer."

"We have no time to wait," she informed him somberly. "Here it is important to mate and produce children as soon as possible. If we were to wait, every tribe would soon pass from being. Even on the third level people die frequently, and young.

"If anything were to happen to me, I know that Dwell and Kiss would care honorably for my place in the Tree. They would maintain the balance."

"More talk of balance. If the human tribes increase, doesn't that upset the balance here?"

She blinked at him. "Of course not. For each human there is a furcot."

"Right. I'd forgotten about that." No need to tell her he still didn't understand that special relationship between human and beast. She would just try to explain further, or think of him as more ignorant than she already did.

Her voice was as gentle as the rain dripping off the lip of the shelter. "One can mate without forswearing permanence, Flinx."

He would have backed away, but there was nowhere to go. "What, here?" he stammered skittishly. As he pushed up against Saalahan, the big furcot grunted in its sleep. "Your children are right there. So are the furcots."

Her smile enlightened the darkness. "What a strange place it must be where you come from, where people hide natural things from each other. To think of mating with me here makes you uncomfortable, doesn't it?"

She didn't need any special talent to sense that, he knew. "We have something called privacy."

"So do we, but mating is more important than privacy."

"If we were at your Home-tree—" he began.

"But we are not," she interrupted him. "We are here, where there is still some safety in numbers. So everything must be done in numbers."

"Sorry. I do things in private, on a one-to-one basis. Not," he added quickly, "that I find you unattractive."

"Then you *do* find me worthy of mating with?" Her tone was at once ingenuous and coquettish.

"Of course."

"Then that will have to be enough for now." She contented herself with the small victory. "Tomorrow I will show you something that may make you not worry about such things so much. I saw them when we found this place but had no time to gather any. Tomorrow I will give you a treat, and you will not worry so much about privacy."

Flinx started to explain that he not only enjoyed but needed his privacy, that he was in fact one of the most private people he knew, but he didn't want to disappoint her any further. Since he didn't know what she was talking about, he saw no point in prolonging the encounter.

But he didn't object when she laid her head on his chest and closed her eyes.

The rain ceased early. It seemed that he'd just dropped back off to sleep when their overnight refuge was once again awash in yellow-green light.

One at a time they climbed out, Saalahan effortlessly giving Flinx a boost to the top of the branch. Their emergence was greeted by a flock of opportunistic aerial predators. Soaring low on silvered wings evolved to blind prospective prey, they beat in frustration with meter-wide wings at the curtain of protective vines.

Saalahan dismissed them with a derisive snort that was mimicked in comical fashion by the two younger furcots. Meanwhile Teal had leaped lithely from the broad branch on which they stood to a smaller one nearby and slightly lower down, indifferent to the thirty-meter drop between.

As Flinx looked on, she shinnied up a thigh-thick vine that was striped with blue, carefully avoiding several nearby that to his eye looked exactly the same. Reaching a knot formed by two woody creepers, she vanished into an explosion of enormous purple and red blossoms whose oversized stamens were a bright, metallic gold.

"What's she doing?"

Saalahan only grunted, leaving it to Kiss to explain. "Mother is gathering something." She toyed with her chestnut tresses.

"Food." It struck Flinx that his stomach was not aching because Teal had spent some time resting her head against it, but from a demanding emptiness.

"No." Morning muted Dwell's gruffness. "No food in a Tolling bush. Maybe beyond."

"Is that what those flowers are called?"

"Of course." The boy's sharp-edged tone returned. "Don't you know anything?"

"Very little," Flinx confessed.

Teal wasn't gone long. She retraced her steps, making the same death-defying leap back to the main branch with the same casual aplomb as before. With a prideful smile she opened one of her gathering pouches, filled now with thumb-sized yellow fruit, and then found a place to sit. Saalahan chided her, urging that they move deeper into the forest before pausing to eat.

"Oh, hush, Saalahan. Set your big green backside down somewhere and relax. This is a special place. Maybe we'll spend another night here."

"Lazy." The big furcot sniffed. It lumbered off into the arboreal veldt, the two younger ones following like a pair of six-legged green bears trailing their mother.

Thanks to their coloring, they vanished from sight almost immediately.

Looking on, it was difficult for Flinx not to envision some sort of familial relationship existing between them. Once again Teal insisted it just wasn't so.

Idly stroking Pip, he stared out through the curtain of vines across the valley in the forest. "Won't we be in danger up here without the furcots?"

"People can look after themselves without furcots." She gestured to her son. "Dwell, sit sentry."

The boy beamed as his mother handed him the long tube she had been carrying strapped to her back. For the first time Flinx got a good look at the snuffler. Hewn from a special hardwood that remained green even after curing, the tapering weapon was a deft blend of half-remembered high-tech and determined improvisation. Keeping his fingers clear of the hand-tooled trigger, Dwell also took charge of a sack of gas-filled membranes and a quiver of poisoned darts.

Settling himself in a crook where a smaller branch met its parent, he steadied the snuffler on his legs, stuffed one of the globular membranes into the opening in the rear, closed the cover, and let his gaze rove the surrounding environment. Unless something in the way of an immediate threat manifested itself, the lethal darts would remain safely in their protective quiver.

Thus positioned, Flinx decided, the boy looked considerably older than his ten years.

Kiss wandered freely, studying crawlers and plants but never straying far from the two adults or her brother. No matter how focused she became on any object of curiosity, she always looked up to check and evaluate her surroundings every couple of minutes.

Sitting across from Teal, Flinx watched with interest as she removed a hand-carved wooden disk from her backpack. It looked as if it had been sliced whole from a benign gourd. From her water jug she poured a small amount of liquid onto the center of the disk. Instantly it began to swell and thicken, the sides curving upward. Once it had absorbed all the available moisture, the result was an impermeable bowl that, when dehydrated, could be packed flat for easier transport.

Taking the small yellow fruits from her pouch, she carefully squeezed them over the bowl one at a time, discarding the pulp. When she was through, she removed a small sack from her backpack and dumped the flourlike contents in with the juice. A small mixing stick stirred the combination to a thick paste.

When Kiss returned with a double handful of blue-black berries, her mother added them to the mash. The result was not only visually pleasing but smelled of a promising alien tartness.

"Now what?" asked Flinx when it seemed that no additional ingredients were to be forthcoming.

Teal smiled. "We wait."

"For what?"

"For the sun to work its magic."

It didn't look much like magic to Flinx. As the morning wore on she added a second species of berry, this one orange and pear-shaped, and more water.

Eventually the furcots returned, the young ones exhibiting an unexpected delicacy of touch as they dumped two unbruised mouthfuls of some heavy cream-colored tuber on the branch. Saalahan's contribution was a stubby-legged two-meter long tree-dweller that looked like a giant nude mink, which Teal expertly gutted and filleted.

The furcots then filled a space atop the branch with dried wood and tinder, and the mink fillet joined the tubers in an embracing fire. There was no fear of it spreading. Not when every centimeter of exposed vegetation existed in a condition of permanent damp.

Flinx found the meal nourishing if without excitement. After the first swallow, Pip downed choice bits of meat without hesitation, though she balked at the roasted tuber. A few unsoused berries completed her breakfast, leaving her bulging contentedly in the middle. The fact that the flying snake was an opportunistic omnivore surprised most who encountered her, but Teal and her children accepted the minidrag's diet without question.

The moisture in Teal's fermenting surprise kept the bowl hydrated and prevented it from returning to its original shape. Only when they had finished eating did she offer it to him, eyes shining.

"Disiwin," she told him, as if that explained everything.

He eyed the syrupy red-orange liquid dubiously. "What's it supposed to do?"

"Make you feel good. Help you to see clearly. Drink, and forget about silly privacies." She giggled like a schoolgirl.

He wondered how he could politely refuse the local beer or whatever it was, and decided he couldn't. Not after she had gathered the main ingredients and brewed it herself. Mindful as he accepted the bowl of the precipitous drop on either side of the branch, he prayed it didn't contain a powerful hallucinogen, or if it did, that he'd retain sense enough not to see if he could fly.

Sensing his discomfort, she reassured him. "Don't worry, Flinx. Saalahan knows how disiwin affects persons. The furcots will watch over us." When still he hesitated, her expression fell. "You won't try it with me?"

"I don't know. It's just that I haven't had a headache since I've been here. Not even a twinge." He studied the colorful concoction. "I'd hate to induce one voluntarily."

"Headache?" She frowned. "What's that?"

He touched various places on his head. "Pain, throbbing aches, here and here."

Her reaction was a mixture of concern and amazement. "I've never heard of such a thing."

"Are you telling me that your people don't get headaches? All humans get headaches."

She shook her head guilelessly. "I don't know what you're talking about."

He steadied himself. "Maybe after I drink some of this stuff you will." He brought the rim of the bowl to his lips, then lowered it slightly. "How much should I take?"

"Half. There isn't a lot."

There really wasn't. When he'd taken his share he handed the bowl back to her, wiping his lips with the back of one hand. He watched as she slowly, almost ceremoniously, drained the remainder of the bowl's contents.

He felt no different. Surely a few swallows of berries, juice, and water couldn't upset his equilibrium *that* much. It wasn't as if he'd chugged a liter or two of hard liquor.

She patted the wooden surface next to her. "Here, Flinx. Come and lie down beside me."

Wary of the children's proximity, he moved to comply. The hard, unyielding wood beneath his spine was reassuring. Overhead, the brilliant mottled green of the hylaea soared another hundred fifty meters to meet the sky.

Without question the most extraordinary world he'd ever visited, he decided. Too extraordinary to have been overlooked and forgotten. Feeling his eyelids growing heavy, he allowed them to close. Something like a living rainbow flashed by on wings of translucent carmine.

A sleep potion, he thought. Nothing more. Or perhaps it affected Teal's people differently. If so, she was about to be disappointed. He determined that a midday siesta was a fine idea.

He felt Teal take his left hand in her right and squeeze gently. That was the extent of physical contact, allowing him to relax even more.

A bath, he avowed silently. He was floating in a warm bath of carbonated milk, not a muscle tensed in his body. Yellow-green warmth enveloped him completely, permeating his entire being. It blossomed to encompass Teal, the branch they were lying on, and the gigantic tree beneath whose crown they were reposing.

Billions, trillions, of individual growths paraded in grand and leisurely procession at the edge of his awareness. Their fronds reached out to caress him; sometimes tickling, sometimes soothing, at other times healing wounds he hadn't known he'd had.

How, he found himself wondering in the midst of his bath, did the bases of the great boles keep from rotting? The soil at the surface must be saturated all the time. How deep went the dirt that formed the top of what Teal referred to as the Lower Hell? A few meters, a dozen, a hundred? If the latter, what colossal equivalent of earthworms probed and prodded and turned the unimaginably productive loam? He thought he could see them, blind and pale and wide as whales, working their way over and around roots the size of starships.

He saw the Home-tree with its symbiotic vines-of-own, now modified to accommodate the presence of people. The people of the six tribes were there also, living and loving and, most important of all, surviving in a place where no human was designed to survive. All living things great and small he encountered while floating in the warm bath of himself.

Teal lay next to him, drifting but not distant. The children were nearby, alert and watchful, understanding if not quite comprehending. They weren't old enough, not yet. A little farther off he sensed the comforting, slightly fuzzy mental meanderings of the furcots, attentive and independent, and something more.

Pervading the entire surging, bloated, deeply interlocked ocean of life was a maternal greenness that made him feel as if he were an infant nestled once again safely against its mother's bosom. That was remarkable because try as he sometimes did, he'd never been able to remember her.

Here was a different kind of mother; the boundless, globe-girdling forest, matriarch and life-giver to all who dwelled within, be they the monarch of all trees or the smallest peeper clinging to the tip of a bare branch. The furcots were a part of that, perhaps a more important and less enigmatic part than Teal's people or anyone else suspected.

Her ancestors had bent and twisted themselves to fit into that forest. Those who hadn't, who had fought against accommodation and assimilation and sought to remain apart, had perished.

A stabbing pain made him wince in his sleep. It had no physical source and it went straight through him. Not a headache, though. It was a touch of the darkness he had experienced not so very long ago, a splinter of that vast, amorphous evil that existed far beyond the range of any human perception.

Except his own. Even that was not entirely valid, he knew, since he was not wholly human, having suffered callous prenatal modifications over which he'd had no control.

As before, it frightened him, just as it frightened the all-pervading greenness that cradled him. Impossible as it seemed, there was a chance it could be dealt with, manipulated, turned aside. Even as the bright spark bloomed in his mind it began to dissipate before he could fully grasp it. Away it fled, into the deepest recesses of his mind. But this time it was not lost.

He was that spark, he realized. Only he could do battle with that incomprehensibly immense evil. Not alone, but with assistance. With the aid of a triangle of great forces.

One flashed instantly to mind, startling him because it had been so long since he'd thought of it. A single machine, an ancient device left behind by a civilization clever enough to build but not to survive. It continued to function, dormant and waiting, on a far-distant world. Just as he knew it, it knew him, for he had once unconsciously utilized it to save friends. It remained resting, and Flinx knew he had not been forgotten.

Second was the greenness, expansive and eager to help, but innocent of much of its power. Anarchic by definition, it required another source to supply focus. Not what he was, Flinx sensed, but what he could become.

Completing the triangle was a mind he felt he knew but did not recognize. Greatly expanding and hugely developed, it dwelled in ignorance of its importance to the triad. If the effort was to have any chance of success, all three components of the triangle had to be brought together, for a two-sided triangle cannot stand.

The triad was a weapon, the most impressive never envisioned. Once brought together in a harmonious whole, all that would be lacking was a single vital component.

It was not what those well-meaning but misguided thinkers who had tinkered with him while he was in the womb had intended when they had vectored his genes, but it was what had resulted.

I am a trigger, he realized with stunning clarity.

A unique destiny, he realized—if indeed he was thinking. It was probably fortunate he was not, at least not in the commonly accepted sense. The evil he would one day be forced to confront could not be comprehended by a mere human mind, however singularly adjusted.

Terrifying and soul-destroying enough to know that it was preparing to move.

He thought that was the end and saw that it was not. Because there was another device; not a component of the triangle, but one that had been left behind on another world eons ago by a race of daring and resourceful builders. Having sourced the location and strength of the evil and realized they were incapable of resisting it, they had constructed a much larger device to transport themselves to a place where not even it could follow. And not only themselves, but their immediate neighborhood.

Flinx was shown the device, and its still functioning consequentialities, and was left breathless and awed.

Even as this was taking place, a part of him wondered how the greenness had come to know about it, and how it was presently being imprinted on his own mind and soul. His wonderings were swept aside by an overwhelming, imploring urgency.

The triad must perforce be joined, before it was too late.

This was something he would have to do on his own, he saw. For while the greenness was expansive of thought, it was constrained by what it was.

A dream, he mused. A dream of a bath of carbonated warm milk. Nothing more than a product of his imagination, fired by the disiwin Teal had fed him. He smiled in his bath. Disiwin—dizzy wine. Suitable.

With the realization that one is dreaming comes inevitably a reassessment of one's condition, followed by an urgent desire to Wake Up.

He blinked and sat erect. A smiling, contented Teal lay next to him.

"Did you have good thoughts, Flinx? Do you feel all right?"

"Yes. Yes, I do." Fully awake, he took in the enveloping hylaea, the glistening arboreals, the brilliant-hued flowers, the vines and lianas and epiphytes and symbiotes. Each flaunting independence, it seemed impossible they could all be tightly interconnected. Yet there was no denying that they were, the whole unimaginably greater than the sum of its parts. It was an analogy that could be extended further, beyond the boundaries of any single world, to encompass entire systems, star clusters, galaxies.

And all of it under threat.

He shook his head. That had been *some* dream. Why should he think of the Krang, in a place like this? Years ago, it had been. The Tar-Aiym weapon was real enough, as was the evil the Ulru-Ujurrians had thrust him toward. What was their place in all this? Were they the third component of the triad? Somehow they didn't seem to fit, though he could hardly rule them out.

What triad? It was only a dream. He rubbed his palm along the branch, scraping skin on the rough bark. The pain was reassuring, a sharp not-a-dream.

Feeling a tickle on his cheek, he glanced down to see Pip anxiously caressing him with the end of her tongue. Smiling, he ran two fingers down her head and neck, along her spine.

Her triangular head.

Now he was drawing absurdities out of a dream, he admonished himself angrily. He was twenty years old. Absurd to expect him to deal with anything more dangerous than a taloned flier or sharp-toothed climbing carnivore. How could he bring together forces as vast as individual world-minds and the ultimate product of Tar-Aiym civilization? He had trouble enough trying to decide if he wanted to sleep with the woman next to him!

What was the critical third component of the triad?

Damnably *persistent* dream!

How many millennia before the threat made itself dangerously proximate? Or was Time nothing more than an indifferent observer here, to be paid off with cheap visceral reaction and hastily cast aside? When was too late? he wondered.

When he was no longer available to participate?

He'd spend some time with Teal, he told himself. Help her the rest of the way to her home, spend some time with her people, study and enjoy this world, and then depart. Back to Moth, perhaps. A place he could understand, comprehend. Or maybe Terra, or New Riviera, worlds where mind as well as body could find rest. Worlds that wouldn't torment him with incomprehensible dream scenarios on a cosmic scale, that wouldn't try to fix him with unwanted, impossible responsibilities.

Gingerly he felt his head. There was no pain, no lingering side effects, no dreaded pounding. As was to be expected if all had been nothing more than an elaborate dream.

If only he could forget some of it, any of it, even a little of it.

Teal's smile had faded and she was sitting up now, inspecting his face with concern. "Are you sure you're all right, Flinx? You look—strange."

"Just a dream." He forced a smile of his own.

She responded hesitantly but hopefully. "Many dream deep while under the influence of disiwin. Was it a good dream?"

"I don't know." He brought his knees up to his chest. "I don't know if it was a good dream or a bad dream. All I know for sure is that it was a big dream. Food for thought."

" 'Food for thought,' " she repeated. Then she nodded knowingly. "Ah! You have had a vision. They are also a consequence of drinking disiwin."

"I've had *something*," he told her. "I'm just not sure what."

"A vision is a blessing."

He looked at her sharply. "Believe me, I'd be more than happy to share this one. Have you had visions, Teal?"

"Oh, yes!" Her expression turned wistful. "Of flying, of fighting a baranop, of other people's children. What was your vision like?"

"It's not easy to describe. It concerned something I may—have to do."

"Have to do? But why?"

He looked away, out over the depression in the forest, at the fliers and gliders and brilliant-winged inhabitants of the canopy. "Because there may not be anyone else able to do it. I don't particularly want to do this thing, I might very well be able to avoid doing it, but I'm afraid I may have no choice."

"Having an important vision confers responsibility." Shifting on the branch, she sat next to him and put her arm around his shoulders. There was nothing sexual about it, nothing even especially friendly. She was just holding him, trying to help even though she didn't, couldn't, understand. It made him feel worthy in a way the disiwin dream had not.

He couldn't linger, he knew. Not because of the dream, but because there was something inside him that was always pulling him on, dragging him to the next world, the next experience, the next place. Irresistible, inexorable, it frequently led him away from comfort and ease into danger and difficulty. It was as much a part of him as any organ, and to him just as real.

Nor could he conceive of taking her with him. Away from her hylaea, her all-encompassing forest, she would be as lonely and helpless and sorrowful as a bird-of-paradise suddenly dropped in the middle of a desert. True tropicals could not make friends with buzzards. The sounds and stinks of a city would be enough to impoverish her soul.

Under the circumstances he did all he felt he could; he put his arm around her and held her in return.

Nearby, the big furcot watched the two humans while munching on the last of the nude mink.

"What are they doing, Saalahan?" Tuuvatem inquired respectfully.

The great, tusked head inclined in the youngster's direction. "Comforting one another."

"But neither is wounded," Moomadeem pointed out.

"I know. It is a strange way of human persons. They comfort each other even in the absence of injury. They imagine pain for themselves, invent agonies where there is no cause."

"Why would they do that?" Tuuvatem's three eyes were wide with innocence.

"I don't know," Saalahan replied candidly. "It is a characteristic peculiar to human persons. No other creature does such a thing."

"It seems wasteful," commented Moomadeem.

"I agree. I don't pretend to understand it. I'm not sure the human persons understand it themselves. It is just a thing that is."

"This odd new human person," Moomadeem asked, changing the subject, "do you think he will stay with Teal and her cubs?"

"I don't know that, either."

"Impossible," declared Tuuvatem. "He has no furcot."

"No, but he has the pretty flying thing. The bond between them is not unlike that between human and furcot. Similar, yet different. Maybe it is enough."

"Perhaps where this Flinx human comes from the human persons all have little flying creatures instead of furcots," Moomadeem suggested.

"Perhaps," Saalahan admitted with just a touch of condescension.

They watched the persons for a time before Moomadeem spoke again. "Saalahan, I know that Dwell is my human, but humans come out of other humans. Where do we come from?"

"The same place that gives life to everything: from the great forest."

"I know that everything comes from the forest *originally*," Moomadeem replied. "Even humans, originally. But I have seen them born into the world, and I have learned that it takes two adult humans to make one new one. What does it take to make a furcot, and why is a furcot made whenever a human is born?"

"Balance," the elder explained. "Balance is everything. Without a person a furcot dies. Without a furcot a person may live, but never for as long, and only with great difficulty. Without furcots I think all the persons would die out."

"And what would be the danger of that?"

Saalahan considered thoughtfully before responding. "Perhaps it is important for the balance of the world for there to be persons in it. Certainly they make life much more interesting."

"Yes, that's true," Moomadeem admitted. "Dwell has never failed to amuse me with his antics, nor Kiss, either."

"Then perhaps that is our purpose." As Saalahan shifted its great bulk, bark was rubbed away beneath it. "To be amused by persons and to help them survive. There are far worse kinds of existence. You could be a panic beetle, for instance, growing inside in a tree for years only to come forth and flash the light for a few days, frantic to mate before death overcomes you."

"That would be a poor existence," Moomadeem had to admit.

"Much better to be a furcot with a person of your very own." Saalahan turned back to the humans and the gamboling children. "No matter how deeply this flying creature satisfies the needs of the new person, I feel badly that he has no furcot to look after him. At times he seems content, and at others, very troubled. I sense that he is happy with his small companion yet unhappy within himself." A huge claw dug idly at one nostril.

"And that, Moomadeem cub, is worse than being a panic beetle."

Following Teal's suggestion, they ended up spending another night safe within the spectacular surrounds of the burnt-out cavity in the side of the branch. That night, the rain clouds did not gather for several hours after sunset. For the first time since he'd entered orbit, Flinx was allowed a glimpse of the world's two large moons. As viewed from the planet's surface, their dominance of the night sky was total.

They cast a doubled glow across the valley in the trees, occasionally illuminating the passage of some great nocturnal predator as it passed by on silent wings. Their pure, unsullied light revealed for the first time the remarkable night-blooming plants that had heretofore been concealed by darkness and rain. Tinted a thousand shades of gray, an entirely new and compelling vista burst forth to satisfy his hungry eyes.

Like a fistful of knives flung at the inner canopy, a flock of sharp-spined predators slashed into the trees. Out of many, just a few emerged victorious, only to have their catch contested by those of their companions who had failed. Their eerie, piercing cries echoed across the moonlit valley, fading as they covered distance in their battle for aerial supremacy.

Several broke away to pursue a cluster of thickly feathered fruit eaters. Instead of wings, their torpedo-shaped bodies were entirely surrounded by a cylindrical tube that pushed them through the air in fits and starts. Capable of phenomenal but brief bursts of speed, they plunged with much agitated squawking into the canopy in search of cover and safety.

"*Quinifers.*" Teal rose on one arm to point. "They can turn very sharply, but they have poor vision. Once, an entire flock flew into our shaman's house. We picked them off the ground, dazed, and caressed them until they recovered. They are not good to eat. Too many tendons and ligaments."

Flinx's talent had chosen to take some time off, and try as he would, he couldn't sense what she was really feeling. So he simply nodded understanding as something with three enormous yellow eyes went flapping past, looking like a runaway pawnshop symbol with wings. Everywhere you turned, another zoological or botanical wonder manifested itself, fairly begging to be classified. Once again he realized that this planet was a xenotaxonomist's dream—or nightmare. He would be very much surprised if it did not contain the most extensive and diverse biota of any world yet discovered.

He leaned back against Teal and half closed his eyes. It was a terrible thing to be cursed with curiosity. "A vision of responsibility," Teal had more or less called it. Try as he might, he knew he would be unable to cast it aside.

On balance, he would far rather have had a headache.

Chapter Fourteen

The morning dawned clear, beautiful, and sultry, as the last of the night-rain dripped and coursed from the tips of leaves and down the flanks of trees and creepers, beginning its long journey toward the distant regions of the Lower Hell. The majority of the moisture would never reach the surface. It would be caught and trapped along the way by expansive bromeliads, enterprising epiphytes, aerial roots, and thirsty fauna.

The sleepy occupants of the cavity stretched and yawned. It was Dwell who announced that he would be first to see if he could find something fresh and surprising for breakfast. Nimble as a cat, he scrambled over the back of a drowsy Saalahan and up over the edge of the opening.

Still suffering from the effects of his epiphanic vision of the day before, Flinx did his best to loosen cramped muscles as the youngster's feet disappeared from view. A fall from the branch could have been fatal, but he no longer worried about the children's safety. They were infinitely more agile and confident clambering about the forest tangles than he ever would be. For a few moments they heard Dwell rustling about atop the branch. Then his movements grew muffled and faint.

Flinx glanced back at Teal. She was truly lovely, he decided. Difficult to believe she had two half-grown offspring. Trying to assay her emotions, he found that he could not. At the moment, his frustratingly erratic abilities were not functioning. Tomorrow likely would be different, or tonight.

No matter. The look on her face conveyed a good sense of what she was feeling.

Mother Mastiff would have approved of her, but then Mother Mastiff would have approved of anyone. All that irascible old woman had ever wanted was for her adopted son to find someone to share his life with, settle down in one place, and be happy. Unfortunately, the older he grew the more unlikely it seemed that there would be room in his life for any such charmingly domestic developments. He'd been born to something else, and was still in the process of finding out what that might be.

The shouting from above came as a surprise. Howls and screeches, bellows and roars he would have expected, but not shouts.

"There he goes! . . . Grab him! . . . Don't let him get away! . . . The net, use the net . . . !"

Teal sprang to her feet, eyes staring upward as if they could pierce the solid wood. "I don't understand. The accents are strange and sound like more of your kind. Skypersons." Subsumed in the frenzy of struggle, the shouts and urgent cries were diminishing.

"Skypersons, yes," he murmured, "but they're not relations or friends of mine." Now intensely alert, Pip hovered protectively near his shoulder. "They're enemies."

"Enemies," Moomadeem growled softly. Claws securing a firm grip on the wood, the young furcot swung out onto the side of the branch.

"No, wait!" Flinx grabbed at the clipped green fur.

Moomadeem hesitated and looked expectantly back at Saalahan. The big furcot reached out to put a massive paw on the cub's middle shoulder as it explained.

"Flinx speaks smart. They already have your person. Better not to charge blindly into something we do not understand."

Teal was teetering on the edge of the cavity, trying to see upward. "Don't hurt him! He's just a child!"

"Hey, there's a woman!" To his regret and embarrassment, it was a voice Flinx thought he recognized.

His suspicions were quickly confirmed. "Philip Lynx, come on out of your hole! We know you're down there."

"How'd you learn my real name?" He had to restrain Pip from rising to the attack.

"There's a lot of information on your shuttle," replied the voice of Jack-Jax Coerlis. "Not everything I'd like to know, but enough. Are you coming up?"

"There's nowhere else to go. Just don't hurt the boy."

"Why would I want to hurt him? He's a funny-looking little savage with a nasty temper, but I don't hold that against him. I'd be on edge myself if I had to spend much time here. Now, where there's a boy this age, there's usually a mother, so why don't all of you come on out? You know what's between you and me, Lynx. Hurting ignorant bystanders isn't a part of it—so long as you cooperate."

"There's no one else here." Flinx did his utmost to make the declaration sound convincing.

"Don't try me, Lynx. We've been listening to you gab down there for the last ten minutes. I know there's a woman and a girl. I heard you talking to the woman."

Heard me, Flinx thought anxiously. Then it struck him that Coerlis knew nothing of furcots, nor had Saalahan or Moomadeem uttered anything above a whisper.

"Surely these people will not harm Dwell." Teal's eyes were wide with disbelief.

"I hate to tell you this, Teal, but where I come from there's a surplus of persons. It's not necessary to cooperate in order to survive. Sensible and rational, yes, but not necessary. We shouldn't take any chances. It'll be all right, you'll see. It's me they want to talk to."

"You first, Lynx," Coerlis shouted down to him. "We have weapons out and ready, so I suggest you put a hand on the minidrag if you want to keep it alive."

Flinx gripped Pip just below her head, gently but firmly. "Easy," he murmured to her. She was taut as a wire, fully conscious of his discomfort. He whispered tautly to Saalahan. "They don't know you're down here. Let's try to keep it that way. Can you give me a boost?"

The big furcot nodded. Grasping Flinx around the waist with both forepaws, it raised him effortlessly off the floor of the cavity and lifted him outside. Glancing down, Flinx saw that the curve of the branch concealed the heavy paws. His expression grim, he scrambled up onto the top of the branch, heedless of the sheer drop below.

Waiting to confront him was an alien of a size and countenance he didn't recognize. It was as massive as a furcot but not as stocky. Its emotional state remained closed to him, but at the moment he couldn't even read Teal.

Two of its four arms firmly pinioned a defiant Dwell, while the others clutched a large rifle. Most ten-year-olds would have been thoroughly intimidated by the Mu'Atahl, but not Dwell. Compared to the dangers he knew and lived with every day there in the arboreal heights, he did not find the alien particularly impressive.

For the first time since Flinx had crossed paths with Jack-Jax Coerlis, he saw the man smile contentedly. "Surprised?"

"Yes and no. At your resources, not your obsessive behavior."

"One man's obsession is another man's fortitude."

At that moment Pip tore free of Flinx's grasp and shot forward, taking care to aim straight at Coerlis's eyes before anyone had time to react. As the merchant yelped, a thin stream of pressurized venom gleamed in the yellow-green light.

Shifting the heavy weapon he held, Chaa fired. Dilating as it emerged from the special gun, the weighted net englobed Pip and carried the flying snake to the ground. Eyes burning, she lay there beneath the composite netting, flopping and flapping furiously against the restraint, unable to rise.

Flinx started toward the imprisoned minidrag. "You could've killed her!"

"Hold it there, sonny. Remember me?" A grinning Peeler had his pistol pointed directly at Flinx's chest.

Flinx spared the man a glance. "Yes, I remember you. Where's your associate?"

Peeler's grin evaporated. "Dead. Some little crawling things got him. No," he corrected himself, "this planet got him. But it won't get me, and now we've got you." Keeping his pistol trained on Flinx, he walked over and roughly removed the younger man's equipment belt.

"Aimee." Holding his pistol in one hand, Coerlis used a special industrial cloth to wipe the viscous venom from his protective flip-down face shield. "The minidrag."

An attractive blond woman carrying a gray mesh sack advanced to the spraddled net and its incensed captive. In addition to chameleon suit and helmet with face shield, she wore heavy gloves designed for handling powerful solvents and chemicals.

"I wouldn't do that," Flinx warned her.

She glared back at him. "You don't look threatening. Mr. Coerlis said as much." Crouching, she worked the open mouth of the sack forward beneath the netting. With a hiss, Pip fired a burst of venom in her direction. It struck the face guard and she flinched.

Coerlis frowned. "You okay, Aimee? Any of the poison get under your shield?"

"N-No," she muttered. "Jack-Jax, I—I'm not doing so good. Maybe you should have someone else do this."

"If the poison didn't penetrate the shield then there's nothing wrong. Everyone else is busy. Get on with it."

"R-R-Right. Feeling a little better now."

She continued to work the sack forward along the wood until the flying snake was trapped against a fold of netting. A quick shove, a twist, and Pip was caught up in the bag. The minidrag thrashed about furiously, but the uncommon weave was immune to the effects of the normally corrosive venom. The confident engineer straightened and secured the sack with a flexible slip tie.

"Got it!"

Coerlis removed his helmet and face shield. In the heat and humidity the military headgear couldn't be tolerated for long, but it had more than served its intended purpose. His companions did likewise, stowing the collapsible helmets in appropriate belt pouches.

As Coerlis was packing his away he noticed Flinx watching him. "Special lenses. After what happened on Samstead you didn't think I'd come all this way without making suitable preparations, did you?" When Flinx didn't respond he glanced over at his engineer. "Aimee, are we all secure?"

"In a minute." She carefully slid the sack containing the minidrag into another, heavier bag. "All set."

As if everything that had happened already wasn't enough, a dull pounding had started at the back of Flinx's head.

"You can't take her. We've been together since I was a child!"

Coerlis was singularly unimpressed. "Then I'd say it was time to grow up. Besides, in a little while it won't matter to you anyway." Even though he feared only the flying snake, he kept the muzzle of his weapon pointed at Flinx's chest.

"You can't kill me. There's something I have to do. It's important to everyone. Me, you, the entire Commonwealth."

"There's nothing you can have to do that's important to anyone," the cocksure Coerlis corrected him. "Not anymore. All that matters now is what's important to *me*."

Flinx didn't try to argue. How could he explain the substance of his dreaming to someone like Jack-Jax Coerlis? For that matter, how could he explain it to anyone?

"All right. Let's get it over with." He started down the branch.

"What's your hurry?" A hint of a smile cracked Coerlis's expression. "Did you think I'd forgotten that you're not alone?"

Flinx's stare was so intense the disconcerted Coerlis found himself looking away without knowing why. "You said you wouldn't harm them. Why not just let the boy go and leave it at that?"

"When *I'm* ready." The merchant moved to the edge of the branch and leaned out. Flinx tensed. "You down there! Come on up, *now*."

Flinx could only look on helplessly as first Kiss and then Teal climbed up to join him. Their captor studied them dispassionately.

"You're a pretty little thing, aren't you?" Coerlis's eyes started with Teal's hair and worked their way downward. "Except that you've got feet like a chimp." Flinx's lips tightened, but Teal didn't react. Knowing nothing of chimps or their physiological peculiarities, she wasn't insulted. Come to think of it, Flinx decided, if she had known, she might have been flattered by the comparison.

"You've seen them. Now let them go. Please." Flinx nodded toward Dwell.

Ignoring him as if he was already dead, Coerlis walked a slow circle around Teal and Kiss. "Very pretty. There shouldn't be natives here. Aimee?"

The engineer could only shrug. "According to the charts, there shouldn't be a planet here. So why not natives as well?" She blinked and shook her head sharply, as if something small, superfast, and loud had abruptly buzzed her ears.

"Quite a world, this is." Standing on the edge of the branch, the merchant gazed at the spectacular vista presented by the sunken valley in the trees. "Rife with commercial prospects, if a little on the nasty side. Unlimited quantity of exotic wood products, boundless pharmaceutical potential, the pet trade, who knows what else? Take a fully equipped expedition just to begin basic cataloging."

Teal leaned toward Flinx. "What is the unpleasant skyperson talking about?"

"He's the type of individual who's not happy just being in the world. He has to possess it."

She frowned. "No one can possess the world. It belongs to everyone, just as everyone belongs to it."

"Some skypersons think otherwise."

"Try to possess the world and it will kill you," she deposed knowingly.

Coerlis overheard. "It's sure killed some of us." The way he said it made him sound as if he was referring to a couple of pieces of especially valuable office equipment. "But I'm still here, along with a few of my friends, and we've learned the hard lessons. From now on it's we who'll do the possessing." He put a finger under Teal's chin. "Knowing, however, that the overconfident tend to die young, I'm going to rely on you to lead the way back. We'll choose the route and you can show us what to avoid."

"Then when we reach the landing site you'll let them go?" It took a tremendous effort of will on Flinx's part to keep from jumping Coerlis as the merchant continued to finger Teal. She remained motionless, ignoring the attention stoically.

Captor glanced back at his quarry. "Why not? I don't kill for fun, you know. I have to have a good reason." He nodded at Dwell. "I don't want him. Or her," he added, glancing down at where Kiss stood clinging wide-eyed to her mother's leg.

"Why should I bother with them? As the discoverer, or rediscoverer, of this world, I'm entitled to first exploitation rights as soon as it's been appropriately registered and classified."

"Who're you trying to fool?" Flinx retorted evenly. "You know as well as I that if anyone has rights here, it's these people. Their claim supersedes yours by an order of magnitude."

Having already reached his daily limit, Coerlis didn't smile again. "There are always ways and means of dealing with such awkwardness. A word in the right hearing organ, a financial contribution with the decimal point in the right place, both can work wonders with the bureaucracy. With a whole new planet to develop, I'm not concerned. I don't have to control it *all*." His eyes glittered.

"That gives me an idea. I might just take the woman and kids back with me. It's their lost birthright, and the anthropologists would be fascinated."

"You can't take them off this world. Their lives are too tightly entwined with their surroundings."

"So now you're an anthropologist, too." Coerlis was enjoying himself. "So many talents in such an unprepossessing body!"

You have no idea, Flinx thought coldly, wishing one particular talent would reassert itself.

"I'm sure the children would find the interior of a starship fascinating. As for the mother," he leered objectionably at Teal, "I'm sure we can find all manner of ways to keep her entertained. Dazzle her with the products of modern Commonwealth technology, for instance. As demonstrated by myself."

"Your charm's certain to overwhelm her," Flinx concurred sardonically.

"To be sure. I'm really a very nice person, when I'm getting my way."

Flinx felt the pressure continue to build at the back of his skull. If the situation didn't improve, something was likely to happen. What that might be, he didn't know himself. His singular talents had saved him before, first on Moth and later on Longtunnel. Each salvation had come at a cost. Part of that cost was lack of control. He'd much prefer to resolve the present situation without losing that control, but he didn't have the vaguest notion how to begin.

Patience, he told himself. Coerlis had said nothing about killing him outright. If he persisted he might still convince the young merchant to let Teal and the children go. Then if he lost control, he'd be responsible only for whatever happened to himself. It was a long ways back to the barren mountaintop and the shuttles.

Also, there was Pip's fate to consider. It was the first time he'd ever seen the minidrag reduced to helplessness. Better to know exactly where he stood before he tried anything.

"What about me?"

Coerlis replied pretty much as expected. "Oh, you won't be going back. I'm not sure whether to kill you right here or just leave you. I like the idea of abandoning you to the local life forms. Their killing methods are much more inventive than anything I could come up with. But if I do that, some other happy tribesfolk might find you and keep you alive. I don't like the idea of you being around, even in pelt and loincloth, to welcome the first survey expedition. They would want to ask you questions." He looked thoughtful.

"I've given some thought to cutting one or both of your Achilles tendons. Unable to walk or climb, I don't think you'd last very long here."

"We're not going with you."

Flinx threw Teal a warning look, but she was defiant.

"You'll never make it back to your 'shuttle.' The forest will see to that."

"Oh, I think we'll manage. Admittedly we've suffered some casualties, but the rest of us have made it this far.

With what we've learned and with you to take the lead, I think we'll be all right."

Teal shook her head slowly from side to side. "It makes no difference. You don't know how to walk, where or how to place each foot. You don't know how to look, or listen. You don't know when to not breathe. You don't know how to emfol. You're ignorant, as ignorant as Flinx when first I met him several days ago. Worse than that, you're arrogant. Arrogance will kill a person here quicker even than ignorance."

"That's why I'm going to rely on you to tell us when and how to do all the right things." Coerlis waved his pistol. "I know that you'll do your best to keep us alive."

"It doesn't matter," she replied passively. "I can only give so many warnings, can only do so much. There are certain shortcomings I can try to compensate for. But I can do nothing about your attitude. For example, one of you is already dead."

Nothing Flinx or Teal had said thus far had had any visible affect on Coerlis, but that jolted him. Flinx knew it was so even though their captor's expression had remained unchanged, because his talent chose that moment to spring back to life. He'd sensed the wariness blossoming like a storm cloud in the merchant's mind.

Quickly he shifted his perception, assessing the emotional state of each of Coerlis's minions. Peeler standing bold, but nervous and fearful inside; the female engineer holding her ground but troubled by some unspecified physical distress; the powerful alien calm and analytical as Dwell wriggled in his grasp.

"What are you nattering on about, midget?" Coerlis saw uncertainty taking root in the expressions of Peeler and Aimee. "We're not in any danger. The minidrag isn't a factor, and without it neither is this skinny twit. Are you afraid of the woman and a couple of kids?" He stalked over to Teal. Kiss clung tightly to her mother, her eyes following the threatening skyperson's every move.

"There's only one of us here who's 'already dead,' and that's the geek over there." He gestured in Flinx's direction as he directed his words to Teal. "I still think you're pretty, but I can be fickle. Don't force me into any disagreeable reevaluations." He nudged her cleavage with the muzzle of his pistol.

Teal met his gaze evenly. "The one who is already dead is over there." A startled Flinx evaluated her emotional state and knew this to be true.

Then she pointed at Aimee.

The color drained from the engineer's face. "What's she talking about, Jack-Jax? Make her shut up. Make her take it back!"

Coerlis's lip curled in disgust. "Get ahold of yourself, Aimee. There's nothing the matter with any of us."

"I'm still not feeling well."

"None of us are. Have you taken anything yet?"

She looked past him. "N-No. It comes and goes. I thought it would go away."

"Then what do you expect?" He turned to the Mu'Atahl. "You don't have to hold the kid anymore, Chaa. He's not going anywhere. Break out the big medkit and pull her a max dose of general antibio." His voice dropped to a mutter as he looked back at his engineer. "Should've done it yesterday."

The Mu'Atahl acknowledged in his own fashion and released Dwell, who ran immediately to stand protectively next to his mother. Twisting his sauropodian neck, the big alien began to unfasten a portion of the rain shedder that covered the large pack strapped to his back.

"It will do you no good." Teal was quietly adamant. "It's the cristif."

Aimee blinked at her. "The what?" A worried Flinx tracked the wavering arcs of the engineer's pistol. She could panic at any time and start shooting.

Teal was adamant. "The cristif. In your hair."

The other woman reached up to feel the bouquet of glittering, gemlike flowers. "Is that all you're talking about? The flowers I'm wearing?" Her expression wavered between relief and uncertainty.

"You do not wear the cristif." Teal's tone was solemn. "The cristif wears you."

"I don't know what you're bab—" The engineer staggered suddenly, her extremities going limp. The needler she'd been swinging carelessly about fell to the ground. Flinx winced when it struck the branch but the weapon didn't go off.

Coerlis took a step toward her, stopped. "Aimee! What the hell?"

A blank look on her face, she turned to reply. As she did so, half a dozen wire-thin white filaments emerged from her mouth, wiggling like blind worms. Her gaze fell and the most complete look of horror Flinx had ever seen on another human being's face froze into her expression. Trying to say something, she gagged on the filaments.

Then her eyes rolled back in her head and she crumpled.

While a shocked Coerlis and Peeler watched, unable to react, not knowing how to respond, the filaments pushed farther from the unconscious engineer's mouth, creeping along the surface of the wood. Bulging in a dozen places, her chameleon suit burst forth with dozens, hundreds, of the writhing, twisting tendrils. They exploded from her thighs and shoulders, her neck and chest, belly and pelvis.

Flinx's first thought was that she had been infected by some kind of communal parasitic nematode, but he soon saw that the infestation had a much simpler and more direct source. The exquisitely beautiful cristif bouquet was the blossoming portion of something that was part fungus, part flower, and part something new to Commonwealth botanical science. The woman had unknowingly entwined the seeds of her own destruction in her blond curls, where they had found root. And nourishment. Having spread undetected throughout her body, the developing mycelium of what was possibly an endomorphic mycorrhiza had finally fruited.

The active, motile spawn formed a pale white sheath around the twitching body, the pointed tips digging into the surface of the branch as they secured the fertilizing corpse firmly to the wood. Once the body of the unlucky woman had been pinioned in place by hundreds of throbbing white cords, several of the pale filaments began to swell.

Moments later the darkening, taut skin of the tendrils burst, and the engineer's body lay abloom with the breathtaking radiance of newly blossoming cristif. Deftly turning toward the available light, the gold and crystal blooms enveloped the dead woman in a delicate casket of rainbows. Petals of crimson and gold, azure and purple, flared from her eye sockets. Eventually, Flinx suspected, the remains of the engineer would be thoroughly consumed, leaving behind only the dire wonder of the flowers.

"Beautiful to look at, dangerous to hold," Teal quietly informed the shocked silence. "That is the sort of thing that will happen to all of you if you stay here."

"No!" blurted Coerlis. Behind his defiance, Flinx could feel the fear in the other man's mind. Though the

Mu'Atahl remained calm and his emotional state was more difficult to read, even he was obviously upset by the malevolent miracle of reproduction they'd just witnessed.

Taking a step forward, the merchant grabbed Teal by the neck. Dwell started to react, but his mother waved him off.

"Nothing like that is going to happen to the rest of us because you're going to show us what to avoid as well as what path to take. And if anything, anything at all, happens to one more of us, I'm going to hold you personally responsible. Not that I'll do anything to you, oh no. We need you." He scowled meaningfully at Dwell. "The children, on the other hand, are expendable. Do we understand one another?" He released her neck and stepped back.

Nodding slowly, she reached up to feel the imprints his fingers had left on her skin. Her eyes burned into his.

The corners of Coerlis's mouth curled slightly upward. "That's okay, I don't mind you hating me. I'm used to it. Just pay attention to where we're going and help us get safely back to our ship, and you can hate me all you like." He stepped aside and gestured with his needler.

"You go first. Peeler, stick close to her. And pick up that bag." He indicated the double sack that contained the confined Pip.

The bodyguard eyed it unhappily. "Why me, Mr. Coerlis? I mean—"

The merchant lowered his voice dangerously. "Just—*do it*." Reluctantly, Peeler slung the heavy mesh over his shoulder and fell into place alongside the much smaller woman.

Coerlis smiled humorlessly down at Dwell and Kiss. "You kids stay next to me. I know you want to keep close to your ma, and that's exactly what I plan to do. Chaa, you bring up the rear, as always." The Mu'Atahl responded with a curt gesture of acknowledgment.

"First sign of any tricks, first nub of an excuse," Coerlis informed Teal as he lazily waved the muzzle of his pistol in the children's direction, "and I'll kill the girl first. You understand? I'll fry her pretty little head."

His eyes were wild and Flinx could sense the first hints of a complete loss of control. Hopefully that wouldn't happen. He knew from experience that it was impossible to reason with someone who had gone over the edge.

"Where do you want me?"

Coerlis raised the needler and smiled. "Want you? Our mutual business is finished."

Trying to stall, Flinx gestured toward the sack. "You got what you wanted. Now you owe me."

"*I* owe *you*?" The merchant shook his head slowly. "Oh, very well. How does ten thousand credits sound?" When Flinx didn't reply, Coerlis used the fingers of his free hand to tick off a long list of expenses.

"Cost of tracking your ship, loss of business time on Samstead while I was forced to deal with this, loss of four valued employees; I'd say that at this point you owe me, Lynx. One or two million credits should do it."

"I can cover that," Flinx replied quietly, "but as you may have noticed, adequate banking facilities are somewhat sparsely situated hereabouts."

It was an uncertain Coerlis who returned Flinx's stare. "I'm damned if I can tell whether you're lying or not. Not that it matters. Since you can't pay up on the spot, which is how I usually require payment, I'll have to obtain satisfaction in some other fashion." He gestured stiffly with the needler. "Step over to the edge."

Flinx moved slowly. "You're going to shoot me."

The merchant shrugged apathetically. "Why waste a charge? The fall should be sufficient. Unless you can fly, like your ex-pet. Can you fly, Philip Lynx? Do you think you'll bounce when you hit the first branch, or just lie there, smashed and moaning?" Keeping his needler aimed at his nemesis, he edged over the rim and leaned out to study the drop.

"Yeah, this should do it. If you're lucky, you'll break your neck. If you're not, you'll fetch up somewhere down there broken and crippled. I don't think it'll take long for an opportunistic representative of the local fauna to find you. Maybe it'll have the grace to finish you off before it starts eating." He was quite pleased with himself. "Much better than shooting you." He waved the pistol.

"Over you go, Lynx! You can step off, take a running start, do a flip if you like. Why not jump into the spirit of things, so to speak, and try to make your last moments entertaining?" When Flinx hesitated, the other man's face darkened. "You've got thirty seconds. Then I'll shoot you in both knees and have Chaa throw you over. Who knows? Maybe you'll land in a soft place and can crawl all the way back to your shuttle. But somehow I don't think so."

Out of ideas and options, Flinx steadied himself. He was fast, but not as fast as a needler. Maybe he could catch a strong liana on the way down, break or slow his fall. He took a deep breath. The worst part of it all was that he could sense the pleasure Coerlis was experiencing.

Then he frowned. Suddenly he could sense the emotional presence of others besides those already accounted for. It made no sense. He wished for time to analyze what he was sensing, but mindful of Coerlis's warning, he knew there was no time. It puzzled him as he started forward, wondering what he would feel next.

It was safe to say that neither he nor anyone else expected Coerlis's skull to explode like a ripe melon.

Chapter Fifteen

The headless body stood swaying for a moment, blood fountaining from the raw stump of a neck. As quivering fingers contracted reflexively on the needler's trigger, Flinx dove for the ground, screaming for Teal and the children to do likewise. The single bolt seared open sky, and a severed branch or two tumbled downward. Then the decapitated corpse crumpled forward belly first. Coerlis hadn't even had time enough to look surprised.

The Mu'Athal whirled and simultaneously unlimbered its heavy rifle, but it never had the opportunity to return fire. The attackers were well hidden within the dense greenery. Multiple shots from both projectile and energy weapons blew the rifle out of the big alien's four hands before bringing him to his knees. A last shot inflicted a blackened streak on the long snout before terminating in a neat, round hole in the exact center of the sloping forehead. With nary a sigh, the powerful alien rolled over on its left side and expired. Equipment spilled from its capacious backpack, tumbling out onto the branch.

Firing wildly into the verdure, Peeler flung the sack containing Pip aside and raced desperately down the branch. Shots tracked his flight, missing the frantic, agile human. Flinx lifted his head slightly to watch. If Peeler could escape the immediate ambush, and if he carried a positioner of his own, it was conceivable he might make his way back to the landing site.

At that point the bodyguard missed a step, flailed madly, desperately, to regain his balance, and went plunging off the side of the branch.

A long time passed before his screams were cut off by the first crack of snapping branches. The sounds continued, rapidly diminishing in volume, for nearly a minute, fading into the distance rather than ceasing entirely. For all he knew, Flinx mused as he rose to his feet, Peeler was still falling.

"That's what I call a timely interruption." A glance showed that Teal and the children were unhurt. Around them the wall of green remained unbroken. "Come on out so we can thank you!"

"Thank us?" The accent was clipped, the tone dry and rasping. "I suppose you would."

Why, Flinx wondered, should that surprise the unseen speaker? Without the intervention, he would most probably now be lying somewhere far below, badly injured and possibly dead. The unexpected arrival had saved his life and probably that of Teal and her offspring as well.

Making his way forward, he passed first the headless cadaver of Jack-Jax Coerlis and then the wholly enflowered body of the luckless engineer. Hastily abandoned by Peeler, the mesh sack stirred as Pip sensed her master's approach.

"Easy, girl," he murmured as he started to kneel. "I'll have you out of there in a second." He reached for the tie that secured the opening.

A voice stopped him. "Please do not do that. I believe it would be best if your remarkable pet remained where she is."

Figures began to emerge from the greenery. Two descended from above on swing climbers, reeling in the portable devices as soon as they reached the branch. All wore camouflaged ecosuits.

None were human.

His insides went cold. The source of the peculiar emotions he'd only recently detected was now evident. They were not wholly alien to him, but he hadn't encountered their like in some time.

Teal and the children gathered around him. "What are *those*?" Dwell's curiosity overcame his fear. "They walk like persons, but they don't look like persons."

"They're a different kind of person." Flinx moved to position himself between the new arrivals and the family. "Very different." Within the sack at his feet, Pip was stirring anxiously. Even if she could be freed in time, he knew that if they tried to run, he and Teal and the children would be shot down where they stood before the minidrag could do anything to help them.

He counted seven, eight, eleven in the party as they emerged from the greenery, and there was no guarantee a dozen more weren't keeping under cover. Not even Pip could deal with so many trained, heavily armed assailants. Furthermore, these weren't a young merchant and his hired bodyguards. They were professionals, and comported themselves as such. For the moment, his pet was safer in the sack, where her instinctive desire to protect her master couldn't get her killed.

All of them wore dark goggles and bore sleek packs and weapons. Even had they been alerted to the presence of such as these, Flinx knew that Coerlis and his companions wouldn't have stood a chance against them.

He thought rapidly. Their unexpected saviors hadn't revealed themselves until Coerlis had moved to finish off his quarry. That suggested they wanted him alive. He had no difficulty resigning himself to his new status—it certainly beat lying broken and shattered on a branch fifty meters below.

But what did they want with him, and what were they doing here? Certainly altruism had nothing to do with it. Altruism was a concept alien to the AAnn.

It had been some time since he'd had to deal with any of the noble servants of the AAnn Empire, an interstellar alliance second in scope and power only to the Commonwealth, whose might the AAnn probed with circumspect relentlessness. Bribing, cajoling, occasionally making war and then retreating, the AAnn sought continuously for signs of weakness, taking advantage whenever possible, relinquishing when overmatched.

His last encounter with them had been on Ulru-Ujurr, where the loyal but avaricious servants of the Emperor had busied themselves stealing the planet's surface riches without ever learning of the far greater wealth inherent within the amusing, dangerous, comical, extraordinary dominant native species. Only Flinx had penetrated the secrets of the Ulru-Ujurrians and become their friend. Or at the very least, a curious component in their Great Game. In return, they had included him in their amusements and assisted his mind in reaching further than it would ever have been able to reach on its own.

He wished a few of them were here now.

As several of the soldiers slid their goggles up on their high, scaly foreheads, Kiss pointed to the individual in front. "See, Mother? Isn't it funny-looking? Like a prindeletch without the right number of eyes and legs!"

Teal put a reassuring arm around her daughter's shoulders. "Hush now, Kiss, until we know what they want."

She was watching Flinx closely, trying to read his body language.

The reptiloid halted. It was unusually tall for one of its tailed, armored kind, able to scrutinize Flinx eye-to-eye. Slitted yellow eye to round green one. Flinx stared back without flinching, knowing that to look away would be taken as a sign of weakness.

What he saw was a tapering, scaly snout full of short, sharp teeth. The officer was clad in a green camouflage suit complete with skintight tail sock. Both clawed feet were shod in special webbed grip-boots that greatly enhanced the wearer's footing without reducing flexibility. A long-muzzled sidearm showed prominently on the well-made equipment belt. While the other soldiers wore contoured jungle bodypacks, the tall officer was not similarly burdened. One neatly manicured hand lifted the thick goggles from its face. Like a counterweight, the tail switched reflexively back and forth.

Empire soldiers, all of them, Flinx saw. He counted eleven, could sense none hiding back in the trees. Not that he intended to rely on that estimate. Not given the way his abilities had been functioning lately. Or not functioning.

Coerlis and his people had never had a chance. This was not some wandering exploration team. Judging from the efficiency and forethought with which they'd been equipped, Flinx didn't think they'd stumbled across this world by accident. Certainly their locating and subsequent ambushing of Coerlis and his party had been no coincidence, nor was the fact that he himself had been spared. They had arrived in search of something specific, and were prepared to fight for it. Now that the fight was over, he wondered what they were after. Watching the officer, Flinx felt certain he was about to find out.

Flinx indicated Coerlis's corpse. "If I didn't know your kind better, I would thank you." The AAnn appreciated candor.

"Having no way of knowing what you have been saved for, your ambivalence is understandable." The officer's symbospeech was nearly perfect, with nary a hint of the usual hiss that normally harshed their attempts to enunciate the lingua franca of the Commonwealth.

Flinx deliberately looked past him, managing by means of his visual inclination and concurrent verbal comment to simultaneously magnify and minimize the officer's importance.

"I would've expected there to be more of you."

The AAnn responded with a gesture indicative of third-degree appreciation for Flinx's tactfulness, with overtones of sadness and loss.

"There *were* twelve soldiers with me. One was carried off by something that dropped down on him from above, swept him off the branch we were traversing, and carried him away into the depths before we could react and fire. His cries linger still in our minds. The other stepped on a rotten, shallow place and fell through, to land in the center of a large growth not far below. Though we rushed to his assistance, by the time we could reach him, his nether regions had been consumed up to the hips.

"There are two medics with me, and he might have lived, but we complied with his traditional desire to die with his spirit intact. I administered the injection myself, as I am bound to do." A vertical flick of the tail emotionally underscored the painful memory. The AAnn tended to express emotion through gesture instead of speech.

"Given the immoderate hazards this world presents, I consider it fortunate to have lost only two in catching up to you, Philip Lynx."

So it was him they were after, Flinx decided. He could suspect several reasons for their interest in him but refrained from mentioning any. There was a to-be-hoped-for chance he might be wrong.

The officer performed an elaborate, sweeping gesture with both hands and tail that was meant to be all-encompassing. "A most remarkable biosphere, do you not agree?"

"Considering what you've been through, I wouldn't think you'd be in any hurry to admire it."

The officer responded with a series of incongruously high-pitched cheeping sounds, a form of laughter among his kind. The AAnn had a deep appreciation of irony and sarcasm.

"Your observation is warranted, Philip Lynx. As you may know, we prefer dry, less heavily vegetated surroundings. Even with the use of appropriate climatologic gear, the humidity taxes my troops. Unlike your own, our purgatory is a damp place." He executed an intricate hand salute, appropriately adjusted for the fact that those to whom he was speaking were neither of noble lineage nor military bearing.

"I am Lord Caavax LYD, honored and enshrined servant of his most Revered and Shining Illustriousness, the Emperor Moek VI."

"You seem to know who I am." Flinx nodded in the direction of Teal and the children. "These are my friends."

Lord Caavax's eyes passed over them as though they didn't exist. "Yet another offshoot or subspecies of your regrettably fertile kind." His tone was cool, correct, and devoid of overt animosity. "We have been trying to catch up with you for some time." Turning slightly, he gestured to where a trio of soldiers were rummaging through Coerlis's effects. Several others were examining the unlucky engineer's mycelium-encrusted carcass, careful not to touch.

"It appears we were not the only ones. Do you have a lot of enemies?"

"I seem to have lately," Flinx replied readily.

The AAnn did not smile, but the noble did his best to make his captive feel at ease. "I am not your enemy."

Flinx smiled back, knowing the AAnn would recognize the expression. At the same time, he could sense the antipathy and revulsion that dominated the alien's emotions. Of all the members of the human species, the only one Lord Caavax could not hide his true feelings from was standing before him.

Flinx kept his voice flat. "Are you trying to tell me that you're my friend?"

"Let me put it this way: it would distress me greatly if I were to have to kill you. Surely you can appreciate the benefit of that?"

"I'm overcome with affection," Flinx replied dryly. He gestured at Coerlis. "What intrigues me is that you didn't want him to kill me, either."

"Certainly not! By all the rules of rational etiquette, you should be kneeling at my feet in gratefulness, but as you are human I do not expect you to act in a civilized manner. Among your kind, heartfelt gratitude is a cheap commodity to be bartered and traded like salt."

"You'll have to excuse me." Flinx maintained his inflexible smile. "I would kneel, but I have a bad back. So you don't wish me dead?"

"On the contrary, we are strongly desirous of perpetuating you in a state of healthy existence." White teeth flashed.

"And my friends?" He jerked his head in Teal's direction.

Lord Caavax responded with a gesture of second-level indifference tempered by third-degree curiosity. "*Ssissist.* Their future is yet to be decided. If they are important to you, then they become by inference of mild interest to us."

Flinx folded his arms. "Why don't you tell me what you're doing here? And why the interest in me?" He struggled to monitor the noble's emotions closely.

The AAnn considered at length before replying. "I was not ordered to withhold the information from you, Philip Lynx. Several visits to a proscribed world within the illegally declaimed borders of the Commonwealth were made by another of the Noble House several years ago. A distant relation of mine by marriage, actually. He was a participant in a since terminated mining venture there. You are familiar, I believe, with the properties of Janus jewels?"

A startled Flinx remembered. The aristocrat continued.

"More recently there were interesting developments on a Commonwealth world by the name of Longtunnel. According to the file we have developed for you, *pssissin*, you recently graced both worlds with your presence."

"Your agents are very good," Flinx conceded.

"They have to be, the Commonwealth being so much larger and more powerful than the Empire. For now." Yellow eyes glittered.

Here it comes, Flinx thought as he prepared possible explanations, excuses, and evasions. But how had they found out about him? How had they come to learn of his unique talent? What did they know about him from their observations of what had happened on Ulru-Ujurr years ago and on Longtunnel comparatively recently?

The noble performed a gesture indicative of first-degree interest and admiration. "You travel aboard a most remarkable vessel, Lynx-sir. Most remarkable."

So that was it! Fighting to conceal his relief, Flinx forced himself to relax. This wasn't about his distorted genetic background, about what the outlawed Meliorares had done to his nervous system prior to his birth. It wasn't about his carefully concealed abilities at all. It was the *Teacher* they were after.

Initially relieved, he had to remind himself that this revelation did nothing to enhance prospects for imminent freedom. With Pip still trapped in Coerlis's infernal catch sack, he and Teal and the children weren't about to disarm and disable nearly a dozen highly trained AAnn soldiers.

The situation had changed, but whether for better or worse it was too early to tell. Lord Caavax was nonhuman, representative of a species that was a traditional rival of humanxkind. On the other hand, unlike Coerlis, he was rational and might be swayed or influenced by logical argument. Better to contest with a rational alien than an obsessed human.

To do that, he needed to learn as much about Caavax and his backup as possible. Casual conversation was always a useful way to begin.

"Did you arrive via shuttle? If so, it must be getting awfully crowded on that mountaintop."

"There was only just enough room," the noble replied. "Landing required much delicate maneuvering. You will understand also a desire on our part not to upset or interfere with the situation we found you in until we were able to ascertain the details. We have managed."

"Why the intense interest in my ship?"

"*Pssussk.* You are making jovial. We have reports that it is capable of achieving planetfall, a feat practically but not theoretically impossible for any KK-drive craft. If the reports are accurate, it would seem that you or some others you have had contact with have effectively resolved the theoretical contradictions. Even making allowance for your youth, I do not think I need to explain the interest those of a military bent would have in such a scientific breakthrough.

"Yet our information also suggests that this is a discovery you have kept to yourself and not revealed to anyone who is of the Commonwealth. This is something of a puzzle to us, but one that I assure you we will do our utmost to preserve."

"The ship was a gift." Flinx tried to impart the attitude of one for whom the matter was of little import. "A present. For that and other reasons, I've decided not to reveal its capabilities at this time."

Clearly Lord Caavax did not understand. "But it would give your people a significant military advantage over the forces of the Empire."

Flinx's response expressed confidence rather than military expertise. "The Commonwealth can handle the Empire just fine the way things are. Sure, having ships equipped with drives the equal of the *Teacher*'s would give an advantage, but it would only be a temporary one."

"Why temporary?" Slitted pupils dilated.

"Because I know how good your agents are, remember? Sooner or later they'd manage to bribe, steal, or cajole their way into possession of the necessary information. Soon Empire ships with similar capabilities would be plying nullspace. That would make the military on both sides happy, but only increase the misery of impacted noncombatants. The balance of power would be restored but the potential for destruction increased. So I prefer to keep the secret to myself.

"For one thing, unlike some humans and thranx, I have nothing against your kind. As far as I'm concerned, the issues that inspired historical conflict are as dead as those who disputed them."

The noble twisted in a manner suggestive of second-degree understanding seamlessly infused with first-degree disagreement.

"A very self-centered explication, and therefore also very human. It remains, however, that I am bound by different cultural paradigms. The Empire wants the secret of your drive because it promises advantage. It is the essence of AAnness to seek advantage. Therefore I am afraid that your youthful idealism will have to be set aside should you wish to preserve your continued good health."

"I can't help you," Flinx replied tartly. "I'm not an engineer or physicist. I have no idea how the *Teacher*'s drive operates or how it sidesteps the Kurita-Kinoshita equations, or whatever the AAnn equivalent is."

"*Ssissi.* You needn't worry about that. On board my vessel are many who are competent to analyze the workings of your drive. But as you know, your craft is programmed to defend itself against unauthorized intrusion."

Flinx worked to suppress a genuine smile. "You tried to board her."

"Obviously. Otherwise there would be no need for me to be standing here in these infernal, oppressive surroundings trying to reason with you. We simply would have put a crew aboard your vessel and departed quietly."

"Leaving me stranded here."

Once again the essence of a smile was visible only as a portion of the noble's emotions. "You have friends. You would have survived." He indicated Coerlis's body. "I offer you more than what your fellow human was willing to allow.

"While the weaponry mounted on your vessel is no match for that aboard my own, we were of course constrained from firing by our desire to obtain your craft intact and undamaged, as well as a fear that if disabled and subsequently boarded, it might self-destruct, thereby obviating our whole purpose in coming here. The solution was straightforward: you had to be located and convinced to give us what we wish."

"How did you manage to penetrate this far into the Commonwealth?"

"With great care and difficulty. We were helped by the fact that though this world lies within the self-proclaimed illegal Commonwealth sphere of influence, it is well away from major routes of trade and communication. We were cautious.

"You should also know that the mandate I was given, while all-encompassing, is possessed of a certain flexibility. I was told simply to obtain the secret of your ship's drive. The actual methodology is left to my discretion. I am authorized and prepared to offer you a considerable fortune in return for access. You may even retain ownership of your vessel.

"Should you decline this very generous proposal, I am equally prepared and ready to use other methods to secure our objectives. These will be unprofitable to you except perhaps from the standpoint of experience, and considerably less comfortable. The choice is yours." He took a step forward.

"I do not expect gratitude for having preserved your life from others of your own kind. I do expect, and insist, that you will accompany me back to my vessel and thence to your own in the company of myself and an advance team of designated specialists. Under their supervision you and your ship will retire via nullspace to Blasusarr, where you will be well treated for the duration of your stay."

"So I'm a prisoner?"

"Guest. As for your indigenous friends, they are self-evidently not in a position to alert Commonwealth authorities to what has transpired here. It is also apparent that they have not the slightest inkling of the substance of this conversation. Therefore they may remain and depart in peace."

Flinx replied quietly. "I can't and won't be a party to anything that increases the likelihood of conflict between the Commonwealth and the Empire. Besides, you have no intention of letting me go free, either with my ship or without. Even if I can't explain the functions of the modified drive, I could still alert Commonwealth authorities to your possession of it."

"Do you doubt my word, *Ssisstin*?" Several of the soldiers tensed in tandem with their superior.

Flinx smiled thinly. "Of an AAnn noble? How could I? You said I could retain ownership of the *Teacher* and that I'd be well-treated for the duration of my stay on Blasusarr. It won't do me much good to retain ownership if I'm never allowed to leave."

Amusement as well as appreciation figured prominently in the aristocrat's reply. "Better a life of good treatment in the capital than a swift death by decomposition here."

Flinx drew himself up so that he could stare sharply down at the noble. "That's my choice to make. I can't allow you to have the secret of the *Teacher*. It would be a betrayal of those who gave her to me."

"An interesting problem in and of itself," declared Caavax. "Who 'gave' the vessel to you? Where was this scientific breakthrough accomplished?"

Flinx thought of the childlike yet incredibly advanced Ulru-Ujurrians and had to grin. "You wouldn't believe me if I told you."

"I am not overly credulous, but I am certainly prepared to accept any reality that is supported by evidence."

"What reality?" Flinx argued. "If my ship is capable of the feats you suggest, why didn't I just land her here? There are no cities to damage, no developed areas to threaten."

Lord Caavax eyed him pensively. "I have been wondering that myself. In time I am certain you will enlighten me. Now we will go." He turned.

Flinx took a deep breath as he scanned the surrounding greenery. Surely his conversation had bought enough time? He knew it would be helpful if he could keep the AAnn noble's attention focused on him.

"Sorry. I'm staying here, with my friends."

Lord Caavax LYD turned back to him. "I said that your friends were free to depart in peace. For one who declares himself dedicated to forestalling conflict, you are remarkably shortsighted. How if I were to kill them one at a time, beginning with the youngest child?" A clawed hand rested on the handle of his long-muzzled sidearm.

"How if that doesn't persuade me?" Flinx replied tightly.

"I believe it will. Your human-type is fairly straight-forward in that regard. To save time and display my personal magnanimity I will not kill outright. I will amputate the female child's limbs a joint at a time until she expires. If you still refuse to comply, I will resume with the male child and conclude with the female parent. If your obstinacy persists, I shall then begin on you, but not here. More sophisticated technology is available aboard my vessel." As always, he remained correct and polite, an admirable representative of the AAnn aristocracy.

"Better for four of us to die than thousands or millions."

"That is not logical, but you are not AAnn and will eventually come to realize as much. Why not spare your friends as well as yourself unnecessary unpleasantness? The end will be the same." Flinx noted that emotionally, at least, the noble was utterly convinced of this.

What was delaying the others, he wondered nervously? Caavax was watching him intently, and it was clear he couldn't stall the noble any longer.

He tried to make himself look as resigned and disconsolate as possible. "All right, you win. I'll go with you."

The AAnn gestured second-level gratification. "Of course you will. It was inevitable."

Flinx started forward, only to have the reptiloid block his path.

"Where are you going, Lynx-sir?"

Flinx blinked at him. "To the landing site, of course. The place where the shuttles are."

The noble gestured contrariwise. "Do you think me a complete fool that, having lost two of my party already to the inimical and subtle biota of this world, I would so readily offer up others for similar sacrifice?" With a perfectly trimmed and unpainted claw he pointed in the opposite direction.

"The depression in the forest is more than large enough to admit a shuttle. A skilled pilot interacting closely with a sensitive descent program should have no trouble positioning his ship so that we may board right here. It will be compelled to hover carefully, though I suspect that many of the remarkable growths around us would be quite capable of supporting its weight. Lifting off under such conditions, however, could prove difficult."

Turning, he hissed in his own language to one of the attentive troopers. Flinx knew some of the sibilant AAnn tongue, having studied it on his own, and the noble's terse command was relatively easy to understand.

Responding, the trooper removed a nonreflective cylinder from his duty belt. Telltales winked to life as he activated the communicator and spoke into the pickup. After exchanging a few words with the trooper, Lord Caavax turned back to Flinx.

"In a very few moments we will be gone from this place."

"Programming notwithstanding, your pilot better be good," Flinx replied. Hope continued to dominate his thoughts. Judging from the look on Teal's face, he could see that hers were following a similar course. Since the ongoing delay did not seem to be troubling her, he made an effort to appear similarly indifferent.

Aware of his attention, she addressed him softly. "I don't understand, Flinx. What is happening?"

Caavax watched closely as Flinx put a comforting arm around her shoulder. "These nonhuman skypersons want something from me. It's important that I don't give it to them, even at the risk of our lives. I'm doing my best to convince him that since you're not directly involved, he should let you and the children go."

"That is what I thought." Her gaze probed his own. "If it is that important, you must do what you think best."

She really was beautiful, he mused. "They want me to go with them." He gestured upward.

Her eyes widened slightly. "Into the Upper Hell?"

"No. Beyond that. To—" He really wasn't very good at this, he realized. "—a place beyond the sky. Where your people came from originally. Where I've come from. In a shuttle."

"A skyboat," she declared, sifting ancestral memories for a suitable term.

He nodded. Together, they settled down to wait.

Chapter Sixteen

The AAnn soldiers talked continuously. Flinx could sense their unease. They were anxious to leave what to them was not only an unremittingly hostile environment, but one that they found physically uncomfortable as well. The special fabric of their camouflage suits did its best to wick away the moisture that formed on their skin. Meanwhile their jaws hung slack as they panted, trying to cool themselves down. They were unable to perspire in the manner of a human.

The only lapse in the admirable display of discipline came when two of them fired shots into the hylaeal depths, certain they had seen something large and threatening moving toward them. Flinx had seen it as well, salmon-colored and spiked like a medieval armory. Three maniacal eyes had glared furiously in the group's direction, only to vanish into the green depths in response to the first shot from the agitated troopers. It missed, of course, as did the several follow-up bursts.

After calming his jittery soldiers, Caavax stalked back to confront the humans.

"What was *that*?" To all outward appearances unaffected, the noble's unease was apparent only to Flinx, who found himself inordinately pleased by the AAnn's distress. Lord Caavax was more shaken than he showed.

"Probably a cheleac," Teal replied, as if the apparition's appearance was of no consequence. "They're very fast. And very dangerous."

"Its aspect was indicative of that." Caavax was squinting warily into the verdure. "Do you think it will come back?"

"No. If it intended to attack, some of you would already be dead. The cheleac is a streaker, not a sneaker. Once it has fixed on its quarry, it comes straight at it. With a cheleac it's kill or be killed quickly."

"Is that so? Then how do you explain the fact that my soldiers have frightened it away?"

She turned hard green eyes on the AAnn. "If the cheleac did not attack it was because it had other prey in mind. You cannot 'frighten' one away." She smiled thinly. "Besides, what makes you think it has gone 'away'?"

The noble's head snapped around and slitted eyes once more searched the greenery. "It is still here?"

Teal shrugged nonchalantly. "I don't know. Why don't you send some of your soldiers to look for it?"

Lord Caavax postured appreciation for the jest combined with unalterable determination. "You will forgive me if I say that that is a request in which I choose not to indulge."

Flinx gazed longingly at the double mesh sack that held Pip. It lay on the branch between two of Caavax's troops.

"Put that thought out of your mind, Lynx-sir." Caavax was alert as ever. "Your dangerous pet will remain as it is, ensuring continued comfort for all."

A muted roar reached them from above, echoing through the yellow-green firmament. The feelings of relief this engendered in the AAnn soldiers was strong.

Several of them glanced toward the valley in the forest, but none left his post. There were no wild demonstrations. They were too well trained for such overt displays of exultation. That was a human failing.

Lord Caavax stepped past Flinx. Squinting through the curtain of creepers and lianas, the noble located and tracked the tiny glistening dot in the sky until it grew large enough to identify with certainty.

"It will be a blessing, *sissink*, to get off this homicidal world. I loathe the flora and fauna, the light, the climate, everything about it. Unpleasant day gives way to unbearable night. One might as well try swimming like a human as endure the demonical rain. This is a climate fit only for a thranx, and I believe it too damp even for them."

"It's too wet for me, too," Flinx told him. "I don't like getting drenched every night any more than you do."

"Then you will find Blasusarr infinitely more appealing."

Flinx was watching the AAnn shuttle as it descended. "I tried a desert climate once. Didn't care much for it, either."

Conversation became difficult as the thunder from the shuttle's engines drowned out forest sounds as well as speech. Dwell and Kiss were gesturing excitedly, astonishment temporarily overcoming their fear.

Teal put her lips close to Flinx's ear. "Fire comes from its belly! Why doesn't it burn itself up?"

He turned his head and raised his voice. "The skyboat rides on fire!"

"Fire," she avowed, "is very dangerous! Very threatening!" Her eyes were intent on the descending craft.

To Flinx's regret, it appeared as if the AAnn pilot knew what he was doing. The shuttle descended in a smooth arc that would bring it alongside their branch in a few minutes. At that point his options would be drastically reduced.

Despite the deafening rumble, Teal was still talking to him. "You have lived the rain at night. So you know that with the rain comes sometimes the fire that scars the sky."

He nodded absently, paying only cursory attention to her words. "Lightning."

"Yes, lightning. Haven't you wondered, Flinx, why there are so few lightning-caused fires in the forest? Why there are no large burned places?"

"What?" Mildly irritated by her persistence, he turned to meet her gaze. "I suppose it's because everything is so wet."

"Partly so, but lightning can make anything burn."

"Then why doesn't it?" he asked, only half curious.

He felt her lips touch his ear so that he could hear but no one else. "Because the forest has ways of protecting itself."

For a moment he was uncertain. Then he remembered. "Stormtreader tree," he murmured.

"Stormtreader—and others." She joined him in observing the shuttle's final approach.

It was larger than his own landing craft, but that was to be expected. Stolid and utilitarian of design, it was descending on four vaned lifting jets. Next it would position itself alongside and align itself with the branch on which they were standing. The trooper Caavax had spoken with earlier was holding his cylinder close to his mouth, speaking steadily and evenly into the pickup.

Halting its descent level with their branch, the sturdy landing craft began to hover sideways toward them. It was too loud to talk now. As it adjusted its position, the shuttle's exhaust blasted into the vegetation below, burning and crisping dozens, hundreds, of growing things, scorching a black path eastward through the verdure.

A port opened in its side. Flinx could see armed troops milling about within. An extensible ramp extended toward the branch like a long gray tongue. A moment later the muzzle of a sidearm was prodding him in the ribs. It was a gesture whose meaning was universal.

Shouting to make himself heard, the AAnn noble leaned close. "As soon as the ramp is near enough, you will start across!" Behind him, his troopers were collapsing their perimeter, gathering in a tight, protective mass behind their superior. They continued to watch the surrounding greenery.

Flinx nodded to indicate he understood. Turning to Teal, he tried to think of something final to say. She wasn't looking at him. Instead her gaze, as well as those of the children, was focused on something off to their left.

The trunks of three fairly large trees had swollen to several times normal size. So intent had he been on the descending shuttle that he hadn't noticed the measured but steady expansion. Neither had the soldiers, preoccupied with both the shuttle's arrival and watching the forest behind them.

Amidst the muffled roar of the jets, the ramp continued to lengthen. Flames began to leap from the inner forest canopy as the intense heat from the shuttle's engines inflamed and blistered the exposed vegetation. The spreading conflagration had no effect on the ship's systems and her pilot ignored it, knowing that they would be sealed up and on their way before the blaze could blossom into anything threatening.

As he took his first resigned step toward the beckoning ramp, Flinx could feel the heat from the fire burning below. While he was confident that Teal and the children were in little danger from the blaze because it would quickly die out due to the greenness and dampness of the surrounding vegetation, he still felt sorry for the plants and slow-moving animals below that were threatened by the shuttle's indifferent jets. They would be at the mercy of the flames until the blaze burnt itself out.

That was when Teal screamed, "Get down!" and flung herself flat onto the branch. Dwell and Kiss followed by nanoseconds while a comparatively laggard Flinx didn't begin to drop until the mother and children were already pressing themselves against the wood. Noting that instead of trying to protect their heads, as one would expect, they instead concentrated on shutting their eyes tight and covering their noses and mouths, he endeavored to do the same.

"What is all this?" Lord Caavax bellowed. Keeping his sidearm aimed in Flinx's direction, he turned to roar at his troops, several of whom had already fallen uncertainly to their knees. "There's no danger here. Get up!" Jumpy, but regaining confidence when nothing continued to happen, they straightened.

Flinx felt a heavy foot prod his left leg. "Enough foolishness. I am hot and damp and it is time to board. Don't force me to have you carried. My soldiers are in an ill mood and can be ungentle."

Flinx was pondering a reply when something blew up with enough force to momentarily drown out even the thunder of the shuttle's hoverjets. The eruption had been preceded by a fleeting but intense surge of emotion the likes of which he had never experienced before. As he tried to isolate the source, he felt pressure on his forehead and exposed arms. Keeping his face pressed firmly to the wood, he cupped his right hand over his nostrils and his left over his tightly shut mouth.

The immense bladders incorporated inside the three tumescent trees had reached their limit of containment and ruptured spectacularly. The heavily aerated latexlike sap they had contained spewed forth in truly prodigious quantities, smothering everything within a circle some forty meters in diameter. It was a natural response to the threat of fire that Teal had alluded to, very different from the reaction to lightning of the stormtreader tree but no less effective.

On contact with air, the puffy, sticky white substance began to expand farther, transforming from a fluffy sap into a foaming aerogel. Ethereal but persistent, it clung to Flinx's hair, his ears, his back.

He could feel the bubbles expanding as the original volume of the sap ballooned to encompass ten, twenty times its original volume. Within that space the movement of air was restricted or cut off entirely. No wonder Teal and the children had been so careful to cover their mouths and nostrils. Growing anxious for air, he wondered when or even if it would be safe to part his lips just a little and try to breathe. He envisioned inhaling a mouthful of the sticky foam and having it settle in his lungs.

A small but strong hand was tugging at his shoulder, trying to lift him. Turning, he saw Teal peering anxiously down at him. With her other hand she was tearing at the congealed foam that clung to her face. He rose and copied her movements.

Then they were both thrown to the ground as the branch beneath their feet heaved violently. Crackling, ripping sounds mixed with the rumbling whine of the shuttle's engines. Madly he tore the clinging translucent whiteness away from his face in a frantic effort to see what was happening.

With both portside hydrajet intakes completely clogged and one of those on the starboard side at least partly obstructed by the organic aerogel, the AAnn vessel was skewing wildly to port. Neither its computational navigation system nor its pilot was able to compensate for the abrupt and drastic loss of lift.

With full power to only one jet, the shuttle had swung around to slam into the tree on whose branch the prospective passengers had been waiting. Encased in sticky white foam that was hardening rapidly as it dried, Flinx stared as the shuttle lurched away from them. The deeper-throated roar of the craft's rockets, normally not utilized until a shuttle had left atmosphere behind, coughed to life, intermittent and uncertain, as the pilot tried to bypass the smothered hydrajets and gain altitude.

The rockets appeared to do the trick, as the bulbous craft began to climb. But while it gained altitude, it was at the expense of a continuing loss of maneuverability. Once it cleared the crest of the canopy, that wouldn't matter. All the pilot had to do was break atmosphere and wait to be picked up by the parent vessel.

Simultaneously climbing and sliding to port, it had nearly surmounted the top of the sunken valley when it slammed into the big trees on the far side. A muffled explosion echoed from within the shuttle's underside. Falling backward out of control, it plunged into the vegetation below, landing upside down amidst a great crackling and tearing of greenery. A dull *whoom* obliterated the craft from sight, and Flinx spun away as a gust of superheated air rushed over him.

The fires resulting from the crash stimulated half a dozen of the foam-producing trees in the immediate vicinity to balloon and release their flame-retardant sap. In seconds the wreckage was completely engulfed in an expanding white cloud. Taking into account the crash, the explosions, the resultant fire and consequent suffocating reaction of the foam trees, Flinx doubted anyone aboard could have survived.

Pulling and scraping foam from his face and upper body, he assured Teal he was all right before he began hunting through the pale white, rapidly solidifying dreamscape. Bubbles clung like overripe fruit from every branch and vine, burst with soft popping sounds as he forced his way through them. The all-pervasive whiteness made walking tricky. He was wary of pushing through a mass of congealed foam only to find that he'd stepped clean off the branch.

Eventually he found the sack, knelt to feel Pip moving energetically within. A rush of familiar warmth swept through his mind as he made contact with the flying snake. There was nothing to suggest that she'd suffered an injury, and in fact the mesh sack had probably protected her from the choking effects of the foam.

As he reached down to release her, cool ceramic contacted the back of his neck. The attendant emotions were not filled with warmth.

"Leave the sack and its contents be, Lynx-sir." Lord Caavax LYD took a step back and gestured with the sidearm. "They are fine as they are."

Rising reluctantly, Flinx saw that the noble was covered in congealing foam. His face was unobstructed. Coughing, hacking sounds came from nearby as the soldiers struggled to clear their lungs.

Two of them hadn't reacted appropriately or in time. During the initial blast, each had inhaled a fatal dose of the sticky sap. Expanding within their lungs instead of outside their bodies, the foam had ballooned relentlessly. Now both lay dead on the surface of the branch, the foam oozing from their mouths showing how they had suffocated.

That left nine, including the AAnn noble, to watch over them. Still too many. Flinx waited as Dwell and Kiss, with Teal supervising, plucked congealed foam from their bodies. Angry, frightened soldiers kept a wary eye on the humans while performing similar hygienics.

Brushing at the hardened bubbles coating his own clothing, Flinx was startled when a handful powdered under his fingers. The next mass collapsed of its own accord, releasing as it did so a faint aroma of lilac along with a delicate, tinkling sound.

All around him the aerogel was breaking up as it lost the moisture necessary to support its internal structure. The verdure was filled with an overpowering scent of lilac counterpointed by a symphony executed by a carillon of miniature bells. The final residue was a fine white dust that sparkled like powdered diamonds. The nightly rain would wash it all into the depths, allowing affected growths to resume unobstructed photosynthesis the following morning.

Peering out across the green valley, he saw a thin line of smoke rising from the place where the shuttle had gone down. It was not the only sign of movement. Already the inhabitants of the forest had reemerged to cautiously resume their daily routines. Among the majority, the wreckage in their midst engendered no unusual curiosity. The surface against which the shuttle had impacted and exploded was not solid. Many of the fragments had spilled between trunks and branches, tumbling down to emerald depths unknown. More of the fine white residue overlay the crash site, glistening in the yellow-green sunlight like iridescent snow as the last of the fire-retardant aerogel decomposed.

The AAnn picked at the remaining foam and brushed at the resultant powder as if they were infested with leeches. Their disgust was underlined by their emotional state. Comforted by their more reactive companions, several were still coughing up white spittle.

Flinx struggled with his nascent AAnn as the group subofficer reported. "Two dead, sir. Trooper Keinkavii partially incapacitated, but I think he will be all right." He indicated a choking, wet-eyed soldier who was being supported by two companions.

Caavax responded with a curt gesture indicative of first-degree comprehension and turned to confront Teal. "Female, is this foam toxic to humans if ingested?"

Green eyes flashed. "Only if you swallow a lot of it. Then it clogs up your insides."

The noble indicated understanding, glanced back at the subofficer. "You heard the female. See that all afflicted troops are medicated appropriately. Where indicated, a strong purgative may be in order."

"*Sistik*, honored one." The subofficer looked unhappy. Such treatment would not improve the soldiers' already battered morale, though it was certainly preferable to the alternative.

When Caavax offered no objection, Flinx wandered over to rejoin Teal and the children. "What about me?" he asked her. "I'm sure I swallowed plenty of that powder."

"Don't worry," she whispered. "In its final form it will pass harmlessly through your bowels."

His brows drew together. "But you told the AAnn—" He caught himself. She was smiling at him, and he could do no less than return the grin.

Caavax was gazing solemnly out at the crash site. "More dead. Better this world had remained forgotten. Give me the clean, dry sands of Blasusarr or Sysirkuus." With a hissing sigh he turned back to his prisoners.

"Where were you going when we captured you?"

"To the Home-tree, of course," she replied before Flinx could warn her.

" 'Home-tree.' How appropriate." As he murmured to the subofficer the aristocrat's sarcasm asserted itself once more. "Humans love trees. No wonder they can survive here."

"And they breed like flies," agreed the subofficer.

"Well, I don't like it here," Flinx countered. "Much too humid for my taste. And there are other considerations."

"Sers," acknowledged Caavax. "Everything is eager to poison, dismember, or eviscerate. So we share a common dislike. Perhaps from that a certain modicum of trust may grow."

Flinx said nothing. The noble's words were a flimsy veil through which his emotions could be read clearly.

"The *Keralkee* carried two shuttles," Caavax declared. "Normally that is more than sufficient for any perceived needs. But as has been learned with pain and difficulty, this is not a normal world. The fate of one shuttle you all have witnessed. The other remains sealed and waiting for us at the touchdown site.

"We are now on our own. With no way to reach the surface, we can expect no help from those who anxiously await our return aboard the *Keralkee*. I choose to regard this as a delay and inconvenience, nothing more. With the native human to guide us, we shall return safely to the landing site." He gestured at the catching sack, covered in white crystals.

"One of you take charge of *that*."

The field officer hissed at a soldier. The unhappy individual thus signaled out warily approached the sack. Satisfied that it was still secure, he knelt and proceeded to strap it to his own backpack. Though putting up a brave front, he was clearly unnerved at the prospect of having to march through the alien forest with only a double layer of mesh separating his neck from the toxic jaws of a lethal predator.

This accomplished, the field officer then turned back to Caavax. "Our deceased companions; what shall we do with them?"

"Leave them," proposed the aristocrat.

"We might find a hollow in a tree." The field officer was careful to add a gesture of second-degree deference layered with respect.

"Do you want to linger here?"

"No, Lord, but—"

"I don't want to waste the time." Caavax masked his frustration with impatience. "Scavengers would find the bodies anyway, as soon as we had departed. Or perhaps the tree itself would consume them. Nothing on this world is to be trusted."

Again the slight bow, the honorific lowering of the eyes. "How fortunate we were," the field officer declared when next he spoke, "that we did not try to set our own shuttle down close to our quarry."

"*Sherss,*" Caavax agreed. "We must inform the *Keralkee* of what has happened. Commander Beiraviq will be distraught. Assure him that we are all right and that the prisoner remains safe within our custody. Inform him of our intentions."

The field officer acknowledged and spent some time conversing with the warship via communications cylinder. When he was finished, he reported back to the noble.

"The honored Commander extends his condolences for the discomfort you have suffered, Lord Caavax. His engineers propose utilizing remote control to guide the remaining shuttle from the landing site to our present or any other designated location."

"Commander Beiraviq's concern for my welfare is gratifying, but we cannot risk a repeat of the recent disaster, which would leave us permanently stranded in this diseased wood until another ship could reach this system from the borders of the Empire. Nor can we ascend to the top of the forest, there to await pickup. Commander Beiraviq has no experience of the aerial carnivores that inhabit this world or he would know that we would not last long enough in the treetops for the shuttle to reach us.

"We will simply return to the landing site via our original route. We have already performed a successful landing on this world, and we will shortly execute a successful lift-off. Assure him of our confidence, and that we will continue to remain in contact while we make our way back." Without further ado he checked the positioner attached to his belt and pointed.

"That way. Let us be moving."

Flinx translated as best he could for Teal and the children. "It will be dark soon," she pointed out. "We should find a place to spend the night. It takes time to find a suitable place."

"We'll camp where we stop, when the light has grown too feeble for safe travel." Lord Caavax had no time to waste on human concerns. "That is what we did while we tracked you, and that is what we shall do on the way back. I will brook no delays." He waved the sidearm. "Move, Lynx-sir. Female, I will provide the direction and you will lead the way. Your offspring will remain close to me. For their own safety."

"It's okay." Flinx ruffled Dwell's hair and this time the boy smiled up at him. The three of them fell into position in front of the aristocrat while Teal assumed the point. The troops spread out as best they were able on the broad branch, the field officer sticking close to his superior, the soldier hauling the sack containing Pip shifting to the rear. It had been made clear to the troops that the sack was to be kept under watch at all times and under no circumstances was the adult human prisoner to be allowed near it.

Moving off through the trees, they soon left the valley in the forest behind, with its legacy of confrontation and capture and the still smoldering wreckage of the doomed AAnn shuttlecraft. A riot of uninhibited color and explosive growth filled in the gap behind them, engulfing them all once more in a sea of inscrutable, impenetrable greenery.

Chapter Seventeen

By nightfall they still had not found a suitable site to spend the night, nor had the relentless and determined Lord Caavax called a halt. It was left to the trio of soldiers in the lead, who had been reduced to using their portable beams to find their footing while Teal picked her way along easily without the aid of artificial lighting, to protest. The branch they were currently traversing was narrow, the upper surface of the bark slick and treacherous. If the continued safety of those following was to be assured, they would have to stop until morning.

Caavax was forced to give in. "*Sysumeq.* We will spend the night here."

Teal inveighed immediately. "We can't stop here, out in the open like this. We must find shelter from the night-rain and those who hunt in the dark."

The aristocrat was not moved. "Our suits provide adequate insulation from the nightly downpour, and AAnn soldiers are quite capable of dealing with malevolent primitive life forms. As for you, I am afraid you will simply get wet." He peered over the side of the branch.

"I happen to like this location. The branch on which we are stopping is quite narrow and there are no strong vines or creepers within human reach. Beneath us lies an impressive drop-off. I do not think you will try to use the darkness as cover for an attempted escape. Behave yourselves and we shall all greet the dawn together."

Teal pulled Dwell and Kiss close. "It's not good for children to be out in the night-rain."

The AAnn noble was unmoved. "They will not melt. Find some leaves or something with which to shield yourselves." His voice was thick with fourth-degree irritation.

That night there was no rain delay. The instant the last vestige of yellow-green light seeped into the rising mist, it began to pour. Thunder rattled the branch on which the travelers crouched; the soldiers squatting inside their camouflage suits, Teal and her children huddling as best they could beneath their water-repellent green cloaks. Only Flinx was in danger of a drenching.

Somewhere nearby, lightning struck a stormtreader tree and the smell of ozone stung everyone's nostrils. Someone cursed in guttural AAnn. While not literally translatable, the sentiment would have been recognized by the soldiers of any combative species.

Teal singled out a large epiphyte that grew from a smaller, overhead branch, identifying it for the AAnn aristocrat. "That is a brorobod. Let me gather a few of its leaves for Flinx. Do you want your valued captive to catch sick and die?"

Squinting against the rain, Caavax consulted with the field officer before granting permission. "Go ahead, but be quick." Scaly fingers curled firmly over Kiss's right shoulder, the claw points digging into the skin. The little girl winced but said nothing. "I know you will return with harmless leaves and nothing more."

Teal looked significantly at her daughter, who stood silent and wide-eyed in the grip of the AAnn. Had she told her not to breathe, Flinx was convinced the girl would have held her breath until she passed out. In the green wilds of this world, children were doubtless taught early on that the ability to remain motionless often translated into continued survival.

Flinx watched as Teal jumped to grab a looping, dangling vine. Climbing several meters hand over hand, she swung one leg over the branch above and was soon straddling the wood in front of the flowering brorobod. While Caavax and several of the soldiers kept their eyes on her, she removed several of the plant's large, glossy leaves, twisting them in both hands until they snapped off cleanly at the base.

"Look at this." Idle, damp, and unable to fall asleep so early in the evening, one of the lead soldiers was beckoning to his companions.

The object of his attention was a cluster of powder-blue, bell-shaped blossoms that hung straight down from the underside of a man-sized mossy mass. They were attached to the parenting body by bright red stems no thicker than common sewing thread. As the darkness deepened it became possible to see that the flowers emitted a natural blue phosphorescence. Close to the blossoms it was bright enough to read by.

"Attractive," commented the field officer from his place on the branch, "and useful. Should strange sound or movement strike in the middle of the night, we will not need to use our portable beams to see that which may be moving about near us."

Indeed, by the time Teal returned, having dropped the thick leaves down to Flinx, the natural blue glow had greatly intensified. It provided enough light for the soldiers in front to see all the way to their colleagues farther down the branch. The field officer was delighted.

Grounding the stalks of the leaves as best she could, Teal constructed a crude and none-too-stable lean-to on the exposed branch. Together the four humans huddled beneath the imperfect roof. With no green cloak to shed secondary moisture, Flinx continued to suffer from the water that dripped inside the lean-to, but it was much better than simply crouching outside, exposed to the elements.

While the ambient temperature would remain high all night, moisture still sucked body heat away. He huddled close to Teal. They watched as several of the soldiers continued to admire the now brilliantly glowing blue flowers. A glance at Teal showed her staring intently. He started to ask something, decided instead to keep silent. Events could and doubtless would unfold without extraneous commentary. The children huddled close to her, watching with equal interest.

The soldier who had first pointed out the extraordinary blooms reached out to cup a hand beneath the nearest blossom. The blue light illuminated his entire hand, reflecting dimly off the small scales of his wrist.

"Look at this, *ssuusam*! Is it not wondrous beautiful?"

"Probably serves to attract nocturnal pollinators." The soldier who'd spoken blinked at the night-rain. "Large insects, perhaps."

"I have read that such things exist on the far plateaus of Chisskin," added the third member of the trio, "but I have never seen anything like it myself."

"I wonder if their scent is as attractive as their appearance?" The first soldier twisted the bell-shaped blossom up and around, bringing it gently toward his nostrils.

A blinding flash of pure white light obliterated Flinx's vision. Shouts and yells of dismay and distress came from the soldiers in front. Furious blinking failed to restore his sight.

Fingers gripped his arm to restrain him. "It's no good," she whispered. "Too many of them were looking the other way."

"Teal, I can't see!"

"Hush! It will return."

He forced himself to sit motionless while confusion reigned around them. A hissing scream came from the soldier who had discovered the radiant blossoms as, stumbling about while rubbing frantically at his outraged eyes, he missed a step and plunged over the side of the branch. His scream was cut off as he struck something solid and unyielding not far below.

Lining up along the branch, those of his companions who had not been affected by the blinding burst of light aimed their own beams into the sodden depths.

"Chorsevasin, are you all right?" someone shouted.

"Speak to us!" cried another.

There was no reply. Nor could they, search with their lights as they might, locate the body of their unfortunate associate. The green-black depths had swallowed him up.

Flinx found his vision returning. "What happened?" Large white spots continued to dance before his eyes.

"The one who fell agitated a *dontlook*. The forest world is a closed place and even more so at night. To attract the cocary to its nectar, the dontlook makes a strong light. But the light can also draw plant eaters who would chew up the dontlook for its nectar. If it is not touched correctly, the dontlook will make enough light to blind the unwary who approach too near." She leaned forward to peer over the side of the narrow branch, into the bottomless depths. "Usually those who are so stunned fly away, bumping into trees as they go."

With great relief Flinx found he could once more make out individual shapes. A couple of meters away he had been completely if temporarily blinded by the burst of illumination. The face of the unfortunate soldier had been only centimeters from the flower when it had gone off. The flash must have caused considerable pain as well as blindness.

As a consequence, their escort had been reduced to eight.

Lord Caavax LYD, High Servant of his Most Estimable and Expectant Emperor Moek VI, confronted his abashed retinue. The steady downpour was insufficient to cloak the gestures he performed.

"Listen to me, all of you! From now on I do not care how alluring is the life form you espy. I do not care if you find an apparently solid nodule lying loose that is the equal of the most exquisitely polished cassesha wood. I do not care if you find a depression filled with pearlized ziszai seeds. I care not if you pass a hollow overflowing with precious metals and gems. Do not reach for it; remark on it not, pass it by. Note it for future study, if you are so inclined. But *touch nothing*. Walk around, avoid, evade, circumvent." He glared at each of them in turn, ensuring that he made eye contact with each soldier individually.

"I do not care if what makes you gasp in wonder appears as harmless as a Lieff scallop contoured in the flank of a dreamer's dune. Ignore it you will!" The only response from the thoroughly cowed soldiers was some disgruntled muttering.

They returned to their previous positions, those whose close friend had died adopting a particularly aggressive stance, as if they were angry enough to do battle with the rain. In the company of Teal and the children, Flinx settled back down beneath the inadequate canopy of leaves.

"These will never reach their destination." She was very assured. "You will see. The forest will take care of them."

"Don't underestimate them," Flinx advised her. "The one who just fell made a stupid move. The AAnn tend not to repeat mistakes. I know this species. Once fixed on a goal, they never give up. They're clever and determined. The higher in rank, the more determined."

"The more stupid." Dwell was at once alert and at ease. This was *his* world.

Flinx continued. "The one I've been talking with ranks high in the AAnn sociopolitical hierarchy. If he fails to bring me back he'll lose a great deal of face."

"How can he lose face?" Kiss wiped a trickle of water from her forehead. "Isn't it part of the rest of him?"

Flinx smiled affectionately. "There's more truth in what you say than you know, little one." He turned back to Teal. "Remember that he's holding you responsible for all of us arriving safely at the landing site. If he loses many more troops, he'll blame you."

"How can he blame me for something over which I have no control?" There was satisfaction in her voice. "No harm has come to him or his while I have been leading."

"I know, but from now on he'll expect you to warn them of any dangers in the vicinity, even if you try to lead them safely past. Don't let him get angry. I wouldn't put it past him to kill one of the children just to set an example."

Teal pulled Kiss closer to her side. "That won't happen, Flinx. The forest will get them first."

"What happens if it doesn't?" He brooded on the possibility. "What happens if these very competent soldiers manage to tough it out and most of us reach the landing site? You can't lead them around in circles. Caavax and several others have positioners. We have to travel in the direction they choose."

"I do not know about that. I know only that I must protect the children. About myself I care little." She leaned forward. "All is not yet lost, Flinx. You are forgetting something very important."

"I haven't forgotten," he assured her. "I wonder at the timing, but I haven't forgotten." Water dribbling through his red hair was running down the back of his neck. He shifted his seat on the branch, trying to find a drier spot.

The night was home to active possibilities he was presently unable to sense. That didn't mean they no longer existed.

In actual fact, they were at present quite near.

His thick green coat efficiently shedding the rain, Moomadeem looked up at Saalahan. "Look at them. Just look at them! Spending the night right out in the open like that. They are stupider even than the strange person called Flinx."

"They are not-persons." Saalahan solemnly nodded agreement. "Is one thing to know nothing. Is another to refuse to learn."

Next to him Tuuvatem strained to penetrate the darkness. The furcots had excellent night vision, but even they could not see very far in a heavy rain.

"Where is Kiss? I can't see." The densely vegetated golagola bush in which they were resting rustled with her movements.

"All fine, all well." Saalahan was a huge black hump in the darkness. "They are under some brorobod leaves."

Moomadeem snorted pugnaciously. "Not so good. Better to fix things."

"Did you see the one who shoved his face right into the dontlook?" Tuuvatem could hardly believe it. "What a stupid!"

"A dead stupid now," Moomadeem asserted. "If the others play stupid also, we won't have to do anything."

"They must not reach the other skyboat." Sitting there on the arm of the tree in the midst of the comforting go-lagola leaves, Saalahan resembled a soft, round boulder. "They *will* not reach it."

"Too stupid," Moomadeem reiterated. "All the time the bad skypersons were talking, they never knew we were there, right under them in the cave in the branch. Then these strange not-persons came, and they didn't see us either, not even when the smother trees killed their skyboat." He sniffed. "It died noisy. I thought we were going to be shaken out of the sleeping place."

"You understand now why it is always best to wait and see what happens before trying to bad fix things yourself," Saalahan reminded them sternly. "Sometimes if you leave them alone, things fix themselves." Tilting back its great head, the scimitarlike tusks glistening in the silver scrimmed moonlight, it ignored the raindrops as it considered the rugged green ceiling.

"Soon all will be asleep."

"Surely not all?" commented Tuuvatem.

The big furcot stretched, muscles rippling beneath twin sets of shoulders. "Perhaps they are not completely stupid and will leave some awake to look out for night dangers. It will not matter."

Moomadeem's eyes flashed in the pale light. "How do you want to do the thing?"

Saalahan's triocular gaze shifted from one cub to the other. "You are both young. Have you no unsureness about this?"

"Why should we?" A confident, relaxed Moomadeem shook himself, sending droplets flying. "They are not-persons."

"They have thoughts."

"It doesn't matter." Tuuvatem was licking a front paw and using it to groom her face. "We will do what we must to keep our persons safe."

"That is fine for Teal, and Dwell, and Kiss, but what about the skyperson Flinx?" Saalahan wondered. "He is not our responsibility. He has no furcot."

"No furcot to help or comfort him." Tuuvatem's paw paused in the middle of her face. "It's very sad."

"We have to help him, too."

Saalahan looked surprised. "I thought you didn't like him, Moomadeem."

The younger furcot blinked at the rain. "At first I didn't, because I wasn't sure he was a person. Then I decided he was a person, but just stupid. When I found out he was a skyperson I got mad, because I know the stories of what happened the last time the skypersons came. Since then he has learned much, and has helped our own persons. Whoever helps my person is my friend."

Saalahan smiled knowingly. "Flinx is not the only one who has learned much these past several days. Learning is a good thing, for furcots as well as persons."

Moomadeem looked away, embarrassed. "I didn't say I learned anything. I just said that we ought to help him as well."

"So we will." The big furcot's brow furrowed above the three eyes. "It is the—ethical thing to do."

"How sorrowful to travel through life without a furcot of one's own." Tuuvatem was still mourning Flinx's status. "I can't imagine how awful it would be if Kiss were to disappear."

"I feel the same way about Dwell, but I don't think about it much." Moomadeem scratched under its chin with a claw capable of shredding metal.

"I once heard the shaman Ponder speak about this matter," Saalahan informed them. "He said that humans are mostly active, while furcots tend to be primarily reactive."

Moomadeem snorted. "Then let's do some reacting! I'm bored just sitting here in the rain."

"Patience." Making as little noise as possible, the massive adult let its great bulk slump down into the cushioning boughs and leaves. The rain washed over it, and the two smaller masses crouched close by, the three motionless humps looking in the darkness like green galls growing directly from the surface of the branch.

It was a semblance that went deeper than it looked.

The half of Tatrasaseep QQWRTL that was asleep was enjoying life far more than the half of him that was awake. Consigned to the watch for another hour or so, he had been awakened by his predecessor and posted near the back of the encampment. Tepid rain streamed off the hood of his camouflage suit, spilled off his arms, waterfalled from his knees and trickled down his tail. No matter how he arranged his limbs, no matter how carefully he sat or adjusted the suit's hood, a certain amount still succeeded in working its way inside to dampen both his underattire and his spirits.

Irritated and tired, he wiped rainwater from his muzzle. Perhaps if he bent over more—but then he wouldn't be able to watch the accursed forest for signs of approaching danger. What danger? He mumbled to himself. Virtually nothing was afoot in the saturated landscape. Or a-wing or afloat, he added silently. Any creature that could manage it had sensibly gone to cover, unlike himself and his colleagues, who were reduced to squatting forlornly on the narrow, exposed branch. Strategically he supposed it made sense, but from a practical standpoint it was pure hell.

His thoughts drifted to his barracks bed on the *Keralkee*, lined with fine yellow sand and heated to a nice soothing dryness. He'd had enough of humidity to last him a lifetime. There would be tales aplenty to brag upon when they returned to the ship with the peculiar human in tow. For the life of him, Tatrasaseep couldn't see what was so important about the young mammal or his vessel, much less why a Lord of the AAnn would take a personal interest in the matter. If it had been up to him, the trooper would have shot all the humans on sight and been done with it.

Less than an hour to go now. Then he would turn his post over to Creskescanvi and flatten himself comfortably on the branch until morning. Time enough for his associates to partake of this suffering.

At the far end of the branch he knew Masmarulial was keeping watch. In between, the rest of the expedition slept. A few days march and with luck all would arrive safely back at the dangerous landing site. No more watches then. Only blissful dryness and the promise of promotion.

Resting his chest on his knees, he shifted the pulse rifle to a more comfortable position. His tail twitched restlessly, flicking water from side to side. With little light to see by and only the steady drumming of the rain for company, time passed with agonizing slowness.

Fortunately there was little wind in the depths of the forest and the rain fell straight down. Tiny luminous shapes slithered and crawled and flitted through the sodden night. Occasionally one ate its neighbor.

Leaning slightly forward enabled him to peer into the dark depths, where other naturally refulgent shapes swam like zooplankton in a celestial sea. Stealthy silhouettes plucked the unwary from the damp air or dropped down on them from above. A few specially adapted life forms were active even at the height of the nightly deluge.

Something scratched on the branch behind him. Every sense suddenly alert, he jerked around and aimed his rifle in the same motion.

Something was moving back in the leaves; a lumpish outline half his size. A soft mewling sound came from it, as if it were in pain. As he stared, it rolled over and stopped moving.

It lay like that for some time, utterly motionless. Doing his best to ignore it, Tatrasaseep found that after a while his curiosity, not to mention prudence, dictated that he investigate a little closer. After a glance in the direction of the slumbering encampment, he ventured a soft hiss as he rose.

Keeping the rifle pointed toward the lump at all times and two fingers on the triggers, he approached cautiously. Once he was careful to step around, not over, a clump of what appeared to be harmless grass growing from a bump in the wood. The lesson of the hapless Chorsevasin had not been lost on his fellow soldiers. The grassy blades were spotted with tiny black bumps that for all Tatrasaseep knew were as likely to contain a virulent poison as easily as harmless pollen. One could not be certain of anything on this hell-world, except that if something looked harmless, it probably wasn't.

He kept that thought in mind as he neared the immobile lump. It lay amidst a cluster of epiphytes bright with tiny white flowers whose petals had closed for the night. Black flowers blossoming from the same plants stood open to the rain. It wasn't the first time they had encountered a plant that boasted two distinctly different types of flower, one blooming diurnally and its counterpart nocturnally. In this way the plant maximized its opportunities for pollination. In the face of eternal and relentless competition, individual growths on this world had evolved unique methods of survival.

The lump quivered slightly and the trooper froze. A steady stream of dark liquid was trickling from an ugly lesion on its side. Whatever else it was, it was apparent that the creature was either sick or badly wounded. That would explain why its movements had been blatant and clumsy when every other life form traveling about at night was at pains to move quietly and with stealth.

Taking a wary step forward, the trooper was able to locate the head. The three eyes were closed and more liquid flowed from the half-open mouth. The animal was of a type they had not encountered before.

Should he awaken Field Officer Nesorey, kick this diseased mass over the side, or just ignore it and return to his post? He leaned toward nudging it into the depths as the most conclusive of the three possibilities. A single shove should do it. A quick look around revealed no movement nearby. Taking no chances, he kept the rifle aimed at the creature's skull as he took another step forward. He was prepared and ready to deal with whatever surprises even a near-corpse might proffer.

What he was not prepared for was a surprise from another source entirely.

Dangling unseen from the underside of a branch ten meters directly overhead, Saalahan simultaneously released all six sets of claws. The AAnn never saw the half-ton mass that landed on his head, snapping his spine in several places. The soldier made not a sound, unless one counted the subsequent inconsequential snapping of numerous bones.

Sliding from lax fingers, the pulse rifle bounced once and vanished over the side of the branch, its triggers unactivated, its destructive power still leashed. As a third figure came ambling out of the dense vegetation that lay in the direction of the trunk, the motionless form abed in the black-flowering epiphytes rolled to its feet.

Moomadeem shook sharply, shaking pools of water from green fur. Then a paw reached back to flick the blood-sucking toet from its temporary home atop a rib. Settled onto a host, the parasite looked very much like an open wound. It was a sloppy drinker, spilling as much blood as it ingested. Carefully Moomadeem spat a second one from where it had been clinging to the inside of the furcot's upper jaw.

"Nasty," it muttered with distaste. "Are you all right, Saalahan?"

The big furcot nodded as it climbed off the smashed pulp that had moments earlier been a member of the Empire's elite expeditionary forces. "Not a bad drop. You?"

"I was wondering what was keeping you."

Saalahan indicated the engorged toets that were creeping slowly back down the branch in search of shelter. "Nothing to worry about. They would have stopped sucking soon."

"It wasn't that. The one in my mouth tasted bad and I wanted to get rid of it." Already the two wounds were healing over, a familiar well-known by-product of the toets' anti-agglutination saliva. No successful parasite desires a useful host to perish from infection. Corpses make poor fonts of future nutrients.

As Tuuvatem joined them, the three furcots studied the irregular outlines of the encampment. Saalahan absently used its back pair of legs to kick the remains of the dead soldier off the branch. The rain muffled the noise as it bounced down through the hylaea below, breaking branches and snapping vines.

"What next?" Tuuvatem whispered interestedly.

"They're sleeping." Moomadeem dug its front claws into the wood underfoot. "Let's charge and knock them all off!"

"No." Saalahan did not move. It was studying, observing, analyzing. Or perhaps it was just instinct. "Not all of them may be asleep. Their snufflers shoot thunder, and we are not as quick as thunder. Come."

They melted back into the trees as silently as they had come.

Ceijihagrast BHRYT was furious as he blinked at his chronometer. He was Tatrasaseep's follow-up on watch, and it was the other soldier's responsibility to wake his designated replacement. What was keeping him? Already Ceijihagrast had overslept his posting by an unforgivable margin.

Angrily he fumbled with his rifle. Let Tatrasaseep try to claim compensation for unscheduled watch time! It wouldn't play. Worse still for him if he'd fallen asleep on duty. Field Officer Nesorey would have the scales off his nostrils.

Rifle armed and ready, he picked his way past his sleeping comrades as he strode down the branch. He hadn't gone far before he paused and turned a slow circle. Tatrasaseep should be standing or sitting on this spot, just in front of the little grassy clump that protruded from a woody knot. There was no sign of him.

Either the fool had sneaked back into camp and gone to sleep in violation of every conceivable directive, or more likely, he had simply mispositioned himself. Difficult even in the rain to overlook the grassy knot, but not impossible.

Ceijihagrast walked on past the patch of quasi-grass. The encampment was well behind him now. Where was the lazy *sisstinp*? Had the clumsy idiot gone for a walk to loosen his muscles, only to slip and tumble soundlessly to a green grave? Unlikely. Tatrasaseep would never make underofficer, but he was physically adept.

Leaning slightly to his left, the trooper tried to see into the sodden reaches below the branch. If Tatrasaseep *had* fallen, he might be lying not far below, concealed from view by overarching leaves and blossoms. Even now he might be trying weakly to call for help, his portable beam broken or out of reach, his tail thrashing feebly beneath him.

If a search was to be mounted, assistance was in order. Too easy to become disoriented and lost in the dense vegetation, too likely to meet up with something lethal in the dark.

He called out, not too emphatically lest he wake the Lord Caavax. The thought that his comrade might have been attacked never crossed his mind, knowing for certain as he did that in that event any competent AAnn soldier would have been able to squeeze off at least a burst or two from his weapon which would have awakened the entire camp.

No, either he was sleeping safely back in the encampment, in which case Ceijihagrast would be tempted to shoot him himself, or else he had met with an accident. Satisfied that he had considered every possibility, the trooper pivoted to return to camp.

And promptly encountered an accident, waiting to happen.

Something immense and dark had risen behind him, blocking not only his path but his view. Standing on hind legs, Saalahan scowled unblinkingly down at the soldier. Remnant moonlight outlined razor-sharp tusks.

Ceijihagrast's slitted pupils dilated sharply as he brought the pulse rifle up. He wasn't nearly quick enough. Four massive paws came together, catching the soldier's skull between them and crushing it like an egg. Messily decapitated, the body crumpled to the ground.

With a disdainful snort, the furcot dropped to all sixes. "Clear?"

"All clear." Tuuvatem was scrutinizing the rain-soaked encampment while clinging to the side of the branch, indifferent to the twenty-meter drop beneath her. Thirty-six claws ensured that she did not fall.

"You see?" Saalahan gestured with a bloodied paw. "Each night they do the same thing. Each night we will kill one or two more of them. Soon they will all be dead. Then we can go back to the Home-tree."

Effortlessly grasping the headless body in powerful jaws, it took a step to the edge of the branch and dropped it over the side. Pulse rifle still clutched convulsively in clawed fingers, the dead trooper went bouncing and spinning down in the wake of his predecessor. The forest swallowed both with equal efficiency.

Saalahan considered the sky. "Soon the sun will rise and it will be lightness. Enough for one night. Tomorrow we will kill more of the nonpersons." Shepherding the two youngsters, the big adult led them off into the depths of the verdure in search of a place to sleep.

"There is no hurry."

Chapter Eighteen

Field Officer Nesorey was livid as he confronted his four remaining troops. "None of you saw anything? None of you heard anything?" His burning gaze fixed on Hosressachu. "You! You were on the last posting forward. Nothing disturbed your watch? No sounds, no sights piqued your interest?"

To his credit, the frightened, unhappy soldier replied readily. "No, honored one. I saw only the rain and small glowing things. As did he who watched before me." At this the trooper on his immediate right executed a decidedly sharp gesture indicative of first-degree concurrence.

"Someone should have checked on Tatrasaseep," the field officer muttered.

"Probably Cheijihagrast did just that, honored one." Proper sociomilitary etiquette notwithstanding, the soldier initially berated wasn't about to concede control of the discussion. While he felt first-degree guilt over the loss of two comrades, he wasn't about to take responsibility for their demise. Such unwarranted acquiescence would be decidedly un-AAnnlike.

What fate had befallen the two soldiers, the survivors could only imagine. Nor were the human captives any help, responding to angry inquiries with blank expressions on their flat, soft-skinned faces.

Morning sounds filled the air, a cacophony of creatures rising in endless variety and profusion to take back the forest from the citizens of the night. The music they made was pure dissonance to the surviving AAnn. Yellow-green light grated on their pupils as the unseen sun sucked at the lingering moisture. Several of them were certain they could feel their flesh rotting inside their suits even as they stood patiently waiting for the aristocrat and the field officer to make a decision.

"Something took them both." Lord Caavax's gaze roamed the enveloping forest. "It is likely we will never know what. Evidently our nightly routine must be altered."

Field Officer Nesorey responded with a gesture of third-degree affirmation coupled with an overlay of frustration. "That which served adequately on our initial foray is obviously no longer valid procedure. There are not enough of us left to set out perimeter guards. We will have to keep close together, half of us sleeping while the other half remain on watch." He was staring intently into the surrounding growths, searching for an assailant whose identity remained unknown to him. That was the worst part of it: not knowing what was stalking them.

He was suddenly thoughtful. "Something has changed. There is something different about the forest."

A trooper disagreed. "Most likely it was an isolated, random attack, honored one." Both soldiers looked to Lord Caavax for resolution.

"There is validity to both preceptions," the aristocrat finally remarked. "In any event, we will take additional precautions." His gaze shifted to the four humans.

Flinx kept his expression carefully neutral. A look from Teal confirmed what he'd already suspected. He'd been waiting for the furcots to make their move even before the AAnn had arrived on the scene. Their patience was uncommon. Last night their emotional presence had been stronger than usual. Early in the morning it had peaked, in concert with an emotional jolt from first one and then a second AAnn. That they were alien mattered not. The emotional spectrum he was erratically able to access did not discriminate according to species.

Besides that, death had its own unmistakable emotional signature.

The AAnn knew nothing of furcots, and Flinx wasn't about to enlighten them. He wondered how confident the Lord Caavax would be if he knew he was being stalked not by mindless nocturnal carnivores but by intelligent symbiotes. Rescue wasn't assured, but Flinx felt more confident than he had in days. The trick was not to show it. He would have to warn Teal not to sleep too soundly at night. To Caavax's way of thinking, whatever was out there should be as much a threat to the humans as to their captors. To indicate otherwise would be to raise suspicions in the noble's mind that would do them no good.

As long as he was convinced that they were in danger only from mindless apparitions, Caavax would continue to act rationally. Was he rational enough to be reasonable? No harm, Flinx decided, in finding out.

"Your escort is down to five, honored Lord. Why not give this up as a bad business and let us go? I know the AAnn, and I know it would be hard for you. But there are precedents."

"To which I will not add," Caavax replied promptly. "So long as I live and can lift a weapon, we will continue together toward the landing site."

Flinx had expected nothing less from a high noble, but it had been worth a try. The attempt had been intended not only to secure their freedom but to prevent further deaths. Now he washed his hands of it, feeling that he'd done all he could. From this point onward, everything was up to Caavax. And the furcots.

"Continue," the aristocrat declared. Field Officer Nesorey indicated third-degree assent and hissed at his soldiers. With two troopers taking point and two bringing up the rear, the much reduced-in-strength expedition moved out along the branch.

Flinx glanced frequently in the direction of the field officer. To ensure that his subordinates were free to respond to any threat from the forest as quickly as possible, Nesorey had taken charge of the sack containing Pip. The flying snake could go several days without eating, but by tomorrow night would have to receive nourishment of some kind or she would begin to fail rapidly.

At present Flinx knew she was estivating to conserve energy, something Alaspinian minidrags could do at will. Otherwise they couldn't last a day without food because of their phenomenal metabolic rate. At least, he knew, she hadn't been forced to expend any energy on flying. But conservation measures would only sustain her for so long. Somehow he had to get nourishment to her or free her from the containment bag.

They were less than an hour's march from the site of the previous night's encampment when the soldier walking point on the right side let out a hissing screech and began firing madly into the forest. Before his companion could restrain him, he took off wildly, hissing obscenities as he blasted branches, lianas, fruit, flowers, and anything that moved.

Exhibiting a frenzied surge of strength and agility, he leaped from branch to branch, entering into a maniacal search of hollows and crevices with wide, despairing eyes, firing until his rifle was discharged. Ignoring the pleas of his fellow soldiers and the outraged commands of the field officer, he jammed a fresh energy pack into his weapon and reembarked on his aimless orgy of destruction.

Nesorey roared helplessly at the enraged soldier. "Trooper Hosressachu, return to your position! In the name of the Emperor . . . !"

Neither his words nor those of the other soldiers had any effect on the wild-eyed Hosressachu, who persisted in annihilating anything that caught the attention of his unhinged mind.

The AAnn's preoccupation with their wayward comrade allowed Flinx to whisper unnoticed to Teal. "That's another one gone. If this doesn't convince Caavax, then . . . hey, what's the matter?"

Next to him, Teal had gone cold. Flinx felt her fear, which was genuine and not faked. Casting out with his talent, he discovered an absence of furcotal emotion. That suggested that the furcots had either moved on ahead or were deliberately trailing far behind.

Or else something had scared them away.

He thought of Moomadeem, brave beyond his years, and Saalahan, immovable as a rock, and wondered what there was out there in the forest capable of frightening them. That's when it struck him.

Maybe the feverish trooper Hosressachu wasn't firing at nothing.

Nesorey continued to bellow imprecations of admirable elegance at his berserking soldier. Ignoring him, the determined trooper fired into a cluster of thickly entwined small branches. Wood and sap went flying. Bending low, he advanced on the opening his weapon had made.

At the same instant, what looked from a distance like a coiled rope dropped over him and contracted. Hosressachu screamed hideously as the coil sliced him into a dozen disklike sections, blood spurting violently from around each loop of the coil. Even more than the violence of the attack, it was the speed that was shocking. The poor trooper never had a chance. The muscular power inherent in those coils, Flinx thought, must be on an unbelievable order of magnitude to slice a body like that.

Suspended from an overhead branch by four multi-jointed legs, the perfectly camouflaged quilimot regarded its prey. Even when Teal bestirred herself to point it out to him, Flinx still had trouble separating the predator from the branch beneath which it hung. Clasped in the coil of the killing tail, the smashed body of Hosressachu rose slowly toward the waiting mouth. His rifle went up with him in the unrelenting grasp, the military-grade composites pulverized by the force of the quilimot's murderous contraction.

Two longer, slimmer legs reached down. Each terminated in a single, thin gleaming claw. One pierced the soldier's skull directly between the eyes while the other entered his back. Three bright crimson eyes were visible now, examining the prey.

Badly shaken, the deceased trooper's comrade on point knelt and took careful aim. Balancing his rifle across his knees in the accepted AAnn fashion, he began firing at the quilimot. When the field officer hissed at him to desist, he was ignored. Cursing, Nesorey unlimbered his own weapon and added his firepower to that of the soldier. Both were soon joined by the last heavily armed member of the expeditionary force.

As several shots struck the quilimot it responded with a cry halfway between a cough and a roar. Body jerking spasmodically, two of its four legs lost their grip on the branch above. Snarling defiance, it dropped to a large liana and attempted to find safety in the dense vegetation nearby, still clutching the crushed corpse of the unfortunate Hosressachu in its coiled tail.

A well-directed shot from the field officer struck near or on the head. Losing control entirely, the horrid being shuddered once before plunging from the liana. It fell some ten meters, bounced off a thick branch, and dropped another twenty before coming to rest in a cluster of thick keskes leaves.

When they finally reached the immobile, stinking form after carefully working their way downward, they found the trooper's body still held convulsively in the grasp of the unyielding tail. Field Officer Nesorey performed a closer inspection and reported back to the Lord Caavax.

"One would have to cut Hosressachu loose section by section to free all of the remains, honored Lord." He looked back at where predator and soldier lay entwined in death. "It is as if he is wrapped in metal cable. His bones are crushed, but I think the shock to his system killed him before blood loss or suffocation."

Lord Caavax considered the remnants of his escort, the cream of an entire AAnn martial burrow. The human's words haunted him, knowing as he did that they still had a considerable distance to travel to reach the landing site and the safety of the imperial shuttle. If he continued to lose soldiers at this rate, they wouldn't make it to the halfway point.

He turned solemnly to Nesorey, knowing that these successive tragedies must be taking their toll on the field officer. "There comes a time when aspiration must give way to expedience. You have more experience in the field than I. I await any recommendations."

Tired, angry, and frustrated, the field officer replied without hesitation. "There are now five of us to watch four of them, in addition to maintaining a watch for predators." He gestured at Teal. "It is clear the human female cannot warn us of dangers if, like Hosressachu, we choose to stumble into them on our own, or if she is sleeping when night carnivores attack.

"I therefore respectfully submit, honored Lord, that her usefulness to us has been exaggerated and that as such, her presence and that of her offspring now constitute an ongoing burden rather than a benefit. Killing them will allow the five of us who remain to concentrate our attention on the one human whose return to the *Keralkee* is, after all, the purpose of this much suffering expedition."

Flinx whirled on the AAnn noble. "We had an agreement."

"Abrogated by circumstance," Caavax replied remorselessly. "I am compelled to prioritize."

"Kill them and you'll never get possession of the *Teacher*!"

"That may be," the aristocrat conceded. "However, it cannot be argued that I will also not gain control of your vessel if I happen to die on this *sissfint* pestilence of a world. Given the choice, I prefer to live and take my chances with our advanced methods of persuasion."

"Then just let them go," Flinx pleaded. "What threat can a small female and two offspring pose to you?"

Caavax considered Teal and the children out of cold, yellow eyes. "On this world? I am long past leaving anything to chance." Turning to the field officer, he executed a gesture of fourth-degree consent marked with concurrence.

"I am tired of watching only AAnn die. Proceed."

Field Officer Nesorey gestured to the soldier on his right. Having just witnessed the violent death of yet another of his fellow troopers, this individual was in no mood to question orders, much less feel any sympathy for a clutch of dirty, smelly, damp humans. Advancing, he raised the muzzle of his rifle in Teal's direction.

Responding to her master's agonized emotional state, Pip writhed wildly within the restraining sack. Flinx took a desperate step toward Lord Caavax. The AAnn noble raised his sidearm warningly.

"Do not try anything foolish."

"Kill me and you have nothing," Flinx shot back.

"I have no intention of killing you. This is a neuronic pistol." He gestured with his sidearm. "It is set to paralyze, not kill. If I am compelled to shoot you, you will only wish you were dead."

Incipient sniffles gave way to all-out bawling as Kiss fell to her knees in front of the AAnn soldier. Dwell shifted to stand protectively in front of Teal.

"Please, don't hurt my mother! Kill me if you have to, but leave her alone!"

"Almost like an AAnn." The field officer gestured approvingly. "Don't worry," he told the boy, "you will have your turn." He flexed clawed fingers in the direction of the waiting trooper. "Reward the male child. Do him first. And be clean with it."

The soldier responded by checking the charge on his rifle, ignoring the female child who was now clutching desperately at his legs and sobbing uncontrollably. Flinx contemplated making a jump for the weapon even though he knew he'd never reach it. Caavax was watching him too closely.

The alarm was sounded by another of the alert troopers. Movement in the branches overhead spurred him to shout a startled warning. For an instant Flinx flinched along with the AAnn, but the unexpected sense of calm and assurance Teal projected caused him to relax. Along with everyone else, he turned his gaze upward.

Drifting down through the leaves and branches was what appeared to be a swarm of thin mushroom caps. Brown on top and streaked with bright blue, pale white underneath, they averaged a third of a meter in diameter with hollow centers. Each cap was ringed with tiny globules. If it was some kind of attack, it was proceeding at a pace an active slug could avoid.

"Calm yourself, Masmarulial," the field officer instructed the trooper who'd yelled. "All kinds of plant matter drifts down from above. Seeds and leaves, twigs and empty husks. Just move out of the way."

"Yes, honored one," mumbled the abashed soldier. Stepping clear of the nearest gently tumbling brown disk, he watched it spiral down toward the branch.

He had no way of knowing that his body heat would be sufficient to activate it.

Faster than the eye could follow, the tiny globes rimming the disk ballooned to four times their normal size and exploded. The soldier responded by doing precisely the wrong thing, which was to inhale sharply. Vertical pupils expanding to the maximum, his eyes bugged. Mucus began to stream from his nostrils and he sneezed so violently that he dropped his rifle. It clattered on the branch but did not go off.

Everyone gaped at the unfortunate trooper, who by this time had collapsed on the branch and was sneezing uncontrollably. In imitation of Teal, Flinx once again had clapped his hands over nose and mouth.

Distracted by their companion's distress, the AAnn failed to notice that Kiss's sobbing had ceased with suspicious suddenness. Nor did they see her remove from a pocket concealed in the lining of her cape a child-sized bone blade ten centimeters in length. Demonstrating lightning reflexes and precocious skill, she jammed this with all her strength up between the legs of the soldier she was clinging to.

The trooper screamed like a baby and dropped his weapon to clutch at himself. At the same time, Dwell bounded forward and leaped at the field officer. Wrapping one arm around the AAnn's neck and both legs around its waist, the boy used his own knife to slash several times at the straps that secured the catching sack to the officer's pack. He had to work fast because more and more of the mushroom-puffballs were exploding as the disks drifted within range of those standing on the branch. Sneezing helplessly, locked together, both he and the field officer crumpled onto the branch.

Flinx closed his eyes to try and shut out the irritating spores. At that moment he wanted nothing more out of life than to be able to take a deep, invigorating mouthful of fresh air. He was sure his face must be turning blue.

Having planted her hidden knife where it would do the most good, Kiss scrambled like a little brown-haired bug to the edge of the branch . . . and flung herself over the side, out into empty space. Sneezing painfully, Dwell rolled free of the helpless Nesorey. A last, tenacious tug ripped free the sack containing Pip. Flinging it ahead of him, he followed it over the side.

Seeing this, a wide-eyed Flinx stumbled toward the edge. He couldn't hold it in any longer; he *had* to breathe. As he opened his mouth, someone hit him hard in the middle of the back. Flailing wildly for balance, he looked over his shoulder and saw that it was Teal who had struck him from behind. Her cool, contemplative stare was the last thing he saw before he felt himself falling through space.

Seconds became an eternity before he struck something soft and yielding. Bouncing several times, he eventually came to a halt. Rolling over onto all fours and looking up, the first thing he saw was Dwell. The grinning boy was standing and looking down at him, a now familiar sack slung safely over his shoulder.

"You can breathe okay now." With one hand he pointed upward. "The hac spores are all up there."

Nodding to show that he understood, Flinx sucked in a great, deep mouthful of heavy, moist hylaeal air. It felt wonderful and his starved lungs cried for more. As he climbed to his feet he saw that Teal was laughing at him.

Smiling shyly, he inclined his head and tried to see up into the canopy. They had fallen far enough so that there was no sign, or sound, of their captors. A hand tapped him on the shoulder.

The boy held the sack out to him. "Here is your animal. I knew you would not come without it."

Flinx accepted the sack and tried to think of some way to show the depth of his appreciation. "That was very brave of you, Dwell, to jump the field officer like that."

The ten-year-old shrugged. "I knew what the hac spores would do. He didn't."

Flinx smiled and bent to release the secure seals. When the last had been loosened, a brilliantly colored cylindrical shape slithered out, flaunted multihued wings, and took to the air. It circled three times around the cluster of approving humans before setting down on Flinx's shoulder. He felt the pointed tongue flicking affectionately at the underside of his jaw.

"We have to get her something to eat," he explained to Teal. "It shouldn't be difficult. She's omnivorous—I mean, she'll eat just about anything."

Approaching with a shyness Flinx could no longer accept at face value subsequent to her actions above, Kiss presented him with a handful of thumbnail-sized nuts drawn from still another concealed pocket in her green cape. They were bright pink with ribbed exteriors, but Pip downed them one after another without hesitation.

"Thanks," Flinx told the girl. She smiled back up at him and he could feel a blend of uncertainty and affection radiating from her.

Looking up into the boundless greenery once more, he thought he could just hear the echo of distant popping. "How much longer will the sneeze effect last?"

Teal moved close. "We left before the spores could disperse fully. If the not-persons are still up there, in the same place, they won't be able to do anything at all for a little while yet."

Kiss pressed a finger to her lower lip. "Not-persons aren't very smart."

"Certainly not as smart as you," Flinx told her admiringly. "Who taught you to react the way you did up there?"

Not-so-innocent green eyes peered up at him. "Mommy and Daddy an' Uncle Thil and Shaman Ponder."

"Children's training starts very early," Teal explained. "It's easy to get them to pay attention to their lessons. Those who don't never grow up."

"Lost my knife." A disappointed Kiss pushed out her lower lip, looking for all the world like any little girl who'd misplaced her dolly.

"I'll get you another one," Flinx assured her. "A better knife than you've ever seen. Even if I have to make it myself."

Her eyes grew wide. "Really? Promise?"

"Really. I promise." He smiled fondly.

They had landed atop something Teal identified as gargalufla. The single flower had only two leaves, each of which was three meters thick, five wide, and six long. It would have been incapable of supporting its own weight if the majority of its intercellular interstices hadn't been filled with air. This was what had cushioned their fall.

"How did you know this was here?" Flinx looked from the colossal flower to Teal. "Surely your decision to jump this way was based on more than hope? For that matter, you didn't seem surprised at the arrival of the hac spores. Are they common around here?"

She was smiling back at him. "No, they're not. They usually don't fall in such dense clusters, either. They were carried to the place and then dropped on us."

"Dropped . . . ?" Half-familiar feelings caused him to turn in the right direction several moments before the furcots actually arrived.

With a somber Saalahan in the lead, they ambled out of the verdure to rejoin their humans. A delighted Kiss and Dwell flung themselves at the equally responsive Moomadeem and Tuuvatem, the four of them laughing and giggling as they rolled about, swatting and hugging one another with reckless disregard for the precipitous drop that gaped beneath the gargalufla. While no less pleased to see one another again, Saalahan and Teal restricted themselves to a more formal embrace.

"You almost waited too long." She made a fist and rubbed the big adult between the ears.

Saalahan grunted contentedly. "Easy to gather hac spore caps. Harder to make sure you had a place to jump okay."

Flinx eyed Teal. "So that's how you knew it was safe to throw yourself off the branch."

She nodded. "As soon as I saw so many hac caps falling in one place I knew that Saalahan had to be responsible. Knowing that, I knew my furcot wouldn't dump them right on top of us unless it was safe to get away from them the quickest way possible. Which was to jump." She nodded in the direction of the gigantic flower. "I didn't know what we'd land on. The gargalufla was perfect, Saalahan."

"Thought it would be so." The big adult sniffed.

"How did you know these spores would have the same effect on the AAnn," Flinx inquired. "On the not-persons?"

Three eyes regarded him thoughtfully. "If a thing has a nose, hac spores will make it sneeze."

"Furcots have noses. How come they didn't make you sneeze when you gathered them?"

The social symbiote sniffed. "Use long grasper vines to pick, and carry caps. If hac caps are not brought close to a person's body, where they can be warmed, they stay closed."

The furcots helped them slide safely off the side of the humungous leaf. Teal showed Flinx the stem of the flower, which was as big around as the trunk of an oak. The flower in turn grew atop a branch greater in diameter than the largest tree Flinx had ever seen on Moth. Everything on this world, he reflected, was of a scale to dwarf all the combined jungles of the known worlds. Compared to it, the Amazon basin of Terra was backyard landscaping and the rain forests of Hivehom as thoroughly domesticated as the rough bordering a golf course.

At the limit of his perception he felt he could see an extraordinary jumble of fear, fury, uncertainty, and determination.

"Don't you think we should get moving?"

Teal peered up into the tangle of vegetation. "Do you really think after what just happened to them they will still try to come after us?"

"I don't know, but the AAnn honor persistence. I'd rather not wait around and see."

Lord Caavax's expeditionary force was now down to a field officer, two healthy troopers, and the hapless victim of Kiss's knife, assuming he hadn't bled to death. Given such losses, human pursuers would have opted to execute a strategic retreat. The AAnn thought differently.

"Then we will not linger. Give us a direction, Flinx."

Checking his tiny positioner, he raised an arm and pointed. "That way."

"Your device is a wonderment." She smiled at him. "Perhaps this time we will reach the Home-tree without interference."

"I sure as hell hope so." He scratched Pip under her chin and she closed her eyes in pleasure. They could just as easily head for his shuttle, he reflected, and with the furcots' help, probably beat the leery and weakened Caavax to the landing site.

The drawback to that notion was that there could be several dozen fresh troopers still aboard the AAnn craft, waiting with heavy weapons and eager attitudes for the opportunity to see some action. Perhaps only an imaginary confrontation, but one Flinx intended to avoid. Before attempting anything on his own behalf he fully intended to see Teal and her children safely home.

Dwell was chatting with his sister. "Remember when that dumb diverdaunt tried to *eat* a bunch of ripe hac caps? It nearly sneezed itself to pieces!" Brother and sister shared a giggle along with the memory.

Watching them, serene and safe once again, Flinx mused on what it might be like to grow up in a world like this, never seeing the ground or the sky, surrounded by millions of exotic species where in a lifetime most people were fortunate to encounter a few hundred. The forest supplied everything they needed, in unimaginable plenty and variety. The flavors of foods alone must exceed anything available to even the richest of merchants.

Then a thorn nicked the back of his left hand and he winced slightly. A tiny bubble of blood welled up where the skin had been broken. It was a reminder, small but not insignificant.

This was a place of great beauty, but also a place where daydreamers died. Resolutely, he returned his attention to the track ahead.

Chapter Nineteen

When Field Officer Nesorey finally stopped sneezing long enough to catch his breath, he staggered weakly to his feet. His face was a mess, the usually immaculate scales crusty with drying mucus, normally bright eyes dulled and dark from uncontrolled glandular seepage.

Chorazzkwep was doing his best trying to treat the moaning, badly wounded Jusquetechii, applying disinfectants, antibiotics, and sterile spray-on. Serious medical treatment would have to wait until they returned to the shuttle. Wiping at his eyes, the field officer saw that the quick-thinking Chorazzkwep had at least succeeded in stopping the bleeding. Nesorey would put him in for an appropriate commendation—provided any of them lived that long.

Gazing intently into the green depths below the branch, Lord Caavax was using a moistened disinfecting towel to clean his face and muzzle. He stood too close to the edge for Nesorey's comfort, but it was not the field officer's place to criticize the noble's decision. Suggesting that he step back from the abyss would be equivalent to impugning the aristocrat's courage. Whatever else his faults might be, Nesorey mused, Lord Caavax was not lacking in bravery.

What was in order now, however, was not bravery but common sense.

Cries, whistles, screeches, howls, rhythmic bellowing, and musical calls resounded from below as well as all around the devastated expedition. None provided any clues as to the fate of their former prisoners. Had they all committed suicide rather than submit to the ennobling attention of AAnn weaponry, or were one or more of them lying safe somewhere unseen below, possibly injured? The field officer knew that in that equation only the tall human male mattered.

He peered cautiously over the edge. Green of every possible shade and permutation assailed his still tender eyes. There was ample movement, none of which could be traced to a human source. With a soft hiss he sidled sideways until he was standing next to his superior.

"Honored Lord, what shall we do now? Direct me." He performed a second-degree salute with suggestions of understanding and a touch of sympathy-for-position.

Caavax was touched. Un-AAnnlike as it would have been, given their circumstances, he would have taken no umbrage had the field officer chosen instead to announce himself with several choice curses.

"As soon as Jusquetechii's injury has been stabilized we shall resume pursuit." After a glance down at the tracker attached to his instrument belt, he pointed eastward. "They're moving that way. So long as the human Flinx utilizes his own instrumentation to position himself with respect to his shuttle, he cannot escape us. If he switches the device off, he will become hopelessly lost. He is young, but not stupid.

"When we next catch up with him, there will be no hesitation. We will kill the three native humans from ambush and I myself will see to it that he cannot flee from us without great difficulty. The option of a respected captivity will not be offered."

The field officer acknowledged his superior's designated course of action. "Honored Lord?"

"Field officer?" Caavax was staring off into the impenetrable wall of green.

"The human Flinx is aware of our presence and intentions. As you have observed, he is not ignorant. Therefore he must know that we can track him so long as he continues the use of his positioner. The fact that he does so suggests that he does not fear pursuit. To carry this line of reasoning further, it is not out of the realm of possibility to consider that he may be deliberately tempting us to follow him."

"To what end, field officer?"

Nesorey's tone was one of first-degree assurance. "Our ultimate destruction, honored Lord."

Caavax considered. "The thought had occurred to me. However, all of our losses save a single wounding have been caused by inimical local life forms, not by the humans. We need to take more care. Also, the human Flinx has been relieved of his only weapon."

"I need hardly point out, honored Lord," the field officer replied in a voice that flirted dangerously with impertinence, "that we are running out of soldiers with which to take care, and that this whole world may be regarded as a weapon.

"Even if we were to catch up to the quarry a second time, keeping in mind that he is now fully aware of our presence and intentions, I wonder if we could make it safely back to the landing site. We embarked on this hunt with a full squad of alert, energized troops. Presently we find ourselves reduced to three, one of whom is seriously injured." He executed a profound gesture of disagreement tempered with respect.

"Let the human and his native friends go, honored Lord. Unless he chooses to live out his life in this pestilential morass, he will eventually have to return to his shuttle. Easy enough to disable the craft so that it would do him no good to sneak back aboard. Then we, or any AAnn who may follow us, can take him at leisure." Nesorey turned to gesture in the direction of the wounded Jusquetechii.

"Is principle worth more than the life of an AAnn soldier?"

"Of course it is," Caavax replied readily. "You know that as well as I do, field officer. Yet I take your point. I will lose face if we return without the quarry."

Field Officer Nesorey regarded their surroundings with continued wariness. "Better to do so figuratively than literally, honored Lord." He flinched as three stubby fliers with streaming yellow tails and quadruple wings flitted past the branch. They looked clumsy, harmless, and attractive, which made Nesorey all the more uneasy in their presence. He was learning.

Caavax was silent for a long time. When he finally replied, the resignation in his voice was profound.

"You are right, field officer. It will do us no good to die out here and leave the human free to wander on or off-world as he wishes. A blow to one's pride is a fearful thing, but death compounded by failure is worse.

"We will return to the landing site. The quarry's shuttle will be disabled and a suitable message placed aboard. When he is ready to leave he can determine his own fate." He resumed his contemplation of their surroundings. "Perhaps that would have been the best course of action to pursue all along, but no one anticipated there would be this degree of difficulty in apprehending a single human."

"No one could have, honored Lord." Nesorey's terse reply was ripe with both feeling and sympathy. "Who could imagine a world like this? It will haunt my memories till the day the Dark Dune sweeps over me." His voice fell to a murmur. "I do not like this world, and I do not think it likes me."

"Be careful, field officer," Caavax warned him. "Suffering fear is debilitating. Projecting it is worse.

"Inform the others. We will return to the landing site as rapidly as is feasible, in the course of which we will touch nothing, brush nothing, examine nothing. If the journey could be accomplished with closed eyes and sealed ears, I would order it done so. Our food will be caution and care, which we will consume daily and in copious quantity." He stepped past the field officer.

"Let us see how trooper Jusquetechii is doing. Now that a course of action has been decided, I am anxious to be on our way." He bumped a trio of innocuous pink blossoms and jerked back sharply. They did not laugh at him, but had they in fact broken into audible hysterics, he would not have been at all surprised.

"There is no sign of them."

Saalahan dropped from a liana and ambled up to the campsite, which consisted of several large leaves suspended over a crook where two large triangular cummumbra branches joined their parent trunk. Flinx and Teal reclined beneath the shelter while the children and their furcots played nearby.

"I went quite a distance." Settling down with a grunt, Saalahan folded all six legs underneath.

Flinx's senses had been devoid of AAnn-feel for some time now and he could readily have confirmed Saalahan's observation. There was no need. What mattered was what was: regardless of what the surviving AAnn were up to, they weren't following. This posed other potential difficulties, but he would deal with them later. For now it was enough to know he and his friends were safe from the attentions of Lord Caavax and his minions.

"They've given up. For now." Idly he fingered the softly pulsing positioner.

"Maybe all dead." Saalahan seemed to find this hugely amusing. A deep rumbling issued from within the burly chest. "Hard to follow when dead."

"We were lucky," Flinx corrected the furcot.

"Lucky like Kiss." Tuuvatem took a playful, prideful swat at the child, who ducked easily.

Flinx lifted his eyes. Pip lay curled around the back of his neck, sleeping on his shoulders. They were on the third level, favored of local humans, and the sky was hundreds of meters distant.

"The AAnn aren't always predictable. They might try to fight their way down to us with another shuttle. Next time there might not be the right kind of trees around to clog up its intakes."

"Always such trees nearby." Saalahan grunted knowingly. "Otherwise more fires."

Flinx chose not to elaborate on the options open to the AAnn through the aid of modern technology. It was hard to argue with a furcot. Saalahan always seemed to have an answer for everything.

He envisioned a heavily armed AAnn shuttle blasting its way through the canopy and descending into the depths of the forest. It was a disconcerting image, made tolerable by the certain knowledge that in one way or another, the forest would respond. The consequences of such a conflict could only be imagined.

Something told him it would be unwise when considering the outcome of such a confrontation to bet against the all-encompassing vegetation.

Safe now from Lord Caavax's attentions, Flinx was enjoying himself. Pip was all right, Teal was in good spirits, the children and furcots were consistently amusing, and everywhere he looked something new and extraordinary materialized to astonish the eye. He chose not to dwell on when it all might start to bore, as had everything else new and exciting he'd encountered in his brief but harried existence.

The time would come when he would have to consider leaving. How persistent was Lord Caavax? How desperately did the AAnn desire control of the *Teacher*?

Time yet to work out a plan of reaction. Careful not to disturb Pip, he placed his hands behind his head and leaned back against the trunk. The bogli tree reached nearly to the canopy and put forth a sensuous, pungent fragrance. Not all the wonders of this world were potentially lethal. He and his companions were relaxing in the shade of a six-hundred-meter-high cinnamon stick. It wasn't cinnamon, of course, but that was the scent that came most readily to mind. Wallowing in the sensation, he inhaled deeply and often. A vast feeling of well-being and contentment washed over him, a massage more mental than physical.

It was a situation he was able to savor not because he knew he was safe, but because he enjoyed the company of three forest-attuned humans and three equally alert furcots.

That night he found himself sitting and watching the rain as it pelted the branches and leaves, flowers and bromeliads outside their simple but adequate shelter. Seeing Pip curled like a blue and pink tattoo atop the mountainous Saalahan's spine, he had to smile. Unable to catch or dissuade the persistent minidrag, the furcots had chosen to ignore her. Flinx knew the big adult's back had to be softer than his own unyielding shoulders.

After checking on the children, Teal slid over to sit close to him. "What are you looking at?"

"The rain. The way the bromeliads catch and store it. The little glowing lives that flit and fly among the leaves. The dark shapes that boom hopefully at the night. The silent fliers who steer by the light of concealed moons." Turning, he smiled affectionately at her. "Lots of things. My senses are all filled up with the perfume of newness."

Her face wrinkled. "I don't understand."

He returned his attention to the dark, dripping hylaea. "I have this hunger to learn, Teal. You know how when you're hungry you get a knot, a tight feeling, in the pit of your stomach?" She nodded. "I have the equivalent in my mind. There are plenty of times when I wish I could satisfy it, sate it, but no matter how much I learn, the hunger always comes back." In the shadow of the cummumbra leaves he spread his hands in a gesture of helplessness.

"I need to learn, Teal. I need to see and experience new things. Otherwise, a part of me starts to starve."

She snugged up against his arm. "Is the forest feeding you enough?"

"More than enough," he assured her.

"Tell me, then. Share with me. What have you learned from the forest?"

He reflected. "That with beauty comes also death, and out of death arises new life, and that nothing should be taken for granted because in nature nothing is what it seems." He shrugged. "It's equally true for people."

"Is it different where you come from?"

"No," he told her quietly, "not really. It's just not as passionate. Everything here is intensified: sights, sounds, smells. This world puts all your senses in overdrive." He grinned in the darkness. "It's hard to relax and lose yourself in beauty knowing that at any minute that which you're admiring might gleefully try to rip your leg off."

"I wouldn't let that happen to you."

"Thanks, Teal. I know . . ." He paused, struck by the tone as much as the import of her reply.

She was concentrating hard. Not on the forest. On him.

"I am mateless, Flinx." That was all she said. It hung in the air like a seed, waiting for nurturance.

He looked away from her. "I've never been married . . . mated, Teal. I've told you that."

She shifted against him, her words as well as her body ripe with warmth and promise. Nearby, children and furcots slept soundly.

"I have helped you, you have helped me. I think there is more than help there. We are good for one another."

He had visited many worlds, escaped dangers few could imagine, interacted with the good and the bad of numerous species, but not even his unique abilities could prepare him for Teal's straightforwardness, nor tell him how to reply.

"Teal, I—I hardly know what to say. I'm not looking for a mate." He turned away from her, letting his gaze mark the silhouettes of the great forest. "I'm not even sure it would be fair of me to mate with anyone."

She didn't understand. "Why? Flinx, is there something wrong with you?"

"Yes. No. Something is—different with me. I don't know yet if it's wrong. Sometimes it's a good thing, other times I can't stand being inside my own head."

"That is crazy talk. Where else would you be?"

He started to reply, caught himself. How could he explain that he'd actually been outside his head a few times? Once with the aid of the Ulru-Ujurrians, again on this very world not so long ago. Sleep was not a state he always looked forward to with anticipation. There were times when he was asleep during the day and awake in his sleep.

"You're a very fine person, Teal. A very fine woman." As indeed she was, lying there next to him beneath the commumbra leaves, her skin mottled with diffuse moonlight. Everything about her seemed to enhance the feeble glow. Her face and form were full of promise and shadows.

"But this isn't my home, isn't my world. I like a lot of things about it, but I'm not sure I'd want to settle here permanently." His voice choked and he coughed to clear his throat. "I'm not sure I'm destined to settle anywhere permanently."

Sensing his distress, she tried to comfort him. "Tell me about your home. Is it very different from here?"

"Everywhere is very different from here, Teal. This world is unique. Moth—where I come from—is much colder than this."

Curiosity underlined her response. "I have heard of cold. I don't think I'd like it."

"I know you wouldn't," he told her feelingly. "It's wet, but not as wet as this, and the rain is cold, too. There are trees—"

She perked up. "Trees! Like these?"

He had to laugh, gently. "Teal, there are no trees like these anywhere else in the known universe. Your home is special in so many ways."

"Well, if it is special and you are special, then what better place for you to be?" she argued ingenuously.

He started to reply, hesitated, and had to admit that she was making her case very well. The truly sad part of it was that he *wanted* to give in, wanted to make a home somewhere.

Presently that was impossible. As for the future, his present concern was to learn if there would be one. And just because this world might be a suitable place for him didn't mean that he was suitable for it.

She wouldn't understand any of that, of course.

"There are also places on Moth called plains, where there are no trees at all."

Her eyes widened. "No trees at all!"

"Some of them don't even have grass, and are covered all year 'round in ice."

"Ice?" Her expression twisted. "Isn't that something like 'cold'?"

"It's cold you can pick up," he explained patiently. "Solid cold."

She shook her head. "The old stories—it was always hard to believe some of the things they said. Your home is such a place?"

"It's where I grew up." He was not being intentionally evasive, only truthful. "I need to find out about who and what I am, Teal, before I can inflict myself for any length of time on someone else."

This time there was nothing innocent about her response. "Don't be in such a hurry to protect everyone from yourself."

"I have things I have to do. There's something unpleasant," he looked upward and nodded, "up there. I may be fooling myself, but I think maybe I can do something about it. Or at least help." He ran one hand lightly over the warm living wood on which they were sitting. "This place may be involved, somehow."

She blinked. "This tree?"

Again he had to smile. "No. More than this tree. Much more. I don't understand it all yet. There are so many things I don't understand."

She squeezed his arm. "Then you are more normal than you believe."

If only that were so, he thought. If only it were so.

"Things are happening, Teal. On a very big scale. *Very* big. I seem to be in the middle of it all, somehow. There's a sense of many parts of a whole trying to come together. I don't know yet how I fit into the final equation. Only that I'm a part of it."

"And because of that you can't mate?"

His tone was tender but unyielding. "Because of that it wouldn't be fair of me to mate."

She looked away from him, silent and contemplative for some time. "Afterward?"

"Afterward all things might be possible." *There,* he thought. No lie and no harm in speculating on a nonexistent future.

She sighed. Wee comical snores rose from the two young furcots while Saalahan's great mass rose and fell silently. Dwell and Kiss slumbered in silence and Pip remained curled comfortably atop the big furcot's back.

"Then you will not mate with me?"

He considered carefully. If greatness or tragedy was to be thrust upon him, it still lay sometime in the future. Vast forces in motion had not yet come together, were still in the process of doing so. Meanwhile, reality consisted of the forest, the rain, the warmth, and those around him.

Turning to her more solemnly than he intended, he replied, "I didn't say that. What I said was that I couldn't be your mate."

After a moment's uncertainty her face crinkled into a fresh smile; a provocative blend of shyness and anticipation. Then she reached for him.

Chapter Twenty

It took several days of hard climbing to reach the Home-tree. Flinx followed patiently behind Saalahan and Teal, watching the children and their furcots swing fearlessly across green-fringed chasms that would have given a mature human athlete pause. Occasionally they detoured carefully around dangers Flinx never saw, and once at Teal's admonition he was compelled to all but tiptoe past a slim, smooth-barked growth that appeared no more threatening than its immediate neighbors.

Eventually Moomadeem called out from his position on the right. Joining the young furcot, Teal and Saalahan discussed what appeared to be familiar surroundings. They were sufficiently confident to diverge from the course dictated by Flinx's positioner.

"If we're wrong we can always use your device to return to our former path," she told him. "But I think Moomadeem is right. I think we are very near the Home."

An hour's walk proved the furcot right. The branch that marked the outlying reaches of the Home-tree looked the same as those that he'd initially encountered upon leaving his shuttle at the landing site and descending into the hylaea. But it was not the same.

Without warning a large, powerful form dropped from a cluster of lianas dangling overhead to land directly in front of Saalahan, effectively blocking their path. Startled by her master's reaction, Pip instantly rose into the air and began searching for the source of the alarm, alert and ready to defend against any attack.

A man landed on the branch next to the fully grown furcot. He was little taller than Teal and similarly clad. A finger waved in Flinx's direction.

"Who and what is that?"

"Hullo, Enoch." Stepping forward, Teal put a hand on each of the man's shoulders. Still wary, he kept trying to see past her. Flinx wasn't sure whether the newcomer's attention was directed toward him or Pip.

Saalahan led the younger furcots to greet the second adult. Meanwhile Kiss and Dwell raced past both guards, shouting and calling out gleefully. The man watched them go, then put his own hands on Teal's shoulders. At that moment Flinx realized what the man was looking for.

"Where is Jerah?"

Lowering her eyes respectfully, Teal shook her head. "It was not a good gathering."

The older man nodded knowingly. "We thought you all dead."

"Only Jerah."

As Enoch retreated a step, Flinx noted the snuffler strapped to his back. "I didn't know you knew the returning way."

"We didn't." She turned to indicate Flinx. "This person found us and helped us to return."

Enoch studied Flinx carefully. "It is a person, then." Like Teal and the children, the scout had a gymnast's build, further hardened by a lifetime of climbing trees and swinging from convenient creepers.

"He is from Up There." Teal thrust a finger heavenward.

The man's eyes widened slightly. "A skyperson?"

"Yes, but of a different tribe. In fact, he was being chased by evil skypersons. He came here seeking refuge."

Enoch's deep-seated gaze flicked past the arrivals. "Where are these evil skypersons? What happened to them?"

"Furcots and forest." Her smile was tight. "The little flying creature is a furcot to him. Without him we would not be here now."

Striding boldly and unafraid up to the much taller Flinx, the older man held out his right hand, palm facing up. Echoing the gesture Teal had demonstrated, Flinx placed his own hand atop the other man's, covering it completely. The scout didn't pull back.

"*Feels* like a person," he avowed.

Sensing that her master was once more relaxed, Pip settled back down onto his shoulder.

Enoch stepped back. "You are welcome, and thanked for helping Teal and her children." He smiled affectionately at her. "You will have a tale to tell. Everyone will be glad to see that you and your cubs have survived. There will be mourning for Jerah."

Flinx followed, noting carefully which growths Enoch and Teal avoided. In this fashion he had traveled in safety for the past several days, and he had no intention of letting his guard down now.

It was another hour before they came upon a tree so grand of girth that Flinx thought surely that it had to be one of They-Who-Keep.

"It is the Home-tree," Teal informed him. "The They-Who-Keep are very rare."

Gazing at the gnarled wall of wood, Flinx found it difficult to believe anything so big could actually be alive. Approaching the main trunk at an altitude some four hundred meters above the surface, he saw that it split into half a dozen subsidiary boles, each of which sought its own path to the distant sky. From the multiple trunks, branches greater in diameter than most trees grew in all directions.

The immense structure supported a forest of its own in the form of the thousands of symbiotic and parasitic growths that found purchase upon it. Tons of vines and lianas clung to soaring branches or hung from subsidiary verdure. Flowers bloomed in profusion, attended by hundreds of nectar-, pollen-, and leaf-eaters.

Their guide halted before an impenetrable thicket of vines which sprouted clusters of a peculiar, waxen-petaled blossom. As Flinx looked on, first Enoch and then Teal spat directly into the center of two of the vitreous blooms. The petals closed momentarily over the spittle. A moment later a tremor ran through the obstructing vines. In fits and jerks they pulled themselves aside, contracting far enough in upon themselves to create a passageway between.

Some kind of specialized, acquired biochemical interaction, Flinx mused wonderingly as he followed Enoch and Teal. The children and young furcots had preceded them by several minutes.

A woody chasm opened before him to reveal a spacious hollow formed by the six subsidiary trunks. Within the vaulted enclosure he saw his first signs of permanent habitation.

Using creepers and saplings, leaves and split gourds, hand-hewn planks and thatch, the inhabitants of the Home-tree had fashioned within its protective heart a real village. Storage chambers had been hollowed from parasitic galls, and unusually hard knots served as places of work, trimmed and shaped to serve as living tables and benches.

He was allowed only a fleeting glimpse before Enoch hailed his fellow villagers and they recognized Teal. A helpless Flinx was caught up in the subsequent rejoicing as they swarmed around her. Because most of the men were out hunting or gathering, the celebrants consisted primarily of women and children.

Separating himself from the crowd as best he could, Flinx noted that more formal greetings were being exchanged elsewhere within the clearing as Saalahan's return was acknowledged by fellow furcots. No doubt Moomadeem and Tuuvatem had already announced themselves and retired to the company of their children.

When the initial excitement over her safe return finally subsided, she proudly introduced Flinx and Pip to her people. Wide-eyed but audacious children dared one another to touch him. All were fascinated by his pale skin, red hair, and towering frame. Hugging his neck, Pip hissed warningly at any small hands that fumbled too close. Each time she reacted, two or three children would retreat while emitting squeals of mixed fear and laughter.

Eventually the crowd parted, quieting reverently at the approach of the old shaman, Ponder. Flinx stoically presented himself for examination while Teal stood by approvingly. The old man studied the strange arrival intently, occasionally feeling of his body and raiment. Flinx endured it all in silence, looking past the old man only once to wink at Teal.

When he was satisfied, the shaman turned to the expectant villagers. "That this person has come among us is an important thing. That he is a skyperson and yet comes in peace seeking understanding is more important still. All the tribes must be notified." He turned back to the visitor. "What knowledge do you seek, young man?" The crowd watched and listened intently.

Feeling many eyes on him, Flinx replied with care. "That which I do not have."

"And what knowledge is it that you do not have?"

"Everything."

The shaman Ponder chuckled. "You are not as young as you look. Or at least a part of you isn't." A wrinkled but still vigorous hand clapped him on the shoulder.

"In particular," Flinx added, now that he'd made a good impression, "I'd like to see the place that belonged to the evil skypersons."

For an instant the old man's expression darkened, and Flinx worried that he might have overstepped his bounds. But the shaman's emotional aura was warm, and a moment later he was grinning.

"It never 'belonged' to them. No part of the forest can belong to anyone. According to the old tales, they learned that the hard way. Where they once were is a place to be shunned, but if knowledge of this is something you wish to acquire, then you shall have it. For what you did to help Teal and her cubs, you are owed."

Uncertainty gave way to embarrassment. "They helped me more than I helped them."

"A modest skyperson!" exclaimed someone in the crowd. It sparked murmurs of approval.

Old Ponder's smile widened. "There must be a feast, to celebrate Teal's safe return. Later, I would like to talk with you, young man. There are some questions I have about the sky I would very much like to have answered."

Flinx smiled back. "The brethren of the curious. I'll do what I can." Arm in arm, young skyperson and aged forest dweller strolled off toward the center of the village.

The sheer variety of edibles brought forth at the communal meal that evening was breathtaking in its scope. Flinx hardly knew what to try first. There was meat both dried and fresh, the product of several days' hunt, but it was the fruits and vegetables and a number of unclassifiable growing things that truly teased his palate. A whole spectrum of new flavors was opened. A suitcase full of synthesizable extracts from this world would be worth a fortune to any food conglomerate in the Commonwealth, he reflected as he ate.

Someone handed him an oblong lavender fruit speckled with blue streaks that had been cooling in the depths of a hollowed-out gall. Taking a bite, he was rewarded with soft indigo pulp that tasted of raspberries and cream. Settled on his lap, Pip lay quiescent, her middle swollen, her appetite properly sated for the first time in many days.

He loosely estimated the tribe's population at between fifty and a hundred. It was impossible to be any more accurate because people were constantly coming and going on this or that errand while giggling, laughing children streaked back and forth at random.

To all outward appearances the community was thriving and healthy despite being surrounded by danger enough to give a fully equipped exploration expeditionary force pause. Teal and her people had adapted so completely to a life in the forest that if left alone, in another couple of hundred years any memories of Commonwealth antecedents would probably be completely forgotten.

Whether they would be left alone was doubtful. Where one ship had accidently come, others were likely to follow. Another problem for him to contemplate, as if his problem quotient wasn't bursting mental seams already.

Several days passed before, with Ponder's blessing, he was guided to the blasted place in the forest that had been the site of the evil skypersons' brief sojourn on this world. Beneath a pulsing, fecund blanket of greenery, the ruins of a commercial humanx outpost were clearly visible. How it had come to be here he had no idea, but the stories related by Ponder pointedly detailed the tragedy that had overtaken its hopeful but intrusive builders.

With the aid of the shaman and others from the tribe, a path was hacked through the suffocating vines and roots that had taken possession of the buildings. Branches and creepers had pushed through every port. Doors lay crumpled and twisted, ripped from their hinges by the slow but inexorable action of growing things. Secondary and tertiary trees had burst upward through the floor and continued growing until they'd punctured the roof.

Ample evidence showed where fire had swept through the complex, though the profusion of plant life had healed or obliterated many of the original wounds. He had to smile at the sight of pink and yellow flowers trailing from vines that had enveloped a floor-mounted pulse cannon. Once a brooding weapon, time had reduced it to the status of a decorative planter.

Flinx would have probed deeper, but Ponder restrained him. "Dangerous animals live in the darkest places." It was clear that only his curiosity allowed the shaman to move freely about the ruins. After helping to clear a way in, most of the tribespeople had chosen to remain outside. For them the complex was the location of unpleasant collective memories, and they saw no reason to tempt whatever ghosts might linger in its depths.

"These animals you refer to; they scare you?" Flinx asked the shaman. Ponder nodded solemnly. "Then they scare me as well." He gestured down a half-lit corridor. "Let's see what's up that way. What happened here, anyway?"

"The stories tell that the skypersons came seeking to steal from the forest." The shaman stepped carefully around a twisted lump of stelamic. "They could not emfol, not a one of them. So what happened here was as sad as it was inevitable."

A failed commercial venture, Flinx mused. Carried out surreptitiously, without proper permits, preparations, or safeguards. He edged around a bush whose flowers he'd been told were capable of firing tiny, toxic darts if disturbed. Whoever these people were, they'd come intending to subdue rather than cooperate with the world-forest. He shook his head at the thought. No wonder they'd never had a chance.

Somewhere there would be a record of the failed venture. In company files, in the records of whichever concern had insured the ill-fated House. It constituted a piece of Commonwealth history destined to remain sealed for some time. Any individuals who'd been directly involved and who could tell the true story of what had happened here were probably dead by now.

Until and unless proper protection was extended to Teal and her people, a repeat of that tragedy was certainly possible. How he would manage to secure such protection, Flinx didn't know; only that he would arrange it somehow. Wherever it could be found and whatever the circumstances, happiness was a rare enough commodity that it deserved protection. If it could be done without exposing the tribesfolk to a stampede of Commonwealth attention, from starry-eyed botanists to overeager anthropologists, so much the better.

At the same time he knew that there were areas where Teal's people would benefit from contact with the rest of humanxkind. Flinx was too young and too much a realist to succumb, as certain romantics did, to a fatuous belief in the inherent perfection and nobility of the forest-roaming primitive. The unfortunate Jerah, for example, would have been delighted by the gift of a heat-sensing, compact magazine, rapid-firing pistol.

Somehow a happy medium of contact would have to be found. Surely the quality of life here could be improved without being destroyed. At the same time he was considering the problem, he was acutely aware of his lack of experience in such matters.

Truzenzuzex and Bran Tse-Mallory would know how to proceed, he thought. If only that remarkable pair didn't choose to move about as often as he did himself. With a shock he realized that he didn't know if his early mentors were even still alive.

One day I will have to stop wandering, stop playing, and attend to business, he told himself.

He wasn't going to do much of anything, he knew, until he could figure out a way of getting off this world safely. Reaching his shuttle and lifting off without incident was going to be difficult, and docking successfully with the *Teacher* next to impossible so long as the AAnn kept careful watch. He knew they wouldn't grow tired and give up. The Imperial Authority could always rotate ships on station to relieve boredom among their crews. Precivilization AAnn would watch a hole containing prey until either they or their quarry starved. Their modern, technologically sophisticated descendants were no less tenacious.

Could he strike some kind of bargain with them? In order to do that he would first need something to bargain with. If he was patient, perhaps time and chance would provide it.

He remained alert to any possibility while allowing Teal and her friends to show him the wonders of the hylaea, of which there was a plethora within a day's hike of the Home-tree. He was also pleased to see that the scout who had met them in the forest, the providentially unmated Enoch, had taken an abiding and ongoing interest in Teal's welfare.

For her part, she paid little attention to him, preferring to devote most of her free time to looking after Flinx. He accepted this, knowing that it was only temporary. At present he was a novelty, one to whom she felt she owed something. When it came time for him to leave, she would turn gradually and gratefully to the attentive and worthy Enoch.

At his request they climbed one day to the upper reaches of the second level. Each level was marked by distinctive changes in the type and density of vegetation, much of which he'd come to recognize. A willing Teal and Enoch filled in the gaps in his knowledge.

But none of them, not even Ponder, would go any higher. Nor would they descend below the vegetative border that separated the sixth level from the seventh, where light came more from eerily phosphorescent fungi than from a distant and shadowed sun. Despite his interest in the actual nature of the planet's surface, when he finally found himself poised on that border contemplating the unwholesome, stygian depths, Flinx understood that it was a journey no one would be criticized for postponing indefinitely.

"Terrible things live down there." Ponder stood next to him, his nose wrinkling at the fetid odor rising from the abyss. Teal, several hunters, and their furcots waited uneasily overhead. "We should go."

Beneath the sickly branch on which they stood, something monstrous went scuttling through the depths, a slightly brighter shade of black than its noisome surroundings. Flinx imagined a foamless wave cresting on a moonless night and shuddered. Turning without regret, he followed Ponder upward, toward the light.

Chapter Twenty-one

Two months and a week had passed without any sign of the AAnn. Thanks to the information the *Teacher* relayed to him via the shuttle, he knew they were still about, waiting for him to give up and return.

The fact that the shuttle's relay continued to function suggested that they were content to retire to orbit and await communication. Whether the shuttle would respond to flight commands or not remained to be seen. Easy enough to leave it intact and at his disposal, save for its ability to fly. Disabling it would leave him planet-bound and at their mercy.

If he was going to be marooned, there were several items aboard he very much wished to have; supplies that would make an extended stay on this world a deal more tolerable. Foremost among these were a replacement sidearm and fresh power cells for his positioner and communicator. And while the local foodstuffs were tasty as well as edible, he hungered for more familiar shipboard fare.

A prisoner of my environment, he reflected, even if I carry it around with me.

Enoch, Teal, and two other hunters agreed to accompany him, together with their four furcots.

"I don't think any AAnn will be waiting in ambush," he told them as they made their way through the hylaea. Pip fluttered on ahead, examining each and every fruit and flower. "There's no reason to station troops at the landing site. A shuttle doesn't have room for and isn't designed to accommodate passengers for any length of time."

"Why wouldn't the nonpersons simply set up a camp outside their skyboat?" Enoch asked.

Flinx had to smile. "Assuming they managed to make it back to their own skyboat and lift off successfully, the not-person AAnn who captured Teal and I would share tales of their experience with their fellows. I don't think they'd find many volunteers to spend any amount of time on your world." He ducked under a limb.

"Besides, there's no need for them to go to the trouble of establishing a permanent camp. They know I can't get offworld without their permission. All they have to do is wait me out." He tapped his instrument belt. "I'm sure that's why they've left my communications alone. I can't surrender if I can't talk to them."

"*Are* you going to surrender, Flinx?" Despite his longer stride, Teal kept pace with him effortlessly.

"No," he told her fondly. "Not a chance."

"Then what will you do?"

"Survive. Live. Try to be patient." He put an arm around her shoulders and gave her a reassuring squeeze, noting with amusement Enoch's stolid sideways glance as he did so. "It's not such a bad thing to spend time in the company of good friends." He waved at the surrounding forest. "There's so much to learn here. So much *newness*."

"Only new to those who are ignorant," Enoch groused.

"And I am ignorant, Enoch. That's why I'm relying on experienced, knowledgeable people like yourself to enlighten me."

The other man tried not to appear flattered, but failed.

They made excellent time through the forest, untroubled by wandering carnivores. This wasn't surprising: not with adult furcots flanking the group on either side as well as above and below. Traveling with a party consisting entirely of seasoned adults, Flinx was astonished at the progress that could be made.

Dangerous growths were easily and rapidly avoided, difficult places expertly negotiated as they followed the course supplied by the positioner. Initially dubious as to its efficacy despite Teal's assurances, the hunters soon came to trust the compact device. Each of them wanted to caress it, turning it over and over in their fingers as if mere contact could impart some of its magic to the holder. For their part, the furcots dismissed it with a collective snort, preferring to trust in their own instincts and sense of direction.

In the company of eight capable guides, Flinx found he was able to relax, though his companions still expected him to watch out on his own for the smaller, more easily sidestepped threats.

There was even time for some play, as when they each made a ten meter leap onto the comforting leaves of a close relative of the gargalufla plant that had allowed Flinx, Teal, and her children to finally escape the clutches of the AAnn.

Nearing the landing site, the party was attacked for the first time. The reech consisted of a small, pallid round body from which extended half a dozen three-meter-long arms. As it charged it gave forth an unexpectedly farcical roar that Flinx could only describe as a *squonk*. There was nothing amusing about the mouth, however, which was all hooked, serrated teeth.

The combination of waving, flailing arms and small body made for a difficult target. While the furcots diverted the charge and kept it occupied, Enoch and One-Eye slipped close with their snufflers. Two poison darts struck the reech, one just under the lower jaw, the other square in the center eye. Losing its grip, it fell spinning and tumbling into the green depths, its attenuated arms thrashing convulsively like a starfish on speed.

That night they camped in the shelter of a slyone grove, surrounded by two-meter-tall flowers which were at once incredibly graceful and strong. The tubular stems and blossoms glistened like glass, not surprising since they contained more silicon than carbon. When the night-rain commenced, Flinx felt as if he were sleeping in the woodwind section of a symphony orchestra. Each droplet drew forth from the flower it expended itself upon a different note, all tinkling and gemlike.

Around midnight he was awakened by the muted shush-shush of multiple wings. He watched while Teal explained how the blind hyels, boasting ears big enough to put those of any Terran bat to shame, pollinated the scentless sylone, locating the blossoms by sound alone and feeding on the odorless nectar with tongues as long as her arm. In this way pollinator, plant, and rain were intertwined, as without the rain to strike them the sylone would produce no sound.

Awed yet anew by the synchronicity of nature, Flinx allowed the flower-music to lull him back to sleep.

The following morning the furcot Beelaseec, who had been walking point, returned to announce that according to Flinx's description of the landing site it must lie just ahead, for they had reached a place where the forest was growing directly upon naked rock.

A glance at the positioner confirmed the furcot's supposition. "We should start ascending now," Flinx informed his companions. "Be easier to climb through the trees than on the rock."

"You mean to enter the Upper Hell," Saalahan declared. "That is not for us. We will remain close, but concealed." It was a measure of the terror in which the open sky was held that even furcots refused to present themselves to its openness. Having been exposed to its dangers before, Flinx understood and sympathized.

"No one needs to leave the cover of the trees. I can make it to my skyboat by myself."

Enoch stepped forward. "I will come with you, Flinx, if you need me."

Flinx put both hands on the other man's shoulders, in the accepted fashion. "Thank you, Enoch, but there's really nothing you can do up on the rock or aboard my boat. Better you stay with the others and keep watch. Pip will look after me. Keep an eye on Teal."

A smile cracked the smaller man's face and he responded in kind, grasping Flinx's shoulders firmly.

When they were a hundred meters from the top of the canopy the first glimmerings of blue began to appear through the leaves. Shortly thereafter, a comfortable resting place was located and Flinx bade temporary farewell to his friends. The branches soon grew narrower, the supporting vines thinner as he approached the rock face, making his way upward.

When he had vanished from sight, one of the hunters turned to Teal. "What do you think truly of this tall skyperson?"

"In the ways of the world he is very young." She was looking at the place in the branches where Flinx had disappeared. "In others, he is old beyond his years. Older than is fair."

The hunter nodded sagely. "It's better, then, that he works this thing with his skyboat alone." Satisfied, he found a comfortable place to sit and removed the food pouch from his backpack.

Teal tried to put Flinx out of her mind but found she could not. Horrific creatures inhabited the Upper Hell, alert and ready to snatch up anyone who ventured too close to the sky. Yet Flinx spoke of flying through the sky and beyond it, as her own ancestors were said to have done. Surely he would be all right.

Surely.

Though she had no appetite, she forced herself to join the others in eating.

It was strange for Flinx to stand again beneath a sky in which blue rather than green was dominant. The yellowish-blue atmosphere was alive with colorful, drifting shapes. Some soared on thin, membranous wings, others flapped rainbow-hued feathers, while a flock of peeled spheres coiled through the air like animated corkscrews. A trio of slim fliers boasting six stubby wings apiece shot past overhead, the wind whistling with their passage.

Not every inhabitant of this world's atmosphere was a predator, Flinx observed as he ducked under the tip of a branch and emerged onto bare granite. Seed and fruit eaters dominated the clouds.

Still, he paused to crouch beneath the last protective vegetation as he scanned the crowded yellow-blue for signs of taloned hunters. Weeks of experience had taught him that on this world safety was an illusion, and confidence a sure path to disaster.

It was immensely reassuring to see his shuttle squatting exactly as he'd left it. After so much green, the rudimentary dull gray of it came as a shock to his retinas. Outwardly undisturbed, it hugged its chunk of exposed mountaintop, the boarding ramp still temptingly affixed to bare rock. A flick of the transmitter that was on his belt would open the lock, readmitting him to a world temporarily set aside.

Next to it stood a second shuttle, larger than his own and equally devoid of animation. It was of a familiar design, relatively common throughout the Commonwealth.

Coerlis's ship, he knew. Waiting patiently for a crew that would never return.

Of the AAnn shuttle there was no sign, unless one counted the scorched, blackened section of rock in front of his own craft. Either Lord Caavax had made it back to his vessel with the remnants of his party and had safely lifted off, or else another shuttle had descended and put aboard a reclaim crew to recover the craft. Flinx suspected the former. Caavax was stubborn, but resourceful.

Resting comfortably in orbit, waiting to hear from me, he told himself. Well, that was a communication he intended to delay for as long as possible. Rising, he stepped out of the concealing vegetation and started toward his ship.

Only to halt abruptly as an unfamiliar emotion from *within* his shuttle impacted on his thoughts.

While Pip hovered nearby, alert and wary, he strained for identification. Tumbling the sentiment in his mind, examining it from every angle, he felt the overriding sensation to be one of all-pervasive calm. It *could* come from a waiting AAnn, but there were distinctive differences that suggested another source entirely. One, he decided, that was not human. For one thing, the internalized conflict that was always present in his own kind was absent.

Alien emotions were always difficult to recognize, much less analyze.

Who, or what, had taken up residence inside his shuttle? Certainly nothing local. Not even the cleverest furcot could solve the security of the outer lock.

A furcot, however, would know enough not to stand so long exposed to the open sky. Keeping low and moving fast, Flinx hurried in the direction of the boarding ramp.

Hiding beneath the ramp, he twisted and leaned out far enough to see that, as expected, the lock was still secured. Could some peculiar animal, perhaps one that generated similar frequencies for attack or defense, have accidentally broadcast the signal that would open the lock, only to subsequently find itself trapped inside? It was a far-fetched scenario, but given what he'd seen on this world in the previous few weeks, he believed the creatures that inhabited it capable of anything.

No, he decided. Nothing native was involved. There was too much of the familiar about the emotional condition he was sensing. Nor could it be an AAnn. Only a single mind was projecting. Had it been Lord Caavax's intention to post a guard on board his craft, most surely he would have assigned more than one.

None of it made any sense.

As time passed, nothing occurred to suggest that whatever was within was aware of his presence beneath the ramp. If he could crack the outer lock, slip quickly inside, and reach a certain storage locker, he would be better able to confront whatever had taken possession of his vessel. In any event, there was nothing to be gained by huddling beneath the ramp in expectation of nightfall.

As he stepped out from under cover and started up the ramp, something like a winged, ribbed barrel fell out of the sky. Its beak or bill, which was as long as the stubby body and ended in a needle-sharp point, would have been more appropriate on a fish-eater.

Possibly it reached the same conclusion, because as Pip rose to intercept, it veered off and shot past its intended quarry, the wind of its passing ruffling Flinx's hair.

Another half-dozen steps found him at the top of the ramp. His hand reached for the transmitter . . . and hesitated. Might as well see if the shuttle's vorec system is still functioning, he decided. He directed his voice to the grid set flush in the door.

Responding promptly to his verbal command, the barrier slid aside on permanent low-friction seals, admitting him to the lock. A second command opened the inner door, and he made a mad dash for the storage locker.

"Come on, come on!" he muttered aloud as he fumbled with the recalcitrant latch. Seconds later it was free, allowing him to liberate the sidearm secured inside. A quick check showed a full charge, as expected.

Pip was just settling on his shoulder when the owner of the emotions he had detected from without appeared in the fore portal. His symbospeech was fluent, the accent familiar.

"I really don't think you want to shoot me. At least, I hope that you don't."

A relieved Flinx let out a long sigh. The creature standing before him had four legs, two arms, and a pair of limbs that could be employed as either, according to the demands of the moment. It wore very little; a double pack strapped across its thorax, and leggings that were more decorative than functional. Its insignia was inlaid in the shoulder of one truarm.

From half his height the iridescent-gold compound eyes gazed back at him thoughtfully. Feathery antennae inclined in his direction.

"I am Counselor Second Druvenmaquez," the thranx informed him, "and you are Philip Lynx."

"I'm honored. Also very surprised." He slipped the sidearm replacement for the one Coerlis had taken into the empty holster attached to his belt. "How did you get here, sir? I see only this shuttle and the one belonging to—"

"We know who it belonged to," the Counselor interrupted him. "I arrived by means of personal flier, escorted by appropriately armed military personnel who through dint of considerable effort managed to keep me from being devoured by overly enthusiastic representatives of the local aerial fauna. A more extraordinary assortment of wings, teeth, and claws I have never seen before and hope never to encounter again.

"An electronic bypass allowed me to enter your shuttle, whereupon my escort returned to their waiting craft. With great eagerness, I should imagine.

"What an astonishing world this is. Do you know that in the time I have been waiting for you I have witnessed over a hundred life-and-death battles involving the local flora and fauna, and that on two occasions extremely large predators actually attacked this landing vessel? Fortunately its hull resisted their energetic but primitive assaults. Needless to say, I have not spent much time outside." He shook his head to express wonderment, a gesture the thranx had picked up and adopted at the beginning of their long and intimate association with humans.

Using his tongue against his upper palate, Flinx responded with a clicking sound to indicate understanding, responding to the human gesture with one utilized by the thranx. He did it automatically and without thinking, as would have any human in the presence of a thranx. The relationship between the two species had progressed beyond clumsy, heavy-handed etiquette.

"Imagine a creature of the air big enough to try and fly off with a shuttlecraft! I wonder what its young must look like! Thank the Hive this vessel was too heavy for its intentions. You would think such a formidable predator would realize instinctively that metal and ceramic composites are not very nutritious." The Counselor made a gesture with both truhands.

"I am glad you finally came. I am no explorer and this is not a posting I looked forward to eagerly."

Flinx spoke as he led the Counselor forward and activated the shuttle's food unit. It had minimal capacity, but he was hungry enough for something familiar to eat, whatever the unit chose to dish out.

"If you think the struggle for survival is competitive up here, sir, you should see what it's like down in the jungle." The unit whined and gave birth to a seasoned soy patty, bread, and some steamed, reconstituted carrots. Flinx attacked them as if he hadn't eaten in weeks and had suddenly been presented with the specialty of the house from the finest restaurant on New Riviera. Occasionally he would pause to pass a choice bit to Pip.

"Yet you have survived in its depths." The Counselor was studying the young human thoughtfully. "I have been able to follow your progress with this craft's instrumentation because your positioner has been on continually. You have been moving around quite a bit."

Flinx spared a glance for the tiny device attached to his belt. "I didn't dare fool with it, sir. If I'd lost the signal I never would have been able to find my way back here." He shoveled in a mouthful of carrots. "I suppose it's unnecessary to point out that there's an AAnn vessel in orbit. Probably a warship."

Counselor Druvenmaquez's antennae flicked significantly. "Wrong tense, my young human friend. There *was* an AAnn warship in orbit. Though this is an unpopulated and overlooked world, it still lies within Commonwealth space."

"Wrong adjective," Flinx informed him. "It's not unpopulated."

"There is native intelligence?"

"In a manner of speaking." He finished the last of the soy patty and followed it with more bread. "Must have been one of the first human colony ships to go out. If it was pre-Amalgamation, that means the people here have been surviving, on their own and completely out of touch with the rest of humanxkind, for something like seven hundred years.

"The descendants haven't completely forgotten their origins, but they've been living here long enough to revert to a semiprimitive condition. When word of this world gets out, Commonwealth anthropologists are going to have a field day." A small smile broadened his expression. "If they can survive long enough in the field to complete any work, that is. As for the taxonomists, there are billions of new life forms here that will need to be classified. Whole new classes, maybe even new phyla.

"There's also evidence of a comparatively recent, illegal attempt at settlement and exploitation. It didn't succeed. Nothing survives here for very long unless it learns to cooperate with the world-forest. Try to dominate it and you're plant food."

"Remarkable." The Counselor's antennae bobbed with excitement. "This world will have to be reentered into the Commonwealth catalog. I would think 'for study only—no development,' would be the most appropriate classification. What is the population of survivors?"

"I don't know. They're split into half a dozen tribes. The one I made friends with seems to be doing fairly well."

"Friends. That explains how you have been able to survive in this rain forest of all rain forests."

Flinx bit into the last of the bread. "Wouldn't have lasted long without them. They've not only learned how to survive in the forest, they've evolved the better to fit in to the particular niche they've chosen."

"Humans are extraordinarily adaptable," the Counselor agreed.

Having no antennae to wave, Flinx gestured with the remnants of his bread. "Wait till you meet your first fur-cot, sir."

"Furcot?" Truhands semaphored anxiously. "Please, this is all too much to digest at once, and in any event I am not the one to whom you should be elucidating. I am no xenologist." A truhand and foothand gestured pointedly. "I came here searching for *you*, not alien mysteries, human or otherwise.

"Arriving here we encountered first the AAnn interloper and subsequently another vessel registered to a noted mercantile House on Samstead, in addition to your own craft. When the second vessel did not respond to normal hailings, it was boarded. The presence of the AAnn was self-explanatory, as is that of most trespassers." The triangular, golden-eyed skull cocked sideways. "Perhaps you can explain the presence of the other?"

"I was involved in an altercation with the owner. A personal dispute that he chose to pursue beyond the bounds of reason. He and his people chased me all the way to this world and down into the forest."

"What happened to him?"

"The forest."

The Counselor Second nodded knowingly, executing another useful acquired human gesture. So fond of such gestures were the thranx that Flinx knew they used them often among themselves, even when no human was present. There was a certain cachet to it, just as there was among humans who utilized the click-speech of High thranx as a favorite party patois.

"Having spent much time under difficult circumstances in this remarkable environment, I suspect you would like to immerse yourself in warm water." The thranx understood the philosophy behind water cleaning but had a positive horror of baths, understandable for a species that could not swim and whose air intakes were located just below their necks. A thranx could stand with its head well above water and quietly drown.

"Actually, I've had access to a warm shower every night, sir, but without any kind of cleanser. I'd enjoy that very much."

The shuttle's facilities were Spartan but serviceable. More welcome still was the change of clothing he found in the bottom of the storage locker.

"What happened to the AAnn?" he asked as he changed. The elderly thranx had not even an academic interest in his naked form, and Flinx suffered from no nudity phobia, anyway.

"Ah, the *Keralkee*. I'm afraid we had an altercation of our own. They refused to comply with a request to allow boarding or to cooperate in any way. You know the AAnn. There was a certain Lord Caavax LYD—"

"I made his acquaintance."

"Did you?" The Counselor's eyebrows would have risen if he'd had any. "A typical AAnn aristocrat. Noble of bearing, arrogant of mien. Stubborn and devious.

"They tried to run, covering their flight with undeclared fire. Their vessel suffered a reactive implosion before they could activate their drive. Presently their components are dispersing throughout this system. It is to be regretted."

So Lord Caavax had survived his ordeal in the forest and made it safely back to his ship, only to run afoul of a Commonwealth peaceforcer. A fight had ensued that he and his crew had lost. No doubt it had pleased him to go out in that fashion. His line would acquire honor from the manner of his passing.

Remembering the icy, emotionless tone of the AAnn's voice when he'd ordered one of his soldiers to kill Dwell and Kiss, Flinx was unable to summon a twinge of regret at his demise.

"For an unknown world, it has been very crowded here of late." The Counselor regarded the much taller human thoughtfully. "How did you find it?"

"I didn't. When I was fleeing Samstead I asked my nav system to take me to the next inhabitable world on whatever vector we happened to be pointing." He spread his hands wide. "This is where I ended up. It wasn't planned and there was no intent behind it."

"That's very interesting." The Counselor considered his prosaic surroundings. "As this world has been uncharted and utterly overlooked, its location shouldn't be in your vessel's navigation files. Unless whoever programmed the system knew something Commonwealth Central did not."

The Counselor was quite correct. The *Teacher* shouldn't have known the location of this world, much less that it was capable of supporting humanx life. However, the *Teacher*'s assembly had not been supervised by a recognized humanx concern. The ship had been cobbled together by the Ulru-Ujurrians, who did indeed have access to knowledge that was denied even to Commonwealth Central.

Had his arrival here been as much an accident as he'd come to believe? Or was it part and parcel of another of the Ulru-Ujurrians cryptic and incomprehensible "games"?

Raising his gaze, he stared past the attentive Counselor Second, half expecting one of the massive, furry Ulru-Ujurrians to pop into the cabin expecting to sample the food. It would be wholly in keeping with, say, Maybeso's unpredictable nature. How that singular species negotiated space-time was something so far outside known science as to verge on magic.

Maybe if he played his part in the Great Game to their satisfaction, they would teach him that trick some day.

"What are you thinking?"

Flinx blinked at the Counselor, who was eyeing him closely. "Nothing, sir. Actually, I was remembering a game."

The thranx emitted the clicking sound that passed for laughter among his kind. "Did you win or lose?"

"I don't know. I don't know if there are winners or losers in this game. All you can do is keep playing and hope someday to find out."

"Someday you'll have to tell me more about it."
Reaching into his slim backpack, the Counselor withdrew a sealed thranx drinking utensil and sipped from the traditional coiled spout.

"Speaking of telling things," Flinx pressed him warily, "what brings a Counselor Second to this unrecorded world? You know my name, too."

The Counselor made a gesture of polite acknowledgment. "Why, I should think it obvious. You bring me here, Philip Lynx."

Flinx kept his voice and expression perfectly neutral. "It seems a long and difficult way to come just to make my acquaintance. I'm nobody important."

"That remains to be seen. Do you recall a brief but interesting conversation you had recently with a Padre Bateleur on Samstead?"

Flinx remembered the kindly father. "So he reported my situation? That was good of him, but I wouldn't have expected a Counselor Second in charge of peace enforcement to take an interest in one person's problem, much less command a peaceforcer to try and protect him from the likes of Jack-Jax Coerlis."

"I am not with peace enforcement," declared Druvenmaquez quietly. "I am Counselor Second for Science, with a particular interest in astronomics."

Flinx blinked. "Astronomy?"

"You spoke to the padre of a recurring dream. The average human or thranx would have thought it nothing more than that and soon forgotten all about it, but Padre Bateleur providentially decided to pass it along for analysis. It was deliberated by a couple working for Commonwealth Science on Denpasar, on Terra, before being passed along to Bascek on Hivehom.

"By this time it had acquired a lengthy file of opinion and relevant facts. When it finally came to my attention I was instantly intrigued, and set a formal study circle to working on it. When I was presented with their summation, I became even more intrigued by how someone such as yourself, with no access to extensive scientific facilities, had managed to come to similar conclusions."

Flinx frowned "And that's what you came all this way for? That's what brought you all the way out here?"

Druvenmaquez nodded, the artificial light gleaming off his blue-green exoskeleton. "That is correct."

"How did *you* find this planet?"

The Counselor made the thranx equivalent of a shrug. "I expect that once he had committed to an interest in you, the good padre Bateleur had your position monitored in case he wanted to talk to you again. This interest would extend to recording the departure vector taken by your vessel as well as that of the contentious human pursuing you.

"This solar system was an obvious conclusion, since no others lying anywhere along your chosen outsystem vector contain worlds capable of supporting life. It was assumed that you had come here because there was nowhere else for you to go."

It struck Flinx then that the Counselor knew nothing of the *Teacher*'s unique abilities. He wondered how many AAnn had known, in addition to the now deceased Lord Caavax. Maybe none save his immediate courtiers and family. Humanxkind's traditional enemies could be secretive even among themselves. Perhaps he could yet keep the secret a while longer.

Within the Commonwealth, at least, it seemed he would still be able to travel freely, without drawing undue attention to his vessel.

Meanwhile he still had to deal with the problem of drawing undue attention to himself. How much did they know about *him*? About the Meliorare Society and his damnable personal history? If the Counselor was in any way familiar with such matters, he was, for the moment at least, keeping such knowledge to himself.

"What I told Father Bateleur was the subject of a recurring dream. I don't know what else to tell you. I didn't realize it had any basis in scientific reality." Ignorant of the Counselor's skill level at interpreting human expressions, he adopted his most innocent.

"The Astronomy section of the Commonwealth Science Department believes it does." Druvenmaquez carefully set his drinking vessel aside. "You spoke to Padre Bateleur of a great evil, 'out there.' Not a particularly scientific observation. Researchers in Astronomy and Ethics rarely have occasion to consult with one another.

"However, the section of sky you singled out is the location of a cosmological phenomenon that has been known for some time as the Grand Void. For the sake of convenience in the course of this discussion, I will employ human terms of reference.

"The Grand Void is an area of the cosmos that is barren of the usual astronomical phenomena. No stars, no planets, no nebulae. No *light*. What may lie *beyond* is the subject of occasional speculation. We have no way of knowing because the Void is obscured by a stupendous concentration of dark matter consisting largely of stable, massive, electrically charged particles left over from the beginning of the Universe. 'Champs,' in the common human terminology.

"The result is a gravitational lens of unparalleled extent which effectively distorts any light in the vicinity. Studies of the nonvisible spectrum have been similarly ineffective in detecting what lies behind this lens . . . if anything does.

"You spoke to Father Bateleur of experiencing a 'jolt' immediately prior to perceiving this evil. This leads the imaginative, or perhaps merely the lighthearted, to speculate on whether or not a gravitational lens might distort thought or perception much as it does light. I have heard humans speak of the 'gravity of someone's thoughts' without ever realizing I might someday be compelled to consider it literally.

"All this is so much extreme conjecture. At my age, a charming hobby. In discussing it, I find it necessary to invent new terms in order to be able to forge ahead with further speculation. In meeting you, I was hoping for exposition if not outright explanation. From a scientific standpoint, this Void should not endure. Even allowing for a universe in which matter is not distributed evenly, a vacant region of this size should not be possible.

"Yet it manifestly exists. And you insisted to Father Bateleur that something evil lurks within, although our best instruments insist it is utterly empty. Aside from that subjective determination, your vectoring of the Grand Void was not only accurate, it fully accords with the latest facts and hypotheses, many of which have yet to be released to the lay population. If the mental 'jolt' you say you received accords in any fashion with the location of the recognized gravitational lens, then perhaps the rest of your tale is grounded in something sturdier than mere metaphysics. Truly now, *how did you come to know these things*?"

Flinx responded instantly. "I have sources." *There, that ought to satisfy him!* And without giving anything away.

"Ah. The reply that does not answer. Let us try another approach. You have your own KK-drive ship. The registration has been checked and is in order. Personally, I have difficulty reconciling your obvious youth with such an expensive possession. Perhaps you could enlighten me?"

Again Flinx didn't hesitate. "I have friends."

"Sources and friends." A small whistling sigh escaped the Counselor Second. "You are not under arrest or restraint, so I cannot compel you to elaborate. Is this to be my reward for coming all this way, and saving you from the attentions of the AAnn in the bargain?"

"I'm telling you the truth, sir."

"I do not doubt that. What I doubt is that you are telling me all of it."

"Ask me any question and I'll try to answer it."

"I would rather you were obtuse than clever. It is less slippery. You're a very interesting young human, Philip Lynx, and I think you are worthy of deeper questioning. Anyone who can spark my staff to debating whether or not evil has mass and propounding equations to prove such a theorem is deserving of deeper questioning."

"Come with me to the Home-tree, sir, and I'll show you answers to questions you haven't even thought of. The Home-tree is where the locals live. It's quite a place, one that a person of science like yourself can't but find fascinating."

"You want me to travel to where the local humans live?" Druvenmaquez indicated the greenery visible through a port. "Through *that*?"

A dark brown vine had crept over the left side of the port. Tonight, as it did every night, the shuttle's field cleansers would scrub and scrape clear the rock in the immediate vicinity of its landing struts. For now, though, the vegetation was feverishly trying to colonize this strange new structure. As it did every night.

"There's so much here to study, sir." Flinx leaned forward earnestly, pleased to have succeeded in turning the conversation away from himself, even if only temporarily. "For example, these people do something called *emfoling*."

"Emfoling?"

"I've spoken with their shaman, who is their priest and repository of what scientific knowledge they still remember. It means 'empathetic foliation.' They believe they have the ability to sense what the plants around them are experiencing."

"The plants, you say? Impossible, of course, but an entertaining contribution to human mythology." He hesitated. "Can you promise to lead me to this Home-tree alive and with all my limbs intact?"

Flinx smiled. "It's not a good idea to promise anything on this world, sir. But my escort is an excellent one, and I've made it back this far without coming to any harm. As you must already know, the climate here suits the thranx better than it does humans, so you should be even more comfortable on the journey than I. There is some climbing involved—"

The Counselor started. "Climbing! You know that we are not very skilled climbers."

"Nothing you can't manage, sir," Flinx hastened to add. "Especially with a little help. And along the way, you and I can talk."

Druvenmaquez considered carefully. "A personage of my position—this will have to be cleared with the ship— I admit you tempt me, Philip Lynx. You have interested me ever since I first encountered the report of your meeting with Father Bateleur."

Scratching the dozing Pip under her chin with one hand, Flinx reached out with the other to clasp one of the Counselor's delicate truhands. "Then come with me, sir, and we will talk of green places where life abides and black spaces where less than nothing can exist. And maybe does."

Chapter Twenty-two

Teal, Enoch, and the others were taken aback by the sight of the Counselor. With his eight limbs and compound eyes, feathery antennae and fused vestigial wing-cases, he was unlike anything they'd ever seen before. They were even more astonished when he addressed them in perfect symbospeech. His pleasant body odor went a long way toward muting concerns.

Flinx assured them that the thranx were the best friends that humankind had ever had, and that both species had been working closely together for some eight hundred years. But it was only after the furcots had completed a thorough examination of the new arrival and pronounced themselves satisfied that Enoch and the other hunters agreed to take Druvenmaquez along with them on the journey back to the Home-tree.

The Counselor's fears soon faded. As Flinx knew he would, the elderly thranx quickly adapted to the hot, humid climate and proved surprisingly adept in the tangle of vegetation. Since he could not pull his body weight up a vine, there were places where he required some assistance, but with furcot muscle and human skill available to help, such temporary obstacles were easily and quickly overcome.

When they finally reached the Home-tree, after a journey in which the Counselor's initial apprehension was rapidly replaced by wonder, he was greeted with the same astonishment originally displayed by Teal, Enoch, and the hunters. The children in particular viewed him with a wide-eyed mix of disbelief and uncertainty, which he did his best to overcome.

For his part, Druvenmaquez marveled at the skill and determination with which these lost humans had adapted to an unremittingly hostile environment. His openness and appealing natural fragrance soon saw him trailed by a mob of laughing, gesticulating children and their bumbling but equally fascinated furcots. Granted the freedom of the Home-tree, he was soon a common sight as he moved easily between dwelling and work site, his compact optical recorder always at the ready. From time to time he would pause in his studies to contact the orbiting Commonwealth peaceforcer *Sodwana*, using the relay on Flinx's shuttle to boost the signal from his hand transmitter.

"An astonishing place," he told Flinx, "settled by remarkable people. I believe they can be helped and studied simultaneously. Care will need to be taken. I will see to it myself."

Flinx smiled at the Counselor. "I know you will, sir." He hesitated. "I was wondering if you might know the whereabouts of an acquaintance of mine? The Eint Truzenzuzex?"

Antennae twitched. "That old fraud? Of course I know of him. He's as much a legend as a fraud. Our society isn't as tolerant of eccentrics as is that of humans. Some say his stature exceeds his legend. Never having touched antennae with him, I myself cannot say. As to his whereabouts, I have no idea and doubt few do. You say you know him?"

"From my larval days, yes. I was just wondering."

Druvenmaquez sniffed of a bouquet that was growing directly upon the Home-tree's heartwood. "There has been much wondering going on here lately, young human. We in Science want to know more about your dream. The *Sodwana* did not come all this way to providentially rescue you from the attentions of curious AAnn. We—I—would like some explanations."

"I'm not sure, sir, that I know the questions."

"Don't be circuitous with me, young human!" The Counselor waggled a truhand at him, and Pip raised her head to follow its metronoming movements curiously. "Humans are only just beginning to explore the full potential of their minds—with our help, of course."

Flinx looked away, his voice flat. "You want to take me back for study."

"We want to know how you know what you know."

"I told you: it came to me in a dream."

"That's fine. Dreams are a legitimate subject for study."

"Am I under formal detention?"

The Counselor drew back in horror, which the thranx could express eloquently through body language. "What a notion! You have committed no crime. But having placed yourself in danger, it would not be out of line to say that you may regard yourself as being in protective custody."

Flinx turned back to the Counselor. "I fled from the human Coerlis's unwanted attentions. I avoided the AAnn. If I choose not to comply with your wishes and remain here, there's nothing you can do about it. You'll never be able to remove me forcibly from this world." The confidence with which he delivered these words surprised him.

The old thranx was eyeing him closely. "I will not dispute that because I do not have the information at hand with which to do so. It would be far better, far more agreeable, if you would consent to cooperate. We seek only knowledge." He shrugged. "There may be none to gain. As you say, there may be nothing more here to look at than a dream. A dream of physics and ultimate ethics."

Flinx found himself torn. "Believe me, sir, there's a lot going on I'd like to know more about myself. I just don't want to end up like a smear on a slide."

"Would you feel more at ease if at all times you remained aboard your ship and myself and my staff on board the *Sodwana*?"

Flinx's expression narrowed. "That would satisfy you?"

"I did not say that. But I want to work with you, not against you, young human. It would be a beginning, and perhaps it would suffice."

"I'm not sure I'm ready to leave here yet."

"I can understand that. I am not certain I have any desire to depart immediately myself." A truhand and foothand gestured in tandem. "There is so much here to learn! The forest is home to a billion secrets."

You can't imagine, Flinx mused silently.

The Counselor laid the four chitonous fingers of a truhand on Flinx's forearm. "Consider what I have said. My concern in this is with astronomics. Yours seems to be with evil. If there is any kind of a cojoining here that extends beyond the bounds of metaphysics, is it not worth pursuing? You certainly thought so when you spoke with Father Bateleur." The fingers squeezed gently. "When you are ready, I hope you will speak as freely with me."

He turned and ambled away, heading for a group of women who were cooperatively weaving a large green blanket. The thranx were fascinated by any aspect of human society that seemed to mimic their own.

Leaving the Counselor to his studies, Flinx wandered deep in thought until he found himself standing by his favorite place within the protected bounds of the Home-tree.

A knobby gall grew from the inside of one of the immense growth's subsidiary trunks, forming a flat platform that overlooked a downward-arcing branch some two meters in diameter. The upper surface of the rogue branch was concave, forming a deep groove that ran all the way to the end. The pale green palm sized leaves that were common to the Home-tree sprouted from the bottom of the branch and both sides, but not from the surface groove.

Children had made the aberrant offshoot into a playground. Starting at the top, they settled themselves into the natural furrow and embarked on a winding, spiraling, slip-sliding descent of some twenty meters. Where the branch finally grew too narrow to accommodate their speeding forms, it had been sawn off. Dark, congealed sap showed where the cut had healed over

Shooting out the bottom of this natural chute like a dart from a snuffler, they slammed into a thick pile of transplanted khoumf plants, both the rose-hued and yellowish varieties. With each impact a puff of delicious perfume filled the air, whereupon the laughing, giggling children would scramble back to their feet and clamber fearlessly back up into the heights of the tree for another run.

As in everything else, they were accompanied by their individual furcots, who partook of the activity with a roly-poly dignity that always made Flinx smile. Several adult furcots were always on hand to keep watch, presiding over the frenetic proceedings with silent dignity.

I feel comfortable here, he thought to himself. As comfortable as Pip, sleeping soundly on his shoulder. Could he cooperate with Druvenmaquez enough to satisfy the senior thranx without revealing the secret of himself? That would be the ideal resolution to his present situation. Druvenmaquez was a Counselor Second, and Flinx didn't delude himself into believing he was cleverer than the thranx academician. Only more aware.

There was so much he wanted to know! Exploration of what he knew and what he thought he knew would be so much easier and advance so much faster with seasoned help. But he would have to be very careful.

The all-pervasive warmth he had sensed ever since touching down washed over him; relaxing, calming, reassuring. Emfoling? Or something less, or something more? Since his arrival he'd suffered not one headache, not even a warning throbbing. It was the longest such stretch of cerebral calm he could remember since childhood. This place was *good* for him. For his head, for his thoughts, for his body, and—if it existed—for his soul.

Thousands of light-years distant something abominable shifted and roiled in the absence of stars. It was the antithesis of logic and light. If it would only remain where it was, where it had always been, it would be a simple matter to erase it from his thoughts.

Cold and clear, the unflinching memory lived within him. There was movement out there. In the vicinity of that immeasurable distant horror, matter was stirring. Matter—and other *things*.

Leaning forward, he rested his head in his hands, rubbing tiredly at his eyes. All six feet in the air, a young furcot was swooping down the slide on its back, its rear end forming a blunt and not particularly aerodynamic projectile. Laughing deliciously, a little girl was riding it, clinging to its plump green belly. Flanking the chute, her friends cheered her on, while their furcots maintained a certain juvenile decorum that was absent in their human counterparts. The children's cheers were as loud for the furcot as for the girl.

What he really wanted, he realized as he observed the carefree play, had not changed. To find out all he could about his origins, and to be left alone. Easy enough to do save for one complication.

His damnable sense of responsibility.

If he was right in any measure about what lay out there, at the limits of perception, then long after he was dead and dust, this world and all its wonders would be in dire jeopardy along with every other he'd visited, as well as all those he had not.

Was that his concern? Did he owe anything to a civilization that had failed to protect him even before he'd been born? What he was now was the result as much of calculation as copulation. An experiment gone awry, an experiment that had outlived the experimenters.

It was a great deal to expect someone who had not yet turned twenty-one to cope with.

How long could he keep his secret from the likes of the Counselor Druvenmaquez, from Commonwealth Authority, and from the United Church? There were always aliases, always surgery. More lies to live. There wasn't a day when his headaches, which was the nervous system lying to itself, didn't remind him of his singular status. That is, until he'd arrived here.

Turning to his left and looking down, he considered the triangular, slightly iridescent skull reposing on his shoulder. "How about you, Pip? What do you think?"

The reptilian head rose a centimeter or so. The flying snake couldn't reply verbally, but a deeper pulse of warmth washed through Flinx. So different, he reflected, and yet so mentally attuned.

"That's what I thought."

Rising, he abandoned the gall-seat and strode to the top of the slide-branch. The adult furcot resting there glanced at him out of all three eyes. No words passed between them. Only understanding.

Decisions of great import were not to be taken lightly. That much he had learned from Truzenzuzex and Bran Tse-Mallory.

Plopping himself down in the chute, urged on by the children, watched by dozens of deep green eyes, he let out a whoop as he launched himself forward on the slick wood, letting his weight and momentum carry him forward. Abandoning her master, Pip rose into the air and followed effortlessly, a bewinged pink and blue halo that shadowed his accelerating progress downward.

Down, into the beckoning green depths.

DEL REY® ONLINE!

The Del Rey Internet Newsletter…

A monthly electronic publication, posted on the Internet, GEnie, CompuServe, BIX, various BBSs, and the Panix gopher (gopher.panix.com). It features hype-free descriptions of books that are new in the stores, a list of our upcoming books, special announcements, a signing/reading/convention-attendance schedule for Del Rey authors, "In Depth" essays in which professionals in the field (authors, artists, designers, sales people, etc.) talk about their jobs in science fiction, a question-and-answer section, behind-the-scenes looks at sf publishing, and more!

Internet information source!

A lot of Del Rey material is available to the Internet on our Web site and on a gopher server: all back issues and the current issue of the Del Rey Internet Newsletter, sample chapters of upcoming or current books (readable or downloadable for free), submission requirements, mail-order information, and much more. We will be adding more items of all sorts (mostly new DRINs and sample chapters) regularly. The Web site is http://www.randomhouse.com/delrey/ and the address of the gopher is gopher.panix.com

Why? We at Del Rey realize that the networks are the medium of the future. That's where you'll find us promoting our books, socializing with others in the sf field, and—most importantly—making contact and sharing information with sf readers.

Online editorial presence: Many of the Del Rey editors are online, on the Internet, GEnie, CompuServe, America Online, and Delphi. There is a Del Rey topic on GEnie and a Del Rey folder on America Online.

The official e-mail address for Del Rey Books is delrey@randomhouse.com (though it sometimes takes us a while to answer).